Also by Jennie Marts

HOW TO
Cowboy

JENNIE MARTS

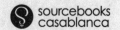
sourcebooks
casablanca

Published by Sourcebooks Casablanca, an imprint of Sourcebooks
P.O. Box 4410, Naperville, Illinois 60567-4410
(630) 961-3900
sourcebooks.com

Printed and bound in Canada.
MBP 10 9 8 7 6 5 4 3 2 1

This book is dedicated to Melissa Marts,
My lifelong friend.
Thanks for always believing in me.

CHAPTER 1

CADE CALLAHAN STOOD IN THE HOSPITAL GIFT SHOP STARING at the colorful display of get-well tokens. A fluffy white unicorn with a purple horn and a glittery pink-and-purple mane caught his eye. Allie had loved unicorns as a little kid—she'd called them "princess ponies." But he was wrestling with the notion that now she might be too old for a stuffed animal.

If she was, she could always toss it. At least he was trying, he thought as he snagged the unicorn from the shelf. He considered a card but figured that might be a little too much. Besides, he doubted he'd find a card that read, *Sorry I was a shitty dad. Get well soon*. For now, the unicorn would have to do.

He grabbed two bottles of water and threw a couple of Reese's Peanut Butter Cups onto the counter, thinking they might want them on the drive up the mountain. He was already dreading the trip. His back hurt from sleeping in the chair next to her hospital bed, and between the two of them, they were grumpier than a grizzly who'd stepped in a hornet's nest.

I'm the grown-up, he reminded himself. Which meant he needed to be the better person, no matter how many of his buttons his thirteen-year-old daughter pushed. And if there were an Olympic event for pushing a parent's buttons, Allison Raye would take home the gold *and* the silver.

As the teenage cashier rang up the items, his eye caught on the shelf of paperbacks behind her. He gestured to the books. "Do you have any YA?" he asked, recalling the conversation he'd had earlier with his daughter about the Kindle app on her phone. It was probably the longest one they'd had yet. Even though she'd rolled her eyes at his lack of knowledge of the young adult genre, he'd still gleaned three important pieces of information from the conversation: one, her phone was at home on the charger; two, her Kindle took the place of any real friendships she might have; and three, she was still a bookworm who loved to read.

The cashier turned to peruse the shelf and pointed to three books along the bottom. "It looks like we only have these three."

"Okay, I'll take them."

"Which ones?"

"All three."

"Sure." She added the books to his total, then slid them into a bag.

Allie was asleep when he got back to her room. He paused in the doorway to look at her and had to swallow back the emotion burning his throat. He and her mother had had their share of struggles, but he couldn't believe Amber was gone. And the thought that Allie could have died in that car accident too hit him like a punch to the gut.

He blinked back the sudden burn of tears as he peered at the dark purple bruises around her eyes and along one of her cheeks. A thin line of stitches ran next to her hairline—they weren't sure if she'd hit her head or something in the cab had flown by and cut her when the car rolled. Her right arm was bandaged and secured in a cream-colored splint, and her left leg was constrained in a blue boot, only sprained and thankfully not broken.

She looked so small, so young, like the little girl he remembered. He hadn't seen his daughter in almost a year. He'd contacted Amber a few years back, told her he wanted to try to see Allie more often, but she'd stalled and always seemed to have some excuse for why it wouldn't work. When Allie got a cell phone, he'd tried to call her, but the few times they'd talked had been stilted and awkward with neither of them knowing exactly what to say.

That's bullshit, he thought as he forced himself to step into the room. *I should have tried harder.*

Her eyes fluttered open, and a hard knot tightened in his chest as he saw the array of emotions flash in her eyes with each blink. They changed from almost glad to see him to confused to angry, then to agonizingly sad as the realization of her mother's death must have hit her again.

She winced as she tried to push herself up in the bed with her good hand but waved Cade off as he took another step toward her. "I got it."

He stayed where he was, not sure how to help her and knowing she wasn't ready to accept his help yet anyway. It used to feel like walking on eggshells around each other—now it felt more like land mines.

The nurse had said she'd be able to leave before lunch, and she'd changed into the shorts and one of the T-shirts his cousin Bryn and neighbor Elle had bought for her when they'd come down to Denver after they'd heard about the accident. The T-shirt was red and yellow and referenced being a Gryffindor on the front.

"Nice shirt," he said.

"Thanks. Cousin Bryn and your other friend Elle bought it for me. Apparently they stalked me on Insta and figured out my size and that I love Harry Potter."

"I don't know what Insta is, but I'm glad you like the things they brought." He held out the unicorn. "Here, I got you something too."

"What's this?" she said, peering down at it.

"A peace offering. And an apology, I guess. And just something I thought you'd like."

"Wow. That's a lot of mileage to get out of one stuffed animal."

He shrugged. "I like to consolidate. I also mix my peas into my mashed potatoes and gravy."

She wrinkled her nose. "Gross."

"What? It keeps them from rolling off the plate." He'd been trying to make her smile—just one instant of her lips curving up—and he thought he might have had it. But then her face shut down again as she pushed the unicorn into the tote bag with the rest of her things. "They gave me a bag with my stuff in it, but I don't know if I want it anymore."

The hospital had given him a bag with his ex-wife's things as well. He'd taken a quick look inside—enough to see some clothes, a pair of sneakers, and a streak of blood across the front of Amber's purse. Being on the rodeo circuit, he was no stranger to blood, but it was different when it belonged to the mother of his child who had been alive and breathing less than twenty-four hours ago. He'd twisted the bag closed and stowed it behind the seat in his truck.

He picked up the plastic bag with his daughter's name written on the front. "I'll take care of it." He passed her the bag of books, as if in trade. "Here. I got you these too. The cashier said they were all YA."

A hint of a smile pulled at her lips as she peered into the bag. "They are. I've read one of them already."

He held out his free hand. "That's okay. I can take it back."

She shook her head and pulled the bag of books to her chest. "No, I'll read it again." She narrowed her eyes, then barely lifted one eyebrow. "The unicorn is cute, but you should have led with the books."

He turned away to hide his smile. At least he'd gotten something right.

A nurse pushed a wheelchair into the room. "You ready to break out of this joint?" she asked Allie.

"So ready." The girl pointed to the chair. "Do I have to ride in that thing?"

The nurse crossed her arms over her chest. She'd been with them since the night before and most of the morning and seemed immune to his daughter's snark. "First of all, yes. It's a requirement. And second of all, you're not going to be walking anywhere today. We're sending you home with crutches, and you'll be using those and that boot you're wearing for the next few weeks at least."

"Fine." Allie plopped down in the seat.

They had already completed the paperwork for her release, and Cade had taken a load of stuff down to the truck earlier that morning. He picked up the rest of her things and followed them down the hall.

The drive up the pass took just over an hour but felt like five. The cab of the truck was thick with awkward silences and uncomfortable attempts at conversation. Mostly his.

To say Allie wasn't thrilled about heading to Bryn's ranch was an understatement. She'd assumed they were going back to her house, but Cade wasn't ready for that. And he wasn't sure Allie was either. He promised her they'd go by her house on their next trip down, but for now, he was trying to keep her mind on her recovery.

Cade's efforts to ask about her school or how she was feeling were met with wisecracks or exaggerated shrugs, so he'd finally just turned on the radio and let his daughter sulk.

She wrinkled her nose at the country music station. "Is this the only kind of music you listen to?"

"No. I'll listen to whatever. You can choose."

She shook her head. "I guess I don't really care either. You can leave it, SD."

He furrowed his brow as he turned the volume down. "So, what's with this SD business?" She'd used the initials several times.

Allie lifted one shoulder. "It's just a nickname I have for you."

"What does it mean?"

She shrugged again and kept her gaze trained out the window.

"I don't think I like it," he told her.

"Oh well."

"Can't you just call me Dad?"

She turned back to him, her eyes narrowed as she leveled him with a cool stare. "No. I can't. You haven't earned that title in a long while. I haven't even *seen* you in close to a year."

He swallowed at the guilt churning its way up his throat like a bad bout of heartburn.

"That wasn't my—" He stopped. He was going to say it wasn't his fault—that Amber had moved them again and hadn't given him her new number for months. And that even when he'd called, she'd always had a reason why he couldn't talk to his daughter. But telling Allie that wouldn't do any good. He didn't want to speak poorly of Amber, especially right now, and it probably was his fault too. He should've tried harder, pushed Amber to put Allie on the phone or insist she return his call. "How about you just call me Cade? I didn't earn it either, but that's my name."

Slumping further into the seat and turning back to the window, she offered him that slight lift of her shoulders coupled with a mumbled "Whatever." Which he now took as her way of agreeing with him.

Glad that's settled. He glanced at the dashboard clock before returning his focus to the road. Only forty-five more minutes of awkward silence to go.

Close to an hour later—traffic up the mountain had been a bear—he turned the truck into the driveway of the Heaven Can Wait Horse Rescue.

Allie lifted her head and sat up straighter in the seat. "Is this it?"

"Yep." He and his brother had been coming here to visit his grandparents since he was a kid, but he tried to see the small farm from her eyes. An old yellow two-story farmhouse with a wide front porch sat on one side of the drive, and a large barn with faded red paint sat on the other. Two nice-sized corrals flanked either side of the barn, and chickens roamed inside the fence surrounding a small chicken coop. The bunkhouse sat beyond the barn, and Cade could see a couple of barn cats lying in the sun on the front porch.

The farm was a little worse for wear, but Bryn had added homey touches in the cheery blue pillows on the porch swing and the array of colorful pots spilling over with flowers on the steps. She had a fenced-in garden next to her house with neat rows of vegetables and tall green cornstalks reaching for the sun. Several of the rescued horses stood in one corral, and a couple dozen head of cattle filled the other and the pasture beyond.

"It's pretty old," Allie said, leaning forward to peer through the front window.

"This used to be your great-grandparents' farm. I came here quite a bit with your uncle Holt when we were kids. Us and Bryn and her brother, Bucky, used to run all over this place."

"What kind of name is Bucky?"

He shrugged. "He just goes by Buck now. I used to see him a lot on the rodeo circuit." Allie's shoulders tensed, and he figured he'd better change the subject quick. She'd always blamed the rodeo for keeping him away and not visiting her more often. "My grandpa left this farm to Bryn when he died. She always loved it, and now she's turning it into a horse rescue. It's pretty cool."

She offered him one of her noncommittal shrugs as they pulled up in front of the bunkhouse. "Is that your dog?" she asked, derision in her tone as she pointed to a mangy canine standing in the pasture behind the bunkhouse. His body was thin, and he stood perfectly still, watching them approach through one good eye. His other was a wreck of scar tissue and damage.

He huffed. "No. Not even close. That's a coyote. He's been hanging around here a lot this summer. I think he's looking to get into the chicken coop and steal a hen. Zane, that's Bryn's fiancé, he's been calling him Jack, for the one-eyed jack in a deck of playing cards. He's pretty small and scrawny for a coyote, probably the runt of his litter. Which is why I think Bryn feels sorry for him and has been tossing him scraps. You'll soon learn your cousin Bryn has a heart the size of Montana, and she can't resist a wounded soul."

"Is he dangerous? The coyote?"

"He could be. Most coyotes are assholes." He held up one hand. "Sorry. I mean jerks. But if you don't mess with him, he shouldn't mess with you. And he's an odd one. You don't usually see 'em this close to the house. I'd be more worried about stepping on a rattler or running into a bear than tangling with that coyote."

"A *bear*?" Her voice raised almost an octave.

Ugh. He was just making this worse. "Don't worry. I won't let anything happen to you." Did he really just say that? The whole reason he'd all but disappeared out of her life was because he *had* let something happen to her.

He didn't know if she was thinking the same thing as she turned away and pushed open the door. This was their new start. He needed to show her he wanted her here. He got out and quickly rounded the back of the truck as she wrestled with the crutch. Her left arm was in a sling, making the use of two crutches impossible. "Welcome home, Allie Cat," he said, as he reached to help her.

"I got it," she said, her mouth set in a tight line as she wedged the crutch into the pit of her good arm. She took a clumsy step forward and had to grab the side of the door to steady herself. "What are you looking at?" she sneered at the row of horses watching her from the edge of the corral.

"I'd say they're staring because you're the first three-legged animal they've seen, but you haven't met Lucky, Bryn's dog. He's missing a leg and runs and hops all over this place." He glanced toward the farmhouse. "I'm surprised he and Zane's dog, Hope, haven't come out to greet us yet. They must not be home. Do you have a dog?" He had a sudden anxious concern that they'd left an animal alone in their house, forgotten in the trauma of the accident.

Allie shook her head. "No. I've always wanted one, but Mom wouldn't let me get one. She said I wasn't old enough for the responsibility. I think *she* just didn't want the responsibility." Her breath caught, as if she'd just remembered that her mom was dead.

Cade caught the well of tears in her eyes before she lowered her gaze to the hand gripping the crutch. He reached an arm out trying to think of something to distract her thoughts. "You want to come over and meet the gang? They seem pretty curious about you."

She looked skeptical but allowed Cade to help her hobble over to the fence, where four horses waited to greet her.

"This is Beauty and her colt, Mack," Cade said, resting a hand on the neck of the quarter horse. "She was Bryn's first rescue. She was waiting on a couple of scumbags at the diner where she works and found out they were taking her to slaughter. Zane left her a hundred-dollar tip for his breakfast so she could buy the horse off 'em."

"A *hundred-dollar tip*? He must have *really* wanted that horse."

"I think he really wanted the girl."

"Ahh," Allie said with a nod that was probably more knowing than her thirteen years should have allowed. "And she got the colt too?"

"She did. Although she didn't know it at the time. The horse was pregnant when she got her." He nuzzled the chin of the gray standing next to Beauty. "This is Prince. They rescued him from an abandoned farmhouse. And this little old man..." he said, scratching the head of the mini-horse who was stretching his nose through the rungs of the fence to sniff at Allie. "Is Shamus. He was dumped here anonymously. But he's real friendly. You can pet him."

"What do you mean by dumped?" She tentatively reached a hand out to touch the side of the mini-horse's neck.

"I mean Bryn came home one day, and this guy was tied to her porch."

"That's awful."

Cade shrugged. "Yeah, but it worked out pretty well for him. He was a mess when he got here, but now he's happy and playful. You gotta watch out for him and Otis, the ornery goat that runs around here. Shamus has a way of escaping the corral, and he and that dang goat are always getting into trouble. Elle found them in the house one afternoon eating a piece of cake."

Allie giggled. He wasn't sure if it was from his comment about the cake or from the way Shamus was nibbling at her hand, but he loved the sound of it. "His nose is so soft. It's like velvet."

The rev of an engine had them turning to watch a small white compact SUV as it headed down Bryn's driveway and stopped a short distance away. A woman stepped out and held her hand up to shade her eyes as she peered around, then offered them a wave. "Is this the Heaven Can Wait Horse Rescue?"

Cade nodded. "Yep. You lookin' to drop one off or pick one up?"

"Neither," she said with a charming laugh as she headed toward them.

She smiled as she approached, and he was struck by the openness of her grin. She was wearing a black pencil skirt, a pink silk blouse, and high-heeled black boots. She looked completely out of place on the farm as the dust of the driveway clung to her fancy boots, but he found his lips curving into a dopey smile as she drew nearer.

His smile didn't matter apparently, because her attention was completely focused on his daughter. "You must be Allie," she said, reaching out a hand to shake, then pulling it back as she realized the move would be difficult for the girl. "I'm Nora. I'm going to be your physical therapist."

Cade turned to Allie and said, "She's a good friend of Elle's and agreed to help us out. She's gonna be staying out here on the farm, so we don't have to drive to Denver every day."

"Whatever." She shrugged in that loose-shouldered way that teenagers had, as if her bones were made of cooked spaghetti noodles. "Welcome to Podunkville, Colorado, otherwise known as the edge of isolation. Hope you don't need cell-phone service."

"It's not that bad," Cade told the woman.

Allie tilted her head toward him. "This is my SD," she said by way of introduction.

Nora's brow furrowed. "SD?"

"It's her nickname for me," he explained, offering his own shrug that he hoped wasn't as annoying as the teenager's. "Except she won't tell me what it means." He cocked an eyebrow at his daughter. "I'm thinking it stands for 'Super Dad.'"

"I can assure you it does *not* stand for Super Dad," Allie said with a snort.

As he'd done with the majority of her salty comments lately, he ignored it and held out his hand to the physical therapist. "Cade Callahan. Thanks for coming."

The woman nodded. "Nice to meet you. Nora Fisher. And I'm happy to help." Her gaze traveled over him in a way that had a shot of heat creeping up his spine. "You're not exactly what I was expecting."

"No?" He had a moment of wondering what she *had* been expecting and if he was better or worse than she imagined. *What the hell?* He couldn't remember the last time a woman's opinion of him mattered. Especially one he'd just met.

She shook her head. "Sorry, that was rude. I just meant from Elle's description, I thought you'd be much older."

He grinned. "Yeah, that sounds about right. She probably said I was crotchety—she likes to tell me I remind her of a grumpy old man."

Allie huffed, then muttered, "She got the grumpy part right."

He ignored her as he shrugged. What could he say? He *was* kind of grumpy most days. And his daughter hadn't exactly seen him at his best. But now they were on the ranch and with the horses, the place where he felt the most at ease. He gestured to the small herd of horses still watching them from the corral. "We just got here ourselves, and I was introducing Allie to the crew. You want to meet them?"

"Sure." Nora nodded and smiled, but the nervous look that crossed her face told him her thoughts were probably more along the lines of *unsure*.

City girls.

He went through the horses' names again, stroking their necks as he repeated their stories to Nora.

"The little one is the funniest," Allie said, scratching the mini-horse's ears. Shamus stretched his neck through the fence again and nudged her hip, sniffing at her front pocket.

"He's checking to see if you brought him any treats."

"What kind of treats does he like?"

"That horse will eat anything. The guy who left him here said his favorites were macaroni and cheese and jelly beans."

"Jelly beans?" Allie chuckled. "I can understand macaroni and cheese—that's my favorite too—but what kind of horse eats jelly beans?"

"Not this one. Not anymore. Now he just gets carrots and apple slices and horse treats. We'll bring him out something tomorrow." Although he just might bring the mini-horse a jelly bean. Shamus was making more headway with his daughter in the last ten minutes than Cade had in the last two days. But he did just find out that macaroni and cheese was still her favorite.

Nora smiled with them but hung back a little, not as bold as Allie had been in petting the animals. "I don't have much experience with horses. In fact, I don't think I've ever been this close to one before."

"Me either," Allie admitted.

"Really?" Cade asked. "I've been around horses my entire life. I get along with them better than I do most people. Present company excluded." He hoped. Although so far in the compatibility battle, the horses were still winning. "You couldn't have asked for better horses to hang out with for your first time. This is a real sweet bunch."

"Which one is yours?" Nora asked, glancing around at the other horses in the corral.

"Mine's in the barn. She's the palomino in the first stall. I'll give you a tour later, but I think for now, I'd better get Allie inside." He reached for her elbow, but she pulled it away.

"I told you, I can do it myself."

He raised his hands in surrender. What else could he do? Her personality was as prickly as a pissed-off porcupine. One minute she was laughing and petting the horses, the next she's firing off a shot at him. "Fine. Do it yourself."

The teenager tried to take a step forward but the crutch slid on some loose gravel, and she started to pitch forward. Cade reached out to grab her before she fell, but after he'd steadied her, she pushed him away again. "I can do it."

"Hold on. I brought you something that might help," Nora said, heading back toward her car. She popped the hatchback and pulled out a wheeled contraption. "It's a knee scooter. It'll make your mobility much easier," she said as she wheeled it back toward Allie. She bent her leg and rested it on the center platform. "You put your knee here, then you can wheel yourself around and not have to use the crutches."

Allie passed the crutch to her dad and positioned herself on the scooter. He watched as she awkwardly inched forward.

"This is much easier," Allie said, getting the hang of the scooter. It was still a little wonky since she could only use one hand, but it offered her much more stability than the single crutch had. "Thanks." She offered Nora the smallest of smiles.

Better than what he'd been getting lately.

"Are you okay to give me a few minutes to get her settled, then I'll come back and help you get unloaded?" he asked Nora.

"Oh, yeah," she said, waving away his concerns. "Take your time. I'll just hang out here with the horses. We'll get to know each other."

He grinned as she inched just a smidge closer and tentatively reached out to pat Shamus's head.

The bunkhouse was small, and it only took a few minutes to give Allie the tour and get her settled in her new room. It was obvious his cousin and Elle had been in there, and they had transformed the second bedroom into a welcoming space. A new floral comforter covered the bed and a mess of matching pillows lined the headboard. Fresh-cut flowers tucked into a mason jar sat on the dresser next to a basket of miniature bottles of soaps and lotions. A fresh bottle of water was on the nightstand along with an assortment of magazines and paperback novels.

"Did you do all this?" Allie eyed him skeptically.

He shook his head. "Nah. I mean I've been working on setting up this room for you in case you wanted to visit, so I got the new bed and the desk and the dresser and nightstand. But the flowers and the bedding and that basket of good-smelling stuff was all your cousin Bryn and her friend Elle. And they definitely get credit for that jumble of useless pillows."

"Why would they do all this? For me?"

"They're good people, and they wanted you to feel welcome. Bryn did all this kind of stuff for me when I first got here too. Maybe not the flowers and frou-frou pillows, but she has the gift of hospitality, just like our grandmother did, and it makes her happy to do things for other people."

"Huh. Just seems like a lot to do for someone she doesn't even know."

"Yeah. It takes a little getting used to, but once she's brought you over a pan of warm cinnamon rolls, you find a way to accept it." He reached out to touch her shoulder, then drew his hand back. "And she does know you. I told you, she met you several times when you were little."

"Oh, you mean before you left us."

CHAPTER 2

NORA SUCKED IN HER BREATH AS SHE WATCHED THE TALL cowboy saunter off the porch and head back her way. She loved the sleek cut of slacks and a dress shirt on a man and never imagined being drawn to the rugged look of jeans and cowboy boots—but holy hot cowboy, did Cade Callahan ever know how to wear a pair of jeans. *Whew.* The fabric of his T-shirt stretched across his broad chest and muscled forearms. His skin was tanned, and she could see the touches of sun in his sandy-brown hair just visible under his Stetson.

She was going to kill Elle. When her old college friend had called and asked her if she'd be willing to spend a few weeks at a ranch in the mountains helping a teenage girl with physical therapy, she'd specifically asked about the teenager's dad, and all Elle had said was that he was salty and crotchety. *Salty?* Ha! Cade was more like pepper and Sriracha sauce blended together in one hot mix of muscles and roguish good looks.

Dang—she was in trouble here.

Stop it. She was here to do a job. To help a teenage girl. And from the looks of Allie and the brief interaction she'd witnessed between the father and daughter, she'd have her work cut out for her. Which meant she needed to stop drooling over the hunky dad with the roguish grin.

She'd been leaning on the fence watching the horses, from a safe and reasonable distance away, and Cade stopped and let out a sigh as he propped his elbows on the fence next to her. "You sure you're ready for this?"

"This?" *Which this?* Spending four to six weeks in the middle of the Colorado mountains trying to help a traumatized teenage girl regain her strength? Or spending four to six weeks in the company of a man who made her pulse race and her head a little dizzy just by standing next to her?

He leaned back and spread his arm out to encompass the ranch. "All of this. Being in the country and on a farm and spending every day trying to convince a stubborn thirteen-year-old to do some exercises?"

Oh. *This.* The farm and Allie. Of course that's what he meant. *Get a grip, girl.* She smiled up at him. "Yes, I'm excited for the challenge."

He grinned as his gaze traveled to her footwear. "I think the first challenge is trying to navigate the ruts in this dirt driveway in those fancy boots. They're not exactly made for the country."

"You're right. But they're my best pair." She lifted one shoulder. "I was trying to make a good impression."

"Nobody around here you need to impress. Just the fact you showed up and agreed to help is impressive enough. And bringing that knee scooter was a stroke of genius. That's gonna be a real lifesaver."

"I'm glad. I figured with her injuries, it would really help."

"You have no idea. Just trying to get her out of the truck and the few steps to the fence, I could tell that crutch idea was going to be a mess. And she's so dang stubborn, she's determined to not let me help her."

She offered him a grin. "Is that stubbornness a family trait?"

He chuckled. "I guess. Considering I'm planning to outstubborn her at every turn and not let her know she's getting to me, it probably is." His expression changed to wistful as he knocked the dust off the side of his cowboy boot by kicking it against the bottom of the fence post. "I don't know how much Elle told you, but I haven't really been in Allie's life much, and we haven't lived in the same house since she was five."

"She just said that Allie had been primarily living with her mother. Elle's a good friend and wouldn't betray your confidence."

"I hope you still think she's a good friend after you've been here a few days. I'm still in awe that you gave up your whole life to come here and help us."

"It's not currently that great of a life," she muttered. "Although let's wait until we get to know each other better before we swap life stories. I want you to hold on to that great impression you have of me, despite my poor choice of footwear." She was sure there was plenty more to his story, but if he didn't want to talk about his mistakes, it saved her from having to share hers.

He gestured to the car. "Why don't we get your stuff in and get you settled, then?"

"Thanks. That would be great." She popped the hatch as they walked to her car. She hadn't meant to bring much but her mother had insisted on packing her pillows, her favorite throw blanket, and some extra groceries. She peered in at the hodgepodge of two suitcases, a box of books, a tub of therapy equipment, and the Keurig she had taken from her ex-fiancé's fancy apartment when they broke up. She'd bought it for him as a moving-in-together gift and probably should have left it behind. But why should she miss out on great coffee just because Geoff was an idiot?

The thought of Dr. Geoffrey Aaron sobered her swoony thoughts right out of her head. She did not need or want another man in her life. She had a job to do, and that's where her focus needed to lie. Pushing the bags of groceries to the side, she grabbed the stack of pillows from on top of the suitcases. But the corner of one of the cases must have gotten stuck under the box because the pillow wouldn't budge. She pulled harder, trying to yank it free.

It gave way with a sudden jerk, and she stumbled backward, right into the solid arms of the cowboy she was trying to convince herself not to think about.

"Whoa there. You all right?" he asked, peering down at her. His big hands were wrapped securely around her waist as her shoulders rested against his firm chest. He felt so good, so solid, she wanted to melt into him.

"Yeah, I'm good," she breathed, all of her senses laser-focused on the heat of his hands as they held her waist. What the heck happened to her voice? She swallowed, her throat making a funny click as she extricated herself from his grip. "Sorry about that."

"No problem," he said, grinning down at her. "You can fall for me anytime." His grin faltered. "I mean fall *on* me." He ducked his head and reached into the car to grab the suitcases. "I'm gonna shut up now and just carry these bags in for you."

She couldn't help grinning as she reached for more stuff. Filling her arms, she followed him across the driveway and up the few steps to the porch of the bunkhouse, trying not to think about how great his butt looked in those jeans.

For all her worries, the dwelling wasn't as bad as she'd thought it would be. The wood of the building was weathered, but it looked like a log cabin with thick log posts supporting the roof and encasing a long front porch. Colorful pink trumpet flowers overflowed antique galvanized steel buckets on either side of the porch and a blue-and-white blanket rested over the back of an old glider sofa. An orange-and-white cat eyed them from the corner of the glider, stretching out one paw to rest on the navy blue cushion and adding to the cozy feeling of the place.

How could she complain about a log cabin on a ranch that came complete with cozy furniture, a cute cowboy, *and* a cat?

Two screen doors sat next to each other, and Cade set down one of her suitcases to open the door on the left. "It's not much," he said. "But it's a heck of a lot better than it was. I've been fixing up both of these spaces for the last few months."

He held open the screen, and she stepped through the door and into her new home.

She let out a tiny gasp, surprised and a little delighted, at the interior. "Wow. I love it."

The space was small but functional, and she noted several more homey touches. The main area was an open concept with a kitchen area to the right, a living room to the left, and a large kitchen island separating the two. A small dining room table was pushed up against the window, and a bouquet of wild flowers in a jar sat atop a light blue tablecloth. A television and a stack of books sat on a small bookcase in the corner. An older sofa sat against the back wall, giving it's occupant a panoramic view of gorgeous, lightly snow-capped mountains perfectly framed in the large picture window on the other side of the door.

A hallway led to two small bedrooms, and Cade set her suitcases on top of the double bed in the first one.

He waved a hand around the room, which had been similarly set up as Allie's. "I'd like to take credit, but Bryn and Elle did all this for you."

"Wow," she said, dumping her pillows on the gorgeous floral comforter. She picked up one of the lotions from the basket and opened the lid to appreciate the citrusy scent. "This is so nice. I wasn't expecting anything like this."

"They both love this stuff, so I'm sure you'll find other little surprises." He pointed toward the door. "Bathroom's across the hall and there's a second bedroom. Not much in there. I think Bryn found a secondhand desk for it, if you want to use it as an office or whatever."

As they brought in the rest of her things, Nora noticed several other of the little welcoming gifts Cade had mentioned—soft towels and fancy soaps in the bathroom and new dish cloths and a pumpkin-scented candle in the kitchen. She set her purse and the bag containing the peanut butter and jelly sandwich her mom had packed for her on the coffee table as Cade brought in the last load of her things.

"There's no central air, but if you leave the bedroom windows and the front door open, you should get a nice cross breeze through the screen door there. And I think there's a fan in the closet," he said as he came out of her bedroom. "You need anything else?"

"No, not right now. This is great."

"I'll leave you to get settled then."

Alone for the first time in her new place, Nora inhaled a deep breath as she peered around the room. Cade had said his grandfather had built the original bunkhouse over fifty years ago. If these walls could talk, she was sure they would have some good stories to tell. The original hardwood floors shone with fresh polish, and she imagined all the bootheels that had trod across the old wood.

She shook her head at her earlier concerns of living on a farm in a bunkhouse with horses as roommates. Instead, she was utterly charmed by the rustic beauty of the whole ranch. It was gorgeous. And the perfect place to escape her current situation.

Situation seemed like a nice way of saying flat broke and living back in her mom's basement. She should have known better than to get engaged to that creep. Geoff had been one of the doctors in the clinic where she worked, and she'd heard the rumors about him being a flirt. But he'd convinced her she was special. Then a big diamond ring and a smooth sales pitch had been enough to get her to sell everything she owned, break her lease, and happily move in with him.

One of Elle's arguments for persuading her to take this job was that no one in the small town of Creedence knew her humiliating situation or had ever even heard of Dr. Douchebag.

Elle had already been sold on the idea of helping the teenager with her recovery, but the Dr. Douchebag comment had sealed the deal.

She sighed. Oh well, no use crying over spilled milk or broken relationships. Or the crappy doctor who'd screwed up her life and she was sure had something to do with getting her dismissed from a job she'd really loved.

But look where I landed. She gazed out at the gorgeous view of mountains as she pulled her attention back to the present.

The only problem was that it was too quiet. There were no traffic noises, no sounds of construction or sirens wailing in the distance. She turned on the television and found a funny sitcom, just to have the noise of other voices in the room while she put the few groceries she'd brought away.

After the kitchen, she moved into the bedroom and unpacked her clothes into the drawers and closet. She pushed the empty suitcases under the bed, then swiped her hand across her sweaty brow and pulled at the back of her damp blouse. She'd wanted to make a good impression by wearing the skirt and dress top, but now she was ready to change into something more comfortable and functional. She laid a pair of black leggings and a lavender T-shirt on the bed, then found her sneakers and a pair of socks. She was itching to explore the farm, but first she needed a cool shower to wash the dust and sweat of the road off.

Twenty minutes later, feeling refreshed and smelling like one of the jasmine-scented shampoos she'd found in the welcome basket, she stepped out of the bathroom. Her hair was wet but combed, and she'd wrapped a towel around herself to cross the hall to the bedroom.

Halfway there, she froze at the sound of footsteps in her living room.

Holding her breath, she stood motionless in place as she listened for another step. Had Cade come back? Surely he wouldn't have just let himself in. A soft scuffling sounded across the hardwood and what sounded like a grunt. Or maybe it was more like an oink.

An *oink*? What the heck?

She scanned the hallway for any kind of weapon. Seeing nothing, she reached back into the bathroom and grabbed the hair dryer from the sink, then took a tentative step forward. She paused as she considered her options—she could shrink back and hope whoever, or *whatever* it was left on their own, she could tiptoe forward, or she could charge loudly into the room in an effort to scare her intruder away.

Her knuckles turned white as she gripped the hair dryer and silently counted to three. Emitting a primal yell, she charged into the room. "Get out of here!"

Her yell turned into a scream as she faced the intruders currently making themselves at home in her new bunkhouse apartment.

She blinked, not quite able to believe her eyes. A giant hog was lounged out across her sofa and a black-and-white billy goat was standing on her coffee table calmly eating her peanut butter and jelly sandwich. A corner of the torn paper sack was stuck to the side of his lip.

"Get out!" she yelled as she brandished the hair dryer like a pistol, then took a quick step back as the goat finished the sandwich, then climbed down from the table and advanced toward her.

"Get away, goat," she commanded as she backed toward the kitchen. The goat took another few steps toward her, blocking her path to the hallway and forcing her toward the front door.

She pushed back her shoulders, attempting to appear taller as she tried to hold her ground. She was bigger than he was, but he had scary-looking horns. She swallowed as she watched his gaze drop. "Don't even think about it," she said. She wasn't sure exactly *what* he was thinking, but she could see that goat's wheels turning and knew he was contemplating something. And it couldn't be good.

The goat licked his lips, then leapt forward and grabbed the bottom corner of her towel. Gripping the cloth between his teeth, he drew back his head…and pulled.

"Ahh," she yelled as she dropped the hair dryer and clasped the towel around her chest. She kicked her foot toward the animal. "Let go, you beast!"

The goat seemed adept at this game and nimbly evaded her kick.

"What's all the yelling about?" a man's voice asked, just as she yanked back and ran smack into a solid wall of muscle.

She shrieked before she realized she'd once again landed herself in the arms of Cade Callahan. "Help, this goat is attacking me."

"It's okay. He's not attacking *you*. He just wants your towel," he said, a hint of amusement in his voice.

"Well, he can't have it. I'm using it at the moment."

"That's Otis, and I have to admit his social graces are a bit lacking. Not like Tiny there." He gestured to the pig lounging on the sofa. "She's a real sweetheart. That was nice of you to turn on the television for her. She loves that show."

"I didn't turn it on *for* her. I just got out of the shower, and she was here. Along with this brute." She leaned back again, pulling on the towel as it slipped further down her chest. "Now that we're through with the introductions, could you please free my towel from that dang goat's grip?"

Cade pressed his lips together in what looked like an effort to keep from laughing. "Sure. Since you said please and all." He wrapped a hand around the goat's mouth and tried to pry the towel from his teeth.

Otis set his feet and yanked back.

"Eep," Nora squeaked as the towel inched even lower. "Cade, I know we just met, but we're about to get to know each other a *lot* better if you don't free my towel from that goat's teeth."

He chuckled. "Now you're just teasing me." His gaze did a quick slide over her bare shoulders and down to the top of her breasts, which were about to break free of the edge of the towel. His lips curved into a roguish grin. "Would you think poorly of me if I admitted I'm half tempted to let the goat have it?"

Heat surged up her spine, and she could feel the warmth coloring her cheeks. Thankfully Cade turned back to Otis, instead of waiting for her to respond. He pried the goat's mouth open again and this time successfully wrested the fabric free.

He let the towel drop, and she quickly hiked it up, adjusting it as best she could to cover all her essential bits. "Oh my gosh. Thank you."

"No problem." He opened the door and shooed the goat outside. "You want the pig out too, or do you want to let her finish this episode?"

She laughed. She had too. This situation was just too hilarious. "I'd prefer to have her out too. At least until I'm dressed."

"Come on, Tiny." He held the door open as he called to the pig, who gave him a huff and an annoyed oink, but climbed down off the sofa. "She apparently thinks she's a dog. She was raised by a teenager who treated her that way."

"That explains it."

"She's a pretty sweet pig though, all things considered."

Tiny shuffled toward the door but stopped in front of Nora, tipping her head up and offering her what Nora swore looked like a smile before trotting outside to lie down on the porch. "I think that pig might have just smiled at me."

"Wouldn't surprise me a bit."

"Everything about this day, and this place, is surprising me." Including the flirty comments from the cute cowboy. She clutched the towel to her chest. "My heart is still racing."

"Your heart is racing? Darlin', I'm the one who just missed out on seeing a naked woman having a tug-of-war with a goat."

That was it. A laugh burst from her, and she couldn't stop. She held her stomach as the laughter bubbled out of her. "Sorry to disappoint," she said when she finally got her chuckles under control.

He offered her a shrug and a coy grin. "There's always tomorrow. And I may get another chance. That goat is always sneaking in somewhere."

"That's a comforting thought."

He surveyed the ruined lunch sack and empty bag of chips left on the coffee table. "Looks like Otis ate your supper. I'm makin' spaghetti next door in a bit. It's nothing fancy, but you're welcome to eat with us."

"Oh, well…" She started to tell him she was fine but changed her mind. Having a meal together might be a good way to ease into getting to know Allie better. Her decision had *nothing* to do with getting to know more about her handsome father. *Uh-huh.* "Actually, I think I will join you. Spaghetti sounds great."

"Good. Let's say half an hour or so? Work for you?"

"Works great. Thank you."

He lifted a shoulder. "It's the least I can do. That thing with Otis and Tiny was probably my fault. I sometimes prop the door open when I'm working in here, so they've wandered in to keep me company before." He flipped the latch on the screen door. "I'll try to secure this better. Not that it will matter that much. Locks don't seem to present much of a challenge if that dang goat smells food."

And she'd thought the stray cockroach in her city kitchen had been a problem. She smoothed down her wet hair. "Thanks for your help. This was maybe not the *best* impression to make at my new job."

Cade chuckled. "Good thing this is a pretty lax place to work. We almost had an HR incident on our hands."

She laughed with him. "Thanks for coming to my rescue."

"Anytime. Always happy to help. Although, I wasn't sure what I was gonna find when I came in. The way you were hollerin', I thought you were being attacked."

"I was." She ducked her head. "And I didn't mean to yell. I was just surprised."

"Course you were. Who wouldn't be surprised to find a goat and a pig watching television in their living room? Although the real surprising thing is that the goat knows how to change the channel."

CHAPTER 3

CADE WAS STILL SHAKING HIS HEAD AT THE GOAT TUG-OF-WAR when he poked his head into his daughter's room ten minutes later. "Hey, I'm making spaghetti for supper, and I wanted to let you know I invited Nora to eat with us."

She was lying in bed with her back to him, her nose stuck in one of the books he'd bought her. "Whatever."

His smile fell. He'd wanted to tell Allie about the goat and pig invasion, hoping to get a laugh out of her, but he could see the teenager wasn't in the mood for laughter. "You okay? You want some Advil?"

She jerked her head toward him as she tossed down the book. It hit the floor with a thud. "No, I'm not okay. And I don't want any stupid Advil. I want my phone. My Kindle is on it with all my books. And my own clothes. And my own house."

"I know. Sorry, kiddo. I told you, we'll make the trip to Denver in the next few days and get your stuff. For now, you'll have to make do with what you have." They were both making do with the new situation. "I thought you liked that stuff Bryn and Elle got you."

"I do. I mean, it's fine." She pulled at the sleeve of the T-shirt. "But it's not mine. Nothing is mine. Nothing feels right. I don't feel right. Plus I feel like I smell weird."

He'd spent enough time in hospitals and emergency rooms to know what she meant. "I get that. But with the stitches, you can't take a shower yet. Not until tomorrow."

"I know. But my hair is disgusting, and it stinks like the hospital too." She tipped her head back into her pillow and whined, "I just want to wash my hair."

"I can do it."

"Do what?"

"Wash your hair."

She offered him a snarl. "Yeah right."

"What? I'm serious. I used to wash your hair and give you a bath all the time when you were a little girl. It's not that hard."

She narrowed her eyes as she studied him as if she were judging his hair-washing skills. "How? I can't bear weight on my foot or lean over the tub."

"No, but I've got another idea." He passed her the basket of toiletries from the dresser. "Looks like there's a bunch of fancy shampoos and stuff in there. Pick out which ones you want, and I'll be right back."

A few minutes later, he stepped back into the room. "Come on, I've got it all set up."

She eyed him with suspicion as she pushed up from the bed, then winced as her foot touched the floor.

He took a step toward her. With the splint on her arm and the bandage and bruising on her face, she looked so fragile as she stared miserably at her injured leg.

She held up her hand. "I can do it myself. I don't need you."

Okay. Maybe not that fragile. Her words stung, but his logical mind knew they came from a place of hurt. "Dammit, Allie, just let me do this for you." He took another step closer and when she didn't stop him, he reached down and lifted her into his arms. She was surprisingly quiet as he carried her into the kitchen, where he'd cleared off the counter next to the sink and laid down a thick towel. "Toss those shampoos into the sink," he instructed.

"One is shampoo and one is conditioner," she said as he gingerly set her on the counter. "Make sure you use the green bottle first then the white one."

"Green one first, got it," he said as he positioned a rolled up towel at the edge of the sink. "Here, put this under your neck."

She lowered her back onto the counter, so her head hung over the sink. "Did you wash out the sink first?"

"Yes. I scrubbed out the sink and washed off the counters. Now be quiet and just enjoy your experience at the Callahan Spa."

She rolled her eyes, but her shoulders settled and a ghost of a grin teased her face. "You're a dork."

"I know." But at least he'd made her smile. Or almost smile.

He turned on the water and held his hand under the faucet, waiting for the water to warm. Lifting the mass of her blond hair, he used the sprayer to wet it down, being careful to avoid the bandage on her forehead. He froze as he caught sight of the thin line of scar tissue above her eyebrow. Her bangs had covered it before, but the sight of the scar brought back memories that twisted Cade's heart like it was being squeezed in a vise.

He let out a breath and tried to focus on the task at hand.

Allie closed her eyes as he gently massaged in the shampoo—from the green bottle. The scent of eucalyptus and something slightly minty filled the air. He was glad his daughter's eyes were closed so she couldn't see him blink back the sudden well of tears. It was stupid. He didn't know why he was getting so dang emotional. But the act of washing his little girl's hair in the sink brought back a flood of memories—memories he'd spent years trying to suppress.

He swallowed as he watched the suds swirl down the drain. This was the first time she'd let him offer her any kind of affectionate touch. He'd wanted to hug her when he first saw her lying in the hospital bed, but it had been so long since he'd seen her, he wasn't sure how. Then the moment had passed, and he didn't know how to get it back.

He could confidently climb onto the back of a two-thousand-pound bull bent on bucking him off, but spending time with this slip of a girl who probably weighed a hundred pounds soaking wet scared the hell out of him.

For whatever reason, he was getting a second chance with his daughter, and he didn't want to blow it. He filled his hand with the conditioner and carefully worked it through her hair. It had been lighter when she was little, so blond it was almost white, but she'd always worn it long, and from the pictures he'd seen of her on Facebook, she had about a million ways to wear it up and down and with braids and little top-knot ponytails. She was the only reason he'd started the account. He probably had less than ten friends on it, and she wasn't one of them. No way was Amber going to allow that. But he could look her up and see her photos, her smile.

If he caught Amber in a good mood—usually when she was seeing a new guy—she might agree to let him see Allie once or twice a year. But the visits were always awkward and weird and neither of them knew what to say. He usually took her to a movie, then out for pizza. He asked the same questions: *How's school? Got any new friends? What do you like to do for fun?* And got the same answers: *Fine. Not really. And watch television or read.*

Amber moved them around a lot, so he didn't often see the same friends, or many friends at all, in Allie's photos. She seemed to be a bit of a loner. Hmm. Maybe they were more alike than he thought.

Nora had changed into the leggings and T-shirt, but then opted for her flip-flops over sneakers since she was just going next door. Her toes were painted a glossy strawberry pink thanks to the pedicures she and her mom had gotten the week before. She'd recovered the dropped hair dryer and done a quick blow dry, then swiped on a bit of mascara. She didn't want to look like she was trying too hard. And why was she even worried about how hard she was trying at all? It was just a polite offer to join Cade and his daughter for supper—it's not like he'd invited her out for dinner.

So why were her hands sweating and her nerves jumping around like kangaroos on speed? She wiped her hands on her leggings as she got ready to leave. Wait—she shouldn't show up empty-handed. She should bring something. Opening the pantry, she spotted a package of Oreos her mom had covertly tucked into the groceries in the back of her car. Perfect. At least she'd have something to hold.

Grabbing them, she let herself out her door, careful to not let it slam behind her, then raised her hand to knock on Cade's door. She paused, not wanting to interrupt the tender scene of Cade washing his daughter's hair she could see through the screen.

He turned off the water and carefully wrung out her hair, then gently wrapped it in a towel. Sliding his hand under her back, he eased her up, then held her arm to steady her.

"You okay, darlin'?" he asked, his voice soft and low.

Allie nodded.

"All right now, take it easy. You might feel a little dizzy. I got you." He lifted her off the counter and helped her into a chair at the table.

Nora was surprised the girl let him help her after she'd seen her being so standoffish earlier. There was a story between these two, but Nora hadn't quite figured it out yet. Elle had said they were estranged—that was obvious. But at least for the moment, they both seemed at ease.

She stood transfixed, knowing she should knock, but she didn't want to interrupt as she watched Cade carefully untwist the towel, then gently draw a brush through the girl's wet hair. He looked up and waved as he saw Nora standing at the door. "Hey. Come on in. The Callahan Spa is open for business. You looking for a cut or just a wash?"

Allie shook her head at Nora, but at least she was smiling. "He is so weird."

"I think I'm good," Nora said, then held up the Oreos. "I brought over dessert and thought I'd offer to help with supper."

"Great," Cade said, wiping his hands on his jeans and crossing to the kitchen. "It's nothing fancy, just spaghetti and some bread, but the sauce is homemade. Bryn makes our grandma's recipe, and she gave me a couple of jars." He pulled a stockpot from the cabinet and set it on the stove. He pulled at the front of his shirt, which was soaked from washing Allie's hair. "If you want to get some water started, I'll just change my shirt and be back to help with the sauce."

"Sure," she answered, glad to be put to work and have something to do with her hands. She took the stockpot, then stopped as she caught sight of him stripping off his T-shirt as he headed down the hall. Her mouth went dry. His back and shoulders were ripped with muscles, but his waist was lean where his jeans hung low on his hips. He had the body of a man who worked, who used his muscles to build and haul and swing tools. It wasn't perfect—even from across the room, she could see white lines of scars marking his tanned skin—but it came darn close.

He was back by the time she'd filled the pot with water and had the stove turned on. The kitchen seemed to shrink in size with the two of them in it. She was all too aware of his presence as they shifted and moved around each other.

It wasn't a complicated meal, and Nora kept up a steady stream of small talk with Allie while she set the table and Cade cooked the noodles and heated up the sauce. Nora put the sauce on the table while Cade filled their plates with spaghetti from the pan. He set their plates in front of them, then dropped into his chair and picked up his fork.

Allie made a sound like she was clearing her throat as she folded her hands together and stared expectantly at Cade.

"Oh yeah, sorry." He put down his fork and folded his hands. "Thank you, God, for the food."

Allie made a huffing sound of disapproval.

Nora had her head bent but could practically hear him floundering.

"And thanks for bringing us Nora. Please let her experience and guidance help Allie to recover quickly. Amen."

Nora raised her head, but Allie kept hers lowered and her eyes closed. "And please watch over Mom. She's new and probably doesn't know what to do."

Oh gosh. *Poor girl.*

Nora swallowed at the emotion burning her throat. Some of Allie's cutting remarks were pure teenager, but right now, sitting at the table with her hair wet, her sweet face bruised and bandaged, as she prayed for God to watch over her mother, she looked like a little girl.

Cade must have thought so too. His voice was husky and rough as he choked out another "amen," then focused on tearing off a piece of french bread.

"Wow, this sauce *is* amazing," Nora said after another few minutes of silence.

Allie shrugged, but Cade nodded in agreement. The girl seemed to have shrunk back into her earlier place of anger and sadness. Any attempts Nora made at conversation were met with curt one-word answers or more shrugs.

———

Cade kept his head down, shoveling in the food from his plate. He may have forgotten to start this meal with a prayer, but he was sure praying for it to be over now.

For her part, Nora was giving it the old college try at engaging Allie in conversation, but his daughter had reverted back to her usual snarky self. At least she wasn't being flat-out rude to Nora, like she was to him.

"Is that your only television?" Allie asked, looking at the small set in the corner of the living room. "Do you at least have cable or streaming?"

He jerked a thumb toward the door. "If you're looking for streaming, there's a creek running down from the mountains and into the west pasture."

She offered him a deadpan stare. "Funny. So I take that as a no?"

"Sorry, kid. I don't watch a lot of television."

"What do you do around here?"

"I read. I listen to music. But mostly I work. I've spent most of my evenings the last few months renovating this bunkhouse, plus I help take care of the cattle and feed the horses and run fence and fix stuff that's broke. In fact, I've still got to take care of my evening chores after we finish up supper. There's never a shortage of work to be done around a farm. If you're worried about being bored, I'll bet I can find something for you to help out with tomorrow."

"Great," she said with a huff and an impressive eye roll. "Can't wait."

His phone buzzed in his pocket. He pulled it out and chuckled as he read the text. Pushing it back into his pocket, he looked up to see Allie's rolling eyes had turned to shooting daggers aimed straight at him.

"What's so funny? Was that one of your girlfriends messaging you with a booty call? Is that what you meant by *evening chores*?" she spat. "Too bad you have me here to mess up your plans. Sorry I'm such an inconvenience."

"Whoa." He jerked his head back at the venom in her words. Stopping himself before he fired back an admonishment, he took a calming breath then spoke. "First of all, you are *not* an inconvenience. You are my daughter, and I'm happy you're here. Well, I'm not happy for what happened to you, but I'm glad to have you with me. Second of all, I'd appreciate it if you watched your tone with me. I'm a patient man, but you, darlin', are sorely trying mine."

She lifted one shoulder and muttered a quiet, "Sorry."

"And third of all," he continued, "not that it's any of your business, but I do *not* have a girlfriend, nor have I taken any booty calls as of late." He cut his eyes quickly to Nora, who was pressing her lips together to keep from laughing. "Besides the mares around here, the only women I know in Creedence are Bryn, who is my cousin, Elle, who is my friend, and Aunt Sassy, who is eighty if she's a day. Although now that I think about it, she is a bit of a flirt."

"We have an aunt that lives here?" Allie asked, perking up a little and ignoring the other parts of his statement.

"Well, not by blood, but I think Sassy James considers herself an aunt to the whole town. She's the actual great-aunt of the guys who run the Triple J Ranch up the road, but everyone around here calls her Aunt Sassy."

"Was that her texting you?"

He sighed. "No, Allison. It was Bryn. And if you would have just waited before you jumped down my throat, I would have told you what the text said."

The teenager crossed her arms over her chest and offered him a sullen expression.

She was testing him. He knew it, but it was still getting under his skin. He'd worked with broody horses before, but none had tried his patience like this thirteen-year-old girl. *I'm the adult here*, he reminded himself. "Bryn texted to say that it was killing her not to come over here and smother us in squishy hugs—her words, not mine. She said she was giving us some space tonight but to be prepared for the onslaught of embraces tomorrow."

"She's weird," Allie said.

"Yeah, but she's a good weird." He smiled as he shifted his gaze to Nora. "And you should be prepared for the hug assault too. My cousin has never met a stranger, and she's thrilled you're here. Get ready to have a new best friend by tomorrow night."

Nora grinned. "I love it. I can't wait to get smothered in some squishiness. Doesn't it make you feel great to know that we all have someone who is just dying to give us a hug?"

Allie's expression softened, and she uncrossed her arms. Cade swallowed. Well, Nora had certainly changed the spin on that conversation. Dang, he liked this woman.

CHAPTER 4

CADE FOUND HIMSELF THINKING ABOUT NORA AS HE WORKED through his nightly routine of chores. As he tossed hay to the horses, his thoughts drifted to the softness of her skin. And he reflected on the way she'd smelled fresh out of the shower—like honeysuckle and something flowery—while he hauled bales of hay out to the cattle.

He needed to stop and get a grip. Nora Fisher was here for one reason. And it wasn't for him to fantasize about her soft skin or how amazing she smelled. She was here to help his daughter.

So why was his face breaking into a grin as he approached the bunkhouse and found her sitting on the glider on the porch? "Hey," he said.

"Hey," she said, smiling in return. "Did you get everything done?"

He shook his head. "Like I said earlier, around a farm, you're never gonna get *everything* done. But I got done what needed to be taken care of tonight. How did it go with Allie after I left?"

"Great."

He cocked an eyebrow her direction.

"Well, pretty good. She let me help her get ready for bed, and we talked through some of the exercises and the physical therapy we're going to be starting tomorrow. I went back to check on her after I cleaned up the kitchen, and she was fast asleep."

"Wow. You didn't have to do all that."

"I know. But I wanted to. The whole reason I'm here is to help."

"To help Allie. Not to do my dishes."

She peered up him, her expression sincere. "I'm here to *help*. However and with whatever I can. I mean it."

"I believe you do." He nodded to the other side of the glider. "Mind if I join you?"

"Be my guest," she said, scooting over a smidge. "It's so pretty out here, I haven't been able to convince myself to go inside." She let out a small shiver. "But it is cooler here than it is down in Denver."

Reaching inside the door, he grabbed one of his hooded sweatshirts from the pegs on the wall and handed it to her before he sank down beside her. He scrubbed a hand through his hair. "What a day."

"I haven't had a chance to say it yet," she said as she wrapped the jacket around her shoulders. "But I'm sorry for the loss of your ex-wife."

He let out a sigh. "Thanks. We had a wreck of a marriage, and she's been a giant pain in my ass for the last nine years, but it's still weird, knowing that she's gone."

"I'm sure."

"The hardest part is knowing how tough this is on Allie. And I don't have a clue how to help her." He offered her a sideways glance. "I don't know how much Elle told you about me, but I haven't been much of a father. Truth is, I barely know my own daughter."

"Hey, I'm not here to judge. Like I said, I'm just here to help."

"We're gonna need it. Both of us. Lord help me. This girl of mine has tried my patience more in the last few days than any other woman has in the last ten years."

"But you love this one," Nora said softly.

Cade nodded, suddenly unable to find his voice. He wasn't usually rattled by a woman, but Nora seemed to get him. He'd spent less than a day with her and being this close to her had his nerves a little unsteady, but she was easy to talk to. And there weren't many people in his life he found easy to talk to.

"I do," he said, finally regaining his voice. "I do love her. Sass and all. And whether I'm ready for it or not, I feel like I've been given a second chance with her, and I don't want to blow it. Again."

"You won't. You can't change what happened yesterday, Cade. But you can choose to make the most of tomorrow."

"Sounds like you offer people more than just *physical* therapy," he said with a teasing note in his tone. "Should I be expecting a bill for this session?"

She shook her head. "My fee is one spaghetti dinner so you're already paid in full."

"Perfect." He liked her sense of humor and the way she put a positive spin on things.

"I know this is all new to you, but I can imagine Allie is scared too," she told him. "She's dealing with a lot, and I have a feeling all that sarcasm and sass is coming from a place of hurt. She's not too excited about the exercises I was telling her about. She said they sound like a lot of work." Nora chuckled. "She has no idea."

"I don't think she's going to be your easiest patient. You're probably used to people coming into physical therapy who *want* your help."

"Not necessarily. Not everyone is there because they want to be. And most everyone I deal with is in some kind of pain. Otherwise, they wouldn't be there. I've dealt with plenty of patients who are sad and angry at the situation that brought them to me, so they're dealing with grief along with the physical pain. Although grief can be like a physical pain as well. I just need to figure out what Allie likes to do and how to incorporate that into our therapy regime. I don't think she's going to be excited about rolling a ball or doing wall stretches, but if I can get her to do some things she enjoys that will naturally work and stretch those muscles, that would be ideal."

"Good luck."

"I've got some ideas that I want to try with her. I realized earlier that I forgot to pack my yoga balls, but I can always order a couple when we get to that point. My goal is for her to think we're just doing normal stuff and not even recognize that we're actually doing therapy exercises. I brought some equipment with me and we'll use that, but I really want to incorporate things from her environment into her therapy, like feeding the animals or maybe brushing a horse."

"We've got plenty of opportunities for that kind of thing here. Bryn's got tons of animals around this place, from chickens to pigs to that funny mini-horse. Heck, she's got six dogs over in that farmhouse and one of them only has three legs."

"*Six* dogs?"

"Well, to be fair, three of them are puppies."

"*Puppies?*" Her face got that dreamy look, and her voice went up a notch as she said the word.

"Oh geez. What is it about puppies that makes people go crazy? Although they are pretty cute little buggers. She had five, but she's given a couple of them away."

"Oh, I can't wait to see them tomorrow. And that kind of stuff is perfect. You don't think about working the muscles in your hand when you're petting a puppy."

"You're smart, Nora." He leaned back against the glider and felt some of the tension he'd been carrying in his shoulders all day ease. "I'm glad you're here."

She settled back next to him, so close their shoulders almost touched. And close enough that he could smell her shampoo. "I'm glad I'm here too."

———

Cade was up the next morning and halfway through his chores before the sun made its way into the sky. He'd spent the night tossing and turning as he'd worried about Allie, then worried more when images of Nora snuck into his thoughts, especially when those images had her half-naked and wrapped back in a towel.

Bryn was walking from the direction of the bunkhouse as he came out of the barn. "Hey Cousin," she said. "How'd it go last night?"

He offered her a weary shrug. "About as good as you'd expect. Allie's mad and sad, but every once in a while, I coax a smile out of her."

"I know it's hard, but keep trying. You'll get there." She pointed toward his place. "I made you all some cinnamon rolls. They're still warm, so I left them on your stove top."

He shook his head. "You didn't have to. You've already done so much."

"I know I don't have to. I *want* to. You and Allie are my family. And that means something to me."

"It does to me too," he said quietly, staring down at his boots.

"Hey, don't knock those cinnamon rolls," Zane said, coming up behind him and clapping him on the shoulder. "I'm reaping the rewards of her baking for you."

Cade chuckled. "So is Nora. She came over to have spaghetti with us last night, and she thought your sauce was amazing."

"Oh? She had supper with you?" Bryn asked. "That's nice. Elle said she's a real sweetheart. Is she pretty?"

"Don't even start," Cade told her. "The only reason I invited her to supper was because that dang goat of yours snuck into her place while she was in the shower and ate hers."

Bryn covered her mouth with her hand. "Oh no."

"Oh yes. She came out of the bathroom to find Otis eating her food and Tiny sprawled out on her sofa watching television."

Bryn pressed her lips together to keep from laughing. "Tell her I'm sorry. And make sure you share those rolls with her. Is there anything else you guys need?"

"Nora said something about wishing she'd brought some yoga balls. You have any idea what those are and where I can find a couple of them?"

"Yes, I know what they are." She chuckled as she made a large circle with her arms. "They're sort of like giant bouncy balls. I think you can find them at Walmart. I'll check for you."

"Sounds good. Let me know."

Zane nodded his head toward his truck. "We gotta go, babe."

"Okay," she said, giving Cade a quick hug. "I've got to help Zane get the trailer hooked up. We're going to pick up an abandoned horse this morning."

"Oh yeah?"

"Yeah. Apparently this guy used to run a riding stable then he got too old to do it, but still kept a few of the horses around. Then he got sick and passed away after a few days in the hospital. He'd thought some neighbor was going to take care of the horses, but no one did."

Cade winced. "That's rough."

"Yeah, we don't know how bad a shape they're in. We're taking one and another horse rescue from Durango is taking the other two. We should be back in a few hours."

"Sounds good. I'll get one of the stables ready."

"Appreciate it," Zane said with a wave before turning toward his truck.

———————

Thirty minutes later, Cade had prepped a fresh stall for the new horse and was headed back to the bunkhouse for another cup of coffee and one of Bryn's rolls. He was pleasantly surprised to see Nora sitting out on the front porch again. She had on black leggings, sandals, and a hot pink T-shirt that matched her toenail polish. Her hair was loose and fell around her shoulders, and she wore a smile so bright and happy, he couldn't help but grin back. "Mornin'."

"Good morning." She held up her mug. "Can I interest you in a cup of french roast?"

He raised an eyebrow. "Is it from that fancy coffee machine I hauled into your kitchen yesterday?"

"Yep. And it was worth it." She stood. "I'll bring you a cup, and you can decide."

"Why not?" He nodded toward his door. "Bryn dropped off some cinnamon rolls while I was doing chores this morning. I'll trade you a roll for the coffee."

"Sounds perfect. I love this place. How do you get home-baked goods dropped off in your kitchen?"

"This is small town livin'. Especially out here on the farm. We leave our doors unlocked and everyone kind of treats everyone else's house like their own."

"Yeah, but you must be special, because I tried that already, and you got cinnamon rolls and I got a sandwich-pilfering goat and a television-watching pig."

He chuckled. "So who's the real winner here?"

A hearty laugh burst from her—a sound that made Cade's smile broaden. She was still cracking up as she opened her door. "I'll be over in three minutes with your coffee."

"I'll check on Allie, then serve the cinnamon rolls. Come on in when you're ready."

The bunkhouse was quiet and smelled deliciously like cinnamon and fresh, yeasty bread as he slipped through the front door. He poked his head into Allie's room and found her still in bed but awake and staring at the ceiling. "Good morning."

"Yeah? What's good about it?"

"The sun is out, and your cousin made homemade cinnamon rolls."

She narrowed her eyes as she glared at him. "Who cares about some shitty cinnamon rolls? My mom is dead."

He sucked in a sharp breath, his chest aching as if he'd taken a hard punch. "I know. I'm sorry, honey. I wish there was something I could do."

She rolled away from him. "Just leave me alone."

He turned and strode down the hall and into the kitchen.

His pulse pounded in his ears, rage and powerlessness coursing through him. More upset than he could remember being in a long time, he wasn't paying enough attention and tripped on the folded up corner of the rug. His shoulder slammed into the wall next to the refrigerator so hard that one of the pictures came loose and fell to the floor with a crash. As he tried to regain his balance, he inadvertently kicked it across the floor. It went flying toward the door, where Nora stood, her face pale as she held two cups of steaming coffee.

CHAPTER 5

Dammit. He could *not* catch a break.

Nora looked terrified. The last thing Cade needed was to scare off his daughter's physical therapist, but the anger was still pumping through him.

Nora's hands trembled as she swallowed. "You said it was okay to come in."

"It's fine," he said a little too gruffly. He let out a heavy sigh, then slumped back against the wall and slid down to the floor as the adrenaline rush turned to weariness.

She set the cups on the table and hurried toward him. "What happened?"

He dropped his chin and pressed his forehead into his knees. "My girl is hurting and there's not a damn thing I can do to help her. The person she's used to relying on is gone."

Nora sunk to the floor next to him, putting her back against the wall as well. She scooted closer so their shoulders touched. "I'm sorry."

He shook his head as he clenched his fists and pressed them to the sides of his legs. "I just want to be able to say something, to *do* something, instead of feeling so damn helpless."

Nora didn't say anything—what was there to say anyway?— but she gently covered his fist with her hand. He turned his hand over and clasped hers in his. He was probably squeezing it too tight, but she didn't seem to mind. She was squeezing back just as hard.

He wasn't sure how long they sat like that—neither of them speaking, just holding tightly to the other's hand. But his breathing settled, and the tension in his shoulders eased.

A crash came from Allie's room, and they both dropped the other's hand and pushed up from the wall.

"You okay?" Cade asked, hurrying toward her.

"I'm fine. Some books fell off the shelf, but it's fine. You don't need to hover," Allie said, knocking into the wall again as she maneuvered the knee scooter through the door. "I just had to pee."

He stood back and let her pass, then turned back to the kitchen. "You might as well have a cinnamon roll, since you're up anyway."

"Fine, whatever," she said before shutting the bathroom door.

Nora had picked up the picture and hung it back on the wall. "Good as new. Didn't even break." She offered him a small smile as she handed him one of the cups of coffee.

He nodded, thankful for her steadfast positivity, and tried to ignore the fact that his hands were still shaking slightly as he accepted the cup and took a sip. The coffee was hot and strong, and helped to soothe his dry throat. "It's good. Thanks."

"There's going to be good days and bad. You just have to focus on the good ones and hope they start to outweigh the bad."

He nodded as he went to the cupboard and pulled out some plates. He placed cinnamon rolls on them and was carrying them to the table when Allie emerged from the bathroom. She had a brush in her hand and set it on the table before slumping into the chair.

"You want milk?" he asked, turning to the fridge.

"Sure." She picked up the brush and tried to pull it through her tangled hair. "I shouldn't have gone to bed with wet hair."

Cade set the glass of milk in front of her, then held his hand out for the brush. "Give it here. I can get the tangles out and put it in a braid for you."

She eyed him with skepticism. "You can braid hair?"

"I am a font of talents and abilities."

"And a nerd too. Who says font?" she sneered, but she handed him the brush.

Score one for nerd dad. He stepped behind his daughter and offered Nora a wink. "Someone who reads a lot of books." He gently drew her hair back over her shoulders and carefully pulled the brush through it. "And I learned how to braid on my horse's tail and mane."

"Oh, that's nice."

"Gypsy thinks so."

"Gypsy?"

"My horse. I'll take you over to meet her this morning." His fingers deftly wove the three sections of hair into a plait. He tilted his head toward Nora. "Could I trouble you to find me a rubber band in that junk drawer next to the stove?"

"I'll do you one better." She pulled a ponytail holder from her front pocket and held it out to him. "I always carry one in my pocket. Especially when I'm working."

"Thanks." He twisted the elastic band around the end of the braid. "There. You look almost as good as my horse."

"Almost?" Allie asked.

"Hey, that's high praise. I have a pretty good-lookin' horse."

Allie smiled reluctantly, her lips curving into a wry grin.

"Why don't you get dressed, and we can go over and meet this good-looking horse?" Nora suggested. "I'd like to meet her too."

Cade held his breath, thankful Nora had made the suggestion instead of him.

Allie shrugged. "I guess."

He let out his breath and stood to take their plates, turning his back before Allie could see the relief he was sure was written on his face. He tried to keep his voice nonchalant. "Great. I'll get this cleaned up while you change."

"Do you need a hand?" Nora asked her just as casually.

"I got it," Allie said, pushing to her feet and wheeling the scooter toward the hallway.

"If you want, we can stop in at Bryn's and I can also introduce you to her puppies," Cade said.

Allie's head whipped back. "Puppies?"

"Didn't I tell you Bryn has some puppies at her house?"

"No." Cade noticed she was wheeling a little faster to her room. "It will just take me a minute to get dressed, then I'll be ready."

He hazarded a glance at Nora once Allie had made it into her room, and this time it was Nora who winked at him.

———

Nora laughed as the wriggling puppy in her lap nipped and licked her chin. "Oh my gosh. He's so cute," she gushed.

"So is this one," Allie said, cuddling a sleepy puppy to her chest. "They all are. But this one is my favorite." She nuzzled her nose into the fur of the fluffy brown-and-white one.

"The mom's name is Grace," Cade told them, scratching the mother dog under the chin. They were sprawled out on Bryn's living room floor, each with a puppy in their lap and Grace curled against Cade's leg. She rested her head on his knee, keeping an eye on both him and her pups. "She's a cattle dog, but from the pup's markings, I'd guess there's some border collie mixed in somewhere on either her or the sire's side." He grinned down at his daughter, thankful he'd found something that made her laugh. He couldn't believe how fast she'd gotten ready once he mentioned the puppies.

Allie had on the same shorts and flip-flops as the day before, but today she wore a light pink T-shirt. Between the pink color and the bright smile she wore, she reminded him so much of the sweet little girl he remembered that it made his chest hurt.

"What happened to the other puppies?" Allie asked.

"One of them went to Aunt Sassy, the lady I was telling you about last night. And there was a chunky one named Peanut Butter who went to a girl named Mandy. She's Elle's boyfriend's daughter, and she's always running around this place."

Allie perked up. "How old is she?"

"Ten or eleven, I think. You'll like her. She's a real sweet kid, and she likes to help out with the horses and the animals. She somehow talked her dad into letting her have *two* puppies."

"Huh" was all Allie replied.

"I think one of these guys is going to some neighbor kids down the road."

"I wonder what will happen to the other two," she said wistfully, cuddling the puppy under her chin.

Cade was fairly certain he knew what was going to happen to that one.

———————

"This is where I first learned to ride a horse," Cade said half an hour later as he led Nora and Allie into the barn. "My grandpa taught my brother and me how to ride when we were younger than you."

Allie wheeled the knee scooter behind him but stopped a few feet from the palomino's stall. "It's hard to imagine you ever being younger than me."

He chuckled. "I know, but I haven't always been this hardened, rough cowboy. It's taken a lot of years to become this cynical."

"I'm sure." Allie peered around the barn. "I wish I could have met my great-grandparents."

His sardonic smile softened. "I wish you could have too. You would have adored my grandma—she was the sweetest, kindest person I've ever known, but she didn't take crap from me or my brother. She made the best lemon meringue pie you've ever tasted, and she was one of the hardest working people I've ever met. Same with my grandpa. That guy worked from sunup to sundown taking care of this ranch and all the animals. He used to have several hundred head of cattle that he ranched and a bunch of horses. He taught me to ride and rope and how to drive a wagon and bucket-feed a calf. He's the one who taught me pretty much everything I know about how to cowboy."

"He sounds like a great guy," Nora said.

"He was a good man." Cade cut his eyes to the stall where his horse stood, the memories of those summers spent here with his grandparents closing in on him like the clouds of a thunderstorm. *Too bad I didn't take after him.* He swallowed, pushing the memories away as he turned back to Nora and his daughter.

He gestured to their sandaled feet. "Gramps would lose his mind if he saw those flip-flops in the barn. First thing he did every summer was take us kids into the Mercantile in Creedence and get us a new pair of cowboy boots."

Nora laughed as she brushed hay from her foot. "I can see why."

"*I* can see I've got my work cut out for me if I'm gonna try to teach a couple of city girls like you two how to cowboy." His comment earned a grin from Nora and an eye roll from Allie, but he was starting to be able to read her eye rolls and could tell this one didn't hold as much as annoyance as some. "A good cowboy always starts by taking care of his horse. Gypsy has been with me for fifteen years."

"That's a long time to have a horse," Nora remarked.

He offered her a wry grin. "Longest and most committed relationship I've ever had with a member of the female persuasion."

"It's longer than you stayed with Mom and me," Allie muttered.

Ouch. "Besides feeding them and giving them fresh water, you also need to groom your horse," Cade continued, choosing to ignore Allie's muttered comment. What could he say anyway? Her dig, though hurtful, was true. He gestured to a bucket of brushes and combs he'd set out earlier that morning. "There's all sorts of brushes and curry combs you can use." He grabbed a round brush, put his hand through the leather strap on the back of it, then stepped through the stall door. "I already fed and watered Gypsy this morning, but she still needs a good brushing today."

He gestured for them to come closer. Nora took a tentative step into the stall, but Allie hung back where she was. "I'm good from here," she said.

"Suit yourself." Cade drew the brush down the horse's neck. "Easy, gentle strokes," he explained. "The horse might sometimes stamp their feet, but they enjoy the attention." He held the brush out to Nora. "You want to give it a try?"

She shrank back. "She seemed tall from over there, but now that I'm closer, I realize she's enormous."

"Yeah. She's a hard worker too. She's gotten me through a lot of tough times and always pulls her weight when there's work to be done. But she's also a sweetheart. And she loves to be groomed." He held out the brush again. "Come on. She won't hurt you. And I'm right here."

Nora took the brush and lightly touched it to Gypsy's neck. "Good horsey," she cooed, her voice a little breathless.

Cade put his hand over Nora's and drew it across the horse's coat. His shoulder brushed against hers, and he was suddenly all too aware of the floral scent of her shampoo. Gypsy turned her head back and gave Cade's chest a nudge.

"Oh, gosh," Nora said, taking a step back.

"It's okay," he told her. "She's just saying hello." Nora might have been unnerved by the horse's movements, but he was more shaken by the feelings of heat surging over his skin from standing so close to Nora and touching her hand. He took a step back as well and turned his focus to Allie. Which was where his focus should always be, he reminded himself. "You ready to give it a try?"

"I'll pass," Allie said, wrinkling her nose.

Cade had a feeling it had more to do with a fear of the size of the horse than disdain.

"Oh, come on. How am I gonna turn you two into cowboys if you're afraid of horses?"

"I didn't say I was afraid," Allie told him, then she let out a shriek as a velvety nose nudged her back. She whipped around to see Shamus standing behind her. "Holy crap. You scared me."

Cade chuckled. He'd seen the mini-horse come in the front door of the barn and had been waiting for Allie to notice him.

Now that her initial fright was over, she smiled down at him. "How did you get in here?" The horse nuzzled into her side, earning a laugh and a neck scratch from her. He reveled in a few pets, then trotted over to the basket of brushes. He nosed through the choices, then daintily picked up a brush in his teeth and carried it back to Allie.

"I told you they like being brushed," Cade said, grinning at the sound of his daughter's laughter and the antics of the little horse.

Shamus shook his head then dropped the brush at Allie's feet. She bent down and picked it up, then tentatively drew it over his back. He nodded his head and scooted closer to her. She giggled and did another long stroke from his neck to his rump. Shamus let out a contented huff, then turned around and nudged her with his backside. She laughed as she obliged his obvious request. "This guy is hilarious. But he likes this. He really does like it."

"I told you. Horses enjoy affection just like dogs and cats. And people for that matter." He loved watching his daughter interact with the little horse. Shamus was doing in ten seconds what he hadn't managed to get her to do in ten minutes.

The horse turned his head and nudged her hip. "Why does he keep doing that?"

"He's checking your pocket for snacks. He's used to all of us giving him treats. I usually have some carrots or apple slices for him."

"Do you have any today?"

"Not on me. But I've got some apples back at the house we could slice up for him."

"Cool. I'll go get some."

"I can…" Cade stopped as Nora rested a hand gently on his arm. "I can wait here."

Nora squeezed his arm. "We'll be out here if you need us," she told Allie.

Allie raised a skeptical eyebrow. "What would I need either of you for? I'm not a child. I'm just slicing up an apple and there was a whole bowl of them on the counter."

"Yeah, of course," Cade said, turning back to Gypsy. "Why would you need us?" He focused on taking deep breaths as he stroked his horse's neck and listened for the sound of her wheeling out of the barn.

Nora patted his shoulder. "Good job, Dad. I know it's hard, but the more things she does for herself, the better off you'll both be. And just making the trip to the bunkhouse and back is good for her. The more she gets out walking and doing stuff, the better. We've made great progress this morning with the horses and the time we spent with the puppies."

"I know. You're right."

The sound of a truck engine drew their attention. Shamus turned and trotted out the barn door to fulfill his duties as official ranch greeter. Cade closed up Gypsy's stall, then he and Nora followed.

Zane and Bryn were back with the new rescue horse. Zane had his window down and was waving Shamus out of the way as he backed the trailer up toward the front of the barn. Bryn got out and hurried around to the back end of the trailer. "I hope you got the stall ready," Bryn hollered in Cade's direction. "She's been pissed about being in this trailer the whole drive back."

"It's ready for her," Cade said, stepping forward to open the back door of the trailer.

The horse inside was a small quarter horse, and she was indeed pissed off. Her body was gaunt, and her eyes were wild as she huffed and stamped her displeasure at the trailer. She was tied to the side bar with a weathered lead rope that looked like she'd been chewing on it. She reared back and the rope snapped, and she charged out of the trailer.

Zane was coming around the far side of the truck, and he held out his arms to try to calm her. He reached to grab what was left of the dangling rope but missed. His border collie, Hope, ran around his legs, letting out a sharp bark as she tried to herd the horse toward the barn.

Wild-eyed, the horse tossed back her head and reared up on her hind legs. Zane and Cade were standing to the left of the trailer, blocking the horse's way.

Cade hollered to Nora as he took a protective step in front of her. "Get back in the barn." From the corner of his eye, he caught sight of Allie, who had just come off the porch of the bunkhouse and was heading their way, holding a bowl full of sliced apples.

The horse bucked again and took off in a terrified gallop heading straight for his daughter.

CHAPTER 6

CADE STOOD FROZEN IN PLACE, HIS HEART SLAMMING INTO HIS chest, as he watched the horse race directly at Allie.

Bryn let out a warning shout, and the sound finally spurred him into motion. His boots felt like they were pulling through peanut butter as he sprinted toward the bunkhouse. He saw Zane take off running around the far edge and instinctively knew he was going to try to head the horse off and force her back toward the barn.

He should have followed his lead and closed in on his flank, but all he could think about was getting to his daughter.

Allie froze, much like he just had, her eyes wide as the horse galloped full speed at her.

Cade was sprinting full speed as well, but the horse reached the girl first and came to an abrupt stop about two feet in front of her. She shook her head, rearing back for a second, then took a tentative step toward Allie and stretched out her head toward the bowl of apples.

Cade and Zane stopped at the same time, both recognizing that the horse had quieted and neither wanting to spook her again.

Something about the horse must have touched Allie—maybe it was her gaunt and frightened appearance, but the girl reached into the bowl and plucked out a thick slice of apple, then slowly held it out to the horse. She kept her hand flat like Cade had taught her the day before.

The horse sniffed at her hand, then delicately took the chunk of fruit. The horse's body stilled and all her attention was focused on Allie as she took another slice of apple from the bowl and held it out on her outstretched palm.

Bryn, Zane, and Cade stood perfectly still, watching the

exchange as if they all knew something special was happening. Cade had been around horses all his life and could read them well enough to know this one had calmed and was more interested in the fruit than in causing any harm to the girl feeding it to him.

"You okay, honey?" he quietly asked his daughter.

"I'm fine," she said softly, keeping her eyes on the horse, a look of awe on her face. "I was scared at first, but I think this horse likes me."

As if in answer to her statement, the horse lightly nudged her arm. Allie laughed as she passed her another slice.

When the bowl was empty, the horse stood still and let Cade approach her. He gently ran his hand over her neck, murmuring soothing sounds as he hooked his fingers under her halter. "There's a good girl," he said. Now that he had the horse firmly in hand, he looked down at this daughter. "That was really brave."

"I didn't feel brave at first. I was so scared I thought I was going to pee my pants," Allie said, reaching out to touch the horse's cheek. "But then all of sudden, I wasn't afraid. It was like I just knew she wasn't going to hurt me."

He smiled at her. "Maybe you have a little more cowboy in you than either of us realized."

A grin broke across her face before she had a chance to stop it.

"Wow, you did really great with her," Bryn said, coming up on Allie's side and putting an arm around the girl's shoulder. "I'm so proud of you."

Allie beamed up at her cousin, eagerly accepting the praise from her that she could only hesitantly take from him. "Thanks."

"You did a good job," Zane said, approaching the group. "That horse was just as scared as you were. She'd been uprooted from her home less than an hour ago and wasn't happy about riding in the trailer. She's not a bad horse, she was just afraid." He tipped his cowboy hat toward her. "I'm Zane by the way."

"I'm Allie," she said, then turned her attention back to the horse. "Why'd you take her from her home?"

"We rescued her," Bryn answered. "Her owner died, and no one was taking care of her."

"Is that why she looks so skinny?"

"Yes, but she doesn't look as starved as some of the horses we've taken in. We got to her before she got too bad." Bryn ran a hand gently over the horse's neck.

"That must be why she stopped for me. She was probably real hungry," Allie said.

"I think she knew you were safe and wouldn't hurt her," Cade said. "Sometimes horses will just connect with people, and I think this horse knew you were a friend. That's something special."

Another small smile tugged at Allie's lips. She stood a little taller as she confidently stroked the horse's neck. "I think you're special too." She turned back to Bryn. "What's her name?"

Bryn shrugged. "We don't know. Would you like to pick a name for her?"

"Me?"

"Sure. You seem to know her the best already. Why don't you think about it, and you can let me know if you come up with an idea?"

"Okay."

Cade wanted to hug his cousin. And he was *not* a hugger. But the way she was talking to Allie and offering her the important job of naming the horse made his heart swell. "Why don't we get this girl into the barn?" Cade said, giving the halter a little tug. "She can see her new home, and you can give her some grain," he told Allie. The horse obediently followed him as he turned around and started toward the barn.

He had to smile at Nora, who stood about six feet back. She had Shamus standing on one side of her and Tiny, the pig, stood on the other. "Evidently she came out to see what all the commotion was about," Nora said, nodding toward Tiny. "I guess now that I let her watch her show at my place, she considers us friends."

"I love it," Bryn said, swooping in to throw her arms around Nora. "I'm Bryn, and I'm so glad you're here. I can't apologize enough for my goat's rude behavior, but I hope we'll be great friends too."

"Told you so," Cade muttered behind his cousin's back as he led the horse around her and into the barn. He got her settled in a stall on the other side of the barn from Gypsy and let Allie feed her some grain while he got her some fresh water.

Zane went to move his truck while Nora and Bryn hung back and let Cade and Allie take the lead with the horse. Cade crossed to where the two women stood chatting with each other. "Thanks, Bryn," he told his cousin as he leaned against the fence next to her.

"For what?"

"You know. For this. With Allie and the horse."

Bryn put a hand on his arm. "This is our family's farm. I want her to have some ownership in it too. She hasn't got to grow up here like we did, but she's here now. And that's what's important." She squeezed his arm. "I'm going to go help Zane get the trailer unhitched and put away. I'll catch up with you guys later."

"You were right," Nora said, leaning against the fence next to him after Bryn left. "I do already feel like I'm best friends with your cousin."

He huffed out a laugh. "I told you so."

"You already said that," she told him, giving his arm a playful nudge.

"Yeah, but it bears repeating because I'm so often wrong when it comes to reading women and what they're going to do."

"You got a lot of things right this morning."

His smile turned to a sigh. "I don't know about that. If that horse hadn't been half-starved, we could have had an entirely different scenario on our hands."

"But it turned out okay. And you still seemed to know how to handle the situation. I watched you back off as if you could read that horse's intentions."

"I could, I guess. But it's my fault it got loose in the first place. I should have been paying closer attention." He shook his head. "I don't get how I can have such natural instincts when it comes to horses, yet I seem to know nothing about taking care of a child. Why did I even open that trailer door without checking to see where Allie was?"

"You're being too hard on yourself. You're not used to having a child around and having to take note of that sort of thing. You'll get better. You just have to cut yourself a break."

As much as he appreciated her encouragement, he was uncomfortable with so much of her attention focused on his lack of parenting skills. He needed to change the subject. "Why don't we *all* take a break? I'm starving. What do you say I take you and Allie into town and treat you both to a cheeseburger?"

"I'd say yes. I'm starving."

———————————

Nora was surprised at the ease the three of them had with each other as they powered through cheeseburgers, chocolate shakes, and a mountain of crispy fries. Even Allie's spirits seemed to have perked up a little, especially when she was talking about the animals.

Cade had brought them to the Creedence Country Café, the diner where Bryn waitressed. Her shift didn't start until later that afternoon, but it seemed like it was the place to be because half the town was eating lunch there and a good number of them knew Cade. Several people waved and a few came by their booth to say hello, including the infamous Aunt Sassy.

"You must be Allie," the older woman said after she had greeted Cade. "It's nice to meet you. You can call me Aunt Sassy. Everyone does."

"Nice to meet you too."

"I knew your great-grandparents, and they were good people. In fact, I spent quite a bit of time out at their ranch when we were younger. They used to hold a barn dance there every fall to celebrate the end of harvest, and I've boogied with several of the ranch hands who lived in the very same bunkhouse you're living in now."

Allie's eyes went wide, and she leaned forward. "You did?"

"Yep." She winked as she planted a hand on her hip. "I may have even kissed a few."

Nora chuckled. This woman was a character. And it seemed she'd already won over Cade's daughter.

"All right. That's enough talk about kissing," Cade said, obviously uncomfortable with the direction of the conversation by the pink color on his cheeks—which was seriously cute as heck. He nodded toward her. "Aunt Sassy, this is Nora Fisher. She's a friend of Elle's and the physical therapist who's staying out at the ranch with us to help with Allie's recovery."

Aunt Sassy turned her attention to Nora and narrowed her eyes as she studied her. "Nora, is it?"

"Yes, ma'am."

"You're not from around here?"

"No."

"You a city girl or from the country?"

"City, I guess. I'm from Denver."

"You go to college in Colorado?"

Nora nodded.

"Buff or a Ram?"

"Ram. Go CSU." She raised her fist in a little air bump. But it seemed as if Aunt Sassy wasn't finished with her rapid-fire questions.

"Coffee drinker or tea?"

"Coffee."

"Favorite season?"

"Summer."

"Popcorn with butter?"

"Always."

"Peanut butter chunky or smooth?"

"Extra chunky."

"Glass half-empty or half-full?"

"Full."

"How often do you stay up past midnight?"

"Rarely."

"Biggest pet peeves?"

"Non-apology apologies, pushy vegans, finding a single sock in the dryer, people who chew with their mouths open, and mansplaining."

"What are you afraid of?"

"Spiders, snakes, and the Broncos never getting another quarterback as good as Peyton Manning."

Sassy nodded wisely. "That's a valid concern. Do you play an instrument?"

Nora shook her head. "Can barely carry a tune."

"What are you good at?"

"Breaking my diet, charades, and looking on the bright side."

"How many books do you have on your Kindle?"

"Too many to count."

"What's the first thing you'd save in a fire?"

"My mom."

"You'll do." Sassy offered her a wink and a satisfied grin before patting Cade on the hand. "I'll come out to see you in the next few days, bring you a pan of my famous macaroni and cheese."

"That'd be real nice. You know how I love it."

"What was all that about?" Nora asked after Sassy had gone back to her table.

"The twenty questions?"

Nora nodded. "I'm not sure I wasn't just interrogated by a CIA intelligence officer."

Cade chuckled. "Right? Apparently, it's just a thing she does. You should have heard some of the stuff she asked me the first time we met. She wanted to know if I preferred blonds or brunettes, if I knew how to tie a fly, and even asked my hat size."

"So which did you tell her?" Nora couldn't help but ask as she fought to not smooth her chestnut-brown hair. "Blonds or brunettes?"

He laughed again and offered her a roguish wink that sent shivers of heat coiling in her stomach. "Honey, this wasn't my first rodeo. I said silver of course."

Despite the heat, Nora laughed with him. "Of course."

The waitress came by with their check. Cade handed her a couple of twenties and told her to keep the change. Nora knew how much their meals should have cost and liked that he was a good tipper.

"I appreciate the gesture, but I can cover my own meal," she told him as they headed out of the diner. Although just barely. She hadn't collected her first paycheck yet and she knew her account was slim. Apparently her bank account had no trouble keeping on its diet.

"I know you can," he said as he held the door for her and Allie. "But I invited you, and this one was my treat." He walked slowly along the sidewalk, patiently waiting as Allie wheeled herself along next to them.

The downtown area of Creedence was patterned in a square with the courthouse in the center. The sidewalks were dotted with old-fashioned streetlamps and planters overflowing with pansies and trumpet flowers. Several shops had cute benches in front of them where either dogs were tied or people could sit to chat. Nora was charmed at the number of shops that had dog bowls sitting outside their stoops filled with water.

The diner was on one corner of the main street and they passed a hardware store, a bank, and Carley's Cut and Curl as they walked back to Cade's pickup. He stopped on the sidewalk outside of the Creedence Mercantile. "As long as I'm feelin' generous, I think we should stop in here and get you each a pair of cowboy boots."

Allie pointed to the scooter. "How am I supposed to wear cowboy boots?"

"You can at least wear one boot on your good foot," he told her as he held open the door to the mercantile. "Because if you're gonna be spendin' any time with that horse, you need a pair of boots on. She'd feel awful bad if she stepped on your foot. And her hooves could rip your toenail clean off."

Allie winced. "Gross. Okay, you convinced me. I'll let you get me some boots. Although how I'm going to get them on is a mystery." She ducked under his arm and wheeled into the store.

"Nice touch with the toenail," Nora told him quietly as she stepped in front of him.

The sound of his chuckle did funny things to her insides. "I thought that would do it. Now what's it going to take to convince you to let me buy a pair for you too?"

"A lot more than the threat of a sore toe," she told him. "But I'll look around." She wandered the aisles, surprised at the selection of moccasins and boots available. The store was huge inside and divided into two sections, as if the owners had purchased two stores, then added a large doorway between them. One side of the store carried boots, hats, and western clothing while the other side seemed to focus on hunting and fishing.

Cade led them down the aisle to a section of short-topped boots. "I think you should each get a pair of these Ropers. They're shorter, so they're easier to put on and take off, plus they've got good soles, are comfortable, and won't pinch your toes."

"And they come in pretty cool colors," Allie said, picking up a pair of brown boots with dark pink and purple sides. "I like these."

"Good choice," he said, then pointed to a chair. "Sit down. I'll help you try one on." He grabbed a packet of socks. "You're gonna need these too."

Allie sat and only fussed a little as he pulled a sock on her foot, then helped her push her good foot into a boot.

He pulled her to a standing position. "How does it feel?"

"Good," she said. "I like them. They're more comfortable than I thought they'd be." She nodded to the black-and-teal pair Nora was admiring. "Are you going to get a pair too?"

She voiced the question as if her accepting a pair depended on Nora's answer. Nora ran her finger over the dark teal stitching. They *were* cute boots. And they were a much better option for walking around the ranch than either her sandals or her dress boots.

Cade nudged her arm. "Just try 'em on."

She sighed and relented, knowing if they were half as comfortable as Allie said they were, she'd have a hard time turning them down. She was such a sucker for a cute pair of shoes, even if they were cowboy boots. She found a box in her size and a pack of socks and sat in the chair next to Allie. "I don't know. I've never had a pair of cowboy boots before. I'm not sure I need them." She pulled on a sock, then took out a boot and tugged it on. Dang it. It was surprisingly comfortable.

"Oh, you'll need them. You both will. It's an essential part of being a cowboy, or in you all's case, a cowgirl." Cade peered down at Nora's feet as she pulled on the other boot and stood to take a few steps around. "Those look good on you. How do they feel?"

"Good, actually. I thought they'd feel weird, but they're pretty comfy."

"I think so too," Allie said. "Those are cute."

"So are the ones you picked," Nora told her. She could see the indecision on Allie's face and the need in Cade's to do something nice for his daughter. It felt a little weird to be accepting this gift from him, but she could see how much it meant to him to buy them for Allie. She could always take them and then later talk him into taking the cost out of her first paycheck.

A saleswoman stopped behind their chairs. "Anything I can help with?"

Cade offered Nora a questioning, and hopeful, look. She chewed her bottom lip as she glanced from Allie to her feet, then back up at Cade. She smiled as she gave him a nod. "I guess you can ring up a couple pairs of boots."

"And the socks," Cade told the saleswoman as he hoisted the boot boxes into his arms. His face shone with a wide smile as he turned back to her and Allie. "Unless I can talk you all into looking at hats."

Allie made a barfing sound, and Nora laughed as she shook her head at Cade. "Don't push your luck, cowboy."

He chuckled as he followed the saleswoman to the counter to pay for the boots.

"He's weird," Allie said.

"Yeah, I know. But getting these boots does seem like a good idea to protect our feet around the animals. And it sure seemed to make him really happy."

"I know," the girl said, looking down and picking at a loose seam on her shorts. "That's why I let him."

Nora smiled even though Allie wasn't looking at her. "Me too."

———————

A surprise was waiting outside their door when Cade, Nora, and Allie got back to the bunkhouse.

"What the hell are those?" Cade asked as they approached the porch.

"They're yoga balls," Nora said, obviously delighted. "But how did anyone know we needed them?"

"I think I mentioned it to Bryn. But I was asking her where I could get a pair." Although he wouldn't have guessed this was what he would be buying. The balls were huge, one blue and one gray. "There's a note," he said, pulling a folded paper from between the jamb and the screen door. "It's from Elle. It says she's sorry she missed us. She stopped by to see Allie and catch up with Nora, and she heard we needed yoga balls so she ran to Denver and grabbed a couple." He shook his head. "That woman constantly surprises me."

"Me too," Nora replied, agreeing. "She's about the nicest person I know."

"Put her together with Bryn and it's like rainbows and teddy bears float in the air around them. She also picked us up a baked ziti and said she put it in the oven on low and stuck a lemon meringue pie in the fridge."

Nora offered him a grin. "You have to admit, she's not a bad friend to have. Baked ziti *and* a pie. I mean, come on."

He chuckled. "She said don't give her too much credit, they're from the diner. Then she drew some hearts and stuff and signed her name." He passed the note to Nora.

"Why do people keep bringing us food?" Allie asked, her brow furrowing. "Mom and I have never had anyone drop off anything at our apartment."

"It's different up here. Small towns are a community, and they like to take care of each other. And one of their own has been hurt, so their way of helping is to drop off food."

"*I'm* not one of their own. And neither are you. You only moved here a few months ago."

"You're right. But my grandparents lived here all their lives, and you can bet your great-grandma dropped off plenty of baked goods for folks in this community. The Callahans are family around here, and you're a Callahan."

"In name only," she muttered before pushing through the door and heading for her room.

Cade flinched at the sound of her bedroom door slamming. He leaned his shoulder against the side of the house and let out a sigh. "I don't get it. What did I say?"

Nora put a hand on his arm. "Nothing. She's a teenager, so her moods are going to be all over the place."

"But I thought things were going so well. She was even laughing at lunch."

"Which might be part of the problem. Remember, she just lost her mom and has been uprooted to this new place. She might feel guilty for having fun or for enjoying this farm—like if she starts to like you and Bryn too much, it will be a betrayal to her mom."

"You might be right." He offered her a smile. "What's that advice gonna cost me?"

She grinned up at him. "One baked ziti dinner."

"Done. I'll even throw in a slice of pie." He tried to laugh, but the anguish of the situation was getting to him, and he dropped his chin to his chest. "Ya know, I consider myself a pretty tough guy, but this parenting stuff is rough."

Nora took a step toward him. "I have to warn you that I'm a hugger by nature, and it's killing me not to be able to offer you a hug. Like I'm totally comin' in hot, so if you don't want to be smothered in a hug, you need to stop me now."

The idea of wrapping his arms around Nora had emotion burning his throat. Which was weird since his feelings toward women weren't generally led by his heart. But something about this woman, with her sunny attitude and her giving nature, was getting to him. He opened his arms, and she stepped into them and wrapped herself around him.

He let out his breath as she sank into him, and he bent his head and buried his face in her hair. "You feel good," he whispered, then cleared his throat. "I mean *this* feels good."

"So do you," she murmured into his chest. Or at least that's what he thought he heard. She might have said, "This does too."

She pulled back, but he wasn't ready to let her go and kept his arms circled around her waist. She looked up at him from under long eyelashes, and he couldn't tear his eyes away.

There was something here. He knew it, and he was sure she did too. The electricity between them was almost visible, as if it shimmered in the air. They'd been teasing and flirting and touching the last few days, but this felt different. This was more than playful flirtation.

He dropped his gaze to her mouth and wanted to groan. Her lips were plump and parted, as if just begging to be kissed.

He leaned down and softly grazed her lips with his—not quite a kiss but enough to feel the soft catch of her breath and the delicious enticement of her mouth.

"What's this going to cost me?" he whispered, but he already knew the answer.

It was going to cost him everything.

CHAPTER 7

"ARE WE GOING TO EAT OR WHAT?" ALLIE YELLED FROM INSIDE the bunkhouse.

Cade jerked back, dropping his arms from around Nora's waist and thanked God that they were to the side of the screen door so Allie wasn't able to see them from the hallway. "Yeah, we're coming in," he hollered back to his daughter, then turned back to offer Nora a sheepish grin.

But she wasn't smiling back. She'd raised her hand to her mouth, the pads of her fingers barely touching her lips. She looked a little dazed, but he couldn't tell if it was in a good way. Or just a dazed way.

He touched a hand to her hip. "You okay?"

"Yeah, of course," she said, dropping her hand and shaking her head as if to snap herself out of it. She took a step back and reached for the bag containing her new boots. "Just give me a second to put this stuff away, and I'll be over."

"Sounds good. I'll set the table," he said to her back as she vanished into her own side of the bunkhouse.

Shit. He'd blown it. What the hell had he been thinking? He hadn't. That's what. He hadn't been thinking at all—he'd been reacting to the feel of a beautiful woman in his arms. A soft woman with gorgeous eyes and a perfect mouth.

He only prayed she wasn't in there packing her stuff as fast as she could and preparing to tear out of there. He couldn't take that. She was making such great progress with Allie. His daughter was actually comfortable with her and taking direction, which she balked at from him.

Please, God, don't let my idiot need mess up the opportunity for my daughter to get the help she needs for her recovery.

He contemplated following Nora into her place to try to convince her he was an idiot but decided to give her some space instead. He hoped he wouldn't regret that decision.

Ten minutes later, he'd washed up and he and Allie had set the table. The two of them were in a tentative truce again, which basically meant she was only being semi-pouty and he was ignoring her earlier comments.

A soft knock sounded on the door as he was putting the pan of ziti on the table.

"It smells amazing in here," Nora said as she let herself in. "I could smell the garlic and basil all the way over in my place. Anything I can do to help?"

Oh-kay. So they were going to go the ignoring route with the earlier almost-kiss as well. Avoidance Central around here. Which was fine with him. He was usually a *take the bull by the horns* kind of guy, but that was with a bull, not a teenage girl and a gorgeous woman he might have just stepped over the line with.

"Nope." He pulled out a chair for her. "Just sit down and eat."

"I already poured you a glass of water," Allie told her.

"Thanks," Nora said.

"I think I came up with a name for the horse," Allie announced.

"Good. What'd you decide?" Cade grabbed a serving spoon, then sank into his chair.

"I wanted to name her something happy sounding, since she seems to have had a lot of sad stuff happening to her lately."

"Makes sense."

"So I was thinking a flower name would be kind of cheerful, and Mom's favorite flowers were daisies, so I thought I'd name her Daisy."

"That's perfect," Nora told her with an encouraging smile. "I really love it."

"What do you think, Cade?" Allie narrowed her eyes, regarding him as if daring him to say something negative.

I think I wish you'd stop calling me Cade. "I think it's perfect too. Great choice. Good job kid."

She kept her gaze trained on him for a few seconds more, then she may have started to smile before she caught herself. But it was enough for him. He cut off any further discussion or any opportunity for a sarcastic comment by bowing his head to pray.

It had only been a couple of days, but Cade couldn't help but wonder if anyone else felt like they were starting to feel like a family unit—sitting down to meals together, shopping, already knowing some of each other's likes and dislikes, and the way Nora picked up the serving spoon and both he and Allie automatically handed her their plates.

The conversation was a little stilted at first, but they eventually eased back into their normal flow as they made it through supper and into dessert.

"I've never had lemon meringue pie before," Allie said, squinting at the two-inch-high glossy layer of meringue. "What is that stuff anyway?"

"It's a mixture of egg whites and sugar beaten to within an inch of its life," Nora said. "And sometimes a pinch of cream of tartar."

"Eww," Allie said, pushing her plate away. "Like you put on fish sticks?"

"No, like you use in baking. Completely different stuff." Nora scrunched up her nose. "I think. But they taste totally different anyway." She picked up her fork and carefully cut into the tip of her slice. "The key is to take that perfect bite that has all three components in it—some crust, some lemon, and some of the meringue." She stuck the bite in her mouth and closed her eyes as she sealed her lips over the tines of the fork. "Mmm. Perfection," she declared as she opened her eyes. "It's delicious. I promise."

Allie took her fork and cut off the tiniest bit. She squinched up her eyes as she cautiously took a bite, then grinned at Nora.

"You're right. It's good." She took another bite. "It's really good. Try it," she told Cade.

He took a giant bite, heedless of the proportion of crust to meringue. "Good," he said, since both Nora and his daughter were waiting for his reaction to the pie.

They both smiled and dug in. His phone buzzed as he was taking his last bite of pie. He pulled it from his pocket to check the screen. "It's a reminder text that your doctor's appointment is at eleven tomorrow. They're going to do a checkup and take your stitches out."

Allie's shoulders tensed. "So we're going to Denver?"

"That's where the doctor's office is."

"Can we go by our apartment so I can get my phone and some of my stuff?"

Cade tried to keep the tension from his own shoulders. "If you want."

"I do. I really want my phone. And my own clothes." Her voice lowered as her chin fell. "And some other stuff."

"We can bring some boxes, and you can take whatever you want."

She looked up at Nora. "Will you come with us? Please."

Nora blinked, then looked from Allie to him. He gave her a slight nod. "Um, yeah, sure. Of course. If you want me to."

"I do," Allie said, then pushed the rest of her pie away. "I'm not very hungry anymore. Is it okay if I just go to my room?"

"Sure. That's fine," Cade told her. He stood and picked up their plates, the pie now sitting like a hard lump of lemon-flavored rock in his gut. "I'll clean this stuff up, then I need to go outside to take care of my evening chores. I'm going to feed the horses if you want to come along."

"I don't think so."

"Why don't I help your dad clean up, then you and I can do a little therapy session while he's out with the animals. Would that be okay?" Nora asked Allie.

She shrugged. "Yes, I guess."

Allie disappeared into her room, and he and Nora quietly took care of the dishes. He reached for his hat when they'd finished. "Thanks for this. For everything."

"Of course."

"I'll be back in a bit."

———

This is a very bad idea, Nora chastised herself, even as she carried a blanket and a glass of wine onto the porch. She should just go to bed—so what if it was barely after nine? She could read a book, or play Candy Crush, or contemplate world peace—anything other than planting herself on this chair on the porch.

She wasn't necessarily waiting for him. She was just enjoying the night air. So what if she'd changed into a cute pair of pajamas and slicked on a little lip gloss? That didn't mean she was hoping Cade would come back and sit down next to her on the glider and try to kiss her again.

Her pulse fluttered as she saw his tall figure walk out of the barn and come sauntering toward her. And lordy, could that man ever saunter. As he got closer, her gaze traveled from the dust on his cowboy boots up his long jean-clad legs to his lean waist, then over his muscled chest and broad shoulders and finally landed on his chiseled jaw, where he wore a panty-melting grin that told her he was giving her the same appraisal—and that he liked what he saw.

She took a sip of her wine, trying to cool her suddenly dry throat as he dropped into the glider next to her.

"I was hoping I'd find you here," he said.

A soft "Yeah?" was all she could muster.

"Yeah." He shook his head. "I know it's wrong and probably up there on the list of world's worst ideas, but I was still hoping you'd be out here waiting for me when I got back."

"Who said I was waiting for you?" She had to at least *try* to sound coy about it.

He grinned and held out his hand for her glass. Passing it to him, she watched as his mouth touched the marks her lip gloss had left on the glass. He grimaced, then rubbed his lips together. "Terrible wine, but the minty lip gloss made up for it."

Oh boy. She was in big trouble here.

Gah. Why couldn't she take her eyes off his mouth? The man had great lips.

"How did it go with Allie?" he asked, bringing her screeching back to reality.

"Good. We went through the whole group of exercises, then she brushed her teeth and went to bed. I checked on her a little bit ago, and she was out like a light. She's got a lot going on. I think her body knows when it needs the rest."

"Good." He leaned forward, resting his elbows on his knees. "Listen, Nora. About earlier, I wanted to apologize. I was out of line. I hope I didn't mess things up with you wanting to work with Allie."

"Of course not. What happened earlier has nothing to do with Allie."

He turned his head, catching her in his dark gaze. "You sure?"

"Yes. Positive. And I was right there at that line with you." She took another sip of wine, this time draining the glass. "I need to tell you something. The reason I was available to drop everything and come up here was because I recently quit my job."

He furrowed his brow. "Okay. What does that have to do with me?"

"The reason I left my job was because I got romantically involved with one of the doctors at the clinic where I worked. So involved that he asked me to marry him. And even though we hadn't been together that long, I sold everything I had and moved in with him."

Cade's eyes flicked to her bare hand.

She wiggled her fingers. "I sold the ring. Our relationship ended several months ago in a spectacularly volatile burst of flames that left me living back in my mom's basement with no job, no furniture, and very little pride." She pressed her lips together to keep them from trembling. "But I did manage to swipe his expensive coffee machine."

"The one…" He tilted his head toward her screen door.

She nodded.

His lips curved into a wicked grin. "I thought that coffee tasted extra good."

A laugh escaped her, and she covered her mouth with her hand. "I enjoy every cup I make."

"From where I'm sitting, it seems to me like he lost out on more than just a fancy cup of coffee."

Emotion seared her throat, and she swallowed as she leaned forward. "You do surprise me, Cade Callahan."

He lifted one shoulder in an offhand shrug. "One of my many talents."

"What are some of your other talents?" she whispered.

"You sure you want to know?" His voice was husky and reminded her of raw timber. He hadn't moved any closer, was still leaning forward with his elbows on his knees. Only his head was turned her way, his gaze dark and ominous under the brim of his hat. And sexy as hell.

She squirmed in her seat, parts of her coming alight that she'd spent the last several months trying to diminish. Her heart was hammering against her chest, and her voice seemed to have completely left her. Along with her good sense. What the hell was she playing at? "Yes," she whispered.

He lifted his hand to cup her cheek, his long fingers twining around the back of her head and through her hair. "This feels like a really bad idea."

"Yes," she whispered again.

He leaned in as he pulled her toward him, then covered her mouth with his. The first kiss was soft, tentative, testing. The second more insistent. The third filled with a controlled hunger as his fingers tightened in her hair. His lips were warm, and he tasted like cinnamon gum and danger.

He pulled back and leaned his forehead against hers, his breath ragged. "You okay?"

"Yes."

His lips curved into another wicked grin. "Darlin', so far I'm three for three in the yes department. If I carry you inside, am I gonna get a fourth?"

YES. She couldn't say it. His kisses seemed to have taken her voice, but she took a deep breath, then nodded her head.

A sound similar to a growl came from his throat as he kissed her again, then lifted her into his arms. She couldn't tear her gaze from his as he pulled open the screen door and carried her inside.

He made it as far as the island separating the kitchen from the living room before stopping to kiss her again. "I need to get my hands on you," he said, setting her down on the counter.

In seconds, she had her arms wrapped around his neck and her legs around his waist, eliminating any space between them. He felt better than she'd even dared to imagine. His strong hands explored her body, roaming over her back, her waist, digging his fingers into her hair as he cupped her scalp to deepen the kisses. His tongue was warm as it pressed between her lips, and she could taste a hint of wine.

Everything about him was warm and exciting, and she melted into his embrace, ignoring every shred of sense that was screaming at her that this was a terrible idea. The needs of her body overruled the logic of her head as she lost herself in the man she'd been fantasizing over since the moment she'd stepped out of her car and seen him standing by the fence.

A soft moan escaped her as his hand slipped beneath her pajama top, his fingers grazing across her stomach before sliding up to cup her breast. Her nipple tightened against the fabric of her bra as Cade dipped his head, trailing a line of hot kisses down her neck.

The front of her shirt had pulled to the side, exposing the deep vee of her cleavage and the silky fabric of one side of her bra. A shudder of need passed through her as Cade's lips brushed over the lacy trim, his breath warm against her skin as his mouth skimmed over the plump crest of her breast pushing to escape the cup.

She dropped her head back, giving him more of herself to taste and discover. His fingers slipped under the straps of her bra and tank top and slowly—oh, so deliciously slowly—drew both down her shoulder as his lips drifted over the bare skin left behind.

"You are so beautiful," he whispered against her neck, sending coils of heat surging through her.

Her hands had found their way under his shirt, and she marveled at his lean waist and the array of hard muscles her fingers traveled over, then gripped as his mouth found another spot on her shoulder to kiss.

She barely knew him, yet she could not get enough of him. And maybe the length of time they'd known each other didn't matter. Something about this man spoke to her, and she'd felt they'd had a connection from the moment they'd met. She felt like she already knew him, and knew enough to know that Cade wasn't the kind of man who let people in easily. Yet he'd shown her parts of himself, parts of his relationship with his daughter, things that made her feel like she saw the man underneath the rough exterior.

Either that or she was just inventing an excuse for why she was considering getting naked with him. And make no mistake, she was in deep consideration.

His lips found hers again and his hand was back under her shirt, his fingers just reaching for the clasp of her bra when they froze as a terrified scream ripped through the air.

CHAPTER 8

"ALLIE," CADE SAID AS HE LET HER GO AND SPRINTED FROM HER kitchen.

Nora pushed off the counter and raced after him, straightening her clothes and smoothing her hair as she ran. He was already to his daughter's bedroom by the time Nora made it through the front door.

"You okay? You hurt? What's wrong?" The light from the hallway spilled into the room, and Cade was on his knees next to the bed.

Nora hung back in the doorway as Allie pushed up on one elbow. Her hair was damp and tangled around her head, and her cheeks were wet with tears. "Mom," she called out reaching for Nora.

Oh no. She stumbled back, out of view, not wanting to upset the girl anymore.

"Honey, it's okay," Cade said. "You had a nightmare. You're okay."

She heard Allie suck in her breath, then let out a sob. "I was in the car with Mom. We were just driving. We were arguing about what station to listen to on the radio. Mom wanted this stupid oldies station, and I wanted pop. We were laughing. And then—" She couldn't speak as another sob ripped through her.

"Shh, it's okay."

"It's not okay. Mom's gone. And she's never coming back."

"I know, baby."

Nora leaned against the wall as she fought back tears. *Poor sweet girl.* She wished she knew how to help. For now, it seemed the best thing to do was to give them space to be together.

She could hear Cade murmuring soothing sounds and Allie's sobs lessening. She didn't know what to do. Especially since Allie had mistaken her for Amber. Should she let her know she was there?

The girl's breathing seemed to even out, and she cautiously leaned her head into the room. Allie was curled into a ball, clutching a stuffed unicorn, her head on a pillow in Cade's lap. He was sitting on the bed, his back to the wall as he tenderly combed his fingers through her hair.

"You okay?" Nora whispered.

Her heart tore in two as he blinked back tears. But then he slowly nodded. She wanted to go to them, to take both of them into her arms and tell them everything would be okay. But it wouldn't be okay. Not for Allie. Not for a very long time.

She pressed her hand to her chest as if trying to send him some kind of message that her heart ached for them. "I'll see you in the morning," she said softly.

He nodded again, and she backed out of the room and quietly slipped out the front door.

━━━━━━━

The next morning, Nora was up early. She heard Cade leave to feed the animals as she was heading for the shower. Her normal morning routine wasn't very complicated—she didn't do much makeup beyond moisturizer, lip gloss, and mascara, and the natural waves in her hair usually allowed her to give it a light blow dry and finger comb it into place. She found herself taking a little extra time this morning and tried to pretend it had nothing to do with Cade. Taking time to pick out her clothes and do an extra little spritz of scent could have been to look nice for him or could have been a stall tactic.

She'd tossed and turned the night before, replaying every

moment with him from the first kiss on the glider to the heated groping on the counter. In the middle of the night, their time together had seemed hot and fantasy inducing, but in the light of day, she suddenly found herself embarrassed at the way she'd practically climbed up the man's chest. Where was her humility? She'd seemed to have left her modesty and restraint on the front porch because once he'd carried her inside, it was nowhere to be found.

What would he be thinking of her this morning? Only one way to find out. She took a deep breath and pushed through her front door.

Cade was heading back to the bunkhouse when she stepped outside. "No way," he said, his brow furrowing as he shook his head.

At first, she thought he was talking about her and what happened the night before, then she followed his gaze to the ground in front of the door.

"Oh, shoot," she said, holding back a laugh as she caught sight of the two new yoga balls sitting next to the door. A note tucked into the screen was from Bryn. Nora picked it up and read it aloud. "I'm working at the diner today but found these yoga balls at Walmart and wanted you to have them ASAP. Also made you a breakfast casserole—it's in the oven. Have a safe trip today. Love to all, Bryn."

"Got any ideas for PT using *four* yoga balls?" Cade asked.

"No, but I have some ideas about that breakfast casserole."

He chuckled as he pulled open the screen. "Me too. You want to take care of these silly things while I dish up breakfast?"

"Sure," she said, grabbing one of them and kicking the other one through her door. She'd put the others in the spare bedroom and tossed these two in after them. She was surprised to see Allie up and dressed when she entered their kitchen a few minutes later.

"Good morning," she said. "You're up early. I like that top on you. It goes good with your coloring."

"Thanks," Allie told her, a shy smile tugging at her lips as she smoothed down the fabric of the light blue shirt. "You said we were going to do a physical therapy session this morning, and I wanted to still have enough time to brush Daisy before we left." She pushed back her shoulders as she faced Cade. "I told you I would."

He put a plate of breakfast casserole in front of her. "I believed you. We should have plenty of time for you to groom Daisy, do your PT, *and* eat some breakfast. You want milk or orange juice?"

"Milk's good," she said, digging into the casserole.

Nora was glad to see her appetite returning, especially with what she had to face today. It was hard to resist the combination of eggs, sausage, and cheddar cheese covering her plate. "This smells delicious," she said, scooping a bite onto her fork.

Cade set a glass of milk in front of Allie, then slid into the chair between them. "You're not the only one who thinks so." He nodded toward the door where Shamus and Tiny stood staring through the screen. A bright pink ribbon with a yellow-and-white flower affixed to it was tied in a bow around Tiny's neck. The flower stood up jauntily next to one of her ears.

Allie laughed. "Look, Tiny likes daisies too."

"Doesn't surprise me," Cade muttered. "What does surprise me is the way my cousin keeps putting ribbons around that sow's neck."

"I think it's cute."

"What surprises me," Nora said, "is that Otis isn't with them. That silly goat seems to be able to smell food a mile away."

As if in response, a loud bleat sounded, and Otis crowded his way in between the pig and the mini-horse. He bleated again and licked his tongue up the front of the screen.

"Nice. Real appetizing," Cade told the goat. "Just ignore them."

Nora laughed and turned back to her plate, trying to concentrate on the casserole instead of how close Cade's knee was to hers.

Cade felt like he'd been holding his breath the entire day as he waited for the next thing to blow up in his face. So far, he'd avoided any explosions, but there were a lot of hours left in this day.

Even though every moment of it had felt amazing, he knew he was sliding along a slippery slope by kissing Nora. He'd been known to make some whoppers of bad decisions in his time, but this one might take the cake.

She might be gorgeous and funny and have a smile that frickin' lit up his entire day, but she was also his daughter's physical therapist. Allie's health and recovery depended on the care she got from Nora. Not that Nora would let their actions affect how she treated Allie—he knew she was too much of a professional for that. But he could easily drive her away. Hell, his track record with women had proven that.

Not that the women he'd been with had always been the ones running. He'd done his share of sprinting too.

He hadn't known what to expect when he saw Nora that morning, whether she would be happy to see him or if he'd be able to read the regret written all over her face. But she'd seemed like her normal self.

He also hadn't known what Allie would be like this morning, but she seemed to want to pretend the nightmare the evening before hadn't even happened. And hey, avoidance worked for him. He was almost chipper to see her up and dressed and taking an interest in the horse. Heck, if it took a broken-down, skinny mare to get her out of bed and into the barn, he'd take it. He'd been surprised to find her propped up on a couple of hay bales outside of Daisy's stall, a barn cat curled at her feet and a book open on her lap as she read it aloud to the horse.

"What?" she'd said. "She likes it when I read to her."

"Okay, I'm not judging," he'd said, then tilted his head to see the cover of the book. "What are you reading?"

"One of the westerns I found on your bookshelf. It's not bad, and she seems to like the parts where they ride the horses."

"Seems reasonable."

She'd narrowed her eyes as she regarded him. "So you don't think it's stupid to read to a horse?"

"No. I think it's pretty smart actually. Especially if she seems to like it and it appears to settle her. It's good for her to interact with people too." He'd given her a proud smile. "I think you're going to be a horsey girl yet."

As they had the past few days, their ease with each other ebbed and flowed, but she seemed to get more quiet and sullen as the trip to Denver got closer. Nobody had done a lot of talking on the drive down the pass. It was as if they all knew the task at hand was going to be tough and each was giving the others the space they'd need to process it.

Allie's doctor's appointment had been first, and thankfully, it had gone well. The stitches came out easily, and Cade could already see a difference in some of the bruising on her face. The shiner around her eye was fading from dark purple to a lighter blue and the edges were starting to turn yellow.

Some of the swelling had gone down in her ankle, and the doctor had given them some more sheets of exercises to work on. Cade had shared some of the physical therapy Nora was already working on, and he'd agreed with all of it. Allie had seemed good while she was talking to him, until the doctor asked her how she was coping with the grief over the accident and the death of her mother. He shared she might experience trouble sleeping, mood swings, and even occasional nightmares and suggested she consider getting some grief counseling.

She didn't tell him about the nightmare, and Cade didn't push it. But he took the brochure the doctor handed him with the names of some child therapists.

Allie was especially quiet as they left the doctor's office and headed for the apartment where she'd lived with her mom. Cade didn't know what to say or how to help, and he questioned if he'd made the wrong decision in not telling the doctor about the night-mare. It had really shaken him. Was this hitting her even harder than he'd originally thought?

Nora was quiet as well as they parked the car and trudged up the few steps to the apartment. Cade paused to collect himself. He'd had to open the bag of Amber's belongings to get her house keys from her purse, then he'd resealed it as quickly as he could and shoved it back onto the top shelf of the hall closet.

Amber's father and sister were taking care of the arrangements for her, and Allie had told him their mail came to a secured box in the complex office, so he hadn't given much thought to their apartment. He wasn't sure what they would find inside. Steeling himself, he inserted the key into the lock and pushed the door open.

He heard Allie catch her breath as she peered inside. He took a cautious step into the living room, then waited for her to follow.

The apartment was small, with a living area at the front and a galley-style kitchen in the back. A long hallway led to what Cade assumed were the bedrooms. Several pairs of shoes were haphazardly piled by the door, and stacks of mail covered the small table in the foyer. An overstuffed couch took up most of the living room, with too many throw pillows and a couple of cozy blankets casually draped over the back and sides. A half-empty glass of curdled milk sat on the coffee table next to a plate holding a dried pizza crust and a lone potato chip.

Dirty dishes covered the counter in the kitchen, and crusted pans sat on the stove, as if they'd just made a meal and hadn't time to clean it up yet. The air was stale and smelled of sour milk and the scent of garbage that was just starting to turn.

Allie wheeled the knee scooter into the living room, her fingers trailing over the arm of the sofa. "Mom?" she called into the empty apartment.

"Allie."

She shook her head. "I know. It's just that it looks exactly the same. Like she's either in her bedroom getting ready for work or she's been at work and going to walk in the door any minute." She let out a shuddering breath. "But I know she's not."

He took a step toward her, but she pulled away. "I just want to get my stuff and get out of here."

"We'll give you some space," Nora told her. "Would it be okay if I washed up the dishes and tidied the kitchen?"

"Knock yourself out," she muttered as she wheeled herself down the hall.

"I'll work on the dishes if you want to take the trash out," Nora said, already starting to collect the dirty plates and glasses.

Working together, it didn't take them long to clean the kitchen and tidy the apartment.

"I'm gonna go check on her," Nora told him as she put the broom back in the closet.

"Yeah, good. Thanks. I think I'll stay out here." Although he *was* curious about what her room looked like, what her life looked like.

He paced around the small living room, stopping to peer at the few framed pictures on the wall. Allie on a playground as a toddler sitting proudly at the top of a slide. Amber and Allie taking a cheesy selfie at some pizza place, giant slices of pepperoni in their hands. One of those terrible snapshots people get taken on roller coasters, the two of them with their hands in the air, Amber's face reflecting terror while Allie's exhibited pure joy. So many moments. Allie wearing a goofy grin at her fifth grade graduation—he had that picture. He wasn't at the event, but Amber had sent the photo to him in a spiteful text about hoping the rodeo he'd been competing in instead was worth it. He'd won a five-thousand-dollar purse that night. He'd give it all back plus twice as much to have another chance at that decision and this time make the choice to be there.

Another framed photo of the two of them plus Amber's dad,

Ed, and her sister, Diana, sat on the shelf and he picked it up, wondering where it had been taken. It must have been a special occasion because they were all dressed up and there were fancy decorations and flowers on the tables in the background. Allie and Amber looked pretty. Happy.

There was so much he'd missed. He tried to ignore the fact that there were no pictures of him. Why would there be? He wasn't really part of her life. Amber made sure of that. And he hadn't fought her. Those facts stung even more as he stood in the apartment knowing he was the only parent his daughter had left.

Three photo albums were tucked neatly on the shelf behind the picture. He pulled one out and flipped through pages filled with smiling photos of his daughter in various stages of her life. Allie as a baby, a toddler, a preschooler. There were photos of birthday parties and family trips and first days of school, all chronicling the moments of his daughter's life he had missed.

He snapped the book shut, then on impulse, pulled the other two from the shelf, thinking Allie might want to bring them with her.

Hoping he'd given her enough time, he walked down the hall and poked his head into her room. Her bed was unmade and piles of clothes were strewn across the top of the purple comforter. "Hey, how's it going?"

The room contained a bed, a dresser, a small desk, and two tall bookcases overflowing with books. A stack of books teetered on the edge of her nightstand next to a pink lamp. Splashes of pink and purple were everywhere, from the bedding to the throw rug to the giant poster of a purple rose on the wall. A few stuffed animals sat on the shelves amid the books.

He noticed a couple more pictures of her and Amber and one with her aunt stuck in the mirror on her dresser. But where were all the pictures of her with her friends? She'd said she didn't have a lot of friends—he'd assumed that was just her being dramatic.

But maybe it was true. Did that mean she had a hard time making friends or had Amber's constant need for something new and exciting wrecked Allie's chances to make those important childhood friendships?

"How does it look like it's going?" his daughter snapped. Her eyes were a little wild as she gazed around the room. "I don't know what to bring or how long I'm going to be with you. How many books should I pack? Should I bring clothes for a week? Or a month?" She narrowed her eyes as she stared at him. "How long do you think it's gonna take before you get tired of playing dad and take off again? Like do I just need summer stuff or should I take a chance and bring my winter coat?"

"Allie" was all she let him say before she held up her hand to stop him.

"Don't even say anything. I don't trust what you say anyway."

"Give me a break, kid," he told her. "I'm doing the best I can."

"Are you?" she asked before turning back to her dresser.

"Listen, I saw the landlord when I was taking out the trash, and he said the rent is paid up through the end of this month and next, so you don't have to figure everything out today. We can come back."

"Why don't you take your favorite things," Nora softly suggested. "Say five or six books and the clothes you feel most comfortable in. It looks like you've got the basics here. As long as you have a few weeks' worth of clothes, you can always do laundry." She gestured to the open closet doors. "Is there anything else you want from in here? I can grab it."

She pointed to a few items. "That blue hoodie is my favorite, and I should probably take some tennis shoes. The black Chucks are the ones I wear the most."

Cade held up the photo albums. "I found these in the living room and thought you might want to bring them."

Allie's jaw tightened as she looked at the books. "Those are *ours*. They're not for you. You didn't want to be there when we were taking those pictures, so you don't get to look at them now. Why were you snooping around our apartment anyway?"

He drew back, bewildered by her sudden mood swings and unsure what to say, since apparently everything he'd said so far was wrong. "I wasn't snooping. I was trying to help."

"You're *not* helping. You shouldn't even be here. This is *our* place. Not yours." Her voice cracked as she yelled at him. "I don't want those stupid pictures, and I don't want you."

He glanced at Nora, unsure what to do. He'd thought he could help carry things or just be here for Allie, but it was clear she didn't want or need him. Or if Nora's earlier opinions were true, the thought of wanting or needing him was causing her even more guilt and grief.

"I'll wait in the truck," he told them. "Take your time. Let me know when you're ready, and I can help load things up." He didn't get an argument as he turned and headed down the hallway. Not that he expected one anyway.

He paused in the living room, crossing to the bookshelf to replace the photo albums. In a split decision, he changed his mind and carried them out to the truck and tucked them into the back seat.

Thirty minutes later, Nora texted him they were ready. It didn't take him long to load up Allie's suitcase and the few boxes of things she'd decided to bring. One box felt like she'd packed her entire bookcase, but he didn't complain; he just loaded it into the back. Whatever she needed.

It seemed like some of the spit and vinegar had been taken out of her as he helped Allie into the back seat of the truck. Poor kid looked wiped out.

Nora offered him an encouraging smile as she got into the front seat next to him, and all he wanted to do was pull her to him and hold on to her. He must be getting soft. Since when did a hug solve anything?

Allie held her phone up as he put the truck into gear and pulled out of the parking lot. "Aunt Di called me like twenty times and left me a billion messages. She said she was out of the country, but she's on her way back to get me. And Grandpa called too. He said he wants you to call him. At least I assume you're the rat bastard he was referring to in his message." Apparently she still had a bit of spit left in her.

"I'll call him later," Cade said absently, more concerned with his ex-sister-in-law's threats to come back to get his daughter.

Allie fell back against the seat with a huff, but within ten minutes he heard the steady rhythm of her breathing and knew she'd passed out.

"Poor thing," Nora said quietly. "This has got to be rough on her." She reached across the seat and touched her pinkie to the side of his hand. "On you too. How you holding up?"

"I'll be fine. I just wish there were something I could do."

"You're doing it," she assured him.

He didn't argue, didn't say anything at all—he just turned his hand over and twined his fingers with hers.

———————

Allie stirred as they pulled into the driveway of the farm. The nap didn't seem to help her mood. She was just as prickly when she woke up. "I'm going to go check on Daisy," she told Cade as he unloaded the knee scooter and helped her out of the truck.

He and Nora each took a load of her things and carried them toward the bunkhouse. "You've got to be kidding me," he said, gazing down at the black yoga ball sitting on his front porch. "Another well-meaning citizen of Creedence must have heard we were in need."

Nora picked up the note. "Who's Ida Mae Phillips? And is that her real name?"

"Oh yeah, it is. And she's a force to be reckoned with. Retired school teacher, sweet as apple pie, but had a firm command of the vacation Bible study Grandma made us go to when we were here in the summer." He looked over Nora's shoulder. "Looks like she brought a meatloaf too. You coming over for supper?"

He would be lying if he didn't admit to being a little disappointed when she shook her head.

"Thanks for the offer, but I think I'll eat on my own tonight. I have some paperwork to catch up on, and I think you and Allie could use a night on your own too."

"It could be a quiet night. Not sure when she's gonna be ready to talk to me again."

"Give her time."

Time was okay, but suddenly he had an idea of something else to give her—something she'd really love.

———

Later that night, Cade leaned his head into Allie's bedroom. As expected, they'd had a quiet supper then Allie had gone to her room. Now that she had her phone back, she'd been riveted to the screen and didn't seem to care about much else. He hoped he was about to change that. "Hey, you got a second?"

She was sitting up in bed and offered him one of her noncommittal shrugs.

"I've got a present for you."

Her brow furrowed. "A present? What kind of present?"

He stepped into her room and brought the squirming brown-and-white puppy from behind his back. "A fluffy one that's gonna need to be fed and watered every day."

She let out a squeal as she covered her mouth with her hands. Her gaze bounced from his to the puppy, then back to his. "Is she really for me?" she whispered as if she couldn't quite find her voice.

"She really is. If you want her." He set the puppy on the end of the bed, and it romped across the spread and into Allie's lap. The smile that spread across his daughter's face was worth every second of annoyance having a puppy was going to cause him in the coming months.

"Oh my gosh. She's so cute." Tears filled her eyes as she lifted it up and cuddled it to her chest. "You're so cute. Yes, you are," she cooed into the puppy's ear, then laughed as it licked her face and tried to nip her chin.

"Now, she's your pup. If you want her, you're going to have to be in charge of feeding her and taking her outside. And she's going to need exercise, so you'll have to put that dang phone away and take her for walks."

"I will. I totally will." She held the puppy to her neck as she narrowed her eyes at him. "Wait. Just to be clear, are you using this puppy as some kind of bribe? Like as a way to buy my love or something?"

He raised an eyebrow as he peered down at the puppy, then back up at her. "Hell yes I am. Is it working?"

She laughed. A genuine laugh.

"No, but I'm still keeping the puppy."

Her voice said no but her laugh had been a definite maybe.

———

Cade was still congratulating himself on his clever gift as he lay in bed later that night trying to sleep. He'd wanted to call Nora over to tell her about it, but she'd made it pretty clear she needed some time to herself that night. He couldn't blame her. She'd been spending almost all her time with him and Allie the past few days. The woman seemed to find the positive in everything, but hanging out with a broody cowboy and an irritable teenager had to push anyone's limits.

The clock on the nightstand read close to midnight. He'd been lying there for almost an hour alternately thinking about how to deal with Allie, kissing Nora, and how the current price of beef would affect the upcoming sale of their cattle—not necessarily in that order.

He was just drifting off to sleep when he heard an agonizing cry come from Allie's bedroom as she screamed something he hadn't heard in a long time.

"Dad!"

CHAPTER 9

CADE'S FEET BARELY TOUCHED THE FLOOR AS HE SHOT OUT OF bed and sprinted toward his daughter's room. Was she having another nightmare?

"Dad!" she cried again as he charged through her door. She was in a tangle of sheets and blankets in the center of her bed, but she wasn't asleep. The bedside lamp was on, and she was clearly in distress as she cradled the small dog in her arms. Her hair was damp, and her face was wet from tears as she thrust the puppy toward him. "Take her back. You have to take her back."

What the hell was happening?

"Okay, take it easy." Cade took a cautious step toward her and eased down on the side of the bed. "What's going on?"

Allie forced the puppy into his arms. "She won't stop whining. She's been crying for an hour." From the looks of her tearstained face, so had she, the despair and anguish evidenced in her swollen eyes and red cheeks. She must have felt desperate to call out for him like she had.

"That's normal. She's in a new place, so she's probably gonna do that the first few nights."

"No, you don't get it," Allie said between wracking sobs. "She's crying…" Her breath hitched on another sob. "She's crying because she misses her *mom*. I can't take her away from her mother. I just can't."

"Oh, honey" was all he could manage around the lump in his throat. He reached out an arm and pulled her to him, surprised and thankful she let him.

Then his heart ripped in half as she leaned into him, her fingers clutching his T-shirt as she let out another grief-stricken sob. "I miss Mom," she whispered against his chest.

Her shoulders shook, and he held her tighter, trying to hang on while being careful not to jostle her injured shoulder. "I got you, baby. Just let it out," he whispered into the top of her head.

"How can I keep her when she misses her mom so much?"

"Honey, this isn't the same as losing her mom. She can go see Grace tomorrow if you want. But this is the process she has to go through so you can become her new mom."

"I don't want to replace her mom."

"Okay, don't think about it like that then. How about she keeps her mom and instead you become her best friend. But the kind of best friend she can always depend on. One who will take care of her and won't let her down."

"Her best friend?"

"Yeah, let's see if we can get her to settle down between us. Dogs can sense if you're upset, and they want to comfort you. Let's see if we can't comfort her." He patted Allie's pillow, and she gingerly rested her head on it. He laid down across from her, leaving a space between them, and settled the puppy into it. They took turns stroking her small back, soothing her to sleep.

Allie's eyes fluttered as sleep tempted them. "Will you stay until I fall asleep?" she quietly asked.

"Sure, kiddo." He watched as sleep overtook her. The puppy had curled against her stomach and was softly snoring.

He'd hoped giving Allie the puppy would bring her joy and laughter. Instead, the first few hours had brought misery and terrible reminders of the loss of her own mother.

As usual, another one of his grand plans had blown up in his face.

―――――――――――

Nora's heart broke the next morning when Cade told her what had happened the night before. "Poor thing," she said.

They were standing outside the fence watching Allie as she led

Daisy around the corral. It had been Nora's idea to get the horse involved to get her walking more. Cade had shown Allie how to put the lead bridle on the horse and instructed her to simply walk the horse in a big circle around the corral. It was slow going since Allie was pushing through the soft dirt on the knee scooter, but the horse was patiently plodding along next to her as if trying to match her speed.

Beauty and Prince ignored them, but Shamus and Mack, the colt, occasionally fell in line as if they were participating in a horsey parade. Cade had hooked a sturdy basket he'd found in the barn to the front of the scooter for Allie to carry things in and so the puppy would have a place to ride. She stood up in the basket now, her paws on the front edge as if she were the captain of her own basket-boat as she occasionally yipped out an order. Which might also account for the mini-horse and the colt following along, curious about this strange, small yapping creature.

"I don't know if I did the right thing giving her the pup or not," Cade said, knocking the dust off his boot by kicking it against the fencepost. "I thought it would make her happy."

"It does," Nora told him, resting a hand on his arm and trying not to focus on the corded muscles under her fingers. She couldn't believe that she could so easily touch this cowboy. And that he seemed to welcome her touch. "Look at her. She's doing so much better than the first day I met her. All these animals are bringing her joy." She gestured toward the girl who was laughing as Shamus nudged her from behind, his way of asking her if she had any treats.

"I thought I was doing the right thing by bringing her here, but you heard her—she said her aunt is planning to come to get her. I'm not ready to give her up."

"Then don't. You're her father. You do have rights."

He shrugged. "I don't know."

The idea of Allie leaving and cutting her therapy sessions—and Nora's time on the ranch—short had panic rising in her chest.

Both because she wanted to help her patient and because she was becoming attached to Allie *and* her father. She wasn't ready for their time together to end. "Do you want her to stay with you?"

He smiled as Allie let out a burst of giggles. The colt had his head in the basket and the puppy was licking his ears. "Yeah, I do," Cade said. "I know I still have a lot to learn about this dad stuff, but dammit, I'm trying. Allie didn't come back to me under the best of circumstances, but I'm glad she's here. And I don't want to lose her again."

"Well, there's your answer. What does her grandpa think? Did he give you any updates when you called him?"

Cade blew out his breath and scrubbed a hand across the back of his neck. "No. But that's because I haven't called him yet."

"Oh?"

"I know," he said, even though she hadn't admonished him. "I *will* call him. But I'm sure as heck not looking forward to it. The man never liked me to begin with, and I can't imagine his opinion has changed in the last ten years."

Nora's phone buzzed, and she pulled it from the pocket of her jeans. She had on the boots Cade had bought for her and a pale yellow shirt that, thanks to her mom's macaroni and cheese, fit her a little snugger than she'd remembered. Cade hadn't seemed to mind when he'd given her an appraising once-over when she'd shown up after breakfast. She'd wanted to hunch forward and cross her arms, then he'd leaned in and whispered that he liked her shirt *and* the boots and that both showed off some of her best assets. His warm breath against her neck had given her a shiver, and she'd found herself grinning like a fool and walking a little taller as they'd left the bunkhouse.

She heard Cade's phone buzz a moment after hers, and she peered down at a message from Bryn inviting her to supper at the farmhouse that evening. She turned her screen toward Cade. "Bryn just invited me to supper."

"Me too."

"Are you thinking what I'm thinking?" she said, grinning at the idea that her host was playing matchmaker.

He nodded. "Yep. No cooking for either of us tonight. Nice."

"Uh, yeah," she said, her grin falling. "That's exactly what I was thinking too."

"And knowing Bryn, she's probably invited half of Creedence to supper as well, since so many people are dying to meet you."

"Me?"

"Course. I'm sure you're quite the hot topic. People pay attention when there's a new gorgeous woman around town."

Heat flushed her cheeks, and she nudged his side with her elbow.

The color must have been noticeable because he offered her one of his wolfish grins as he tipped his hat and leaned closer. "Just so you know, you've got my attention too."

"The house isn't as full as I was expecting," Cade said later that night as he, Nora, and Allie stepped through the door of the farmhouse. He paused to hang his Stetson on one of the free hooks inside the door. Neither of the girls had time to reply before they were engulfed in hugs by Bryn.

"You all are just in time," Bryn told them. "The guys are out back taking the burgers off the grill. And Aunt Sassy is putting the finishing touches on her famous apple pie. We're having a pretty simple meal tonight."

"I'll bet," Cade said, passing her a tray of assorted cookies. He could already see the dining room table stacked with delicious-looking, and -smelling, food. "We wanted to contribute something. Well, Nora did. This is mostly from her. She went into town and got them from some bakery. I didn't even know Creedence had a bakery."

"Thank you," Bryn told Nora. "You didn't have to, but I'm glad you're supporting a local business, and I've yet to see a cookie go to waste around this bunch. They look delicious."

"They are," Cade said with a grin.

Nora offered him a side-eye. "You ate one already?"

"I had to make sure they were good before we brought them over."

Her lips tugged up in a grin. "I thought the same thing. That's why I had one too."

"Me too," Allie said, smiling as she pushed the knee scooter between them.

Bryn laughed at the three of them, but something in Cade's chest tightened with emotion. It was that same feeling he'd gotten two days before when they'd sat down to a meal together. Like a family. The kind of feeling that could get a guy in trouble if he hoped too hard for it. He needed to push that back down and lock it up.

Aunt Sassy wiped the back of her arm across her forehead as she bustled out of the kitchen. "I'm so glad to see you again," she told Nora as she wrapped her in a bear hug.

"Wow, you smell like cinnamon and sugar and apples," Cade told her as she threw her arms around him next.

"You'd better not go out into the barn then," Allie said. "Daisy and Shamus might attack you. They love apples."

"Maybe you'll have to take that horse of yours a piece of pie after dinner then," Sassy told her, gingerly giving the girl a hug too. "Who's this?" she asked, giving a quick pet to the puppy sleeping soundly in Allie's front basket.

"This is Scout," Allie told her.

"I didn't realize you'd come up with a name for her," Cade said.

"Yeah, I was thinking about it this afternoon and one of my favorite books is *To Kill a Mockingbird*, and Scout is one of my favorite characters. It doesn't matter that she's little or a girl. She's smart and confident and curious about everything, and she always seemed so brave. Just like this pup."

Cade smiled down at her. "It's a good name."

"I like it too," Aunt Sassy said. "You know, I've got her brother. He's curious too. But I wouldn't go so far as to call him smart. He fell in the toilet the other day because he was trying to catch a moth. He must have thought it was a flying toy."

Allie laughed but something about the way she held her shoulders had Cade sensing something was going on.

Aunt Sassy must have sensed it too. "Is everything okay?" she asked the teenager.

Allie crinkled her nose, then lifted one shoulder. "I was just wondering why you didn't ask me any of those questions like you did Nora the other day. It seemed like some kind of test, to see if she belonged or something. And I was just wondering why you didn't ask me anything. Was it because you already knew I didn't belong?"

"Oh, no. Quite the opposite," Sassy told her, lifting a hand to Allie's good shoulder. "It was because I already knew that you did. You're Cade's daughter, so you're already like family to me. I didn't need to ask you anything because you already passed every test just by being you." She narrowed her eyes as she studied the girl. "Would you *like* me to ask you the questions?"

Allie nodded. "Yes, ma'am. If you don't mind, I'd rather *earn* my way into your good graces than get there through my connection to *him*." She tilted her head toward Cade.

For his part, he was both proud and slightly miffed at her comments. Good for her that she wanted to earn her own respect, but did she have to act quite so offended at being related to him?

"Okay then," Sassy said, straightening her shoulders as if gearing up for a fight. "Do you consider yourself a morning person or a night owl?"

"Night owl, normally."

"Favorite kind of breakfast cereal?"

"Lucky Charms."

"Winter or summer?"

"Summer."

Sassy winked at Cade as she ramped up her rapid-fire questions. "Team Edward or Jacob?"

"Jacob."

"Favorite Taylor Swift song?"

"'Shake It Off.'"

"Nick Jonas or Harry Styles?"

"Harry."

"What house would the sorting hat put you into?"

"Gryffindor, no question."

Aunt Sassy aimed a grin at her. "You'll do."

Allie offered Cade a smug grin, but he didn't even care about the saltiness; he loved the look of pride on her face and the way she held her chin higher as she pushed the knee scooter into the living room.

"Do you want to let the pup see her mom now?" Cade asked as he gestured to the back door. "I can let her in."

Allie's face paled a little as she picked the puppy up and cuddled her to her chin. Then she gave him a small nod.

He helped her settle on the floor and then set up a throw pillow barricade around her booted leg to protect it before letting the mama dog inside.

Grace came barreling through the door and ran straight toward Allie. The puppy tumbled over its own legs in her frantic attempt to get to her mother. Scout whined and wiggled as Grace licked her head and ears.

Cade's heart broke as he watched his daughter's face crumble.

"I have to give her back, don't I?" she whispered, her eyes full of desperate longing and misery.

Cade lowered himself to the floor next to her. He wanted to

put his arm around her, to offer her comfort, but he wasn't sure she'd let him. "Just give her a few minutes. Of course she's gonna be excited to see Grace. That's natural."

They watched as the puppy crawled over her mother, and Allie even let out a small laugh as Scout chewed on Grace's ears. But then, after several minutes of play, Scout waddled back over to Allie and crawled into her lap. Settling into the folds of her hoodie, the puppy let out a baby yawn before resting her head on Allie's belly and closing her eyes.

Allie stared at the puppy, then peered up at him. Her eyes shone with tears as she softly spoke. "She came back to me. She saw her mom, then still came back to me."

He cleared his throat, searching for his voice. "You're her home now."

She smiled, then looked back down at the pup as she leaned her head on his shoulder.

Bryn had gone outside to check on Zane, and Cade could hear Nora and Aunt Sassy chatting as they finished preparations for the meal, but he didn't care if they ever ate. He was content to sit here, with his daughter's head on his shoulder and her small body leaning against him for the rest of the night.

Unfortunately, Bryn blew in from the back door and her voice woke up the puppy and had Grace racing across the room to prance around her legs. "Brody and Elle are almost here. I saw their truck coming down the road."

Cade was surprised, and happy, that Allie let him take the puppy and put her back in the scooter basket, then help Allie to her feet.

Brody Tate's pickup pulled into the driveway and had barely pulled to a stop when the side doors opened and Elle jumped out and dashed up the porch steps. Juggling two gift bags and a nine-by-thirteen pan in her hands, she still managed to get the screen door open and squeal at getting to see Nora.

Cade had to chuckle at the two women who seemed to shuffle the gift bags and maneuver around the dish to throw their arms around each other, all while talking in a nonstop stream of questions and greetings.

"Oh my gosh, I'm so glad to see you," Nora said.

"I'm so glad you're here," Elle told her. "You look amazing."

"I love your outfit."

"I love your boots."

"Your hair is so cute."

"How are you settling in?"

"The bunkhouse is great. I love it here."

"I knew you would."

"You and Bryn did so much to make me feel welcome."

"I didn't even know you owned a pair of cowboy boots."

"They're new. Cade bought them for me."

At this, Elle paused and turned to offer Cade a questionable side-eye before letting go of Nora and giving him a quick hug too.

"I got Allie a pair too," he told her by way of greeting. "I had to. I've been trying to teach these two city girls how to cowboy, so I had to start with getting some boots on their feet."

"If you really want to teach them how to cowboy, why don't you take them out to run fence tomorrow? That's where the real glamour in the job is," Zane said coming in the back door with a tray laden with steaming hamburger patties.

The scent of grilled beef wafted through the door, and Cade's stomach growled. "Maybe I will if I can figure out how to get Allie on a horse or a four-wheeler."

"I'm not sure she's ready for a horse yet," Nora said, following the group as they filed toward the table.

"She could borrow our Gator," ten-year-old Mandy Tate said as she leaned down to pet the puppy in Allie's basket. She'd followed Elle in and had been inching her way toward Allie. "Hi, I'm Mandy. I live about five minutes away, but I come over all the time to help volunteer with the horses. That's my dad," she said, pointing to the tall veterinarian who was stomping the dust from his boots as he removed his hat and hung it on the hook next to Cade's. "His name is Brody. He's a vet, and he's pretty cool sometimes. For a dad."

"Huh," Allie said, her trademark sneer back as she stared pointedly at Cade, their time with the puppy only moments before now obviously dismissed. "I wouldn't know."

"Is this little cutie yours?" Mandy asked, oblivious to the deeper message Allie had just sent Cade.

Allie's sneer changed to a look of pride as she peered down at the puppy. "Yeah, isn't she adorable? I named her Scout."

"I gave her the pup," Cade said, ruffling Mandy's hair while trying to nonchalantly remind his temperamental daughter that he wasn't so bad. "So I'd vote that I'm pretty cool sometimes too." Allie's comment shouldn't have rankled him, but it did. He *had* been trying. And it seemed that every so often, they had a moment of genuine affection, like the time they'd just spent with the puppy. But apparently a puppy and a few days of staying with him wasn't going to erase the years he'd been absent.

Bryn called them all to eat, and they finished the introductions as they took their places at the table. She'd put Allie at one end so she could maneuver easier with the knee scooter, and Cade helped her get settled in the chair. He was glad to have Nora take the seat on his other side. She didn't need to say anything, but something about her quiet presence next to him settled him. And he liked that she wanted to be near him.

At least someone did.

Allie's puppy was squirming out of her lap, either trying to get into his, or onto the floor. "You want me to take her for a bit?" he asked his daughter.

"No, I can handle her." She soothed the puppy with a few gentle strokes, and it let out a quiet sigh and nuzzled its head against her stomach. Within a few seconds, it had closed its eyes and fallen asleep.

"You're really good with her," Cade said.

"You're good with that horse too," Zane told her. "Her coat looks good, and I saw you working her on the lead this morning. She really responds well to you."

"Thanks," Allie said, ducking her head at the compliment. "She's a good horse. I mean, she's the only horse I've ever been around, but she seems like a good one." She jerked a thumb at Cade. "SD helped me give her a bath yesterday. I think she liked it."

Elle leaned toward Nora. "SD?"

Nora shrugged. "It's some kind of nickname."

"She is a good horse," Zane said. "From what I gather, she used to be used for trail rides, so at some point, when you're feeling up to it, we can toss a saddle on her and you can see how she rides."

"I've never ridden a horse before," Allie said.

Aunt Sassy gasped. "Are you kidding? How can you be Cade's daughter and not have ever ridden a horse?"

"I've never ridden a horse either," Nora chimed in as if she knew the question would open another can of absent-dad worms and wanted to save both him and Allie from having to answer. "But I'd love to learn." She smiled at Allie, but Cade felt like it was aimed at him. "Maybe your dad can teach both of us."

Bryn surprised them by letting out a heavy sigh. "Daisy is such a good horse. They all were. There were three of them there, and it kills me that I couldn't take the other two."

"Why didn't you then?" Mandy asked.

"Because I can't afford to feed them all. Every horse I take in can run me another hundred dollars a month in hay and feed alone."

"Don't you have donors?" Nora asked.

"Sure. And we get donations through the website Elle set up. But it's not a consistent amount that we can count on. Although Elle does a great job of budgeting out the donations to make sure we have what we need for each horse. And when we've had an added expense, the money somehow always seems to come in."

She looked pointedly at Elle, who suddenly seemed very interested in the seam on the tablecloth.

Cade knew all about Elle's generosity with the life insurance money her husband had left her.

"Why don't you have a fundraiser?" Mandy asked, reaching for another stalk of celery from the relish tray. "That's what we do at my school when we need money for something." She wrinkled her brow in concentration as she bit down on the crunchy stalk. "We usually sell chocolate bars or cookie dough or do some kind of raffle thing. You got anything good to raffle off?"

"They're going to have a ten-year-old to give away if you don't stop talking with your mouth full," Brody told her.

"She does make a good point though," Nora said. "Could you do some kind of fundraiser? If not a raffle, maybe an event of some kind, like a craft show or a benefit run?"

Bryn laughed. "Folks around here don't do a lot of running, unless it's after a cow who got loose. But I like the idea of a craft show."

"That sounds like a lot of work," Zane told her. "And harvest season is starting soon, so folks aren't gonna have a lot of time or energy to put into crafting."

"First of all, you're sorely underestimating crafters, but I get your point. What could we do that wouldn't take too much effort to put together, that would make real income, and wouldn't put people out too much?"

"Didn't Aunt Sassy say that she used to come to dances out here when she was younger? What about having a dance?" Allie asked offhandedly, her focus more on getting the tall cheeseburger she'd built to her mouth than on the discussion.

The conversation stopped as they all turned to look at her.

Allie froze, the cheeseburger half in her mouth as ketchup dripped onto her lip and a ring of onion tried to escape out the backside of her bun. "What?" she asked around a mouthful of meat.

"Aren't you a clever girl?" Aunt Sassy with an approving nod.

"That's a great idea," Bryn told her. "And something we could easily put together. All we'd need is a good band."

Zane frowned. "And some people who want to show up."

"That's easy," Elle said. "We can do a pop-up event on social media to get the word out and put up a couple of flyers in town at the post office and the grocery store. We'll have to charge an entry fee, but if folks know it's for a good cause to help with the horse rescue, I'll bet we could charge twenty dollars a person and get away with it."

"Then all you'd need is a hundred people to show up and you'd have two thousand dollars," Mandy said, bouncing in her chair as she got into the excitement of the idea. "That would practically cover two more horses for a whole year."

"We could also sell food and drinks," Elle suggested.

"Or we could get Amy Curtis to bring out her new food truck."

"Amy Curtis has a food truck?" Zane asked. "I thought she managed the coffee shop."

"Yes, she does. But apparently she's branching out on her own. She just started it this summer and Mayor Hardy has let her park it at the courthouse a few times a week. Her pulled pork sandwiches are to die for. Plus she serves mac and cheese."

"Pulled pork sandwiches?" Brody asked. "She should park down by the sale barn on Tuesdays and Thursdays. Those fellas would clean her out."

"Great idea," Bryn said. "I'll tell her. In fact, I'll text her right now to see if she's interested."

Brody pulled out his phone. "I know a couple of guys who play in bands. I can see if we can get one to come out and play. What night are you thinking?"

"How about this Saturday? That gives us four days to pull it together."

"So are we really doing this?" Zane asked. "Putting together a last-minute barn dance? In four days?"

"I say if we can get the food and the music, heck yeah. We're really doing this."

Excitement bubbled around the table. Nora seemed to always get behind a fun idea, but Cade was surprised to see even Allie was joining in on tossing around ideas.

"We could rent a popcorn machine."

"How about dragging out some hay bales to sit on?"

"Too bad we can't serve beer." That last comment was Brody's, and Cade nodded in agreement.

"I think we might have to have a liquor license for that since it's sponsored by a nonprofit," Elle said. "But I'll check to see if that excludes if guests bring their own booze." She had her phone open and was taking notes. "I have to run to Denver tomorrow to pick something up, so I can stop at the party store and get some decorations."

"I have tomorrow off so I can come with you," Bryn told her.

"I'm in too," Aunt Sassy said. "I could use a day trip."

"Can I come?" Mandy asked.

"Why don't we all go?" Elle said, looking toward the end of the table. "We'll make it a girls' day. We can shop for party supplies in the morning, grab lunch somewhere fun, then shop for new outfits in the afternoon. Allie, would you like to come with us?"

Allie had her head bent as she pet the puppy in her lap, but she snapped her chin up at Elle's invitation, her eyes wide. "Me? Yeah, I guess I could go. Except I would probably be a hassle with this dumb knee scooter."

"Oh no, we'd manage that. No big deal," Elle said, waving away her concern. "If it's okay with your dad, we'd love to have you."

Cade's emotions warred with the idea of wanting Allie to have a good time with these women who were so obviously trying to include her and his fear of letting her out of his sight and worrying about her getting hurt. But she'd been doing shopping trips with her mom for her whole life and he hadn't gotten involved then, why start now?

Because now she's my responsibility. He pushed the thought away. Spending time with these women and a girl close to her own age will be good for her. "Yeah, sure. You should go. It sounds fun. For you all, I mean. To me, spending *any* time shopping for an outfit sounds like the ultimate torture."

"That's why you're not invited," Bryn said, needling his shoulder with her arm as she leaned in between him and Nora to clear the plates. "How about you, Nora? Could you use a little shopping therapy?" She paused in reaching for a bowl of potato salad and turned to Nora. "Oh, *therapy*. Ha-ha. That's funny. Oh wait, are you okay with therapy jokes or do they totally annoy you?"

"I usually think physical therapy jokes are a pain in the neck," Nora deadpanned with a shrug.

Bryn's smile fell, then she laughed as she got the joke. "You're funny. I like that."

"You should totally come with us tomorrow," Elle told Nora. "It'll be so fun."

Cade watched the indecision on Nora's face as she looked from Elle to Allie to him, then she shook her head. "No, I wish I could, but I've got tons of paperwork to catch up on, and I have a few things I'd like to do around here tomorrow. You all go on and have fun without me. And it will be good for Allie to do the extra walking. Just don't wear her out too much."

"We'll take great care of her," Bryn said, wrapping an arm around Allie's shoulder. "I'm so excited, this is going to be so much fun."

Allie beamed up at his cousin, but Cade was having trouble concentrating on anything other than the fact that Nora had just nudged his knee with her leg when she'd said she had "a few things to *do* around here."

CHAPTER 10

"So what's a gator?" Allie asked as they headed back to the bunkhouse later that night. The puppy was sitting up in the basket and the knee scooter left a three-wheeled trail in the dirt behind her.

"A scaly reptile with a long tail and sharp teeth," Cade answered absently, his mind still thinking about Nora's earlier comment and the way the back of her hand kept brushing his as they followed behind Allie.

"No," she said, stopping to turn her head and give him an eye roll. "Not that kind. When Zane was talking about us riding on some fence, Mandy said maybe I could do it if she loaned us her gator. At least, I think that's what she said."

"Oh, that. First of all, it's just riding fence, not riding on it. And it just means walking, or riding your horse, along the fence line to find places where weather or animals have broken it loose or knocked it down."

"You just watch for places where's it's broken?"

"That's about it."

"Well, I could do that. That doesn't sound too hard."

"No, it's not. Spotting the problem isn't hard, it's the work it takes to fix it that's the tough part."

"You can say that again," Nora muttered more to herself than to them.

"And to answer your question," Cade continued, "a Gator is like a little utility vehicle cart deal that a lot of ranchers use around their places to haul things around."

"A cart? You mean like a ranch golf cart?"

"In a sense. Although I don't think any self-respecting ranchers would call it that. It's a lot tougher than what you'd see out on a golf course. It's more like a cross between a four-wheeler and a little truck. They usually have a small flatbed on the back to haul stuff."

"Like a girl with a busted-up ankle?" she asked, a twinge of hope in her tone.

Cade chuckled. "I think that was the idea Mandy had in mind, yes."

"Cool. That actually sounds kind of fun. Will you see if we can borrow theirs, and you can take Nora and me out on it?"

"Sure. If you want." Cade tried to keep the surprise out of his voice. His daughter actually *suggested* doing something with him? Maybe they *were* making progress after all.

"I mean if you can make time in your busy schedule or if you don't have any of the kind of pressing issues you seemed to have had for the past nine years, that is."

Or maybe not. Baby steps, he reminded himself. *One day at a time.*

He opened the door of the bunkhouse, then hung back after Allie wheeled herself in. "I'm gonna talk to Nora for a minute. I'll be there in a sec."

"Knock yourself out," she called over her shoulder. "I'm getting ready for bed."

He waited until she'd pushed her bedroom door shut before turning toward Nora, glad to see she'd waited before going in. "Hey, uh, I know you said you had a lot of paperwork and stuff to do tomorrow." He tried to keep the emphasis off the word *do*, just in case the knee nudge had been coincidentally timed. "But I was wondering if you might be interested in taking a ride with me." Oh man, did he have to say *ride*? "I mean a horseback ride. You said you were interested in learning to ride. A horse."

Just close your mouth, dude. He was making it worse.

Nora laughed. "Yes and yes. I am interested in learning to ride a horse, and I'm also interested in taking a ride with you."

He tilted his head. Okay, that totally felt like a flirty comment. Was she doing that on purpose? She had to be doing that on purpose. "Okay. It's a date then. Er, I mean, not a date-date. Unless you want it to be a date kind of thing." He cleared his throat and took a step back. What the hell was wrong with him? He never had this much trouble talking to women. In fact, he didn't usually have to talk at all. The buckle bunnies hanging around the rodeos weren't usually interested in his sparkling wit or clever conversation.

But Nora was different.

He knew that. Felt it. He didn't know exactly why, but he knew he wanted to make a good impression.

"Great. There's a cool lake up in the mountains behind the ranch. It's got a waterfall, and it's real pretty. We could pack a lunch and head up there. There's also a neat old homestead that might be fun to ride around."

"That all sounds perfect. How about I put together some sandwiches and we'll make a day of it?"

"Great." *Quit saying great.* "I mean, sounds good. What say we meet in the barn around eleven? That'll give me time to get some stuff done around here in the morning, then I'll feel better about taking the afternoon off."

"Perfect."

Yeah, she was. And that thought both thrilled and terrified him.

━━━━━━━━

The next morning, Cade was up early and had fed the horses and taken a couple of bales of hay down to the cows before he came back to make breakfast for Allie. Nora had given her the morning off from therapy, since she'd be doing so much walking and moving as she shopped and had lunch. So he was glad to see she was still up and dressed and seemed excited about her day with the girls.

"Are you *sure* Scout will be okay?" she asked for the third time as she finished the plate of scrambled eggs Cade had made her.

"Yes, I'm sure. I'll keep an eye on her this morning, then she'll be with her mom at Bryn's this afternoon. And Zane said he's working on paperwork most of the day, so he'll be right there in the house. She'll be fine."

A horn beeped in front of the bunkhouse, and Cade spotted Elle's SUV through the front window. "You'd better go." He helped get her and the knee scooter loaded into the car, then waved as Elle, Bryn, and Allie drove away. He was tempted to knock on Nora's door. She hadn't popped in for breakfast like she usually did, and he hoped she was feeling okay.

Hell, who was he kidding? He just wanted to see her. She'd been on his mind all morning and most of the night before. He'd been so distracted, Otis had snuck up on him in the barn and swiped the granola bar he'd absently set on the workbench. The dang goat had eaten the whole thing, wrapper and all, before he had a chance to rescue it. Cade couldn't remember the last time a woman had had him so discombobulated.

Or the last time he'd so looked forward to spending time with one.

Three hours later, he was saddling the horses and trying not to check the time on his phone—again—when he heard her come into the barn. He knew it was her even before he'd turned around—he could smell her scent in the air, the light floral perfume she wore and the citrusy aroma of her shampoo.

"Hey" was all he could manage to say as he turned to look at her. She took his breath away. Her hair was loose and curled gently around her shoulders, and she was dressed simply in a pair of jeans, her new boots, and a soft pink T-shirt, but the denim hugged her curves in ways that had his mouth going dry. The look of excitement and slight nervousness on her face added to her beauty.

His daughter was around during most of the time they spent

together, so today felt different, special. It was just the two of them, and the possibilities of the afternoon felt ripe in the air.

"Hey," she answered, suddenly seeming shy. Their usual easy banter was gone as they stared at each other, and he wondered if she could see in his eyes how much he wanted her. She lifted the small tote she held. "I brought lunch. It's nothing fancy—just sandwiches. And cookies."

"You made cookies?"

"No, I'm a terrible cook," she said with an easy laugh. "But I ran into the bakery again and bought some really good ones."

He liked the way she could laugh at herself and not be embarrassed by her shortcomings. He wished he could do the same, instead of getting hung up on all the bad decisions he'd made and all the ways he'd failed his daughter. "Does that mean you tested them as you were packing our lunch?"

"Come on," she said with mock offense. "Would I do such a thing?" She planted a hand on her hip. "Do you think I'm the kind of woman who eats her dessert before her meal?"

He chuckled but wisely kept his mouth shut.

She laughed with him. "Of course I did. And I brought you one too." She pulled a single cookie from inside the bag and held it out to him. "It's peanut butter. I remember you told me once that was your favorite."

"Nora Fisher, I do like you," he said, leaning forward to take a bite of the cookie. He groaned and licked the sugar from his lips. "This cookie tastes almost as good as you look."

"And it's about as nutty as you are." She teased him as she playfully swatted his shoulder, but he noted the way the pink rose to her cheeks as he grinned and took the remaining bite of cookie from her hand. "And just as sweet."

He wiped the crumbs from his mouth with the back of his hand and took the lunch bag from her. "You ready to learn how to ride?"

"Yes. No. I mean yes." She twisted her hands together in front of her. "I mean, I want to, and I think I'm ready, but I'm still nervous." She followed him over to where he'd saddled Gypsy, his palomino, and Bryn's horse, Beauty. Her gaze traveled up the horse's tall body. "They're just so big."

He brushed a hand over Beauty's neck. "Yes, but this girl is one of the sweetest horses I've ever met. She's really gentle. Bryn doesn't know her history, but Zane thinks she must have been ridden quite a bit because she's so calm with a rider."

"I like calm. And sweet seems good too."

"You're going to do great. It's just like riding a bike."

"Oh sure, if the bike were a thousand-pound, living, breathing animal that had a mind of its own and a possible aversion to a human being climbing onto its back."

Cade chuckled as he tightened the cinch on the saddle. "You're going to do fine. Let's go through some safety measures though before you get on." He talked her through the best way to mount and dismount the horse and went through the proper terminology of the horse's tack.

She rubbed her hand over the horse's neck and leaned in toward her ear. "Hi, Beauty. You're a sweet horse, aren't you? I'm Nora. Remember me? A few days ago, I brushed you and gave you that sugar cube at the fence? I'm nice too, and this is my first time riding a horse, so take it easy on me, okay?" The horse nodded her head and gave a huff, almost as if in agreement. Nora shifted her gaze to Cade. "You think I'm crazy? Talking to a horse?"

He shook his head as he put the tote containing their lunch into one of his saddlebags. "Not at all. I talk to my horse all the time. She's a great listener."

"And probably one of the few women in your life who doesn't talk back."

He chuckled. "Oh, she talks back plenty." He patted Beauty's rump. "Just like this one will talk to you. She'll try to get away with a few things at first, you just need to show her you're the boss."

"How do I do that?"

"With a firm hand on the reins and steady commands in your voice." He held her gaze. "You got this. And I'm right here with you." He held out his hand. "You ready?"

She inhaled a deep breath, then put her hand in his. Trusting him. He squeezed it, noting the softness of her skin compared to the rough callousness of his. Drawing her hand up, he placed it on the saddle horn, then used his other hand to hold out the stirrup. "Just stick your foot in here, then use the saddle horn to pull yourself up until you can swing your leg over the horse's rump."

"That's easy for you to say," she muttered as she gripped the saddle horn tighter and raised her foot toward the stirrup. "Oh gosh, that's high," she said, stumbling a little and almost tipping backward.

Cade took a step closer and slid his arm around her waist. "I got you." She leaned into him, and as another flash of heat surged through him, he realized he didn't *really* have her. Sure, he had her in his arms and was holding her steady as she leaned back into him. But it was more like she had him—all twisted up inside and nervous as heck.

The warm pressure of her back against his chest had his pulse racing. He'd had butterflies in his stomach before, but this felt like killer bees, buzzing and swarming and dive-bombing his gut. And all he was doing was helping her onto the horse. Imagine what was going to happen later when they got to the lake and he had her all to himself, really alone with her for the first time. The thought of it had his hands shaking as he gripped her hip.

She took another deep breath, then let go of the saddle horn and turned toward him. Reaching up to rest her hands on both sides of his face, she pulled him down and pressed her lips to his.

He felt that kiss all the way to his toes as they threatened to curl inside his boots. Tilting his head, he deepened the kiss, enjoying the warmth of her mouth and the press of her soft breasts to his chest. She tasted like coffee and spearmint and the feel of her against him was as intoxicating as a cold beer on a warm summer night.

She pulled back and peered up at him, her breath catching a little as she pressed her fingers to his cheek. "There. I just needed to get that out of the way. I was just as nervous wondering about if you still wanted to kiss me as I was about climbing onto this horse."

He grinned. "Well, now you can put that out of your mind. There's no doubt at all that I want to kiss you, darlin'." Her lips curved into a satisfied grin as she turned back to the horse, and he kept his voice low as he leaned in close to her ear. "And if it helps, I plan to kiss other parts of you today beyond just your lips."

She stumbled again as her foot missed the stirrup. "Holy hell. I thought that would take the edge off my nerves, but that comment has my heart practically pounding out of my chest."

He chuckled. He liked the light flush of pink creeping up her neck and the way she couldn't seem to catch her breath. "To tell you the truth, I'm glad to hear I make you a little nervous. I'm feelin' as jumpy as a teenage boy out on my first date."

She turned her head to the side. "You? Mr. Cool and Collected? You never strike me as nervous about anything."

"Well then, I'm glad I've got you fooled."

Another self-satisfied smile stole across her lips, and she raised her chin as she turned back to the horse. The sight of her bare neck was too tempting, and Cade bent forward and pressed a kiss to her skin. She closed her eyes as she stilled and tilted her head slightly away as if to give him more space to nibble. He placed another kiss on that soft indent just below her earlobe and was rewarded with a soft kitten-like sound. He felt the vibration of it in her throat. She was pressed back against him, and if he didn't stop, she was going to feel the vibration of him rising to the occasion.

"If we don't get you on this horse soon, I'm going to have to pull you into that stack of hay over there and strip you out of those snug jeans. With my teeth."

"Promises. Promises," she said with a laugh. But it was more of a breathy giggle—a sound that he liked more than he thought he would. She reached back up for the saddle and this time managed to get her boot into the stirrup. He slid his hand under her perfectly curved butt to give her a boost as she pulled herself up and landed in the saddle. "I did it."

"You sure did."

She squirmed around as she settled into a comfortable spot in the saddle, then he handed her the reins. "Hold these while I go take a quick cold shower."

She laughed again, this one more bawdy than giggly. "As much as I loved both the stroke to my ego that comment gave me *and* that stroke of my ass as you just *helped* me into the saddle, don't you dare leave me alone up here."

He chuckled with her. He liked that she could surprise him with an occasional unexpected comment. "I'm not going anywhere." Adjusting himself as he walked, he crossed back to his horse and swung up into the saddle. "We're gonna take it nice and slow and head across the pasture first before we work our way up the trail on the mountain. Beauty has taken this trail hundreds of times, so trust her that she knows what she's doing." *Then at least someone around here will know what the hell they're doing*, he thought as he tugged the reins to the side, leading Gypsy out of the barn and toward the pasture. Because he certainly didn't have a clue.

There was not one single shred of intelligent thought that made sense for him to get involved with his daughter's physical therapist. Besides the fact that he was dealing with being a real parent for the first time in his life, he was totally jeopardizing his daughter's recovery by falling for the one woman who she seemed to trust the most in this awful situation. Yet for some reason, he was letting his second brain make decisions that could threaten to topple the fragile house of cards he'd been building with Allie.

And make no mistake—he *was* falling.

He slowed to let Beauty come abreast of Gypsy and snuck a glance at Nora. She was sitting tall in the saddle, the reins gripped tightly in her hands, but her cheeks were flushed and a proud smile covered her face. She was beautiful in her own right, but sitting astride the horse with the blue sky in the background and the soft breeze blowing a strand of hair across her cheek, she was gorgeous, and he had to swallow at the sight of her.

"I'm doing it," she said, the pride evident in her voice. "I'm really doing it."

"You sure are. You're doing great," he told her as he led them through the pasture and toward the mountainside rising behind it.

They made it across without incident, the two horses content to plod through the field. Beauty occasionally tried to bend her head to nibble a blade of grass, but Cade instructed Nora to pull up on the reins and urge her forward with a gentle pressure of her legs.

"I think I'm really starting to get the hang of it," she said, then faltered a little as they headed into the trees and up the mountain trail. "Oh, gosh. This trail seems steeper when you're on the back of the horse."

"Trust the horse. She doesn't want to fall any more than you do. Her feet are steadier than you think."

Nora let out a small yelp as Beauty's front foot slipped on a loose piece of shale. Her knuckles were white as she gripped the saddle horn.

"Relax. She can feel how tense you are." Cade turned in his saddle to address her. "Look around at the trees. It's a gorgeous day. Take a deep breath and try to settle as you take in this cool forest around you."

Nora took a deep breath, then slowly let it out as she rolled her shoulders. "It is beautiful in here. You can smell the pine trees and the scent of sage and wildflowers. And it's cooler with the clouds coming in."

The sudden shift in sunlight had him searching the sky through the breaks in the trees, and he noted the black clouds moving swiftly across it. He frowned as he urged Gypsy forward at a slightly faster pace. "We may have to make a detour on our way to the lake. This area is known for sudden thunderstorms coming over the mountains, and it looks like we may get caught in one. There's a hunting cabin right over this ridge we can take shelter in to wait out the rain. I think we should have plenty of time to make it there before the storm hits."

He thought wrong.

CHAPTER 11

THE RAIN STARTED OUT AS A SOFT SPRINKLE, AND NORA WONdered if Cade hadn't been exaggerating about the intensity of the summer thunderstorm.

Then a sharp flash of lightning lit up the sky followed immediately by a loud crack of thunder, and the sky opened up. Torrents of water poured down on them, and they were both soaked to the skin in seconds.

Lowering her head to shield her face from the rain, she trusted Beauty as the horse plodded after Gypsy. Nora raised her head as Cade shouted over the deluge. "It's just in this clearing. We're almost there."

They emerged from the trees and the rain hit harder without the break of the leaves. A small log cabin sat at the base of the next ridge, pine trees ringing its back side. A flat roof jutted off one side of the cabin, offering a shelter for the horses, and Cade headed them that direction.

Another crack of lightning had Nora wincing and hunching into her saddle. Cade didn't seem affected by the rain at all as he took charge of the situation, slowing his horse to the pace of hers, then taking the reins from her and leading Beauty under the shelter. He jumped down from the saddle and tied both horses to a post.

Her hands were shaking and numb as she tried to grasp the wet saddle horn. She was so cold. Her fingers refused to listen to her commands, and she was thankful Cade had taken the reins from her. She blinked against the water dripping into her eyes, then Cade was there, reaching his arms up to support her as she practically fell into them. They'd probably only been in the rain for about ten minutes, but she wasn't dressed for the freezing water that soaked through every scrap of her clothing.

"I got you," he said, wrapping his arm around her shoulders as he led her to the front of the cabin. Kicking over a large quartz rock on the stoop, he uncovered a single key on a ring. Snatching it from the porch, he inserted it into the lock and quickly hustled them through the door. Rain water poured off the brim of his cowboy hat as he took it off and tossed it on the table, then rubbed his hand brusquely over his wet hair.

The air inside the cabin was musty and cool, and Nora wrapped her arms around her stomach in an effort to contain her chills. Cade grabbed a wool blanket from the back of the couch and draped it around her shoulders. She pulled the edges closed as she peered around the interior of the cabin.

Rough timber walls framed a large open space with a living room and kitchen separated by a wooden table and five mismatched chairs. The wood plank floors were scattered with area rugs, including a thick sheepskin one in front of the giant stone fireplace that took up the majority of the far wall. The room was decorated in a bear and cabin motif with little touches of pinecones and bear paws throughout. A pair of sturdy sofas faced the fireplace, their surfaces and backs laden with a random assortment of throw pillows and cozy blankets. A rustic chandelier fashioned from deer antlers hung above the dining room table, and blue-and-white gingham curtains framed the large picture window facing out onto the meadow. Two doors appeared to lead to a bathroom and a small bedroom.

Lightning lit up the room as rain pounded the rooftop, the steady downpour visible through the big window, and she flinched at the loud crack of thunder. "That sounded c-c-close," she said, trying to keep her teeth from chattering.

"It was," Cade said, striding into the kitchen and yanking open the cupboard above the stove. "These storms can get real nasty, real quick. I'm thankful we didn't get hit with hail too. But we're safe now." Spotting what he was looking for, he grabbed a half-empty bottle of Jack Daniels from the cabinet and a juice glass from the next one over. He opened the bottle with his teeth and poured two fingers in the glass as he walked back to her. Pushing the glass into her trembling hands, he told her, "Here, drink this. It'll help."

She lifted the glass to her lips, the scent of alcohol filling her nose. She wasn't normally much of a shot taker, but this wasn't a normal circumstance. She could barely keep the glass in her hand, it was shaking so badly. *Bottoms up.* She tipped the glass, swallowing the amber liquid in one gulp. It burned all the way down. "Gah, that's terrible."

"Yeah," he said, tipping the bottle to his lips and taking a swig. "I'll get a fire going, get this place warmed up." He set the bottle on the table before hurrying toward the fireplace and grabbing several logs from the bin next to it. He tossed the wood onto the grate, then grabbed a handful of newspapers from the stack, quickly crumpling them and forcing them into the crevices between the logs. A box of matches sat on the hearth and the slight tremor in his hand as he took one out and struck it against the stone wall was the only indication that the cold was affecting him.

She might be wet and freezing, but she wasn't too cold to notice the way his wet shirt clung to his muscular frame or the flex of his biceps as he'd pitched those logs. Or the fact that they were alone in a cabin in the mountains wearing wet clothes that would eventually need to come off. Dispensing with the glass, she swiped the bottle of Jack from the table and took another quick slug while Cade's back was still turned as he focused on starting the fire.

Ugh. Her throat burned, and another hard shiver ran through her as she replaced the whiskey to its spot on the table.

Flames licked the dry newspaper, the crackle of the fire catching filling the quiet cabin, and Cade opened the flue as thin wisps of smoke drew upward into the chimney. He waved her toward him. "Come over by the fire. Let's see if we can get you warmed up." He tended to the logs, adding more small kindling and newspaper until the fire took.

Nora sat on the edge of the hearth and held her hands out to the heat, but they were shaking so badly from the cold that the tremors went all the way up her arms. She tried to keep her teeth from chattering, but she was losing that battle as well.

Cade pulled her boots off and rubbed her feet between his hands. He frowned down at them. "Damn, you're soaked to the bone. Even your socks are wet." He peeled her socks from her feet, then stood and lifted her into his arms. "We've got to get you out of these clothes and into a hot shower." Cradling her to his chest, he carried her into the small bathroom, stopping to toe his own boots off on the way.

The bear theme extended into the bathroom with a log cabin light switch cover and a mama bear and her cub on the curtain of the shower stall. Cade tore back the curtain and wrenched the knob. A groan and a creak shuddered through the wall then a stream of water poured from the shower head. "That should heat up in a minute."

He set her down and turned to go but she reached for his arm. "Don't go. You're soaked too."

The kind of heat that no fire could generate surged through her chest as he stared intensely into her eyes. He held her gaze for what felt like hours but was probably seconds, then he gave her a solemn nod and pushed the door shut behind him. The sound it made as the latch clicked into place was louder than any crack of lightning. Not taking his eyes from hers, he pulled his T-shirt over his head and dropped it to the floor.

Nora's mouth went dry at the array of solid muscle and hard abs. *Holy hot cowboy*. She stood frozen, unable to do anything but stare as he unhooked his belt buckle, drew down his fly, and shrugged out of his jeans.

Left in only a pair of black boxer briefs, he looked like a Greek god. His skin was tanned, and his shoulders seemed as broad as the doorway behind him. A dark purple bruise smudged across his side, and his chest was marred with a few scattered scars. Nora's gaze followed a white line of scar tissue that crossed his ridiculously hard abs and ended somewhere below his waistband. She swallowed as she prayed she would get to see where.

Wanting nothing more than to fling herself into his arms and commence licking him, she found she couldn't move. She seemed to be frozen—not just cold and wet, but held captive by his gaze as it raked over her body, his eyes narrowing with hunger and desire. He looked at her as if she were a four-course meal and he hadn't eaten in months. Her limbs might not be able to move, but inside she was aching and couldn't wait for him to taste her.

Moving slowly, he reached for the hem of her shirt and gently tugged it up, easing it over her head. Like a rag doll, she let him undress her, holding his gaze as he ran the back of his fingers down her arm. Goose bumps broke out across her skin as he paused at her waist, then drew his fingers across her stomach. A gasp escaped her lips as he slid his hand under her waistband to release the snap on her jeans.

It might have been the rain, it might have been the whiskey, but it was most likely the pure lust she felt for this man that had her shimmying out of her wet jeans and backing into the shower with him in just her bra and the tiny slip of her lacy thong underwear.

Not that they mattered. She hazarded a quick glance at herself. The white fabric of her bra was practically clear as the thin material molded to her breasts and outlined the hardened tips of her nipples. The sight of the rosy-pink nubs peeking through the sheer fabric was somehow more erotic than if she'd been totally naked.

He paused at the edge of the shower, his voice husky as he spoke. "I'm dying to get in there with you, darlin', but I have to stop."

Stop?

Oh shit. Had she made another colossal mistake? Had she completely misjudged this whole situation?

Her shoulders shrunk in, and she wrapped her arms around her belly, which a moment ago had felt curvy and sensual and now just felt flabby and soft. She dipped her chin to her chest.

"Hey now," he said, his fingers gently touching her chin as he raised her face to look at him. His eyes were so blue and radiated with sincerity. "Don't do that. Don't shy away from me."

His thumb grazed her bottom lip, and she fought to keep it from trembling. She was confused and embarrassed and wanted to melt and wash away with the water swirling into the drain. "But you said you wanted to stop," she whispered.

He shook his head, the ghost of a rogueish smile curving his lips. "No. I didn't. I said I *had* to stop. Because as much as I wanted to step in and take you against the side of this shower, I wanted more to stop and just look at you." He reached for her hand and pulled it away from her stomach. "I needed to stop and convince myself this was really happening." He took her other hand and pulled it away as well.

Oh. Her breath caught in her throat as his stare moved over her body.

"You are so beautiful," he said, his voice gravelly with need. "More beautiful than I'd even imagined." Her confidence blossomed as his smile grew, then transformed into an expression of wolfish desire. "And I've imagined a *lot.*"

His words, and the look of hunger in his eyes, gave her the courage to stand taller. The expression on his face told her everything, but a quick glance at his briefs was further proof that his appreciation of her body was real. Those two things combined emboldened her, and she lifted her chin and pushed back her shoulders, giving him a better view of her plump breasts. "Well then, stop imagining and get in here and start doing."

He laughed a hearty laugh that sent another flurry of sensations racing through her. The sensations might also have to do with him kicking his briefs off and pulling her to him.

She grinned up at him, a grin that she hoped was seductive and coy. "Now, what was that you were saying about taking me against the side of the shower?"

He laughed again, but this time it sounded more like a growl. The warm water rained down, but her body heated from the inside as he pressed his lips to hers. The kiss was deep and demanding, full of yearning and need.

He tasted like whiskey and desire. And she couldn't get enough of him. Her body was his for the taking as he kissed her neck, her shoulders, the tops of her breasts. He cupped one in his hand, grazing his thumb over the hardened tip of her nipple as it pushed through the soaked fabric. He dipped his head to suck the tight nub between his lips. Even through her bra, she could feel the heat of his mouth.

She braced her hands against the wall behind her as he unclasped her bra and peeled it from her wet skin. Taking his time, he knelt in front of her and slowly drew her panties over her hips and down her legs. Ignoring the water streaming down her body, he pressed a hot kiss to her stomach, just below her belly button, and heat swirled and coursed through her in anticipation.

Another kiss, lower this time, then another. The sharp scrape of his whiskers against her thighs had her biting her lip and trying not to beg him to touch her.

He stood, replacing his mouth with his hand, his sure touch sliding between the vee of her legs. The tile was cold on her back as she pressed against it, but she didn't care. All she could think about was this man and the feel of his hands on her body.

She moaned as she surrendered to the relentless ache between her legs when he finally made that connection, circling and stroking, sending sensations rushing through her.

One hand pressed against the wall while the other gripped his shoulder. She was utterly at his mercy, holding on to him, a tide of heat rising in her with every secret caress.

A hot flush swept through her, and her thighs trembled as he commanded more from her, bringing her closer to the edge. She couldn't think straight as tingles of pleasure ripped through her. She was drowning and flying at the same time as the sensations rushed up and seized her muscles, pushing her higher and higher until she shattered in surrender. She cried out as the pleasure swelled, pulsing and hot, as wave after wave raged through her.

He kissed her again, hard and greedy, as he caught her next moan in his mouth, stealing her breath as he inhaled her. She clung to him, her legs shaking, unraveling from the inside out, as she kissed him back with an abandon she didn't know was possible.

She let out a tiny shriek as the hot water ran out and cold liquid streamed down her back.

Cade let out a whoop as she jumped out of the shower, and he rushed to turn the faucets off. Her breath was ragged, and she fought to stand up as he folded her into a scratchy towel that he grabbed from a cabinet next to the sink. She used one corner to soak up the excess water from her hair. He dragged a second towel over his wet head, across his chest, then wrapped it around his waist.

She reached to pick up her wet shirt, but he put a hand on her arm. "I'll take those out to put them by the fire. Not just to get them dry, but because I'm not ready not to be naked with you yet."

Oh.

"I mean, that shower was a-mazing," he said, giving her one of his roguish grins. "But I'd like to try that again horizontally instead of vertically. And in a real bed."

Offering him a seductive smile, she let the towel fall to the floor. "Horizontal sounds good." So did sideways, right side up, and upside down. She'd take this man whatever direction he wanted—or be taken *by* him.

She'd thought he'd sapped every ounce of energy from her but his comments, and that dang grin, had her body heating up and ready for more.

What had gotten into her? She wasn't usually this brazen. But with Cade, everything felt different. *She* felt different. At this point, she probably couldn't blame it on the whiskey anymore, but something sure had her letting her defenses—and her towel—drop.

CHAPTER 12

CADE QUICKLY DRAGGED A COUPLE OF CHAIRS OVER TO THE hearth and hung their wet clothes over the back rungs. He tossed another log on the fire. The cabin was warming up, but it was nothing compared to the heat that was surging through him as he hurried to the bedroom where Nora was waiting.

He paused in the door, taking a second just to look at her. She was lying on her side, the sheet falling softly over her waist and barely covering her perfect breasts. Hell, everything about her was perfect. Especially that coy smile she was giving him as she patted the bed next to her.

He approached the bed, dropping the condom, which he'd pulled from his wallet, on the nightstand before sliding under the sheets with her.

"Hey, cowboy," she murmured, her voice soft and sultry as she drew the tips of her fingernails over his chest.

"Hey" was all he could manage as he drew her close to him, her soft curves molding perfectly against his body. He dipped his head, teasing her lips as he skimmed over her mouth with his. She kissed him back, playfully dragging her teeth against his bottom lip and eliciting a soft moan from him.

He paused to look at her, and her tender gaze crashed into his soul, as if she were trusting him with her heart. He wasn't good with words, but he tried to convey his feelings through his actions, like in how he looked at her and the way he touched her as if she was a treasure to be cherished.

Holding her gaze, he trailed his finger down her chest. Coils of lust and want swirled through his belly as he ached to touch and explore her. He loved the soft kitten-like sigh she made as he grazed the tight nub of her nipple with his thumb. Lowering his head, he circled the perfect pink bud with his tongue before drawing it between his lips. She arched her back, silently offering more of herself. He cupped her breasts—they filled his hands, and mouth, perfectly.

Her fingers clutched his back, and he could see her pulse quickening at her throat. He laid a kiss there before burying his face in her neck and inhaling the intoxicating scent of sin and skin.

He took his time, exploring her body, discovering what she liked, what made her sigh, and what made her writhe beneath him. Then he couldn't take it any longer. Demand throbbed between his legs—he had to have her, to feel her.

He grabbed the foil packet from the nightstand, cursing himself that he didn't carry two as he covered himself, then settled between her legs. Pausing to savor the moment, he peered down at Nora, trying to memorize the way she looked at that exact second—her perfect kiss-swollen mouth, her tousled hair spread across the pillow, the come-hither smile she wore on her lips.

Then he lost himself in her, drowning in the sensations he'd spent so much time dreaming about. He closed his eyes, only for a second, to focus on the intensifying feelings, but then he had to open them again, had to see her face, her body as she arched beneath him.

The rest of the world fell away. It was only him and Nora, and he couldn't get enough of her as he found his rhythm, *their* rhythm, building in tempo as the pleasure coursed through them.

Then her head tipped back as her fingers clutched the sheets next to her, twisting the fabric into her fist. She said his name as a tremor quaked through her, and he was gone. His chest expanded as a growl ripped from his throat, and he gave in to the delirious ecstasy as he surrendered himself to her.

Everything about being with Cade was different than Nora had imagined. She knew it would be wonderful, but she hadn't anticipated how it would shift from gentle to raw, from teasing to pure desire. He had been attentive, caring, but also hungry and carnal in his need for her. And she loved every second of it.

They lay together for a long time, their naked bodies entangled, holding each other as they talked softly and made each other laugh. She reveled in his sweet touch, the way he brushed her bangs from her forehead, the way he kept pressing soft kisses to her shoulder.

He got up once to check on the horses and came back with their lunch, and they ate in bed, still talking and sharing stories about themselves. The day had been perfect. Even with the rainstorm. Who knew a torrential storm could turn into such a tranquil, lazy afternoon spent in bed? After many sparks of lightning.

She would never think about thunderstorms in the same way again.

They cuddled together again after their lunch, and she couldn't help but touch him. She was fascinated with the array of scars covering his body and the stories that accompanied each one she pointed out. Most were from his time spent in the rodeo, some were from stupid childhood stunts or times spent tangling with a horse or a cow, and a few were from his brother. Those were the stories she liked best—the ones that shared his history, his life growing up.

She ran a hand through his hair, noting the inch-long scar that ran just below his hairline. Skimming her finger over the thin white line, she asked, "Is this one from another fight with your brother?"

He shook his head. "No, that one was from a fight with a two-thousand-pound bull named Rose Petal."

"*Rose Petal?* I'm confused. I may not know a lot about ranching, but I'm pretty sure bulls are males, right?"

He grinned. "Yes, they are. The name was ironic. And I can

assure you he is not the dainty flower his name implies. Especially when the side of his hoof catches you on the forehead."

She gaped. "You got kicked in the head by a bull?"

He chuckled. "By more than one. Kicked by, bucked off, and stomped on—sometimes all in the same round. That's the world of professional bull riding. That's why my knee and shoulder are so jacked up as well. Tangling with animals that size can result in all sorts of injuries. Hell, you can get injured messing with animals half that size." He pointed to the bruise across his stomach. "I got this yesterday when I was loading a couple of cows into a trailer and one of them decided she didn't want to go."

"And she kicked you?"

He shrugged. "Nah, I think she got me with her head. Either that, or I got this when Zane and I were wrestling with that tractor engine. I'm not exactly sure."

She shook her head. "I had no idea ranching was such a dangerous business." She touched the scar again. "I think Allie has a scar similar to this one, in almost the same place."

Cade stiffened, and his easy smile fell. His eyes narrowed, and his voice hardened. "Yeah, she does." He sat up and pushed off from the bed. His back was ramrod straight as he strode from the room. "We should probably get going," he said, his voice tight, before he walked out the door.

What the hell? Like the flip of a switch, his personality had changed from easygoing to hard as nails in one second's time. She crawled out of bed, dragging the sheet with her and wrapping it around her body as she padded barefoot into the living room.

The sun was back out and sunshine lay in square patterns across the floor as it shone through the large picture window. Cade was sitting on the hearth by the fire. He already wore his jeans and was tugging on his boots. He stood, and Nora noticed the top button of his jeans was still undone. She swallowed at the display of male perfection as he reached for his shirt and pulled it over his head.

"Cade, wait. What's going on?"

"Nothing's going on. It's just getting late, and we need to get back." His voice held a new edge, and he wouldn't look at her.

He strode toward the kitchen, and she reached out a hand, catching his arm as he passed by her. He stopped but still wouldn't look her in the eye. "We were fine just a minute ago, and now you're stomping around here like you can't get away fast enough. What did I do wrong?"

He cringed and pulled his arm away as if her touch burned him. "*You* didn't do anything wrong. It's me."

She shrank back, flinching as if he'd struck her and suddenly conscious of the fact he was dressed and she was still naked and her hair was probably drying in crazy winged-out curls all around her head. She pulled the sheet tighter around her and focused on breathing. She'd heard this before. Geoff had pulled the old "it's not you, it's me" line and her whole life had gone down the tubes.

She didn't think Cade would be as ruthless as Geoff had been with his callous words, but he could still break her. "I don't understand," she finally managed to say.

Scrubbing his hand over the back of his neck, he let out a hard sigh. "Look, I'm sorry. I got carried away. You're just so... I shouldn't have... I mean I wanted to but..."

Oh my gosh. He *was* giving her the line. Granted, he wasn't doing it very well. She stared at him, not believing what he was saying. Not after the afternoon they'd just had. Her emotions wavered from heartbroken and sad to confused and angry. Pissed off inched out into the lead and she planted a hand on her hip. "What are you trying to say, Cade?"

His expression looked pained, like the words were actually hurting him. "I don't know. I don't know what I'm saying or what I'm doing."

Confusion stepped back in and took over. "I don't get it. What is happening?"

He pulled his hair back from his forehead. "This. You asked me about this scar and Allie's scar, and it hit me like a punch in the gut. Nora, you're one of the kindest, smartest, and most beautiful women I know. You deserve so much more than a guy like me."

"Don't you think that's for me to decide?"

"No, I don't. Because you don't have all the facts. All you know about me is the guy you've seen the past week. You don't know what a real shit I can be. That scar on Allie's head, the one that looks like this one?" He pointed to his forehead again, then pounded his fist against his chest. "That scar is *my* fault. I'm the one who gave it to her."

Nora took a step back, tendrils of fear curling in her belly. *His* fault? How did *he* give Allie the scar? Had he hit her?

No way. She couldn't believe it.

She watched Cade stride to the door, his head down, avoiding her eyes as he yanked it open. "I'll be waiting outside with the horses." He pulled the door closed behind him, leaving her with only the sound of the latch clicking into place.

Earlier, that sound had thrilled her—but that was when Cade was closing them in together, not shutting her out.

She sank onto the edge of the sofa, dazed by all that had just happened. It seemed like just a few minutes ago, she was in the afterglow of amazing afternoon delight, lying naked in the arms of a man she really liked. A guy who she was falling for, and falling hard. But now, she wondered if she even knew that guy at all.

What was wrong with her? Why did she always do this? She led with her heart, trusted too easily, fell for the wrong guy. Feeling embarrassed and angry at herself for jumping in with both feet, just like she always did, she stumbled to the fireplace and collected her clothes. Taking them into the bathroom, she avoided the mirror as she got dressed. Her jeans were still damp, but the rest of her clothes were dry enough.

Hazarding a glance in the mirror, she groaned, her fears

confirmed. Mascara was smudged under her eyes and one side of her hair was smashed against her head, while the other stuck out in wavy curls. Rummaging through the drawers, she found soap and toothpaste and washed her face and used her finger to do a quick scrub of her teeth. Thankfully, she had an elastic in her pocket, and she gathered her hair back into a loose knot at the nape of her neck.

Feeling a smidge better, and with fresher breath and less bed-head, she headed back into the living room and pulled on her boots. She did a quick sweep of the cabin, gathering her phone and what was left of their lunch and taking a few minutes to remake the bed. She swallowed back the emotion as she took one last look at the room, the bed neatly made, the pillows back in place, as if nothing had happened there. Which was exactly how Cade was acting.

She drew her shoulders back. If he wanted to act like that, fine. Whatever. His loss. She wasn't here for him anyway. She was here to help Allie, not get tangled into a romance with a broody cowboy. It didn't matter how hot or muscular he was. *Or what kind of magical things he could do with his tongue.*

Grrr. Not going there. Taking a deep breath, she turned the handle of the door. She needed to focus on the task on hand. Which started with getting back to the ranch.

With a determination to face him head-on coursing through her, she gritted her teeth and pulled the door open, resolved to be brave and act like she wasn't bothered a bit. She took a step forward, then stopped in her newfound courage's tracks.

Cade was standing in front of his horse, his eyes closed, his head bent forward as he leaned it against Gypsy's forehead. A deep sadness pulled at the edges of his mouth, and his fingers curled around the horse's bridle. He struck her as this tall, strong, and handsome-as-hell cowboy who looked broken and grieving as he drew comfort and solace from his horse.

She didn't want to move, didn't want to break the moment. Her heart ached for him. Even though, a moment ago, she was so mad at him she could have spit nails, she knew, as sure as she knew her own name, that there was more to Cade Callahan than he let people see. More to the man whose defensive walls were so high, he rarely let anyone in.

Although she'd felt like he *had* let her in. Maybe not past his walls, but he'd at least opened the gate and met her there.

The horse whinnied as if alerting Cade to her presence. He opened his eyes and stood up, letting out a deep breath as he patted the horse's neck. "You ready?" he asked, but she wasn't sure if he was talking to her or the horse. Or both?

She handed him the tote. He stowed it in his saddlebag, then untied Beauty and led her into the sunshine.

———

Cade still couldn't look at Nora as he handed her the reins to the horse. It hurt too much. He never should have let himself get involved with her.

This time at the cabin already felt like a dream—like they'd carved out this little place in time in the middle of the storm where they could let go of everything else and just be together.

But that dream had come crashing down at the mention of Allie's scar, at the reminder of his past and what a shitty dad he was. Nora might be able to find the good in a lot of things, but it wouldn't take her long to see the not-so-good in him. He was surprised she hadn't figured it out yet. The way Allie treated him, the name his ex-father-in-law had called him. She had to know there was a reason he was estranged from his own daughter. And that the reason wasn't a good one.

When they'd been in bed, lying tangled in the sheets together, she'd looked at him with this thing in her eyes—something a little too close to adoration. As if he were really worth something, worth the devotion she was offering him. He'd gotten sucked into believing they could have something, drawn in by her essence and blind to the fact that, sooner or later, she would figure out that he was just a broken down rodeo cowboy who'd let his family down.

He snuck a quick glance at her, and even now, after he'd walked out on her, she was still gazing at him with a look of tenderness mixed with concern. He turned away. "I need to check the door and put the key back," he told her as he walked back to the front of the cabin.

After securing the front door, he bent to pick up the quartz rock to replace the key. A slight movement caught his attention, and he jerked his head up, alarm ringing through his body.

Nora stood next to Beauty, the reins held loosely in her hands. The horse's back end was facing the rocky side of the trail that led up the mountain behind the cabin. Beauty must have seen it at the same time he did, camouflaged against the layers of shale, because her eyes went wide and she huffed out a startled whinny.

The sun glinted off the smooth, scaly skin of the rattlesnake as its body coiled and its tail rose as it let off a warning rattle.

CHAPTER 13

TIME SEEMED TO PAUSE FOR JUST ONE SECOND, THEN ALL HELL broke loose. Beauty reared back, letting out a frightened neigh as she lifted her front feet off the ground. Cade didn't think—his body just reacted as he hurled the chunk of quartz he was holding at the snake. Nora screamed as she dropped the reins, then sprinted toward him.

Beauty's eyes were wild as she pawed the air, then stamped at the ground with her front hooves. She gave another frightened neigh, then took off at a gallop, heading toward the ranch.

The snake was gone. Either the thrown rock or the horse's hooves scared it back under the rocks it had probably been sunning itself on.

Nora had launched herself into his arms, clinging to his neck as her body trembled against his.

Cade tipped his head until his forehead touched hers. "Hey, now. It's okay. It's gone."

Her arms wrapped tighter around him, and her eyes squeezed shut as she shook her head. Her words came out in a shaky tumble. "That was a rattlesnake, wasn't it? I heard it rattle. Have I told you how much I hate snakes? Like I really, really hate snakes. Especially big scary venomous snakes. And that snake was really freaking big."

"It's all right. I've got you." He held her for a moment, breathing in the scent of her and relishing the feeling of her in his arms. "We probably need to get going though. I don't want Beauty to get too far ahead of us."

Nora hung her head as she took a step back. "I'm so sorry. I can't believe I dropped the reins."

"It's okay. Really. It happens. And believe me, that horse knows how to find her way home. She can see the barn once she gets to the top of the ridge, and that's where both her baby and her next meal are. She'll race right to it. Don't worry about it." He pulled out his phone and shot off a quick text, then pushed it back into his pocket. "I just texted Zane to let him know Beauty got spooked and was heading back to the ranch and to keep an eye out for her."

He gave her arm a reassuring squeeze, then walked slowly toward the hillside. "I've got to get the rock so I can finish putting the key back."

"Be careful," she told him, wrapping her arms around her stomach.

"That snake's long gone by now," he told her. But he still kept a watchful eye on the layers of shale and rock. Just in case the snake, or one of its pals, was still slithering around. He grabbed the rock and returned it to its rightful place, with the key to the cabin tucked securely beneath it. He crossed to Gypsy, untied her reins, and swung easily into the saddle. He held his hand out to Nora. "Come on. You'll have to ride with me."

She cautiously approached the horse, then held up her hand and placed it in Cade's. He pulled her up and settled her in the saddle in front of him. Holding his arms around either side of her, he lifted the reins, and clicked to the horse as he squeezed her sides with his legs.

Nora gripped the saddle horn as Gypsy plodded forward. Cade could feel her still shaking. He pulled her back to lean against his chest. "You're safe. I've got you."

They rode in silence to the top of the ridge. Several times Cade had started to say something then stopped himself. He knew he'd hurt her feelings. Which was maybe for the best. Best she figured out now he wasn't a guy she'd want to get mixed up with. But still—he hated that he hurt her. Hated that their perfect afternoon had ended on such a crappy note. And hated that she thought any of it was her fault or due to something she did.

No, it was all on him. As usual.

He rested his chin on her head. "She was barely four when it happened." He spoke softly, but he felt Nora stiffen then force herself to relax. "The scar, I mean." Like she didn't know what he was talking about. "You have to understand. When Amber and I had her, we were practically kids ourselves. We didn't have a clue what we were doing. Especially me."

He blew out a sigh. "You know I was barely nineteen when I met her. Amber. I was a young buck, just starting off in the rodeo, running roughstock events. I'd won a few rides, and I was full of spit and vinegar, walking around like I owned the place, showing off for the steady stream of buckle bunnies by blowing every purse I won. I'd seen Amber a couple of times. She was pretty but also self-assured. She knew what she wanted, and she apparently had her sights set on me. We hooked up for a while, then she told me she was pregnant."

"Oh."

"My dad took off on us when my brother and I were still in grade school, and I didn't want to do that to my family. I cared about Amber, and I figured we could make a go of it. You know, for the kid." He sighed as he looked out over the mountains. "I never truly knew what love was until the nurse put that little baby girl in my arms. She was crying and her face was all scrunched up and red, but she was mine. I'm a pretty tough son of a bitch, but I'd never been more terrified of anything in my life. She weighed less than seven pounds, but she had a hold of my heart like a socket wrench to a bolt. She might have been a red-faced baby, but as she grew, she turned into the cutest little bugger—all big blue eyes and tons of blond hair."

"It sounds like you were happy."

He let out a hard grunt. "No. We were never really happy. Allie might have been a cute baby, but she was colicky and cried all the time. And Amber was always yelling at me. I suppose we were probably tired and worn-out and didn't know what the hell we were doing, but we fought all the time. And nothing I ever did was good enough. I went back on the road, just a few rodeos here and there, trying to make some money, but Amber had a jealous streak a mile wide. She was sure I was messing around on her—I wasn't. But she never believed me. We were miserable, and I found it was easier to be gone than it was to be at home."

A cool breeze blew across his heated cheeks. He hated talking about his screwed-up marriage.

"I'd spent a lot of summers with my grandparents, so I'd seen at least one example of a healthy marriage, and I knew we didn't have one. Amber never trusted me. Not when I was gone, and not when I was home. She was always telling me to be careful, not to let the kid do this or that. She had me so scared I'd hurt Allie that I was afraid to be alone with her. Even though I tried to play with her and read her books, Amber told me daily what a terrible dad I was, how I didn't know how to do anything right with her. Then one day, all her convictions came true."

Nora sucked in a quiet breath but didn't say anything. She just waited for him to go on.

He swallowed back the emotion that day always brought up in him. "Amber left me alone with her. She was only going to the grocery store. Hell, she wasn't even gone an hour. But it only took two seconds for Allie to fall." He shook his head, thankful Nora couldn't see his face. "She tumbled down the stairs and hit her head—split her forehead open. She wasn't very big, but dang that girl could scream. I heard the thump and knocked over my chair trying to get out of it. I'll never forget rounding the corner of the hallway and seeing her at the bottom of the stairs. We lived in one of those splits levels, so there were only like five or six stairs, but she must have hit the bannister or something. I'm still not sure. She split her lip too, and there was so much blood, I thought I was gonna pass out."

"Head wounds always tend to bleed more," Nora said softly.

"I know. And my rational brain might have got that, but my dad brain just saw his little girl screaming and blood everywhere, and I just lost it. I didn't know what to do, so I picked her up, put her on my lap, and raced her to the emergency room. Forgot to grab ice or even a towel. I used my shirt to try to stop the bleeding."

"Was she okay?"

"Yeah. She ended up with six stitches and a scar that still hurts my heart every time I see it."

"Sounds like that wasn't the only scar that day left."

He huffed out a sigh. "No, that was the end of our marriage too. By the time Amber made it to the hospital, she'd completely lost it. She'd just gotten home and seen all the blood when I'd called her. She walked into the emergency room spitting mad, and she walked right up to me and slapped me across the face."

Nora gasped.

"I deserved it. I'd taken my eye off her, even if it was just for a second, and I let our little girl get hurt."

"It wasn't your fault. It was an accident."

"It *was* my fault. I knew it. And Amber knew it. And that was the excuse she needed to kick me to the curb. I moved out and she moved back in with her parents. Between her and her dad and her sister, they kept me away from Allie for almost a year."

"They couldn't do that. You were her dad."

"Not much of one. I missed her like hell, but I felt so guilty about what had happened and I was afraid to be alone with her— afraid something would happen again. I went back on the road and threw myself into bull riding and competing."

"And hoping that if you got hurt, it would somehow make up for Allie's injuries."

Nailed it. He shook his head. "There you go, getting all therapist on me again."

"It doesn't take a therapist to see what you were trying to do. It seems obvious."

"Maybe to you. But I don't think I even realized what I was doing until it was too late. I didn't make the effort I should have with trying to see Allie those first few years. Then Amber used that against me to keep her from me after that. I still made the effort, cards and lame gifts for her birthday and Christmas, and I never missed a single child support payment. I ate canned ravioli for weeks some months just to make sure I had that check to send her. But Amber had turned the fall into a whole thing and threatened to take me to court for neglect if I didn't go along with her."

"Could she do that?"

"I don't know. I told you, I was young and dumb, and I'd convinced myself that Allie was better off without me."

"Do you still think that?"

He shrugged. "I don't know. I hope not. I feel like I've been given a second chance, and I'm older now and maybe a little wiser, and I *want* to make this work. I'm the only parent she has left, and I don't want to let her down again."

She put her hand over his. "You won't."

They'd been talking as they made their way down the side of the mountain. As they entered the pasture, Gypsy gave a whinny and Cade knew she was ready to get back to the barn. And he was ready to be done talking about himself and what a mess he'd made of his life. "You want to see what this horse can do?"

The muscles in Nora's back tensed, but she gave him a tentative nod. "Um, okay, sure."

He wrapped his arms tighter around her and gave the horse the lead. "Hold on," he said before nudging Gypsy with his heels.

Nora let out a tiny squeak and gripped his arms as the horse took off, galloping across the field. Cade had taken Gypsy on this same ride so many times, she knew the path and raced across it with speed and confidence.

They galloped up to the ranch, and Cade pulled back on the reins and slowed the horse to a trot, then an easy walk.

"Wow. That was amazing," Nora said, her voice a little shaky as it came out in a breathless rush.

"She's a great horse. I'll give her a good brushing and an extra scoop of grain for bringing us both home." He patted Gypsy's side. "I just hope we beat Allie back," he said glancing toward the bunk-house where a large blue yoga ball sat propped against the door. "Aw hell, not another one."

Nora turned her head, following his line of sight, then her shoulders shook against his chest as she let out a laugh. "At least they only brought *one* this time."

"Not quite," Cade said, directing her attention to Bryn's front yard, where Tiny was rolling a hot-pink yoga ball around with her snout.

Nora laughed harder. "I think we should let her have that one."

"I just hope she didn't also help herself to whatever food I'm sure was dropped off with those balls."

Zane's border collie, Hope, came running out to greet them as they approached the barn door, her owner ambling out a few steps behind her. Zane raised his hand in greeting as he nodded toward the barn. "I just got Beauty in and settled. You guys okay?"

"Yeah, we're good," Cade told him. He wasn't sure if he and Nora were good with each other again, but they had made it safely back to the ranch.

"I'm so sorry," Nora said to Zane. "It's my fault that Beauty got away. I let go of the reins."

"I told you it's not your fault," Cade said. "The horse just got spooked by a rattler near her feet."

"Dang. That's scary for anybody," Zane said. "Did it strike?"

"Nah. It slithered away."

"Because Cade kept his cool and threw a rock at it," Nora told him. "All I did was scream and run away."

Zane shrugged. "Understandable. I've seen grown men scream and run away from rattlesnakes. They're a nasty thing to run into. Where'd you see it?"

"By the hunting cabin. We got caught in that thunderstorm and holed up in the cabin for the afternoon."

Zane's gaze raked over their disheveled appearance, and a slight grin tugged at the corner of his lip. "I can think of worse ways to spend an afternoon."

Cade avoided his eyes as Nora swung her leg over the saddle horn.

"That would account for why Beauty's saddle and blanket were damp," Zane said as he raised his arms to help Nora off the horse. "By the way, Bryn called an hour or so ago, and they're on their way back from Denver. She said they picked up a mess of Italian food from her favorite restaurant. And knowing Bryn, she got enough to feed the entire congregation of the United Methodist Church of Creedence. So you all are welcome to come for supper."

"I might sit this one out," Nora told him, rubbing her rear end. "Right now, all I can think about is soaking in a hot bath and putting on some dry clothes." She waved as she headed to the bunkhouse. "I'll see you later."

Cade swung out of the saddle and led the horse behind him as he followed Zane into the barn. He opened the stall door, and Cade guided Gypsy in and unbuckled the straps of her saddle.

"You all right, brother?" Zane narrowed his eyes and studied him as he leaned casually on the gate. "You look like you've been rode hard and put away wet."

Cade shook his head—although the first part held a note of truth to it. He eyed Zane. "You ever done something that seemed like a good idea at the time, but then you started to regret it almost right after?"

Zane chuckled. "Almost daily." He glanced back toward the bunkhouse. "But I wouldn't think that little filly seems like a decision to regret. She's about one of the nicest people I've ever met, she obviously loves your daughter, and she's dang easy on the eyes. What's the problem?"

Cade pulled the saddle and blanket off and balanced them on the top edge of the stall. "So many problems." He scrubbed a hand over the back of his neck. "Besides the fact she's only going to be here for a few weeks and that the whole reason she's here is to take care of my *daughter*, not *me*, there's the issue of me not being the kind of man any self-respecting woman should take a bet on. I don't have a real great track record when it comes to sticking around for relationships."

Relationships? Since when did he start thinking about this thing with Nora as having a chance at a relationship?

Zane shrugged. "Seems to me that's her decision to make, not yours." He chewed on a piece of straw he'd pulled from the hay bale outside of Gypsy's stall. "Besides, people can change."

The sound of an engine had them turning their attention to the barn door as Elle's SUV pulled into the drive.

Cade unbuckled Gypsy's bridle and pulled the bit from her mouth. He hung the bridle on a nail outside her stall, then drew the gate shut and followed Zane out of the barn. He could see Allie's excited face in the back window as she waved happily at him as he approached the car.

He was tempted to look behind him to see who she was waving at, then she opened the back door and said his name. "Cade, you've got to see what we bought. We had so much fun. And I even got my nails done." Her eyes were bright and carried none of her usual hostility toward him as she waved her painted fingernails in the air. Not that it wouldn't or couldn't come back, but he was going to enjoy it while he could.

Maybe people could change.

"Wow, those look nice," he told her, not sure what the exact response was to compliment a manicure.

She was hopping toward him, her booted foot held off the ground. "And we brought back food. So much food. Bryn said it was enough to feed her whole church."

"Told ya so," Zane muttered as he opened the hatch of the SUV, sticking a hand out to prevent the cascade of shopping bags and takeout boxes from falling as he pulled out Allie's knee scooter.

The girl hopped to the back and grabbed several of the bags, barely taking a breath as she chattered on about their day. "We had lunch and we went to the mall and we stopped at this really cool bookstore." She passed him three of the bags. "I got a new shirt and two new books and the cutest dress for the dance on Saturday."

Cade gaped at the plethora of bags. "How did you get all this stuff? I only gave you forty dollars to help with lunch."

"Sassy bought lunch, so I spent my money on books. And Elle bought the clothes."

"This is too much."

"I know. I tried to tell her, but she wouldn't take no for an answer, and she somehow convinced me. You know what it's like to argue with her."

He peered through the window to where Elle was standing and doing a pretty good job of avoiding his eye. "Yes, I know what it's like." And even though he wanted to argue now, to tell his daughter they couldn't accept all these things, the look of joy on her face was worth the price of his pride.

━━━━━━━━━━

Later that night, a knock sounded at Nora's door. Her pulse raced with hope that it was Cade, but instead she found Allie on her doorstep, holding a shopping bag and a small takeout box of food.

"I brought you some chicken Alfredo, and I wanted to show you my new dress," Allie said as she wheeled the knee scooter into the kitchen.

"Thank you. You're so sweet. I can't wait to see what you bought," Nora told her as she grabbed a fork from the drawer and pulled back the lid of the container. The scent of garlic and parmesan filled the air, making Nora's mouth water. She twisted a strand of linguini around her fork and took a bite, then let out a groan. "Oh, yum. This is amazing. I didn't realize I was so hungry. Your nails look gorgeous by the way."

Allie waved her fingers in the air. "Aren't they so pretty? I've never had a manicure in a salon before. It was really fun."

"It is. I love to treat myself to a mani and a pedi every few months."

"A pedi wasn't exactly an option with this," Allie told her, holding up her booted ankle.

"Not yet," Nora said. "But you're getting closer. You did really well in our therapy session yesterday, and I've got some new exercises for you to try when we get together in the morning. Since we've got all these yoga balls, I came up with some fun ideas of how to put them to good use." She took another bite as she dropped into a seat at the table, then pointed to the bag with her fork. "Okay, tell me everything about today, and I'm dying to see the dress."

Allie grinned as she put the shopping bag on the table and drew out a packet of folded tissue. Peeling back the layers, she lifted a deep purple sundress from its folds and held it up in front of her.

"Oh, wow," Nora said. "It's beautiful. And that color is perfect for you."

"Thank you. I love it." The dress came to right above Allie's knees. "I got a supercute pair of sandals to wear with it, but I also thought it would match my purple cowboy boots. Which might be better for a barn dance thing."

"It absolutely will. It will be darling. And perfect for the barn dance." She wrinkled her nose. "And now I'm jealous that I didn't go with you all. Now I want a manicure and a new dress for the dance."

"Elle said there's a cute dress shop in town. Maybe you can run into town tomorrow and still find one."

"Good idea. I just might do that."

"You should." The girl's hair fell over her shoulder and into her face as she tried to fold the dress and put it back into the bag. She huffed and blew her bangs from her face. "Urgh. My hair is driving me crazy."

"Do you want me to braid it for you?"

"Would you?"

"Of course."

"That would be great. Thanks."

Nora took the last bite of her pasta, a little surprised at how quickly she'd demolished the serving, then gestured to the other chair. "You sit down, and I'll grab a brush. You can do your shoulder exercises while I braid your hair."

She heard Allie groan again, but the teenager was sitting at the chair with her splint off and already doing the first stretch when Nora returned with a brush and some elastics a few minutes later.

"It's such a pain to try to do my hair with one hand," Allie told her.

"You must be figuring it out though," Nora said. "Because you've had your hair in braids the last few days."

The girl shrugged. "Cade did it for me."

"Oh, really?"

"Yeah, it's good that he can do it but also kind of annoying that he's so good at it."

Nora grinned as she twisted the girl's hair into a neat plait. "It must be all that practice on his horse's tail."

Allie giggled. "It's not *just* that. I also caught him watching a YouTube video on how to do your daughter's hair last night when I got up to go to the bathroom."

Oh, Cade. You old softie. "Aww. That's so sweet."

The teenager shrugged again. "Yes, sometimes he's an okay guy." She winced as she moved her arm through the exercise, but she completed the stretch. "He's not really the way I've always thought he would be."

"What do you mean?"

"I don't know. I haven't spent a lot of time with him, not like I do now, but my mom and my aunt have never said anything good about him. They've always just told me what a selfish jerk he was and that he never cared about me. But I remember a few things, like him reading books to me and sitting on the floor in my room doing a stupid tea party thing."

Nora had a hard time imagining the tough cowboy drinking out of a tiny teacup.

Allie raised her hand and touched the scar above her eyebrow. "My mom said I got this because of him. And that this is why he left."

"What happened?" Nora didn't want to say that Cade had already told her the story about that day.

"I fell down the stairs and hit my head. My mom said my dad wasn't watching me and that he left because he couldn't handle taking care of me." The girl had ripped a piece off Nora's napkin and was twisting it between her fingers. "She said she begged him to stay, but he said I was too much trouble and that he never wanted me in the first place."

Nora sucked in a breath. That Amber was a real piece of work. Placing a hand on Allie's knee, Nora sat down in the chair next to her. She had so many things she wanted to say, and all of them would be her standing up for Cade. But this beautiful, fragile girl had just shared something important with her, and Nora knew she needed to tread carefully. "That's a hard thing to hear" was all she said.

"Yeah, I've been mad at my dad for a long time, but now that I've been around him, it doesn't seem like all that stuff was true."

"Have you talked to your dad about this? Asked *him* what happened that day?"

Allie shook her head. "No. But why would my mom lie?"

To make herself look better in her daughter's eyes. "I'm not sure, honey. That's a tough one. And I didn't know her, so I can't say for sure."

"I know my mom hated my dad, but he doesn't seem all that bad. It's just that every time I start to kind of like him, I feel like I'm hurting my mom."

"Come here, sweet girl." Nora held open her arms, and Allie practically fell into her lap. Her shoulders shook as she let out a sob, and Nora wrapped her tighter and pressed a kiss to her head as she let the girl cry herself out.

"Sorry," Allie said, sitting back and wiping at the wet spot on Nora's shoulder.

"Don't be," Nora said, passing her another napkin. "My shoulder is always available if you need a good cry." She brushed the girl's hair from her forehead. "I'm so sorry this happened to you."

"Me too," Allie whispered.

"I may not have known your mom, but I know that she would want you to be happy. And Cade seems like he is really trying. I think you should talk to him. Tell him how you feel and ask him what happened that day you fell. I think he would give you an honest answer."

"Yeah?"

"Yeah. I mean, heck, the guy is watching YouTube videos at night to figure out how to do your hair. He can't be all bad."

───────────

After Allie left, Nora changed into her pajamas, brushed her teeth, and fell into bed, exhausted. It had been quite a day, and even though she was tired, she knew it would take a while to process everything that had happened before her brain would shut down and let her sleep.

Her phone chimed, and she was excited and nervous to see a text from Cade. Although her excitement may have been premature.

Hey was all it said.

Wow. He was such a great conversationalist. There were so many ways she could take that one word. She tapped her phone to her chin. How to respond? Hey yourself she typed back but added a smiley face emoji.

I was just thinking about you.

I was just thinking about you too. Gosh. This conversation was getting really deep. Thanks for teaching me how to ride a horse. Sorry I was such a failure at it. She hit send just as another message popped in from him.

I just got out of the shower. Alone. I preferred the one I
    took this afternoon with you.

Oh. Okay. Those were two very different directions of conversation. Before she could figure out what to respond, another message came in from him.

You weren't a failure.

At the shower or the ride?

Either one. An emoji of a wide-smiling face popped on the screen. You earned a gold star from me on both.

What? I was terrible with the horse. She ran away from me.

Oh, you meant THAT ride...

Her cheeks warmed as she let out a laugh.
A winky-face emoji popped up on her screen. Her phone chimed again and the next message was just five gold stars.

Gah. How did she respond to that? She sent back a laughing emoji, then typed another message. I'm not sure how many stars you earned.

His return message was just a question mark.

She leaned back against her pillow, the flirty conversation and the texting format giving her courage. I might need another afternoon in the saddle to make a confident recommendation. She hit Send before she changed her mind.

She got another winky face emoji followed by the message, I'm a rodeo guy so I'm always up for another ride.

A giggle escaped her lips. A giggle? Really? She hugged her pillow to her chest as the smile she'd had on her face since he first texted her started to hurt her cheeks.

Her phone chimed with another message. Good night, Beautiful.

Emotion stung her throat. She was in so much trouble here. She really liked this man. He was tough and tender and strong and funny. He was in the middle of this terrible life situation, and he needed his concentration to be on his daughter. Her head warned her of what a terrible idea this flirting was and that this afternoon was probably a terrible error in her judgment. But her heart swelled with feeling for the man who had held her so tenderly in his arms and kissed her with such passion. And called her beautiful.

Good night, cowboy. She sighed as she set her phone on the nightstand and cuddled down into the pillow.

She'd just started to drift off when her phone chimed with another text. A smile was already on her lips as she drowsily picked up the phone. But her smile, and her stomach, fell as she saw the name on the screen.

Wide-awake now, her fingers tightened on the phone as she sat up. Dread swirled in her stomach as she opened the message from Geoff.

I can't stop thinking about you. I miss you and I still love you.

CHAPTER 14

NORA SAT ON THE FRONT PORCH THE NEXT MORNING, HER coffee cooling in her cup as she stared out across the pasture and the landscape of mountains. Geoff's message had really thrown her for a loop. Heck, the whole day had, from the time at the cabin with Cade to her conversation with Allie to the stupid text from Geoff. Which she hadn't answered.

It felt too much like another one of his games.

But his text *had* made her think. What was she doing here? And what the heck did she think she was playing at with Cade? This was supposed to be a job. And a temporary one at that. In a few weeks, she'd be going back to Denver. Ugh. Back to her mom's basement. At least until she could find another apartment. The money from this job would give her enough for a deposit and a few month's rent. And then she'd probably never see Cade, or Allie, again.

The thought made her chest hurt, and she rubbed a hand against it, as if to push away the pain. She was doing it again. Jumping in with both feet and forgetting to see if there was even water in the pool. Why did she let herself fall so easily? And make no mistake, she was falling hard for the cute cowboy.

Her gaze was drawn to a movement, and she watched a horse and rider come down the path along the side of the mountain, then gallop across the field toward the barn. Cade's features came into view as he got closer, but she'd known it was him. She recognized his hat and jacket, but also his body and the way he carried himself in the saddle. He rode with such confidence, his movements fluid, as if he and the horse were one.

He was so dang hot. But in the same way flames were hot, she knew the closer she got to him, the better chance she stood of getting burned.

She'd felt things for Geoff too. He'd been handsome and charming and had wooed her easily into his bed and his home. It wasn't until she'd moved in that she'd realized his compliments and sweet gifts were often tinged with control.

"You look nice in blue, but you look amazing in red," he'd told her the night she'd worn her favorite soft teal dress out on a date with him, the one that usually made her feel confident and sexy. The dress had a high neckline but dropped low in the back, showing off her shoulders. He'd run his fingers teasingly over her neck, sending a shiver down her spine that turned from heated to cool when he'd followed the first offhand comment with another. "You've got great boobs, baby. You should show more cleavage." He'd slid his hand around and covered her breast, squeezing it just a little too tightly. "I would love it, and it would show all those other assholes out there what I've got that they don't."

Even though the day was warm, the memory of that night had Nora feeling chilled. She fought the reaction, squishing further into the glider's cushions. She touched the ends of her naturally wavy hair, worn the way *she* liked it best, loose around her shoulders after letting it dry naturally.

She realized after they'd broken up that she'd been subtly changing her appearance over the last year to match *his* desires. She'd often get up an hour early so she'd have time to straighten her hair or to pull it back into a severe chignon, another style he liked, before heading into work. She found herself buying and wearing more red. And he'd given her a couple of lower cut tops, then pouted if she didn't wear them to work. So she did, often covering up with cardigans if he wasn't around since the tops made her uncomfortable around clients.

And it wasn't just the way she wore her hair or her clothes. It was the way she loaded the dishwasher and brushed her teeth. He even had an opinion on how she drank her coffee, so she gave up her favorite hazelnut-flavored creamer in favor of his soy-based mocha one instead.

Looking back, it was hard to pinpoint exactly when or how she had changed herself for him, but she had. A *take that, Geoff* smile crept to her lips as she thought about the container of hazelnut creamer in her fridge and how none of the clothes she had brought with her had a smidgen of red in them.

Gypsy's hooves beat a thunderous sound as Cade galloped up to the barn, and Nora's heart thumped almost as loud at the sight of him. His command of the horse combined with his sweet affection for the animal added to his appeal. Plus he was just so damn good-looking.

But Cade hadn't used his looks or his charm to try to change her. She sipped her coffee, made just the way she liked it, and continued her musings. He came out of the barn a few minutes later, and she enjoyed watching him amble toward her, whacking the dust from his well-fitting jeans and wearing a faded blue T-shirt that hugged his broad chest.

"Good morning, gorgeous," he said as he took off his hat and dropped it on the table, then sank into the seat next to her.

"Good morning," she replied, trying not to be flustered by the warmth of his shoulder pressed next to hers.

He gestured toward her cup. "It's dry out there. Can I bum a swig?"

She passed him the mug. He took a sip and wrinkled his nose. "What?" she asked, her voice coming out a little harsher than she'd intended.

"Nothing," he said passing her back the cup. "I needed something wet, and that filled the bill. I just wasn't expecting it to be cold or with that fancy creamer crap in it."

She bristled as she leaned forward. "Do you think I should drink it some other way?"

He furrowed his brow as he studied her. "No. I don't give two hoots how you drink it. It's your coffee, you can drink it however you damn well please."

"You bet I can."

He narrowed his eyes. "You okay?"

She let out her breath as she leaned back against the seat. "Yes. Sorry. Weird morning. How was your ride?"

"Good. I went up to check on the cattle in the west pasture and fix one of the gates up there." He lifted his arm and rested it across the back of the glider chair and the scent of him swirled around her. All masculine with hints of cedar and musk mixed with the subtle scents of hay and saddle leather. He lifted a curl of her hair and twirled it around his finger. "I like your hair like this."

"But?" Dang, there was that angry, slightly miffed tone coming out of her again.

Cade noticed too. He raised an eyebrow in question, then a roguish grin curved his lips and he leaned closer, his breath warm on her neck as he said, "*But* I'd like it spread across my pillow even better."

She laughed—at his comment and at herself for trying to put Cade in the same box as her ex. This cowboy was nothing like Geoff.

Cade brought his arm back around as the screen door opened and Allie pushed through it, the puppy tumbling around her feet. She did a little butt wiggle at seeing Nora and Cade, then raced out into the grass to do her business. Finished, she ran back to Allie, tripping on her feet as she got close. She let out a little yip as she ran around the table, stopping to sniff Nora's toes and Cade's boots, then running back to the girl's side, toppling over as she crashed into Allie's boots. The teenager was looking more like a farm girl, wearing her cowboy boots with jean shorts and a Hogwarts T-shirt.

Allie held her hand up to the dog. "Scout, sit." The puppy obediently plopped down on its bottom, its tail brushing the planks of the porch as it wagged furiously back and forth.

"Hey, that's pretty good," Cade told her as Allie gave the pup a small piece of a dog biscuit she'd had stuffed in her pocket. "You're doing really well with her."

"She's a really smart dog. I watched some videos, and I've been googling a lot of stuff about puppies—cattle dogs in particular. They're a supersmart breed and they like to work, so they can be pretty easily trained if you keep at it."

"Sounds like you've got a smart dog for a smart girl. But it's not just the dog. I've seen you now with the horses and with some of the animals around the ranch, and you're really good with all of them. You've got a real gift."

She stared at him for a moment as if trying to figure him out, then ducked her head and leaned down to pet the puppy. "Thank you," she muttered softly.

They were interrupted by the sound of an engine as a car turned into the driveway.

Nora shaded her eyes with her hand. "Oh, geez. I hope this isn't someone bringing out another yoga ball. I'm running out of space in the spare room."

Cade shook his head as he recognized the blue compact that pulled up in front of the bunkhouse. "I doubt it. They're the ones who dropped the two off yesterday."

"Oh. Best not to tell them we gave one to the pig then."

Cade chuckled. "Actually, they'd probably get a kick out of it."

A tall woman climbed out of the driver's side, and a boy of about ten opened the passenger door. Most of the woman's curly brown hair was corralled into a single braid resting on her shoulder. She wore khaki shorts, tennis shoes, and a T-shirt that read *Librarian because Book Wizard isn't an official title*. Her hips were curvy but her long legs were tan and toned. She had an open and friendly smile on her face as she waved and approached the porch, and Nora immediately liked her—partly because of her smile, but mostly because of her shirt.

"Hey, Cade," she said.

"Hey, Jillian." He nodded toward Allie, then Nora. "This is my daughter, Allie, and her physical therapist, Nora Fisher. Ladies, this is Jillian Bennett." Nora noticed he failed to mention the yoga ball that Tiny had absconded with.

Jillian's smile grew as she held out her hand and shook Nora's, then nodded at Allie. "I'm so glad to finally meet you both. Elle and Bryn have told me so much about you."

"Jillian works at the library," Cade explained. "And this nerdy kid is her son, Milo." He gestured to the boy who was walking up the porch carrying a tall stack of books.

The boy grinned. He was tall like his mom, but his shaggy hair was blond and in his T-shirt, board shorts, and Converse sneakers, he looked more like a surfer than a nerd. "Takes one to know one," he said, giving Cade's insult right back to him.

"Hey, I'm not the one holding a stack of books higher than my head." Cade teased him good-naturedly as he took the top half of the pile and set it on the table in front of them.

"Hey, I brought 'em for you," Milo said.

"You brought those books for my *dad*?" Allie asked, staring at the heap of hardbacks.

"Actually," Jillian said, "we brought them for you." She picked the top few off the stack and passed them to the girl.

"Me?" Allie turned the books over in her hands.

"Yep. Your dad told us you love to read, so he had my mom open a library card for you," Milo explained. "Then he asked us to pick out some books for you. He was gonna pick them up this afternoon, but we decided to bring them to you instead."

"You picked all these out? For me?" She leaned forward to get a closer look at the titles.

"Milo picked out most of them," Jillian told her. "We grabbed some new releases and then he threw in a bunch of his favorites."

Allie gawked at the boy. "You've read all these?"

He shrugged. "Most of them." He glanced at Cade. "He's read some of these too, you know. Your dad is always checking out books."

Allie gave Cade one of her usual side-eyes, but Milo kept talking as he shuffled through the books.

He picked up a thick hardback. "My best friend, Mandy, I think you already met her, she loves to read too. This is one of her favorites. I think she's read it three times."

Allie had tucked the puppy into her lap when their car had pulled up, and it squirmed and wiggled now as it tried to sniff and lick at the books she held. She held it back to keep it from jumping off her knees.

"Oh wow, you got one of Grace's puppies," Milo said, holding out his hand to pet the dog's chin. "I just got a puppy this summer too, but it was hard to choose. These guys were all so cute, but this one has always been really sweet. You're lucky you got her."

Allie's smile widened as she peered down at the pup. "Yeah, she is the sweetest. My dad gave her to me. I named her Scout."

"Nice," he said, nodding approvingly. "Hi, Scout." He laughed as the puppy chewed on his finger.

"How did you know about Grace and all her puppies?" Allie asked.

"Milo and Jillian volunteer here at the horse rescue," Cade explained. "They moved here earlier this summer from California."

"But don't hold that against us," Jillian said, a grin on her lips as she ruffled Milo's hair. "We got here as soon as we could."

Nora laughed. Her instincts had been right. She liked this woman. She was friendly and Nora admired the way she was so easily affectionate with her son. And it touched her that they'd brought the books out to Allie. "What brought you to Creedence?"

"My sister, Carley. She runs the Cut and Curl beauty shop in town. She's been bugging us to move here for years. So when the job opened up at the library, I applied and here we are. I'm still not sure my sister didn't bribe the selection committee with apple pie or free haircuts for a year if they chose me." She laughed, then gazed out at the ranch. "We're so glad we came though. Creedence is a great town, and we love the community. We've met some really wonderful people. Present company excluded, of course." She nudged Cade's foot with hers as she teased him.

Nora pushed down the sudden niggle of jealousy at the ease with which this woman and her son joked with Cade. A minute ago, she'd thought she was great, and now the green-eyed monster was trying to get in her head. *Stop it*, she scolded herself as she nodded at the feisty librarian. "I agree. I've met some really nice people just in the short time I've been here."

"I've heard. You've made quite an impression," Jillian said. "Sassy James can't stop talking about how the physical therapy exercises you gave her worked wonders for her hip, and Sam down at the feed store said you were in there a few days ago and gave him some tips to help with the arthritis in his hand. I'm surprised you haven't had more people calling you to try to schedule therapy appointments."

"We're keeping her to ourselves," Cade said. "She's really helped Allie."

His compliments warmed Nora, but she shook her head. "I haven't done that much. She can't move her shoulder much but we've done some simple range-of-motion exercises to help with the muscles."

"Haven't done that much?" Allie gaped at her. "She's just being modest. Nora is awesome. When I first got here, she and Cade kept me on a steady routine of ice packs and ibuprofen, and she made a schedule for me to do exercises. And she tries to trick me into doing things like pushing a ball with my foot or brushing the horse a certain way and acts like I don't know she's making me do some kind of stretch for my shoulder or my ankle."

Nora put on an innocent expression. "Who? Me?"

Jillian laughed. "I'm just saying that word is getting around that you're good at your job. And we don't have a physical therapist here, so I wouldn't be surprised if you got a little extra side business while you're in town."

Nora hadn't even thought of that. Allie was her first priority and the job she was being paid to do, but after her time with the Callahans was over, she was still going to need a job.

Cade's phone buzzed. He pulled it from his pocket, then held up his hand. "Sorry. I'd better take this. It's Bryn."

Nora sat forward, hoping they hadn't had car trouble. Bryn and Zane had left for Denver early that morning to pick up some supplies.

"Yeah, okay," Cade said, as a tan pickup hauling a horse trailer pulled into the driveway and up to the bunkhouse. A Creedence County Sheriff Department logo was on the door and a dark-haired man got out. He pulled a brown felt cowboy hat from the cab and placed it on his head as he strode toward them. He was tall, confident in his stride, and his handsome face was clean-shaven. He wore cowboy boots and blue jeans, but his tan shirt was crisply ironed with a shiny gold star pinned above his left torso pocket.

"He's here now," Cade said into the phone. "Don't worry. We'll take care of it. I'll call you when we get back." He pushed the phone back into his pocket, then held out his hand as he stood to greet the newcomer. "Ethan."

The man nodded. "Cade."

"This is Deputy Ethan Rayburn," Cade said, then introduced him to the rest of the group.

"Nice to meet you all." He shook Nora's hand, then paused for just an extra beat as he took Jillian's. "You can call me Ethan," he told her.

Nora noticed the small shy smile he offered her, then his grin widened as he read her shirt. "Nice," he said. "You must be the new librarian. I heard we'd hired one, but I hadn't made it down to meet you. You're not quite what I expected."

Jillian smoothed her hair. "I get that a lot. I think most people associate a head librarian with an uptight gray-haired matron who goes around shushing people all the time. Sorry to disappoint."

Hmm. Did Nora detect a bit of a flirty tone in the librarian's comment?

"Oh, I'm not disappointed," Ethan said, shaking his head. "You're great. I mean, you seem great. I mean, you seem like you would be a great librarian." He glanced around as if trying to find a lifeline and gestured to the stack on the table. "Are those your books?"

"Jillian brought them out for Allie," Cade said, stepping in to save the poor guy. "Bryn said you needed our help with a couple of horses."

The deputy nodded, straightening his shoulders as if shifting back into command mode. "Yeah. I'm headed over to the Larson place. You know the one? It's just on the far side of Bryn's property off County Road 36?"

"I know the place," Cade confirmed. "I haven't seen Miss Pearl in years, but she was always nice to us as kids. She used to make these huge chocolate chip cookies that she'd give us when Grandpa took us over there to help her out with something after her husband died."

"Well, unfortunately, she just passed away as well."

"Oh, dang."

"I guess she got sick last month and her daughter drove over from Utah and took her to the hospital in Denver. She died last week, and apparently the daughter got so caught up in everything, she forgot about the horses they'd left behind. I think there's a cat too. Although a cat can fend for itself easier than a horse can." He shook his head. "I don't know quite how you *forget* about animals, but everybody grieves differently. The daughter called us to say she can't take care of the animals and asked for our help. I called Bryn and she said she could take them, at least temporarily."

"Of course she did," Cade said, picking his hat up off the table and placing it on his head. "Well, let's go get 'em. Give me a minute to grab some lead ropes and some sweet feed."

"Can we come with you?" Milo asked. "We came out this morning to volunteer as well as drop off the books. It would be so cool to actually *see* some horses get rescued."

Cade shrugged as he looked toward the deputy. "Okay by me. Ethan, you okay if they come?"

"Fine by me. I'm not promising much excitement though. We're just going to drive over there, load up the horses, and bring them back."

"Don't forget about the cat," Allie said, pushing up from her chair. "We have to find the cat."

"I said there *might* be a cat," the deputy corrected her. "I don't know what we'll find until we get over there."

Cade peered down at Nora. "You want to ride along to see a boring horse rescue and to search for a cat that may or may not exist?"

She popped out of her chair. "Of course. How could I miss out on an opportunity like that? Especially after you pitched it with such an exciting buildup. It sounds like a real adventure."

"Everybody get in the truck," Cade said, heading toward the barn. "We're apparently going on an adventure."

The kids took off for the truck. Milo helped Allie and the puppy into the back seat, then loaded the knee scooter into the back end. Nora nudged Jillian's arm as they followed. "You sure you don't want to ride with the hot deputy?"

Jillian arranged her features into the innocent look Nora had tried earlier. "Oh, was he hot? I hadn't noticed."

"Yeah right," Nora said. "Just like I didn't notice how he stumbled all over his words trying to talk to you." She reached for the door handle. "I could say our truck is full and nonchalantly suggest you ride with him."

Jillian shook her head but couldn't keep the smile off her face. "Oh my gosh, don't you dare."

Nora was teasing her, but it was all in good fun. "Maybe you could steal something from this farm and then he'd have to frisk you?"

"You're terrible," Jillian said, nudging her with her hip and flashing her a grin before she climbed into the back of the truck next to her son. "But I like you already."

———————

Ten minutes later, Cade pulled into a narrow dirt driveway. Rusted barbed-wire fencing lined the long drive, tall grass and weeds almost choking out the path. An old wooden sign hung from one side of the last fence post, the words *Crooked Creek Ranch* etched into dry rotted wood. The farmhouse itself was in a small clearing with a faded white barn and fields off to one side. The mountain rising up behind it engulfed its back and other side, almost as if standing guard over the charming two-story home with the meandering creek running behind it.

The house itself was an old Victorian complete with a cupola that rose along one side, up both stories, then above the attic space. The house had good bones but was in sad disrepair, its wide wraparound porch sagging off the side of the house.

"Oh, wow," Allie whispered from behind his head. "It's like a cottage out of an old fairy tale."

"Old is right," Cade said. "I think my grandpa told me this house has been around for close to a hundred years. It underwent some renovations back in the eighties, updating the kitchen and bathrooms, but it doesn't look like it's had much upkeep since then. Miss Pearl has lived out here on her own for a long time."

"I love it," Allie said, leaning forward and pressing on the back of his seat.

"I do, too," Nora said, peering around the ranch as he pulled the truck to a stop in front of the barn. Two horses were in the corral off the barn, and one walked cautiously toward them.

Ethan pulled the trailer up behind him. He got out and approached the horse, holding what looked like a sugar cube out in his hand.

Cade got out and grabbed the knee scooter from the back end. He passed it to Allie as Milo helped her out of the truck.

"Can we go look for the cat?" she asked.

"Sure. Just be careful."

She and Milo were already heading toward the house, the puppy bounding along next to them. He had no idea what they were going to do with a scraggly farm cat if they found it, but he knew Bryn wouldn't turn it away. She'd probably just add it to the several cats currently chasing mice around her barn.

"Jillian and I are going to look around too," Nora said, coming up to stand beside him. "If you don't need us."

"Go ahead. Ethan and I can handle this," Cade told her.

"Poor babies," she said, shielding her eyes from the sun as she peered at the horses. One was a quarter horse, the other a gray. Both looked in sad shape, their coats dull and their heads hanging low. They must have been able to find some grass around the corral, so they weren't starving, but the outline of their ribs showed on their sides.

"I'm going to try to find them some fresh water." He spotted a bucket hanging off a water pump next to an old windmill. "You all go on. But be careful," he said, repeating the same warning he'd given the kids.

"Holler if you need us," Nora said as she and Jillian walked toward the barn.

"It should be easy enough to open this gate and get them into the trailer," Ethan said as Cade walked back from the pump with a full bucket of fresh water in his hands. He nodded to the gray, who eyed them warily from the other side of the corral. "That one might take a little more convincing, but this one is a sweetheart." He ran his hand over the horse's neck, and she nudged her nose into his chest.

Cade set the bucket down and the horse sniffed it, then took a greedy drink. The gray took a few steps closer. "Let me grab some hay and some of that sweet feed, and I'll bet I can win him over."

Twenty minutes and four handfuls of sweet feed later, they had both horses loaded into the trailer. Cade had been right about the hay and feed. That and some patience and gentle encouragement was what it took to win over the gray, but all Ethan used to convince the quarter horse was his charm and a few sugar cubes.

"I think that horse has a crush on you," Cade told him.

"I think the feeling is mutual," Ethan said, scratching the horse's nose through the grate in the trailer.

"This place is really beautiful," Cade said, peering around at the farm. "Sure it needs some fixing up, but it has a good feel to it. Do you know what the daughter plans to do with it?"

The deputy shrugged. "Not sure. She'll probably sell it. Miss Pearl was in her nineties, so her daughter has to be in her seventies. I can't imagine she'd want to take the place over. Seems like if she was interested in living here, she would have come back years ago."

"True. This land butts up to Bryn's property. I hope whoever buys it wants to farm it and is a good neighbor. This seems like a great place to raise a family." He leaned down to pick up a piece of dried barn wood with a rusty nail in it. "After they've gotten their tetanus shots, that is."

Ethan chuckled.

"All right. Let me round up Nora and Jillian and the kids, and we'll get these guys back to Bryn's ranch."

As if she could read his mind, Nora came around the corner of the house and waved. Jillian was right behind her.

"Did you find the cat?" he called.

"No, but we found these." She held up a bunch of bright pink flowers as they approached the men. "There's a huge gorgeous wild rose bush behind the house. I couldn't help myself. Do you think it's okay I took some?"

"I'm sure Miss Pearl would love it," Cade told her, taking the flowers and setting them on the dashboard of his pickup. "Have you seen the kids?"

Jillian jerked a thumb toward the house. "They were in the back yard with us, but they took off chasing after the cat."

Cade groaned. "There really was a cat, huh?" He wrenched his head toward the house as he heard a banging on one of the windows. Allie's face was framed in one of the windows of the cupola, her mouth open as she yelled his name and waved him frantically inside.

CHAPTER 15

CADE SPRINTED TOWARD THE HOUSE, TAKING THE PORCH steps two at a time. The front door was locked. How the hell did they get in there?

"They must have gone in the back," Jillian said, her voice rising in panic as she raced toward the back of the house, Ethan right on her heels.

Cade vaulted the porch railing, landing hard in the grass and running after her. Nora was right behind him.

The back door was open, and Jillian and Ethan disappeared inside. He ran through the door, fear pounding through his heart. Although it seemed like with this group, they could handle whatever crisis came their way. Between the four of them, they had a dad, a doctor, a mom, and a lawman.

Hardwood floors led from a mudroom into a large sunny kitchen with wood cabinets and cheery black-and-white cow decor. The throw rug was black, spotted towels hung from the stove handle, and a dancing cow cookie jar sat on the counter. The house smelled a bit musty but the air inside still held the slight scent of vanilla.

As a group, they moved from the kitchen into the good-sized living room at the front of the house. A knitted blue-and-gray afghan hung over the arm of a rocking chair which sat next to an older, but still serviceable, chintz-covered sofa. Against the far wall sat a small secretary desk, the chair pulled out and a page of stationery and pen sitting on it, as if Miss Pearl were going to come back any minute and jot down a letter.

The whole place had a hominess to it. It was like the kind of feeling Cade would get whenever he walked into his grandma's house. As if a cute, little old lady was going to walk out of the kitchen with a tray of lemonade and sugar cookies and insist you stay and chat with her a bit.

White french doors opened to the cupola to the left, and he could hear Allie's voice coming from inside the room. "You guys, come in here. You've got to see this," she called.

Cade let out his breath. It didn't sound like she was in mortal danger. He followed Ethan and Jillian into the room, then almost wrecked into the librarian as she stopped midstride and clasped her hands over her mouth.

He heard Nora let out a gasp as she stopped next to him. "Oh, wow," she whispered.

"Isn't this the coolest room you've ever seen in your life?" Allie asked from her perch in the cupola's spacious window seat. Her eyes were wide, her expression a mixture of awe and joy as she grinned like a kid who'd just discovered a candy shop.

She and Milo sat next to each other, leaning back against an array of cushy throw pillows, the puppy nestled between them and an orange-and-white cat curled in Allie's lap. The thick cushion filling the window seat was covered in faded burgundy velvet with antique bronzed tacks along the front edge, similar to the kind of fabric used to cover seats in an old movie theatre.

"It's a library," Jillian said, gazing around at the floor to ceiling custom-made shelves that followed the curves of the room. The shelves were crammed with books, from antique hardbacks of classic literature to paperback thrillers and romance novels.

"It's a reading nook," Nora said, her eyes almost as wide as Allie's. She peered around as she walked past Cade and dropped onto the cushion next to the kids. She ran her hand reverently over the fabric. "It's wonderful." Her eyes shone as she looked from Cade to his daughter. "And you found the cat."

"We did. And she's just the sweetest thing," Allie said. "It's like she's been starved for affection." The cat lifted its head and rubbed her ears against the teenager's chin as if to illustrate Allie's point.

"It's a wonder she's not starved period," Ethan said.

"We found a bag of cat food with a hole in it in the kitchen," Milo explained. "She must have clawed or bit it open. But there's also a cat flap in the back door. We saw her run in here and we followed her in. That's how we found this room."

"It's amazing no other critters have discovered that cat flap," Ethan said. "I'm surprised you didn't find any squirrels or raccoons in here."

"If we did, I'm sure they would be in here cleaning and working because this house is like walking into a fairy tale," Allie said.

"Fairy tale or not, this is still someone else's house," Cade said. "You guys shouldn't have just come in here."

"The back door was unlocked," Allie said. "And we were trying to save the cat."

"We didn't touch anything," Milo said, then sheepishly held up the book in his hand. "Well, except the books when we found this cool room."

"Don't be mad, Cade," Allie said. "I know we probably shouldn't have come inside, but it was almost like the cat was trying to show us this. She led us right in here, and it was like discovering a magical room in a castle."

"I don't know that I would call the widow Larson's house a magical castle," Ethan muttered to Jillian. "But this room is pretty cool."

"It's the coolest room I've ever seen in my life," Allie gushed. "Seriously, have you ever seen curved bookshelves? Or fabric this soft?" She brushed her hand over the cushion. "And just look at that beautiful tea set." She pointed to the delicate pink-and-green porcelain pitcher and cup sitting on a matching antique tray. "I just want to move into this room and never leave."

"Well, it's a pretty neat place," Ethan said. "But we do have to leave. We've got the horses loaded, and we need to get them back to the ranch."

Cade watched the disappointment, then understanding play across Allie's face, and he was glad the deputy had been the one telling her she had to leave instead of him.

Milo picked up the sleepy puppy and put him in his basket while Allie scooted to the edge of the cushion. She held up the cat. "What about Clementine? We can't just leave her here."

Cade tilted his head. "You already named the cat?"

She shook her head. "No. We saw a note on the refrigerator that said to buy cat food for Clementine, so we just assumed that was her name."

Cade looked from his daughter to Nora, but she was no help. She just shrugged as she reached over to pet the cat's chin.

"You know Bryn would want us to take her," Allie said.

He blew out a breath. "Yeah, she would." In fact, his cousin would probably have his hide if they didn't bring the cat back with them. But he wasn't ready to add a permanent cat to his already growing household. He was barely getting used to the dog. "All right. We can bring her. But we're only keeping her until we find a more permanent home or until Bryn comes up with a better solution."

"Agreed," Allie said, passing the cat to Nora so she could get her booted foot settled on the knee scooter. "For now," she muttered not quite under her breath.

Yeah, that's what he was afraid of.

―――――――――

Thirty minutes later, they had the rescued horses back to Bryn's and set up in individual stalls in the barn. Ethan and Jillian had given them fresh hay and water while Cade lined their stalls with straw. Milo and Allie had taken turns feeding them sugar cubes, and Allie had introduced the new arrivals to Daisy and Gypsy.

Nora had taken Clementine back to the bunkhouse and given her some fresh cat food and a saucer of milk. The cat had eaten a little, then curled up in a patch of sunshine on one of the chairs on the porch and fallen asleep.

"All right," Cade said to the group assembled in the barn. "Let's give these two a chance to eat and settle in."

"I'd better get back to the station," Ethan said, as the group wandered out of the barn and into the sun. The day was bright and hot, and he slipped a pair of aviator sunglasses out of his pocket and put them on.

"Thanks for all your help," Cade told him.

"It was nice meeting you," Jillian said, a smile curving her lips as she offered the deputy a little wave.

Nora stood next to her, and Cade noted the way she looked from Jillian to the deputy before stepping forward. "Yes, great meeting you, Ethan. Don't forget about the dance this weekend. We hope to see you out here." She peered back at Jillian. "You'll be here too. Right, Jillian?"

"Uh, yes. We'll be here." She gave Nora a quick side-eye.

Apparently Cade wasn't the only one noticing Nora's subtle matchmaking efforts.

"Yeah, I was thinking about coming out for it," Ethan said, offering Jillian a shy smile. "I was thinking I'd come back out in a couple of days to check on the horses, but I do like to listen to a good band and occasionally take a turn on the dance floor. I'll come if you promise to save a dance for me."

Pink tinged Jillian's cheeks, but her smile spread wider across her face. "Yeah, sure."

His gaze stayed trained on hers as if none of the rest of them were even there. "See you then." He held her gaze for another few seconds, then turned to open the door of his truck. He offered the group a wave as he climbed into the cab. "Keep me posted on how the new horses get along. See you all Saturday."

Ethan pulled out of the driveway as the sound of another engine came from the pasture behind them. They turned to see a small green utility vehicle bouncing across the field, Brody at the wheel and Mandy waving from the passenger seat.

Cade nudged Allie. "*That's* a Gator."

"Where'd they come from?" she asked.

"Brody's ranch is about ten minutes away, but it's only five if you come through the pastures."

The Gator pulled up in front of them, and Brody cut the engine and climbed out of the vehicle. "Hey," he said, waving to the group. "Bryn called and said you all had some new horses arrive. She asked me to come over and check them out, and we figured we'd bring the Gator so Allie could take a ride." He nodded to Milo. "You too."

"Cool," Allie said, glancing up at Cade. "I mean, is that okay? Can I go on a ride with them?"

Cade eyed the Gator. He'd ridden them hundreds of times. They were much more stable than four-wheelers, but he still had a gnawing feeling in his gut. He and his brother and cousins had done all sorts of crazy things growing up. They wouldn't have thought twice about jumping on this thing and tearing up the fields. But it was different when it was his daughter and there was a chance she could get hurt.

He felt a warm arm press against his and looked down to see Nora had come up to stand by his side. How did she seem to always know what he was thinking? "Yeah, okay. But be careful."

"We will," Allie told him, only giving him a small eye roll. Probably because he said she could go with them.

"Stay on the trails in the pastures," Brody told Mandy as she scooted into the passenger seat. "And keep the speed down. Remember Allie still has a hurt foot and shoulder, so she doesn't need to go bouncing around too much."

Cade hadn't thought of that. He took a step forward, ready to change his mind, but Allie must have thought he was stepping forward to help her, and she took his arm to help hoist herself into the passenger seat. They still had a long way to go, but they'd made a lot of progress with each other in the past week. He didn't want to mess this up by being overprotective.

Milo handed Allie the puppy, then loaded the knee scooter into the back flatbed section of the Gator and climbed in next to it. "Ready to ride," he cried, grabbing ahold of the roll bars.

"Are there any seat belts on that thing?" Nora asked as Mandy started the engine.

The puppy sat up on Allie's lap and let out a yip as they moved forward. Allie waved to Cade, then grabbed the bar next to her, holding on as Mandy gave the utility vehicle a little gas and steered them back toward the field.

Cade tried to unclench his jaw as he watched them go. Was this a mistake? Was the Gator too dangerous? Mandy was only in fifth grade—could she really handle the machine?

"Don't worry," Brody told him. "Mandy is a good driver, and she knows to keep the speed low in that thing. We had a talk on the way over about being especially careful with Allie on board. And they're only driving around the pasture."

Cade rubbed a hand over the back of his neck. "I don't know why I'm acting like an old mother hen. My brother and I would have gone crazy for a chance to ride in one of those things when we were kids."

Brody chuckled and nudged him with his elbow. "Maybe that's why you worry. Thankfully Mandy isn't as dumb as we were as kids. And Milo is pretty levelheaded. I trust him."

"Thanks. I do too," Jillian said. "He's a smart boy. And I'll take my kid riding through a field in that solid-looking thing over him riding a surf board in the unpredictable waves of the ocean any day."

Cade looked from Jillian to Brody, suddenly feeling like he belonged in a club that he'd never let himself be a part of before. "Do you ever stop worrying about them?"

The other two laughed. "No," they answered together.

Brody clapped him on the shoulder. "Why don't you show me those new horses?"

He nodded, then took one last glance at the kids before leading the way into the barn.

Thirty minutes later, Brody had given both horses a thorough examination. Nora had brought him the cat, and he'd given her a once-over as well and declared all the animals in pretty decent shape. "The horses are a little malnourished and their coats are a little dull, but they should be fine after a few days of solid meals and fresh water. Thankfully, they had access to some grass, and the bit of rain we've gotten lately has probably helped with their water intake. I've seen a lot of horses in worse shape after they've been abandoned." He ran a hand over the cat's back. "This one looks in good shape. Cats are pretty resourceful creatures. If she's been able to be inside the house *and* out, she's probably been doing a fine job finding herself something to eat."

"You're a good kitty, aren't you?" Nora said, nuzzling the cat's chin. "I'm going to take her back to the bunkhouse. I'm making coffee if anyone wants a cup."

Jillian raised her hand. "I'm in."

Cade's phone buzzed and panic rose in his throat as he saw Allie's name on the screen. "It's the kids," he said, tapping the screen and pressing the phone to his ear. "Allie? You all right?"

"Yes, I'm fine," she said, her voice a little breathless. "But we ran into a little trouble."

"What kind of trouble?" he asked, already heading toward his truck, Brody and Jillian on his heels. "Where are you? Is anyone hurt?"

"No. We're fine. Geez, Cade. Get a grip. We're just stuck in the mud."

He could hear the irritation in her voice, and he tried to relax his tone. "Okay. Where are you? Brody and I will come get you."

"Mandy said to tell her dad we're by pancake rock."

"Got it. We'll be there in five minutes." He clicked off and turned to the others. "It's okay. No one's hurt. They're just stuck in the mud."

Jillian blew out a breath and waved a hand at them. "In that case, I'm going to let you two deal with it while I have a cup of coffee with Nora."

He and Brody climbed into his truck. "Mandy said to tell you they're by pancake rock. You know where that is?"

"Sure, it's a big flat rock toward the top of that outcropping of boulders in the west pasture."

Cade put the truck in gear and headed toward the pasture. "I know the spot." Within a few minutes, they could see the rocks and the Gator. Cade's dread turned to amusement as they pulled up in front of the utility. "Oh shit," Cade said, busting out in laughter as he and Brody got out of the truck. "What the hell happened to you guys?"

The back wheels of the Gator were buried in a large soupy puddle. The three kids had exited the vehicle and stood a few feet away, all three covered in mud. The puppy was gleefully sprawling in the muddy water, but jumped up and ran to the men as they came toward them. She circled Cade's boots, nipping at his heels, then stopped to shake the water from her fur.

All three kids hung their heads. Even Allie had the good sense to look ashamed. "We're so sorry," she said. "It was an accident."

"We got out thinking if the load was lighter, it would be able to move," Milo explained. "And then I tried to push it from behind."

"But when I gave it some gas, the tires just spun." Mandy gestured to the other two. "I didn't know it was going to spray mud all over them. Or that Allie was going to fall into the puddle trying to help him."

"That explains why they're covered in mud," Brody said. "But why are you?"

Mandy shrugged. "I couldn't get us unstuck, so then Milo tried to drive while I pushed."

"Yeah, but didn't you know you would get covered in mud?" her father asked.

Mandy shrugged. "Yeah, but we were in it together. We all got stuck together, so we all had to try to get unstuck together. That's what friends do."

Cade's heart lifted a little as he saw the expression on his daughter's face go from a worried frown to a happy smile. Who cared about a little mud if getting the vehicle stuck and getting covered in mud brought that kind of smile to his daughter's face and had her standing taller as she hopped a step closer to the younger girl?

He knew he had an opportunity here, a chance to show his daughter what kind of dad he was—or wanted to be. He could get mad at them for taking the risk of driving through the puddle and offer an *I told you so*, or he could choose another route. He glanced at Brody, who he knew was a good man and a good dad, and the two fathers broke into grins.

"Let's see if we can get this thing unstuck without ending up covered in mud ourselves," Cade said.

"I'm driving," Brody said, climbing into the front seat. "You're pushing, so be prepared to get muddy."

Cade shrugged and winked at his daughter. "A little mud never hurt anybody." He moved to the front of the Gator. "You want to put it in reverse and let me try pushing you out this way?"

Brody started the engine and put the vehicle in reverse. The wheels spun, shooting dirt and muddy water forward this time and soaking Cade.

He wiped a gob of mud from his face with the back of his hand and looked down at his mud-splattered front. "Perfect." He looked over at the kids who were trying their best not to laugh. "You all think this is funny, do you? Why don't you get over here and help me push?"

Milo put a hand out in front of the girls. "I got this." He splashed through the mud to stand by Cade's side. "Ready," he said, planting his hands on the hood of the vehicle.

"Rock it forward a little, then try it in reverse one more time," Cade told Brody. "I think we got a little traction."

Brody revved the engine and tried to go forward, then in reverse. Ignoring the spray of mud, Cade and Milo leaned their shoulders into the hood and pushed. "You're getting it," Brody called, giving the engine a little more gas. The tires spun a few more rotations, then caught, and the utility vehicle shot backward, and Cade and Milo fell forward into the puddle.

Cade pushed up to his knees and lifted his mud-covered hand to Milo. "Nice work, kid."

Milo laughed and slapped an equally muddy high five against Cade's palm. "You too."

Mandy and Allie clapped and cheered, and the puppy raced back into the puddle and around Cade and Milo as they slipped and slid their way to dry ground.

"Good job," Cade told Brody, clapping a muddy hand onto his shoulder.

"Thanks," Brody said with a wry grin.

"Hey, I wouldn't want you to miss out on all the fun."

"On that note, I think I'm going to take my daughter home and spray her off with a hose. *After* we clean off the Gator."

"Yes, Dad." Mandy scraped her boots on the side of the Gator before climbing into the passenger seat. She grinned and waved at Milo and Allie as her dad put the vehicle in gear. "See you guys later. It was fun."

"Yeah, real fun," Cade said, nodding to Milo and Allie. "You two better get in the truck. I'm sure Jillian and Nora are wondering what's taking us so long."

Milo grabbed the knee scooter and put it in the back end. "Should I ride back here?" he asked Cade. "I'm pretty muddy."

Cade looked at all three of them. "We're *all* pretty muddy. But don't worry about it," he said, holding the door open and helping Allie climb in. "It's a truck. It's not the first or the last time it'll see mud."

"Oh no. What happened to you guys?" Jillian asked when they pulled up in front of the bunkhouse a few minutes later. She and Nora were sitting on the porch, the cat curled in Nora's lap. Jillian set her cup down and stepped off the porch, covering her mouth with her hand as she cracked up.

Milo grinned at his mom as he climbed from the truck, then waited to help Allie. "We got the Gator stuck in this huge mud puddle. But I helped Cade push it free."

"Did you all leave any mud in the puddle?" She motioned him toward the car. "We've got to go home and eat some lunch. Make sure you grab some towels from the trunk before you climb into the seat." She turned back to wave at Nora. "Thanks for the coffee and the chat. I'll see you tomorrow."

Cade lifted the knee scooter out of the back end and carried it to Allie. His jeans were already caking with dried mud. "I think Brody might have the right idea. Why don't we try to clean some of this off with the hose before we go inside?"

Allie peered down at her mud-splattered legs and the clumps of dirt clinging to her boots. "Good idea."

"There's a spigot and hose on the side of the house," he told her.

"I'll grab you guys some towels, then I'll put together some sandwiches for lunch," Nora said. She'd left the cat in the chair and was standing on the edge of the porch. She dug her phone from her pocket. "But first, I have to take a picture. You guys have got to see yourselves. You look hilarious."

Cade looked down at Allie, who shrugged and wrapped her arm around his waist as she offered Nora a cheesy grin. Having his daughter lean against his chest, even if it was only for a picture and they were both covered in mud, still had a smile spreading across his face.

Nora clicked a picture then made a face at them. "Okay, now one silly one."

Cade furrowed his brow. "Are you trying to say we don't look silly enough?"

Allie grabbed one side of her muddy hair and pulled it straight up as she pushed out her lips. "Make a duck face," she told Cade.

"A duck face? How the heck am I supposed to make my face look like a duck's?"

Allie giggled as she looked up at him, pursing her lips together. "Like this," she told him.

"I'm not doing that," Cade told her.

"Come on." Allie was laughing harder as she reached up to squeeze Cade's cheeks together. "Pout your lips and suck in your cheeks."

He couldn't believe he was doing this. It was only because it was making his girl laugh. He pushed out his mouth the way Allie was doing, which sent the girl into another fit of giggles. "You'd better be taking the picture, Nora."

"Don't worry, I am," Nora wheezed. She was cracking up so hard she almost dropped her phone. "Oh my gosh, I can't breathe. I'm going to wet my pants." She doubled over on the porch.

"All right, that's enough pictures," Cade said, nodding toward the hose. "I've got so much mud on my cheeks, I'm afraid it's going to dry and I'll be stuck with this stupid mallard face for the rest of my life."

Allie laughed as she followed him to the spigot. "It's duck face."

He unwound a few coils of hose and turned on the water. A sprayer nozzle was attached to the end of it, and he flipped the setting to soaker, then directed the spray at his legs. He washed the mud from his jeans and boots, then motioned for Allie to hold out her booted foot. "I don't think you're supposed to get mud on this thing. I hope it dries out tonight while you sleep."

"Here, let me get it," she said, taking the hose from him and spraying off her legs and the knee scooter. The hose kinked as she turned around. She yanked on it to get it closer, and the nozzle flipped in her hand and shot a spray of water directly at Cade's head.

"Oh my gosh," Allie said, her eyes going wide as she tried not to laugh. "I'm so sorry." She couldn't contain it, and she burst into giggles again.

He wiped the water from his forehead and sputtered the droplets from his lips. "Oh, that's how you want to play it," he said, making a grab for the sprayer.

She shrieked in laughter and held the hose out in front of her. "No, I didn't mean it." The puppy raced around their legs, yipping and trying to bite the water.

"And I didn't mean this," he said, grabbing the nozzle and turning it toward Allie.

"It's so cold." She squealed again but held on to the sprayer, trying to get another shot at him. Pressing the handle, her shot went wide as Cade ducked and hit Nora as she came around the corner of the house holding a stack of towels.

"Gah," Nora screeched, dropping the towels.

Allie froze, her eyes wide as she stared at Nora, who now had water dripping from her bangs.

Nora's eyes narrowed, and she calmly pushed her sopping hair away from her face as she walked toward them and held out her hand. "That's enough, children. Give me the hose."

Allie lowered her eyes as she handed it over. "Sorry, Nora. I was trying to spray Cade."

Nora took the hose and her stern expression transformed to a sly grin as she turned the hose on him and pulled the handle. "You mean like this?"

Cade yelped as the stream of water hit him, then laughed as he ran around behind Allie. He grabbed her around the waist, using her as a shield as Nora cackled and tried to spray him around the girl's head.

They were all cracking up, and Allie shrieked with laughter as she tried to get behind Cade instead. "Help! Save me, Dad!"

Even through the squeals of laughter and with a shot of water hitting him in the chest, Cade heard the word and a crazy happiness spread through him. Allie had called him *Dad*, and the echo of it made his throat tight with emotion.

That happiness came to a screeching halt at the sound of an enraged voice yelling from behind him. "Cade Callahan—what the hell do you think you're doing?"

CHAPTER 16

HE KNEW THAT VOICE. EVEN THOUGH HE HADN'T HEARD IT IN over a decade, he still recognized the disdainful tone of his ex-sister-in-law.

"Aunt Di," Allie said, hopping around Cade.

Nora dropped the hose and scurried toward the spigot to turn the water off. Cade turned to face his ex-wife's sister. "Diana," he said.

She hadn't changed much. She still wore glasses and her dark hair was pulled back in a long braid. Her figure was still slim and her face still wore the condescending sneer that he remembered. With her bony cheeks and long nose, she'd always reminded him a bit of a vulture, like she was just waiting to peck at the pieces of his carcass.

She had on jeans, hiking boots, and a vest over a black T-shirt. A gray scarf wrapped around her neck, even though it was over eighty degrees outside. She'd been ten years older than Amber, so she was in her midforties now, but she acted more like a snooty seventy-year-old with her holier-than-thou attitude.

Scout raced toward her, running around her feet. "What is that thing?" Diana wrinkled her nose and turned to the side, defending her body from the small puppy. As if it had heard her insult, the dog stopped and shook out her fur, spraying drops of water through the air and toward her legs.

Allie stopped and scooped up the dog as she hopped toward her aunt. "This is my dog, Scout. Isn't she adorable?"

Diana took a step back, peering down at the dog in her niece's arms. "She looks like a drowned rat. And so do you." She grabbed one of the towels from the ground and wrapped it around Allie's shoulders, then turned her fierce glare on Cade. "What do you think you're playing at? This child has been in a serious car accident. Do you realize you could have caused more damage to her already considerable injuries?" She lifted a hand to tenderly trace the bruises still present on Allie's face. "You poor sweet girl. I'm so sorry."

"We were just playing around," he said, but her words struck a chord in him that he had screwed up. What *was* he thinking? He wasn't. Which was why he had no business thinking he could do this dad thing.

"Who is this?" Diana asked, wrinkling her nose at Nora. "One of your floozies?"

"Aunt Di, stop it," Allie said. "That's Nora Fisher. She's my physical therapist. She's helped me a ton."

"I'm not sure what kind of physical therapist would engage in this sort of dangerous behavior." She sniffed her nose at Nora.

"We were just having fun," Allie tried to explain, but her aunt wasn't listening.

"Why don't you give us a few minutes to get dried off and changed?" Cade said. "Then we can talk."

"That's probably a good idea," Diana said, wrapping her arm gingerly around Allie's waist. "Can I help you, honey? Where are your crutches?"

"I don't use crutches," she explained, turning to reach for the knee scooter.

Cade grabbed it and held it steady for her while she got her knee settled on the damp cushion. "*Nora* brought this for her," he told Diana. "It's much easier on her than crutches."

"I see," Diana said as she followed Allie to the porch and tried to assist her up the steps.

"I've got it," Allie said. "I'm going to take a shower. I'll be back in ten minutes."

"Do you need help?"

"No, I can do it."

Nora had grabbed the towels and come up behind them. "Can I offer you some tea or lemonade, Diana? Or I can make you a sandwich if you'd like to join us for lunch."

"Lunch?" Diana jerked back, staring at Nora as if she'd offered her a turd on a plate. "It's well past one o'clock and you haven't fed this child lunch yet? Do you not keep any kind of a schedule around here?" She peered down her nose at Cade, spreading the disdain around. "Or maybe you were making mud pies for lunch."

This woman was really starting to piss Cade off. They normally ate at noon. But everything had gotten off schedule today, what with rescuing the horses and the Gator getting stuck in the mud. He opened his mouth to give her a piece of his mind, but Allie spoke up before he could.

"Don't worry, Aunt Di. Nora was just asking if you wanted to join *her and Cade* for some lunch. I already ate. Cade made me a healthy meal of a sandwich, a salad, some steamed broccoli, a glass of milk, and he even sliced me up an apple. And he made sure it was on the table by noon."

She was avoiding his eye as she flat-out lied to her aunt. He appreciated the effort—was frankly surprised to hear her defending him—but she might be laying it on a little thick. He'd never made steamed broccoli in his life.

Diana stared from Allie to him. "That does sound healthy. I've already eaten, of course, but I think I'd like to try some of that steamed broccoli."

Crap. What was he going to do now?

But Allie saved him again. "Oh shoot. I wish you could, but it was so yummy that we ate it all." She turned and rolled through the door. "I'm getting in the shower. Back in ten."

That sounded like his cue to make his escape as well. "I'm going to get cleaned up too." He heard Nora offering Diana something to drink as he fled into the bunkhouse, stripping off his wet shirt as he headed for his bedroom. Thank goodness for Nora. He owed her a kiss for taking on his ex-wife's sister with such class. Heck, he probably owed her more than a kiss. And that would be a debt he'd be happy to pay.

But later—after they got Diana off the ranch and on her way back to Denver.

———————

Fifteen minutes later, Cade stepped back on to the porch. Allie had been in the bathroom, so he'd used the kitchen sink to wash the mud from his arms and out of his hair. He'd changed into fresh jeans and a clean T-shirt and given his neck a quick squirt of cologne, hoping it might mask the scent of horses Diana would be sure to raise her nose at. He'd heard Allie's door open as he pulled on his boots and followed her out to the porch.

Thankfully, they had purchased an extra shoulder sling, so Allie had a dry one to switch to, but he could see the boot around her leg was still damp. Why did Diana have to show up at the worst possible time?

Although it had been one of the best times for him and Allie, he thought as he remembered the way she had called him *Dad*.

Nora had changed into dry clothes and must have given her hair a quick shot with the dryer. She had brought out a tray with glasses and an icy pitcher of lemonade and stacked a few triangles of mini turkey sandwiches on a plate. Sitting in the chair across from Diana, she looked pretty and much more put together in her jeans, sandals, and flowy blue top. Although she had looked pretty great to him when she'd been soaking wet and laughing her butt off as she pushed her dripping hair from her face.

Allie eased into a chair next to Cade and Scout jumped into her lap. They'd gotten into a routine of him braiding her hair when it was wet, and she absently handed him her brush and an elastic.

He noted the way Diana's face pinched with a skeptical air as she watched him pull the brush through Allie's hair and plait it into a braid.

He'd been working on a fancier french braid style that started on one side and formed a crown around the top of her head, then fell into a loose side braid. He'd watched a tutorial on it, and he wouldn't admit it to anyone else, but he'd been practicing on Gypsy's mane. The horse didn't seem to mind, and she knew how to keep a secret.

He finished Allie's hair and grabbed a couple of sandwiches before sinking down into the empty rocking chair next to her. He was starving and ate the first one in two bites. Thank goodness for Nora. She fit so seamlessly into their lives and always seemed to know what they needed. He wasn't sure how they were going to get along without her after Allie's therapy was finished—how *he* was going to get along without her.

There'd be plenty of time to worry about that later. Best to keep his focus on Allie and his ex-sister-in-law for now. "When did you get in, Diana? Allie said you've been working on a story in the Philippines."

"I have. That's why it took me so long to get home after I heard about Amber's accident. It wasn't easy to book a flight out on such short notice, plus the flight itself is twenty hours in the air. I've spent the last three days traveling and hanging out in airports because I couldn't get a direct flight. But I'm here now and ready to take Allie home with me as soon as you can get her packed up. I can't imagine she brought much with her."

Cade had just taken another bite of sandwich and the bread dried up in his mouth. He forced a swallow. "Home with *you*? What are you talking about?"

Diana lifted her chin to better look down her nose at him as she sniffed. "Come on, Cade. You didn't seriously think Dad and I were going to let her live with *you*. And frankly, I thought you'd be thrilled

I'm here to take her off your hands. You haven't paid any attention to her the last nine years, why would you want to start now?"

Her words hit him like a punch to the gut. "Because I'm her dad. And she's staying with me."

Diana narrowed her eyes. "Is this about the money? Because you should know, we're *not* letting you keep it."

"What money?"

She tsked. "Don't play dumb with me. You might have been able to pull that crap with my sister, but not with me."

What money? Amber and Allie had been living in a small apartment in one of the lower rent suburbs of Denver. Allie had mentioned something about her mom getting a new job earlier that year with great benefits, but nothing about their lifestyle he'd seen indicated that she was making a lot of money.

Before he had a chance to ask more about it, Allie broke into the conversation. "I can't leave now," she said. "What about the dance this weekend? And Clementine? We haven't even found her a home yet."

Diana lowered her voice to a placating tone. "I'm sure your father can find that puppy a home without you, honey."

Allie reared back and cuddled Scout closer to her chest. "I was talking about the cat we just rescued. *This* is Scout. And she already has a home. With me. She's *my* dog."

"Well, I don't think your apartment building lets you have pets. And I thought it best I move in there with you until we figure out a place for the two of us."

"Three of us, you mean. I'm not leaving Scout behind."

"Maybe you can just leave her with your…with Cade for now. Until we figure out a better solution."

"No, the solution is that I'm staying here with Scout and Daisy and Clementine. *And* Nora and Cade."

Nice that she included him. He *was* mentioned after the horse, but at least he made her list.

"You're *not* staying here. You're coming back to your apartment—your *home*—with me. The funeral for your mother is on Monday, and I know you'll want to be there for that."

This was the first he'd heard about plans for the funeral.

Allie turned to Cade with a pleading look in her eyes, and it about ripped his heart out of his chest. She *wanted* to stay here, with him. The idea of it had emotion clogging his throat. He didn't care if it had more to do with the puppy and the horse—hell, he'd be happy if she said she wanted to stay for the damn goat, as long as she wanted to stay.

"Sorry, Diana, sounds like she's staying here. I'll bring her down for the funeral on Monday, of course."

"No, you won't," Diana said. "No one wants you at the funeral. And you have no say in where Allison will be staying."

"The hell I don't." This lady was really starting to piss him off. "I'm her father."

"No, you're not. You gave up that right years ago when you walked out on her and Amber. You haven't been a father to that girl in years."

Damn. Another punch to the gut.

"I'm being a father now," he answered through gritted teeth.

She dismissed him with another cool glare. "Too little, too late."

Nora had been quietly listening, but she set her glass down now and leaned forward. "Diana, if I may, I appreciate that you would want Allie to be with you. And I understand that this is a trying time for everyone. But as a medical professional, and as Allie's physical therapist, it's my professional opinion that she needs to stay here and continue her course of treatment until her health improves."

"I can just as easily take her to a physical therapist in Denver," Diana retorted, seeming almost miffed that Nora would have the gall to insert herself into the conversation.

"Yes, but she and I have already started an exercise regimen.

And I've been with her since the day after the accident. So besides her doctor, I'm the most qualified to judge her daily recovery. I've already seen marked improvement in her range of motion, and I worry that changing her routine and her therapist would be like starting her recovery over. As much as you'd like to have Allie with you, I'm sure you wouldn't want to impede her recovery. Would you?"

Diana sniffed. "Of course not."

"Then it seems like you would have to agree that the best course of action would be for Allie to stay where she is, at least until her health improves. Wouldn't you?"

For the first time, Diana's confidence seemed to falter. "I'm not sure."

Dang. Nora was good. She'd backed Diana into a corner that she couldn't get out of unless she admitted her desire to take Allie back to Denver was more important than the teenager's health.

Nora stood, and Cade and Diana automatically stood with her. She took a step toward the porch steps as if already leading Diana down them. "You can see for yourself that Allie is doing fine. She's eating healthy meals, and she's getting spoiled with attention by Cade's cousin, Bryn. She's even made some friends here. The ranch has got a big event this weekend that she obviously wants to stay for, and it sounds like there are a lot of logistics that still need to be worked out. And I'm sure you're going to be swamped with just getting back to the States and all the arrangements for Monday. Why don't you let Allie stay for the weekend, and we can talk more about her living situation after the funeral? How does that sound for a compromise?"

"I guess that would be all right." She peered at Allie. "Is that really what you want?"

Allie nodded and pushed to her feet. "Yes. I want to stay." She hopped forward to hug her aunt. "But I'm so glad to see you. And I will be there on Monday. Maybe you could call me and tell me the details and if there is anything I can help with or do for Mom."

"Yes, all right." Diana squeezed her niece to her and pressed a kiss to her head. "I can call you, honey." She leaned back to look down at the girl, her nose wrinkled as if she smelled something bad. "You're *really* sure? You want to stay *here*?"

Allie smiled. "Yes. I'm really sure."

Diana hung her head in defeat. "Okay. I guess it's settled then."

Allie plopped the puppy into the scooter's basket. "But I want to introduce you to Daisy and some of the other animals before you go." She led her aunt toward the barn.

Nora sank back onto the glider. "Whew. That was a close one."

"You were amazing. Thank you." Cade moved to sit next to her. He lowered his voice. Not that Diana could hear him all the way from the barn, but he didn't want to take any chances. "That was quick thinking to appeal to her about Allie's health."

"What I said is true. I *have* been with her since the accident, and I *am* the best one to help with her recovery."

"You don't have to convince me."

Nora rubbed her chin. "I'm sorry. I know she's Allie's aunt and all, but that woman sorely pissed me off."

Cade chuckled, wanting to pull Nora into his arms. "You and me both. But you were awesome. You didn't back down and really championed for Allie." Nora's hand was sitting on the cushion next to him, and he entwined his pinkie with hers. "You always seem to know what we need."

Her lips curved into a smile that bordered on bashful. "You mean like sandwiches?"

He laughed. "Don't get me wrong, the sandwiches were great. But that's not what I mean." Turning his hand over, he linked their fingers. "I feel like I can relax and be myself around you, and you just seem to get me."

She squeezed his hand. "I know what you mean. You seem to just get me too."

His shoulders relaxed as he leaned against the cushion. "I just feel good when I'm around you. Happy." He offered her a wry grin. "Well, except when I start to think about how pretty you are or about how much I want to kiss you, then I get nervous as hell."

She tilted her head and gave him a coy grin. "So you get nervous when you want to kiss me, huh?"

He shrugged.

"Are you nervous right now?"

"As a guy going ninety in a thirty who just passed a cop."

A laugh burst from her. "That's pretty nervous."

He squeezed her hand. "*That's* how bad I want to kiss you."

"I'm feeling pretty dang nervous right now too," she said, leaning toward him.

His heart jumped to his throat as he bent his head, already anticipating the soft press of her sweet lips.

Just as they were about to touch, the sound of the barn door clanked. Nora jumped back and dropped his hand as if it had suddenly caught fire. She nodded toward the driveway where Allie and her aunt had come out of the barn and were heading toward Diana's car. "Will you take a rain check on that kiss?"

"Yep. But I hope you have a good umbrella because I think there's a *lot* of rain expected in the near forecast." He winked before getting up and walking to the edge of the porch. He waved as Diana got in her car and drove away.

Allie let Scout out of the basket, and the dog raced toward the porch as the girl rolled after it. She hopped up on the porch as Cade collapsed back onto the far side of the glider, leaving space for the girl to sit between them. He patted the seat. "You okay, kid?"

She sank onto the cushion. "Yeah. She wasn't super impressed with the horses, and I think Tiny freaked her out when she tried to sniff her hand."

Cade chuckled. "I'll bet. For as much world traveling as she does, she still doesn't strike me as much of a country girl."

"I didn't think I was much of a country girl either," Allie said. "But I'm starting to think I might have been wrong because I don't want to be anywhere else right now." She leaned her head on Nora's shoulder. "Thank you for sticking up for me." Her voice lowered, and she snuck a glance at Cade. "And thanks for *wanting* me to stay."

Cade put his arm around her, being careful not to jostle her injured shoulder. "I *do* want you to stay. And not just for the weekend."

"Is it wrong of me to want to stay up here and not want to go with her?" She stared down at her hands. "I mean, she's my aunt, and I love her. And I know she loves me and wants what's best for me."

"Of course she does," Nora said.

She picked at a loose cuticle, and her voice came out as almost a whisper. "Is it bad that I don't want to help plan the funeral?"

Cade squeezed her shoulder. "No. *Nothing* you are thinking or feeling right now is *bad*. It's just the way you feel. This is a tough time, and everyone grieves and processes stuff differently." He glanced up to see Nora nodding encouragingly at him. *Thank goodness.* He had no idea if he was saying the right stuff or not. He was flying blind, but at least he was up in the air and trying to fly. "I would give anything to take this pain away from you. It sucks, and I'm sorry you have to go through this."

She slumped back against the cushion, pinning his arm behind her shoulder. "It does suck. But it also feels like I'm in one of my books where I'm living in two alternate universes. It's like one world is up here, where I get to feel happy and have friends and all these animals and family around. Well, and you guys." Her face crumpled as her mouth turned down in a frown. "And then there's another world down there—the real world—but it's just an empty apartment full of reminders that my mom is gone and my only friends are my books and my somewhat kooky aunt."

"Huh. Kooky is one word for it," Cade muttered.

"Sorry she was acting so weird. She's usually nice."

"Nice like a mother grizzly protecting her young," Cade said. "Speaking of which, thanks for trying to protect Nora and me with that lunch thing."

"Oh, geez, seriously? What was *that* about? Mom and I have *never* eaten on a schedule. That was weird too. I hated the way she was attacking you guys. Especially since we almost always eat at noon on the dot." She poked Cade's leg. "Because if we don't, you get *hangry*."

As if in response, his stomach let out a loud growl. "On that note, let's go eat lunch. I'll try to find something superhealthy for you." He nudged her with his elbow. "Nice touch with the steamed broccoli."

She let out a laugh. "I was improvising, and it was the healthiest thing I could think of. I don't even like broccoli."

CHAPTER 17

It was almost nine that night when Nora heard a soft knock at her door. She'd taken a shower and blown dry her hair, but all she had on was her short silk robe as she peeked out of the bathroom door. Who could be here so late?

Her heart raced. It had to be either Cade stopping by to cash in on that rain check, or the pig and the goat hoping to come in to watch an episode of *The Bachelor*. She hoped it was Cade, since the last time she'd let Otis and Tiny in, they'd hogged all the popcorn.

Her mouth went dry as she opened the door to the tall hunk of hot cowboy standing on the porch. He must have just taken a shower too because he smelled like soap and shampoo and the ends of his hair curled damply at his neck. "Hey," she said, practically sighing out the word.

"Hey." He held his hand up, palm facing the sky. "I know it's kind of late, but I thought I felt a little rain comin' on."

She couldn't hold back her grin as she took a step back. "You better come in then. I wouldn't want you to get caught in a storm."

He sauntered into the room, kicking the door shut behind him before he reached for her and pulled her to his chest. He dipped his head and pressed a warm kiss to that spot right below her ear, the spot that had her knees threatening to buckle. His voice was low as he spoke against her neck. "I'm not afraid of a little rain."

She'd read historical romances where the heroines had been said to swoon, and she'd never really gotten the definition of the word. Until now. Until she felt like melting into the arms of this man. And all he'd done was kiss her neck. Lord help her if he chose to kiss another part of her.

Dear Lord, please let him choose to kiss another part.

He laid another soft kiss on her neck, then another on the line of her jaw, before finally taking her mouth. His hands held her face as if she were a delicate flower as he tasted and sampled her lips. Those kisses, the ones that started out sweet, quickly changed to a hard onslaught of desire as his hands made their way down to her waist and pulled her tightly against him.

She wrapped her arms around his neck and kissed him back, her body keenly aware of the fact that all she had on was a tiny robe that barely covered her lady bits. Her nipples tightened against the slick fabric, the only barrier between them and Cade's T-shirt.

So much had happened over the last few days, and this was the first time he'd really kissed her again after their time at the cabin. But all her indecision, her doubts about if she truly cared about him, fell away as she lost herself in his touch.

His hands felt so good as they moved over her, clutching and caressing as they traveled along her curves. His tongue sought and explored her mouth, then his lips were back on her neck, his breath hot even as it sent shivers of pleasure across her skin.

She clung to him, afraid her knees would buckle and she would sink to the floor if she let go. With how liquid her body felt, she might just slip through the cracks of the floorboards. This man turned her inside out, stealing her thoughts and her inhibitions as she was considering dropping her robe and letting him take her against the kitchen counter.

She squeezed his shoulder, trying to regain some control. "I can't catch my breath."

He kissed her again, softer this time, capturing her words on his lips. "Breathing's overrated."

She laughed, a small puff of air, but it was enough to break the spell. He pulled back, still holding her in his arms but releasing his claim on her mouth. He peered down at her as his thumb grazed over her swollen bottom lip. "You have some kind of hold on me. I can't seem to think straight when I'm around you. Especially when all I can think about is how your skin feels under that itty-bitty robe you're barely wearing."

She swallowed. "I was thinking about that too. I mean how you'd feel against my skin. But I need a minute. Otherwise I might drag you down onto the floor and have my way with you, and that floor hasn't been swept in days."

He laughed this time, but it came out as more of a roguish chuckle. "I'm not afraid of getting a little dirty."

"I wasn't thinking about getting just a *little* dirty."

"Damn," he whispered and she heard the click in his throat as he swallowed. "You do surprise me, Nora Fisher. In all the best possible ways."

She was kind of surprising herself. Since when had she been able to toss out naughty comments like that? Since Cade, apparently. Since being with a man who made her feel sexy and brazen and smart and confident.

Cade dropped his hands to around her waist, still keeping her in his arms as he leaned back against the counter of the kitchen island. His eyes went dark as he studied her. "I can't quite figure you out. Sometimes you act like you're unsure of yourself and your decisions, then other times you charge forward swinging a sword with the confidence of a gladiator."

"Huh. I have never been compared to a gladiator before," she said, tilting her head as if considering the idea. "I think I like it."

"I'm serious. The way you took on Diana, even when she was being such a snot to you was really something. I wanted to thank you again for what you did today. For Allie. And for me."

She let out a sigh. "Don't thank me. I did it for Allie, but I also did it for my own selfish reasons."

"I doubt that. I haven't seen you do a single selfish thing since I've met you."

"It's true." She dropped her gaze to his chest. "I want Allie to stay, for her and for you, but also because if Allie leaves, then my job is over."

"Hey, don't worry about that. We arranged this for a set period, and we'd pay you for the whole time, no matter what happened."

Her eyes went round, and she swatted at his chest. "I don't care about the money. I mean, I do care about money, but that's not what I'm talking about. If Allie left the ranch, then I would have to leave too. And I'm not ready to walk away from this place."

"*Just* this place?" He pulled her closer as his voice lowered. "Is that all you don't want to leave?"

She stared at the pocket of his T-shirt, not quite able to meet his eye. It somehow felt easier to make bold, flirty comments than to admit her feelings for him. "No," she whispered. He lifted her chin, forcing her to look into his eyes. She took a deep breath, then blurted, "That's *not* all. I'm not ready to leave you, dammit."

His lips curved in a wicked grin. "I love it when you swear at me."

A soft laugh escaped her as she rested a hand on his cheek. "I love it when you kiss me as if your life depends on it."

His expression sobered. He lifted a lock of her hair and twisted a curl around his finger. "I feel a little bit that way. My life has changed so much since you and Allie have come into it. I find myself dreaming and hoping for things I haven't let myself hope for in a long time."

"Why not?"

He huffed. "Because I know that a woman like you deserves a man so much better than me. Even though you make me *want* to be better. And I swear I've felt different since you and Allie have been here. I've felt happier than I have in a long time. And I've made an effort in so many ways when before I would have just given up or not bothered. But in my heart, where it counts, I know it's not enough. I know what kind of man I am. And I have no business letting myself get involved with you."

She stroked her finger down his cheek. "I know what kind of man you are too. And there's a million reasons why *I* shouldn't let myself get involved with you. And another million why this thing between us will never work."

"That's a lot of millions. How many reasons are there for you to stay?"

"Only one." Captured by the intensity of his blue eyes, she let the words tumble from her lips. "Because I'm falling in love with you."

He didn't say anything but his eyes widened, and she felt his grip tighten at her waist.

She let out a soft gasp and covered her mouth with her hand. "I can't believe I said that." She turned her head away, heat warming her cheeks. "This is what I always do. I feel too much. I jump in without ever checking to see if there's enough water to catch me."

He bent down, bringing his arm behind her knees and swept her up into his arms. Cradling her to his chest, he peered down at her, his eyes intense as his voice lowered to almost a growl. "Don't worry. I'll catch you."

She buried her face in his chest, inhaling the scent of him, as she fought back tears. His statement was delivered with such passion, his words so sincere, they seared through her chest and went straight to her heart. She couldn't speak. But it didn't matter. The time for words was over. The way to show him how she felt now was through her actions, her touch.

He carried her into the bedroom and yanked back the covers before setting her gently on the bed. The sheets were cool against her heated skin, but his body was warm as he lay down next to her. The front folds of her robe gaped open, barely covering her breasts.

Cade's gaze drifted over her body, pausing to appreciate the glimpses of bare skin. He brushed the back of his fingers down her neck, then across the exposed area of her chest. Skimming over the silky fabric, he stopped at the tied sash and gazed back up into her eyes. "I don't have a very good track record when it comes to relationships. I'm not very good at sticking around. But for the first time, I've found something I *want* to stay for. Something I want to fight for. Being with you and Allie makes me feel good, like I finally have a chance to be the man I've always wanted to be."

His words touched something in her. She'd felt a connection with him from the first day she'd met him. But she'd thought she'd felt connections before. Although none had ever been as strong as the pull she had with Cade. And that intense pull is what terrified her.

"I'm scared," she whispered.

"I am too. I'm in all new territory. And I have no idea what's going to happen tomorrow or next week, but we're here together right now. And I want you—all of you, and with everything in me. I also know this is all a little intense, so if you're not ready for all of this, you can tell me. I can stop."

He started to pull his hand away, but she grabbed it and pressed it back to the bow of her belt. "Don't you dare stop."

He smiled at her, the curve of his grin making promises she couldn't wait for him to keep.

His fingers wrapped around the end of the material, and he slowly pulled at one side of the belt. She felt vulnerable, exposed, and yet a deep desire raced through her, and she wanted his hands on her. All of her.

The only sound in the room was the whisper of silk as the bow loosened and the silk fell away.

In the same moment, a shiver ran through her, and both she and her robe came undone.

———

Nora's limbs felt liquid as she pulled on pajama pants and a soft T-shirt an hour later. Cade had just left, and she'd been tempted to crawl naked back under the sheets just to feel the cool cotton against her skin but knew her brain would never let her fall right to sleep.

She pushed her feet into a pair of slippers and padded into the kitchen in search of an icy glass of the lemonade she'd made earlier. Before she made it to the refrigerator, she heard a frantic knocking at her front door and Cade's voice calling her.

She hurried to let him in. "What's wrong?"

He swept into the room, his eyes wild. "Allie's gone."

"Gone? What do you mean?"

He dragged his hand through his hair, leaving tufts of it sticking up. "I mean she's gone. She's not in her bedroom. Or the bathroom. It's not that big of a freakin' place. She's not there."

"It's okay. We'll find her. Was she upset when you left?"

"No. She was totally fine. I made her some hot chocolate, and when I left she was buried in a pile of pillows on her bed with the dog, the cat, and that stack of books Jillian brought her. Now she's gone, and so is the dog. Her bed is empty."

"Did you call her cell phone?"

"Good idea." He pulled his phone from his jeans pocket and tapped the screen, then held the phone to his ear. He shook his head. "Straight to voicemail." He shoved the phone back into his pocket. "Do you think she changed her mind about staying? Or do you think Diana came back for her? She wouldn't leave without saying goodbye. Would she? What if she ran away?"

Nora took his hands and held them firmly in his. "Cade. She did *not* run away. And I can't imagine she called Diana to come get her."

"But what if Diana came back on her own and convinced her to leave the ranch with her?"

"Allie wouldn't leave like that without telling you. Take a breath, and let's not get ahead of ourselves." She grabbed a sweatshirt from one of the hooks by the door. "Have you checked Bryn's house or the barn? Maybe she just took a walk or went to check on the new horses."

"No, but that's good thinking." He hung his head. "I just panicked when I saw she was gone. I'm responsible for her now. And the last time I wasn't paying attention, she got hurt."

"This is not like last time. And she's a teenager now. You're not expected to watch her every minute." She opened the front door and led him outside. Peering around, she spotted the barn door open and a light inside. "Look, there's a light on in the barn."

Cade sprinted toward the barn. She ran after him and almost smashed into his back as he came to an abrupt halt at the door. His shoulders relaxed, and he took her hand and squeezed it as he nodded to the scene inside.

Allie had brought her pillow and one of her blankets outside and fashioned a cozy nest of hay bales and gunny sacks outside the gate of Daisy's stall. Her voice filled the space of the barn as she read aloud from a book in her lap, her hand absently stroking the various animals surrounding her.

She looked like a teenaged Mother Goose with the puppy in her lap, the cat curled along one side of her legs, and the pig curled around the other. Shamus had somehow gotten out again and was standing behind her as if looking over her shoulder and reading along. Otis was sprawled out near her feet but appeared to be more interested in sneaking bites of hay than listening to the story.

Daisy was standing in her stall, her head leaning forward and her ears bent back as if she were listening intently. Beauty, Prince, and Mack stood at the gate of the corral, and the two new horses both hung their heads over the gates of their stalls, as if they were all enchanted with the teenager and enthralled with the story she was reading.

Allie must have heard them at the door because she looked up and smiled. "Hey, guys."

"Hey, kid," Cade said, dropping Nora's hand as he took a step inside the barn. His voice was low. Nora wasn't sure if that was because he didn't want to startle the animals or because he was overcome with the emotion of finding her.

Allie's brow furrowed. "Everything okay?"

Cade nodded. "Yeah, everything's good. You weren't in your bed, and I guess I got scared that you'd left."

"Left? How could I leave these guys?" She giggled softly as she reached to pat Shamus's head, and he leaned forward and snuffled her neck.

"They do tend to grow on you." He scratched the nose of one of the horses. "Mind if we listen for a bit?"

Allie shrugged. "Sure. If you want. I'm still in chapter two. This book is about a girl who grew up in foster homes, but she just turned fifteen and found out she's a princess. One of the queen's guards just picked her up and brought her to the palace."

Cade held up his hand. "Stop. You had me at princess."

The grin he gave his daughter had Nora's insides melting like goo. Cade grabbed a couple of horse blankets and put them on the ground in front of some of the hay bales. He sat down and patted the spot next to him. Nora sat down and stretched her legs out in front of her. Otis gave her slipper a quick sniff, and the pig shuffled over and rested her head on Nora's leg.

Allie smiled at her, then bent her head and continued reading. "'Julianna…'" She paused. "That's the princess," she explained before continuing. "'Julianna wandered through the rooms of the palace, feeling both in awe and at peace as she munched on the most delicious shortbread she'd ever had in her life. Brushing a buttery crumb from her sleeve, she tried not to let herself get excited about this new adventure in her life. She wanted it. All of it. The new home, the chance at finally having a family of her own. But it all seemed too good to be true—like it could be ripped away at any second and she'd be back in her old life, but this time with the knowledge of the life she could have had. She knew if she let herself believe she belonged here, she would only get hurt. As she took another bite of the flaky biscuit, she contemplated if she should just get out now—dump the rest of the tray of shortbread into her pocket and make a run for it, before she let herself believe this was a life she could truly have.'"

Nora blinked back the tears that sprung to her eyes. It was as if Allie were tearing a page from Nora's own life and reading it aloud. She might not have any delicious shortbread, but she understood all too well the feeling of need and fear and wanting to make a run for it before she got hurt.

CHAPTER 18

NORA SANG ALONG TO THE SONG ON THE RADIO AS SHE DROVE along the winding road heading back to the ranch the next day. She'd had a great morning. It had started with a few stolen kisses from Cade in the kitchen before he'd headed out to help Zane feed the cattle, then she'd met Elle in town for coffee and a little shopping. She hadn't planned on buying anything but had found a gorgeous dress in a cute little shop that would be perfect for the dance tomorrow night.

Shopping always made her hungry, and she'd stopped at Sonic for cheeseburgers and tater tots and had picked up cherry limeades for Cade and Allie. The tots hadn't made it much farther than the edge of town, and she was already halfway through her burger.

Peeling back the wrapper, she took another bite as she rounded a corner, then slammed on her brakes to keep from hitting the mangy dog limping across the road.

Oh no. The poor dog stopped in the middle of the road and turned his head to stare at her. She winced at the sight of his swollen eye and his mud- and blood-streaked face. His tawny fur was matted with dust and dirt, and he held his front paw up off the ground. It didn't look broken, but it was covered in blood as well. He held her gaze for just a moment, then turned to finish limping across the pavement.

Nora's heart was pounding in her chest, and she realized she was holding the drink holder of the cherry limeades against the seat as if she were a mother reaching out to protect her kids as she hit the brakes.

Chewing her bottom lip, she watched the dog hobble along

the shoulder. *Aw, hell.* She lived on a ranch that rescued horses. Surely they could help an injured dog too.

She slowly eased her car off the side of the road and got out.

Cade leaned over the fence as he watched Brody finish examining the horse. He already knew what he was going to say. Daisy had made remarkable improvements to her health. Her ribs were still visible, but she'd filled out more and her eyes were brighter.

"She looks good," Brody said, confirming his assessment.

Cade nodded. "Amazing what buckets of sweet feed and the attention of a teenage girl will do for a horse."

"She really does love Allie," Bryn said from the other side of the stall. "I saw her following Allie around the corral earlier this morning. She didn't even have her on a lead. Daisy just walked along beside her as she wheeled the knee scooter around the arena."

"They've definitely bonded," Cade agreed. It made him so happy to see his daughter connecting to the ranch.

"It's not hard to fall in love with that one," Zane said as he loaded a couple of hay bales into a wheel barrow. "She's a sweet horse."

The sound of an engine speeding down the driveway drew their attention. "What the hell?" Cade spotted a flash of white through the window of the barn. "That's Nora's car," he said, hurrying out of the barn.

His pulse raced as he saw her terrified face through the windshield. She braked to a stop and leapt from the car, racing toward him and launching herself into his arms. "What happened? Are you all right?" He could feel her shaking. "Are you hurt? Did someone do something to you?" His muscles tensed, ready to fight whoever had caused Nora this distress.

She pointed to the car as she gasped for breath. "I picked up an injured dog on the road. I wanted to help him, but the damn thing has been growling at me the whole way here." She pressed a hand to her neck. "I thought he was going to leap over the seat and rip my throat out."

"An injured dog?" He took a step closer to Nora's car to peer into the back seat. "Holy shit" was all he could manage to say before the laugh burst from him.

Bryn, Zane, and Brody had come out of the barn, and he waved them toward the car. "You all gotta see this. Check out the injured dog Nora found on the way home from town," he said between fits of laughter.

They all looked into Nora's back seat. The window, now streaked with drool, was rolled down a few inches, and the animal was crouched in the back seat. He bared his teeth and let out a low growl. Brody chuckled, and Zane's lips curved up, which for him was almost the same as a hearty laugh. Bryn brought her hand to her mouth to cover her gasp.

Nora took a step back, the bewildered expression on her face changing to one of annoyance as Cade couldn't stop laughing. She planted a hand on her hip. "What the hell is so funny? That dog is hurt."

Cade shook his head and tried to catch his breath. "That's not a dog, darlin'. That's One-Eyed Jack. He's a coyote."

Her mouth dropped open, which only made Cade laugh harder. "A coyote?" she whispered.

He leaned forward, placing his hands on his knees as he shook his head. "How in the Sam Hill did you get him into your back seat?"

"It wasn't easy," she said, brushing her bangs off her sweaty forehead. "I led him to the car with little bites of my burger, then I tossed the second cheeseburger I bought into the back seat, and he jumped in. But he got awfully pissed off when I shut the door. So I just hopped in and drove as fast as I could. I was praying the whole way here that he wouldn't try to bite my arm off."

"You're lucky he didn't bite you," Brody said. "Coyotes are real assholes."

"Well, I've found that even assholes need help once in a while," Nora said, peering into the car. "And sometimes a little kindness goes a long way toward changing their attitudes."

This woman. *No wonder I'm falling so hard for her*, Cade thought. She could even find the good in an asshole coyote.

"This guy might have been snarling and growling, but look at him," Nora said. "He's hurt. His foot is bleeding, and his eye is swollen. I think his face is cut up. There's a lot of blood."

"His eye always looks like that," Brody said, putting his face closer to the window. "It's an old injury, but I can see a piece of glass stuck in his front paw. He must have been trying to chew it out. That's why his mouth and head are streaked with blood. He might have cut himself trying to free the glass, but I don't see anything too concerning."

"Can you get the glass out?" Nora asked.

"Not in the state he's in. I'm sure he won't let me near him." His brow furrowed as he studied the animal. "I could probably sedate him though. Give him something to knock him out a little, then I could get the glass out and clean him up." He gestured to his vet truck, which was parked near the barn. "I've got some sedatives in the truck. That should do it. You got any of that hamburger left?"

Nora shook her head. "No. He wolfed it down before I'd even pulled back onto the highway."

"Well, if we can stick it in some food and get him to eat it, that'd be the easiest way to get it in him."

"He likes pancakes," Bryn said.

Zane turned his head slowly toward her and raised an eyebrow. "Just how in the hell do you know that this coyote likes pancakes?"

She lifted her shoulders in a shrug as she offered him a sheepish grin. "I wouldn't know. I'm just guessing. Everybody likes pancakes, right?"

"Bryn Tender Heart Callahan," Zane said, narrowing his eyes at his girlfriend. "Have you been feeding this damn coyote? Is that why he keeps hanging around here?"

Her chin dipped. "I may have given him a few scraps. Not all the time. Look at him though. He only has one eye."

Zane put his arm around her. "I love you for your kind heart and your affinity for the wounded strays of this world, but that is not a stray dog. He's probably hanging around here trying to figure out how to break into your chicken coop. We don't want him around the ranch. He could attack the dogs or even Otis. He may look like a dog, but he's still a wild animal who hunts to eat."

"Zane's right," Brody said. "He is a wild animal. And even if you do feed him, he's not going to suddenly turn tame." He glanced back into the car. The animal hadn't moved. His lips pulled back the slightest, and he bared his teeth. "And even though my opinion of coyotes is pretty low, I hate to see any animal in pain." He nodded at Bryn. "Why don't you go grab something you think he'll eat? Now, don't go whipping up a batch of pancakes, just grab some scraps."

"I've got some leftover biscuits from this morning," she said, taking off for the house.

"Be sure to dip them in some of that gravy," Zane called after her. "We wouldn't want old Jack to have to suffer a dry biscuit."

She blew him a raspberry as she hurried up the steps.

"That's what I thought," he said, crossing his arms and leaning back against the side of the barn. "I can't wait to see how this whole thing shakes out. Is it too late to have Bryn make us some sandwiches? I like a little snack to go with my show."

Cade held back his grin, but only because Nora was glaring at him.

"This isn't funny," she said.

He lifted one shoulder and tried to coax a smile from her. "Come on. It's a little bit funny."

Her lips tugged up in a grin, and she swatted a hand at his arm. "It's not that funny. I bought that second cheeseburger for you."

Oh, dang.

Bryn came back with a handful of biscuits. Brody stuffed one with a few sedatives and tossed it through the window. The coyote gobbled it up. "Now we just have to wait," Brody said.

Zane held up his hand. "Toss me one of those leftover biscuits." Bryn threw half of a biscuit at him, but he caught it deftly in the air and tore off a bite. "Good toss," he told her.

"Not really," she said, giving him a saucy grin. "I was aiming for your head."

Twenty minutes later, the coyote was asleep. The sound of his even snores came through the window, and Brody eased the back door open. Cade had donned a long-sleeved flannel shirt and a pair of work gloves, just in case the sedative didn't fully take, and he helped the veterinarian lift the animal from the car. Bryn had spread out an old blanket, and they set the coyote down gently on its side.

Brody had already washed up and brought his work kit over. He lifted the coyote's paw and examined the wound. "Dang. That glass is really wedged in there. It's stuck between the pads of his paw. No wonder he couldn't dig it out with his teeth." He took a long pair of forceps and carefully inserted them between the pads. He got a good grasp of the shard, then cautiously pulled it free. The group let out a collective breath as the doctor held up the bloody piece of glass. "Got it."

"Thank goodness," Nora said, squeezing Cade's hand.

Cade watched the vet inspect and clean the injury, but his focus was on the woman standing next to him, holding his hand and pressing her body against his side. The others were too engrossed in what was happening with the animal to notice, but Cade was hyperaware of every move she made, every brush of her skin against his.

He had laughed at her city-girl naivety—seriously, who lures a coyote into their back seat, even an injured one?—but he had to admire her spunk. And she had a heart that rivaled the size of the Rocky Mountains. He squeezed her hand back and tried not to think about how badly he was falling for her. Or about how soon she was heading back to that city.

"He's all set," Brody said, grabbing his tools and standing. "I cleaned up the little wounds around his mouth and face and did the best I could with his paw. The cut bled a lot, but it's not deep enough for stitches. I put some antibiotic ointment in there and wrapped a bandage around it. Hopefully, by the time he wakes up and chews the bandage off, the ointment will have had some time to do its work."

"Is there anything you can do about his eye?" Nora asked. She had let go of Cade's hand and stepped closer to peer down at the coyote.

Brody shook his head. "Nah. That's an old wound. It looks a little gnarly, but that's just the way it healed up. My guess is he lost that eye years ago." He gestured to the sleeping animal. "I stuffed some antibiotics in that biscuit too, to help fight off any infection. He should wake up in an hour or so. He'll be a little groggy, but my bet is he'll probably get up and run off into the mountains, find a place to hole up for a few days, and lick his wounds."

"Between the hamburger Nora gave him and Bryn's biscuits, he'll have a full belly at least," Cade said.

"I've got to get back to the clinic," Brody said. "But call me if you have questions. Or if he wakes up and bites one of you."

Nora took a step back.

"He's just kidding," Cade told her, putting a hand on her arm. He couldn't help it. When he was around her, he just wanted to touch her. And seemed to find any excuse to do so. "Like he said, he's gonna be groggy when he wakes up. Give old Jack his space, and I'm sure he'll wake up and just take off."

Zane's pickup was parked a safe distance away. Bryn walked toward it. "I'll sit in the back of Zane's truck and watch him for a while." She dropped the tailgate and climbed into the bed, then waved off Zane and Cade. "I know you guys have stuff to do. Those cows aren't going to feed themselves."

"I'm free," Nora said, climbing into the truck with her. "I can wait with you. Plus, I brought him out here, so I kind of feel like he's my responsibility."

I know the feeling, Cade thought as he watched the gorgeous woman perch herself on the wheel well of the pickup, content to sit and watch the sleeping injured coyote.

———

Later that night, Cade was getting ready to take Allie into town when his phone rang. Bryn, Elle, and Nora were having a girls' night to make pies for the dance the next night, so he, Brody, and Zane had agreed to take the kids out for pizza and ice cream.

His thoughts were on how comfortable Allie was getting around him and the community of Creedence, and he didn't pay much attention to the screen as he pulled the phone from his pocket and held it to his ear. "Cade Callahan."

"Ah. Just the person I wanted to speak with," a man's voice said into his ear. "My name is Michael Slater, and I'm an attorney with the law firm of Kirkland & Slater."

Cade frowned. Why would a lawyer be calling him? "Okay. What can I help you with?"

"I think it's more of a matter of what I can help you with. First, let me offer my condolences for the death of your wife. It's always a tragedy to lose someone so young."

"Well, thank you. She's my ex-wife though. I mean, not that it mattered. It was still a tragedy." Why was he tongue-tied? Not that he'd been around many of them, but lawyers just tended to make him nervous. Seemed to him like nothing good ever came of a situation that started with a call from a lawyer.

"Yes, well, regardless of if you are still married or not, Ms. Callahan named you as the beneficiary in her life insurance policy. It's not a large policy. It's the standard one offered to employees of the corporation where your wife was employed. Still, after taxes and fees, it should end up being close to two hundred and fifty thousand."

"Dollars?" Cade croaked.

"Yes, Mr. Callahan. Dollars. We don't often pay life insurance policies with dog treats."

"That amount would make a lot of dogs pretty happy."

"Be that as it may, I need to confirm your address and get some information from you so I can mail you the check. Or I can take your bank account information if you'd rather we wire you the funds."

"Wait. Hold up. Nobody is wiring any funds. I don't deserve this money. I haven't been married to Amber for years."

"Doesn't matter. She still named you as the beneficiary. Beneficiaries aren't always spouses. Sometimes they are parents or siblings or even friends."

He huffed out a sarcastic laugh. "I haven't been Amber's friend in years either."

"It's my understanding you share a child together."

"That's right."

"And do you now have custody of the child?"

"For now."

"I don't know Ms. Callahan personally, but I can only assume she named you the beneficiary in hopes you would use it to take care of the child."

"Oh." That would make sense. Diana was pretty levelheaded, but Cade wasn't sure how responsible either she or Amber's dad would be if given a quarter-of-a-million-dollar windfall. He scrubbed his hand across the back of his neck. "Can I get your information and call you back? This is a lot to take in, and I need a little time to think."

"Certainly." The lawyer gave him his number and took Cade's address and email. "I'll send you some more information," he said. "And you can always call or email my assistant if you have questions. Like I said, it's a pretty standard policy, and I don't see much in the way of complications once we know where to send the funds."

Cade hung up and slumped into a kitchen chair. All he saw were complications. He couldn't believe Amber had named him as the beneficiary. What the heck was he supposed to do with that money? Could he just put it in an account and give it to Allie? That was a lot of responsibility for a thirteen-year-old girl. And if he did that, how could he ensure that Diana and Amber's dad didn't get ahold of the money? It was enough to send Allie to college and offer her things he'd never had growing up.

No way were Diana and Ed going to take this lying down. This had to be the money Diana was referring to. And she'd already said they weren't going to let him keep it.

"You ready to go?" Allie asked, breaking into his musings as she wheeled the knee scooter into the kitchen.

"Yep," he said, pushing thoughts of the life insurance money aside.

She held up a pink-and-purple band of crocheted threads. "Can you help me with this? It's a friendship bracelet Mandy made me. I want to wear it tonight."

"That was nice of her. She's a sweetheart."

"She is. I really like her. And Milo." Allie scrunched up her nose as she held her wrist out. "Is it weird that I like hanging out with a couple of kids who are younger than me?"

He shrugged. "I don't think so. Especially since both of them seem older than they are. When we were kids, my brother and I hung out with Bryn and Bucky, and we were all different ages. Plus I think it's different in a small town. There're fewer kids to hang out with."

"They're the *only* kids I've been hanging out with."

"Do you have fun with them?"

"Yeah, they like to read the same stuff I do. And they're both funny. They make me laugh."

"Then who cares? Just have fun."

"Yeah, you're right." She smiled as he finished tightening the knot on the friendship bracelet. "Thanks, Cade." She turned and rolled toward the door.

He held back his own smile as he grabbed his hat and set it on his head. His daughter had just asked for some fatherly advice, and he hadn't completely botched it. In fact, he'd done pretty well.

Maybe he was starting to get the hang of this dad stuff after all.

CHAPTER 19

NORA WASN'T SURE WHY SHE'D BEEN A LITTLE NERVOUS ABOUT doing a girls' night with Bryn, Elle, and Jillian. She'd been tempted to beg off and hide in her room with a book while the guys took the kids out for pizza. It had been so long since she'd had a night out or, in this case, in with a group of friends. But she shouldn't have worried. Within minutes of arriving, they were gabbing and laughing like they'd all known each other for years.

"Pass me those glasses," Bryn told Nora over the whir of the blender. "Frozen margaritas are coming right up."

Nora slid the tray of four salt-rimmed glasses across the counter as Jillian finished chopping the last of the lettuce, and Elle took a platter of nachos from the oven. "Those smell amazing," she said as Elle set them on a trivet on the table.

"They are," she said, pulling a cheesy chip from the pile. "Especially dipped in Jillian's homemade salsa. I don't know whose idea it was to get rid of the guys and the kids and have a tacos-and-margarita girls' night, but I love it."

"Me too," Nora said, carrying the tray of margaritas to the table.

"Wait, don't start without me," Aunt Sassy called as she bumped the front door open with her rear end. Her hands were full of a cardboard box, and a gray-and-white ball-of-fluff puppy raced through the door in front of her. Nora had brought Scout with her, and the puppies yipped and clamored over each other in greeting. "I brought fried ice cream and another bottle of tequila," she said, pushing the box onto the counter and pointing to the blender. "Pour me one of those and make mine a double."

Bryn poured her a margarita while Nora took the ice cream dessert and put it in the freezer, then let the puppies out in the backyard to see their mother and the other dogs. "This is so fun. I thought I was just coming over to help make pies."

"Oh, we'll get to the pies," Bryn said, handing her a bowl of crispy taco shells to put on the table. "But they're so much more fun to make after a margarita or two."

"Or three," Elle said with a wink.

"Not that I have far to go," Nora said, setting down the bowl and dropping into the chair next to Aunt Sassy. "But that was sweet of Zane to offer to drive everyone home later."

Bryn nodded, her lips curving up in a grin. "Yeah, he's a pretty great guy. He doesn't really care for drinking, so he often volunteers to be the designated driver."

Sassy leaned toward Nora to whisper, although not very quietly. "He doesn't like to drink because his dad's a big alc-y-holic."

"Aunt Sassy," Bryn admonished.

Sassy held up her hand. "Sorry, I thought I was being kind. Would you prefer I call him an abusive asswipe drunk?"

Oh, gosh. Nora looked from Sassy to Bryn, trying to judge her host's reaction.

Bryn shrugged. "Yeah, I guess that's closer to the truth." She picked up a spoon and waved it in the air like a magic wand. "But nobody wants to talk about Birch Taylor. I declare this girls' night is now officially commencing, and the taco bar is open. Grab your plates and dig in, girls."

Their discussion moved from books to the kids to the latest gossip happening in Creedence as they made their way through several margaritas and numerous tacos. The kitchen was full of laughter and music after they ate as Elle and Nora washed dishes while Jillian, Sassy, and Bryn rolled out and filled piecrusts.

"Okay, the oven's hot," Bryn said once it was preheated. "Pass me the first two pies."

"Speaking of hot," Elle said, handing Nora another margarita, "what's happening with you and Cade? I saw the looks you two were giving each other earlier. I know you're here to help Allie, but are you offering the cute cowboy a little *physical* therapy too?"

"Ohh." Aunt Sassy leaned in. "Now we're getting to the good stuff." She sang the lyrics to an old Olivia Newton John song as she did a few dance moves. "'Let's get physical, physical.'"

Nora ignored Sassy's song and tossed a chip at her friend. "I have no idea what you're talking about."

"That blush creeping up your cheeks tells a different story."

Nora shrugged. "He is cute. I guess."

"You *guess*?" Sassy wiggled her eyebrows. "That man is walking sex on a stick. If I were twenty years younger." She pursed her lips and looked to the ceiling. "Hmm. Well maybe, thirty years younger…" She waved her hand as if to erase the air. "Doesn't matter. That man is hot. And if I were a single woman living next door to him, I'd sure be knocking on his door asking to borrow a cup of sugar." She wiggled her hips. "And by sugar, I mean—"

"La-la-la," Bryn said, covering her ears. "We *know* what you mean." Bryn laughed as she shook her head at Jillian and Nora while jerking a thumb at Aunt Sassy. "You have to watch out for this one. She's got a dirty mind."

Sassy huffed and planted a hand on her hip. "You say dirty, I say flirty. Although my lips do tend to get a little looser after a marg or two."

"Speaking of loose lips," Elle said, "let's get back to Nora. I want to hear what is really going with you and Cade." She tipped up the bottom of Nora's glass. "Swill it and spill it, girl."

"Okay, okay." Nora laughed, then took another sip. "Yes, there *may* be a little something going on with Cade and me. We get along really well together. I feel like he really listens to me. And he's charming and sweet."

"Sweet? That's not a word that's often used when describing my cousin," Bryn said. "He must have it bad for you."

"I don't know about that." What she *did* know was that she had it bad for him. "And it's probably too soon to even mention it. We haven't known each other that long."

"Yeah, but the time you have been together has been pretty intense, so you've seen each other at your worst and your best," Elle said. "And you guys spend *all* your time with each other. You've barely spent a minute apart which seems like plenty of time to really get to know someone."

"And sometimes it only takes a second to make that connection," Aunt Sassy said. "Sometimes you can meet someone, and you just know."

"Been there, done that," Nora said. "Although I've been wrong every time. I'm notorious for leaping before I look, and I just got burned in a big way for jumping into a relationship too quickly with a man I thought I knew." Nora leaned her hip against the counter. "And by burned, I mean sold everything I owned and moved in with him. Then a few months later, we got into an argument and he decided he didn't love me anymore and not-so-subtly suggested I move out again."

"Dr. Douchebag," Elle said.

Nora nodded.

Aunt Sassy put a hand on her shoulder. "Sounds to me like instead of beating yourself up for making the wrong decision about a bad man, you should be congratulating yourself on making the right decision by choosing to be with a good man like Cade."

Nora shrugged again. How was she supposed to know if Cade really was a good man? He seemed to be. But her track record for judging men's characters seemed to be lacking. She could barely trust herself. How could she trust what was happening with Cade? She shook her head. "Enough about Cade and me and my poor life-decision skills."

"We all have those, honey," Aunt Sassy assured her with a wink. "But the real skills we want to hear about are Cade's. Is he a good kisser? He looks like he'd be a good kisser."

Nora chuckled as she picked up a bowl of sliced apples. "Oh, gosh, on that note, these pies aren't going to make themselves. Somebody pass me that cinnamon."

Sassy cackled as she grabbed the tin from the counter and held it in the air. "You're not getting the cinnamon until we get the spice."

Oh crud. She needed to deflect their attention. The alcohol had her saying more than she should have already. She needed to stop talking about the hot cowboy. Or she might end up spilling more than she should—like how Cade could be just as spicy as he was sweet.

Nora pointed to the librarian's half-empty glass. "So, Jillian, you should grab your drink because I think it's your turn to swill it and spill it. You can tell us if that cute deputy has stopped in to see you to get a library card yet."

"Wait, what's this?" Elle said, turning to Jillian. "Why haven't I heard about this cute deputy?"

"Why haven't I heard about this library card business?" Aunt Sassy asked, cocking an eyebrow. "Is 'library card' some new code for hanky-panky, like that Netflix-and-chill business?"

Nora and the other women cracked up. "No, Aunt Sassy. You're not missing out on some new urban slang. I really meant a library card, since Jillian is an actual librarian. And we met him yesterday when he came out to help us pick up the rescued horses. His name is Ethan Rayburn."

"Oh, I know Ethan," Aunt Sassy. "He *is* cute."

"And he's a good guy," Bryn said. "We went to school together."

"Well, he asked Jillian to save him a dance tomorrow," Nora told them.

The librarian's cheeks flushed pink. "I think he was just being nice," Jillian said.

"I'll dance with him," Aunt Sassy, wiggling her hips.

"Sorry, Jillian, this is what happens on girls' night when

margaritas are involved," Elle said. "We start talking men and boundaries get screwed." She put her chin on her knuckles. "But that wasn't much of a 'spill it.' We need more. Have you dated anybody since you've been here?"

"No, and I'm not planning to," Jillian said with a laugh. "I've got enough on my hands with moving across the country, starting a new job, and transitioning Milo to a new school."

"How did your ex-husband feel about you bringing Milo to Colorado?" Elle asked.

"He felt nothing at all because I don't have an ex-husband. Never been married. And Milo's dad has never had any interest in being part of Milo's life."

"That's tough," Bryn said.

"Not really," Jillian answered. "He wasn't that great a guy to begin with. And certainly no role model for my son. In some ways, it's easier. But not a lot of guys want to date a single mom with a ten-year-old boy. Which is fine. If I'm going to have baggage, I'll take Milo as my personal item any day."

"Ugh, I know all about baggage," Elle said. "Try putting two brokenhearted widows together. Poor Brody didn't know what he was getting into when he asked me to move in while they finished the repairs on my house." Elle took another sip of her drink, then gave them a mischievous grin. "Besides dragging in my widow-shaped luggage, I also brought an injured dog, a rambunctious puppy, *and* a horse."

Nora drew her head back. "*You* have a horse? How have I not heard that you have a horse?"

Elle laughed. "She's kind of a new acquisition."

"She was one of our rescues from earlier this summer," Bryn explained.

"She is the sweetest girl," Elle said with a sigh. "Her name is Glory, and she likes to be sung to. She's particularly partial to Christmas carols and anything by Elvis or the Beatles."

"Actually that doesn't surprise me that much," Nora said. "Allie's favorite horse, Daisy, likes to be read to. Cade and I found her out in the barn last night reading to all the animals." She'd finally nabbed the cinnamon and was stirring it and some sugar into the bowl of apples. "But what does surprise me is that I hadn't realized you'd moved in with Brody. I know I've been caught up in my own stuff, but it doesn't seem like you've been with him that long."

Elle shrugged. "Sometimes you just know."

"And sometimes you think you know, but then find out you don't have a clue about the person you've just sold all of your belongings for and moved in with," Nora muttered.

Sassy swiped an apple chunk before Bryn covered the filling with crust. "But you can't live your life in fear of making another mistake. We all make mistakes every day." She glanced down at her outfit. "I probably made a mistake trying to match this hot-pink top with these teal joggers, but who cares? Life is full of mistakes."

"Yes, but shouldn't we try to learn from those mistakes?" Nora asked. "Like surely there's a lesson in here somewhere."

"Yeah, don't date douchesticks." Sassy put an arm around Nora's shoulder. "But the lesson isn't never to date again or to stop believing that you deserve to find someone good. Life's too short to waste worrying about if you're making the exact right decision. I say grab life by the horns and live it. Eat the dessert, dance in the rain, use the good china, light those pretty candles, and for good-ness sakes, if you get another chance to fall in love, take it."

Nora pressed her lips together, blinking at the sudden well of tears in her eyes. "You're a pretty wise woman, Sassy James."

Aunt Sassy fluffed up one side of her hair. "I know."

Elle grinned and pointed to Sassy's face. "I hate to tell you, oh wise one, but you've got apple pie filling on your chin."

The women busted up again and were still laughing a few min-utes later when the front door opened and Cade, Zane, Brody, and the kids filed in. The house exploded with noise and more laughter as the kids raced up to the kitchen island, their words spilling over each other as they told the women about their night.

"Dad dropped one of the pizzas," Mandy said.

"And Cade bet him a dollar that he wouldn't eat one of the pieces off the floor," Allie said.

"Then Zane offered him ten bucks to do it, and Brody ate like half a slice," Milo chimed in.

"Oh, gross," Elle said, swatting Brody's arm. "I kiss that mouth. Just tell me next time you're that hard up for cash, I'll give you a twenty."

"It wasn't the money," Brody said. "It was the principle of the thing. And it barely touched the floor. Easily sneaked in under the ten-second rule."

Allie had wheeled the knee scooter up to Nora, and she put her arm around the teenager's shoulder. "Despite having to watch a grown man eat floor pizza, did you have fun?"

Allie's face lit with excitement as she nodded. "Yeah, it was really fun. They had a little arcade thing in the back of the pizza place, and there were some other kids there that were my age. They go to Mandy and Milo's school."

"Other kids or other *boys*?" Elle asked.

"Both," Allie said, her grin spreading wider across her face.

"Luke Johnson totally likes her," Mandy said. "He even asked me for her number."

"Wait, I didn't hear this part of the story," Cade said. "Who is this kid? And what does he want with your number?"

Allie rolled her eyes. "Gosh, I don't know. Maybe so he can call me and ask if I want to buy some Boy Scout popcorn. I'm assuming he wants it so he can text me."

"I'd rather it be because of the popcorn," Cade grumbled.

Brody swept his finger around the edge of one of the bowls and sampled the filling. "Tastes good. How are the pies coming?"

"Great," Bryn said. "They're all prepared. I just need to bake the last few."

"Good. Because we probably need to take off. I've got an early surgery scheduled in the morning."

"Let me just help clean up a little," Elle told him. "Then we can go."

Bryn waved her away from the sink. "I've got the cleanup covered. I have to wait for the pies to bake anyway. You all go on home. I need you rested and ready for me to put you to work tomorrow."

"Speaking of which," Nora said, carrying some dishes to the sink. "What's the plan for tomorrow? What's left to do?"

"Not much," Bryn said. "We set the hay bales out this afternoon and arranged them for seating. We're borrowing tables and chairs from the church. Zane and Cade can pick those up in the morning."

"That won't take long," Cade said.

"We also borrowed a bunch of café lights, and the guys are going to string those above the area for seating and the dance floor. My idea is that the event will be half in the barn and half out. We'll open the big front doors, and the dance floor, the band, and the table and chairs will be right outside the barn, but the bake sale and the drinks area and some seating will be inside. I want people to be able to roam inside to see the horses."

"And remember you said I could dress Shamus up and walk him around to show off one of our successful rescues," Mandy said.

Allie raised her hand as if she were in school. "I'd really like to help too. Is there anything I can do?"

"Yes, I've got the perfect thing for you. I was going to ask you in the morning," Bryn said. "I have a whole rustic-barn kind of theme. I bought navy-blue tablecloths and for centerpieces I have about a million mason jars that I thought you, Mandy, and Milo could fill with wildflowers and some sprigs of chokecherry from the bushes on the side of the house."

Allie pushed her shoulders back. "Yeah, we could totally do that."

"Great."

"All right, sounds like the chauffeur slash handyman slash barn dance setter-upper has a full day tomorrow," Zane said. "So the Taylor taxi service is leaving in five. Whoever wants a ride home needs to be in the car."

After a flurry of packing up and hugs and last-minute instructions, Zane pulled Elle's packed SUV out of the driveway. Allie had already taken Scout back to the bunkhouse, and Bryn had shooed Nora and Cade out of the house.

Nora didn't realize how that last margarita Elle had poured her had affected her until she tried to walk down the porch steps. "Oopsie daisy," she said, stumbling a little into Cade.

"You all right there, darlin'?" he asked, sliding his arm around her waist.

"I'm just great," she answered, leaning into his solid side. "That was a really fun night. It's been a long time since I've hung out with a group of women I really enjoyed being around."

"I'm glad you had fun." His voice was warm, but he had a pensive look on his face as they walked back toward the bunkhouse.

"You okay? You seem more quiet than usual." She nudged his ribs. "Didn't you have fun tonight?"

"Yeah, it was great. I love those guys, and the kids had a good time. But it was also kind of weird, ya know? Like it's the first time I've ever gone out with another dad and other kids. It just got me thinking about stuff. Like how I've been so focused on the present that I haven't given much thought to the future."

"What do you mean?"

"I saw Allie with those kids tonight, and I realized that school is going to start up in a few weeks, and I don't have a clue where she's going to go. And it's not just school. I'm completely clueless about what happens in her life. I don't know how to make doctor's appointments or when the last time was she went to the dentist. How often are kids even supposed to go to the dentist? Once a year? Once a month? Does she play sports or a musical instrument? I just realized how much Amber has always taken care of. And how in over my head I am."

"It's okay. That's all stuff you can learn. When you get a new horse, you don't know anything about it, do you?"

"Are you comparing my teenage daughter to a rescued horse?"

She shrugged. "Just trying to put it in perspective to your life experience."

"That's fair. Go on."

"I'm just saying that you'll figure it out. Allie doesn't know how to live with a dad in the house either. You guys will adjust, and you'll help each other. And I'm here if you need me. Not that I know anything about school, but I do know that everyone should get their teeth cleaned twice a year." She smiled up at him as if she'd just offered him one of the secrets of the universe.

He grinned down at her. "Good to know. And thanks. Although I don't know if I should be taking parenting advice from my daughter's snockered physical therapist."

They reached the edge of the porch, and she walked up the two steps, then turned to him so they were eye level. She wrapped her arms around his neck. "How about taking advice from a snockered chick who thinks you're really hot?"

He chuckled. "I guess that depends on what kind of advice that chick is offering."

She sighed and leaned her head on his shoulder. "Take me to bed, cowboy."

"That's not really advice. It's more of a directive."

She giggled. "You're funny, Cade Callahan."

"You're drunk, Nora Fisher."

"I know." She leaned forward into him, closing her eyes as her words slurred just the slightest. "And I was thinking of inviting you in for some crazy, hot, sexy times, but now I'm just very tired. That's why I want you to take me to bed."

"I can do that." He picked her up and carried her inside and down the hall to her bedroom. He pulled back the comforter and set her on the mattress. She kicked off her sandals and closed her eyes again as she snuggled into the pillow. Cade pulled the sheet over her and leaned down to kiss her forehead. "Good night, beautiful. I'm glad you had fun tonight."

"Me too," she sighed as sleep drifted closer. "I really like those women. Even though they got me to swill it and spill it, and I sort of told them how much I really like you. And I told them it scared me. Because I really, really like you, Cade."

She heard his quiet laugh and felt his lips brush her cheek. "It scares the hell out of me too because I really, really like you too, Nora."

Her lips curved into a grin as she drifted off to sleep.

CHAPTER 20

Nora gave her hair one last spritz of hairspray the next night, then declared herself ready for the dance. The weather had been gorgeous all day as the group of them worked on setting up the ranch for that night's festivities.

She'd gotten another weird text from Geoff that morning. He'd blown her off for months and now was suddenly texting to say how much he missed her and that he still loved her. She didn't know what was going on with the guy, and she didn't want to know. She'd ignored the text, like she'd done the other ones. She didn't have time for Geoff and whatever drama he was trying to pull her into. She was having too much fun.

Even though they'd worked all day—Bryn had a list a mile long—Nora had still had a great time. She loved being with the group, and even though she hadn't known them all for very long, she still considered them friends. Yes, she and Elle had known each other for years, but she just seemed to click with Bryn and Jillian as well. And Aunt Sassy was like the bonus cherry on top of the friendship cake. The older woman had brought out sandwiches for lunch, and they'd finished right on schedule, giving them all a chance to clean up and get dressed before the food truck and the band arrived.

She figured Allie got in plenty of stretching and moving as she helped with the evening's preparations, but Nora still tried to sneak in a physical therapy session after they'd finished. The teenager was too antsy and excited for the dance though, so they just went through some deep stretches and a few light exercises before heading off to shower.

Nora had a little jean jacket that paired perfectly with the teal-and-dusty-rose floral sundress. The teal in the dress also matched the blue in her boots, and she happened to have brought a layered necklace with teal stones that worked perfectly with the dress. She'd spent a little extra time curling her hair, wearing it loose around her shoulders.

"Wow. You look gorgeous," Cade said when she stepped out onto the porch a few minutes later. He tipped his hat back as his gaze traveled over her.

"You look pretty gorgeous yourself," she told him. He was dressed in jeans, boots, and a pressed blue button-up shirt. The ends of his hair were still damp as they curled around his collar. "How's Allie doing? Does she need any more help?" The girl had come over earlier to get ready with Nora, and they'd had a great time while Nora helped her apply a little makeup and curl and braid her hair.

"I don't know. She wouldn't let me see her until she was all ready," Cade said, then his eyes widened as the screen door opened and Allie wheeled out. "Gosh. You look beautiful, Allie-Cat."

The teenager did a little curtsy. "Thank you. Nora helped me with my hair." Allie had found a picture of a loose braided updo, and Nora had done her best to replicate it. They'd finished the look by tucking a few small sprigs of lavender into the braid.

"You do look beautiful," Nora told her. "That dress is perfect on you."

Cade cleared his throat, and Allie narrowed her eyes at him as he rubbed the back of his hand next to his eye. "Are you crying?"

"No. I just got something in my eye." He offered her a sheepish smile. "You just look so grown-up." He stood and held out his elbows. "And I'm really proud to be escorting the two most beautiful women in the world to the dance tonight."

"You're a dork," she said, but she took his arm anyway.

The sound of a guitar riff ripped through the air as the band warmed up, and Nora's pulse raced with excitement for the fun night ahead. The ranch looked magical, with candles flickering on the array of tables and lights strung out from the barn over the dance floor. Scents of barbecued pork and french fries filled the air, wafting from the food truck already set up behind the tables.

Nora and Elle had made gallons of lemonade and iced tea that afternoon and created a cute drink station using the workbench in the barn. The feed store had donated a couple of new horse troughs to the ranch, and they'd filled them with ice and bottled water and pop. Across from the drink station, checkered table-cloths covered two tables ready to be filled with baked goods and the pies they'd made the night before.

Bryn had created a schedule, so between their group and some of the other horse rescue volunteers, the different tables would all be manned throughout the night. Nora, Allie, and Cade were scheduled to cover the drinks booth for the first hour, then the other kids would help them bus tables the second hour, then they were free the rest of the night. As the night got busier and more cars arrived, Nora was surprised at how many people she'd already met from the Creedence community.

She recognized the woman from the dress shop and some of the other employees from the diner where Bryn worked. There were Theresa and Bob, who she'd helped with physical therapy sessions, and she spotted the couple who ran the grocery and Sam from the feed store. Aunt Sassy introduced her to Doc Hunter, the retired pediatrician who was her date for the evening, and she met Jillian's sister, Carley. The two women had different hair colors and styles, Carley sporting a perfectly coiffed blond mane that she'd probably had blown out at her beauty salon that afternoon, but the family resemblance was there in their smiles and around their eyes.

"You look amazing," Nora told Jillian as she and Milo showed up to take over for them at the drinks booth. The librarian wore a soft-pink sundress that showed off her tanned shoulders and her hair was loose and curled in soft waves down her back. "That dress is gorgeous on you," she told her as she traded places with Milo, then stepped away from the booth so the two women could talk.

Jillian waved away her compliment. "Thanks. It's one of my sister's. She made me wear it, and she did my hair tonight too. I made the mistake of telling her about Ethan, er, Deputy Rayburn, and she begged me to let her do my hair and makeup."

"Well, Deputy Rayburn is not going to know what hit him," Nora said with a wink.

The other woman shook her head. "It's just one dance. And he probably doesn't even remember asking me."

"You're about to find out," Nora said, turning Jillian around to face the barn door where the handsome deputy had just entered. He was dressed in jeans and boots, but wore a black button-down shirt and a gray felt cowboy hat instead of his sheriff's uniform. "Holy cow. A man who looks that good should be against the law." She nudged her friend. "See what I did there?"

Jillian shushed her. "Yes, I get it."

Ethan scanned the barn as if looking for someone, then his face broke into a grin when he saw Jillian. He strode toward her. "Wow. You look incredible," he said, then shook his head as if to clear it. "I mean, hi." He pointed awkwardly at himself. "It's Ethan from the other day."

Jillian grinned. "Yes, I remember."

Relief flooded his face. "Whew. Thank goodness. I mean, yeah, of course."

"I have to say, I was tempted to act like I'd forgotten you," she told him. "Just to give you a hard time."

"But you took pity on me because I'd already made it awkward enough?" He chuckled as he adorably ducked his head. "I'm usually much cooler under pressure." He jerked a thumb toward the band. "Music is pretty good. You still up for that dance?"

"Told you he remembered," Nora whispered quietly from behind Jillian's back.

"Yeah, sure," Jillian said. "But I can't yet. Milo and I are scheduled to take over the drinks booth for the next hour."

"You need an extra hand?" he asked before Nora had a chance to offer to stay in the booth longer so they could go dance. "I'd be glad to help."

"Yeah, sure. That would be great."

"I'm at your service," he said, already unbuttoning his sleeves and rolling them up. "Just tell me what to do."

"It looks like you've got this handled," Nora said, giving Jillian's side a discreet nudge. "I'll check in with you later. Have fun." She waved, then headed off to find her own handsome cowboy.

―――――――

"You having fun?" Cade asked Allie several hours later as they plowed their way through a plate of fries.

"Yeah, I am," Allie told him. "And I'm really glad for Bryn that it was such a great turnout."

"Me too." Cade looked out across the sea of people wandering through the barn and laughing on the dance floor. The line at the food truck had been steady all night, and he'd heard Nora say all the pies had sold for at least thirty dollars each. "I hope they raised a lot of money."

"I know the goal is to find homes for the rescued horses, but is it bad if I'm hoping no one wants to buy Daisy?" She dug a small circle in the dirt with the toe of her boot. "I know she's not really *my* horse, but I love her, and I'd really miss her if she were gone."

"Nah, it's not bad. It's obvious you have a special bond with her."

"Speaking of special bonds," she said, nudging his leg. "Don't think I haven't noticed what's been going on with you and Nora."

Heat warmed his cheeks, and he hoped it was dark enough that Allie couldn't see it. "I don't know what you're talking about."

"Oh, come on. I see the little looks you guys give each other.

And I know you had your arm around her the other night when I came out on the porch." She put her hand on his arm. "I just want you to know that I really love Nora, and I'm okay if you want to ask her on a date or out for drinks or whatever weird thing adults do when they like each other."

A knot of tension eased in his shoulders. "I do like Nora. She's smart and pretty and one of the kindest people I've ever met. Which makes it a real mystery why she'd even be interested in a dope like me."

"You have a few good points."

"Yeah?"

"Sure. You're tall and superstrong, you're sort of funny in a dorky way, you're always on time, and you know how to braid hair."

"That does sound like an impressive dating résumé."

She giggled as she teased him. "See? You're like the whole dating package." She nodded to the barn doors Nora was just walking out of. "So are you going to ask her to dance or what?"

He shook his head. "No way. I'm busy hanging out with you. Do *you* want to dance with me?"

She pointed to her booted foot. "That would be a little tough with this bad boy."

He shrugged. "You could stand on my feet like you used to do when you were little."

She furrowed her brow. "Did I really used to do that? I don't remember."

"Yeah, you really did."

"Whew, what a night," Nora said, dropping into the seat on the other side of Cade. Her cheeks were flushed, but she looked happy as she shrugged out of her jacket and tossed it on the table. "I think this is the first time I've sat down. But it seems to be going really well. Everyone's having so much fun. I can't believe it's almost over. Sorry if I've been ignoring you guys."

"We're fine."

A boy who looked to be about Allie's age hesitantly approached their table. Cade had seen him start to come over a couple of times, then change direction, as if he couldn't get up the nerve. "Hey," he said to Allie, raising his hand in a little wave.

"Hey," Allie said.

"You having fun?"

Allie shrugged. "Sure." Cade cleared his throat, and she tilted her head toward him. "This is my dad, Cade Callahan. And our friend Nora Fisher."

The boy stuck his hand out and gripped Cade's in a solid handshake. "Good to meet ya. I'm Luke Johnson. My folks have a small farm on the other side of town."

"I just met them earlier tonight. I think they bought a cherry pie," Nora told him. "Nice to meet you, Luke."

Cade nodded in greeting but wasn't ready to roll out the red carpet for some young buck who was sniffing around his daughter.

The boy turned his attention back to Allie. His neck was turning red as he pulled at the collar of his shirt. "So, uh, do you want to dance? With me?"

Allie shook her head. "No, I can't."

His eager expression fell, and he lifted his shoulders like it was no big deal. "Oh yeah. Sure. No problem."

"No, it's not that I don't *want* to." She pointed to her booted foot and held up her sling. "I mean I *can't*. Not with all this. But if I didn't have it, I would totally want to. Dance with you, I mean."

His lips curved in a goofy grin, and he gestured to the empty chair next to her. "How about if I just sit with you for a bit then?"

"That would be okay." He pulled over an empty chair, then sat down beside Allie.

Cade turned to Nora and held out his hand. "I think this would be my cue to ask you to dance."

"I would love to," she said, taking his hand and letting him lead her out onto the dance floor.

She felt so good, so right, as he pulled her into his arms and swayed her to the music. Her perfume swirled around him, and he bent his head to speak quietly into her ear. "So I think we got busted."

"Busted?"

He nodded, trying not to be distracted by the bare skin of her shoulders. "Allie told me she knows I like you."

Nora pulled her head back to look up at him. "Is she okay with that? With you liking me?"

He grinned. "Apparently. She encouraged me to ask you on a date or for drinks or for whatever weird thing adults do when they like each other."

Nora's grin had heat surging up his spine. "We've already done that thing. A few times now."

"Speaking of which, I seem to recall you mentioning last night something about wanting to invite me over for some crazy, hot, sexy times." He slid his hand lower on her waist, thinking about how good it had felt lying next to her and brushing his fingers over her lush curves.

Her eyes widened as she cringed. "I said that?"

He nodded and wiggled his eyebrows. "Oh yeah, you did."

She buried her face in his neck. "Oh my gosh, I'm so embarrassed. Remind me never to let Elle mix the margaritas again."

He chuckled as he pulled her closer. "Don't be embarrassed. I'm just hoping that offer's still on the table."

Her fingers tickled the back of his neck as they tangled in his hair. "Oh, it's still on the table, all right. Like a giant floral centerpiece taking up too much space." She shook her head. "That was a weird analogy. I don't know why I said that."

"I kind of liked it. I can't wait to check out your flowers." He cringed. "Yeah, this is getting worse."

She laughed and the sound of it filled up an empty space inside him. The rest of the dance floor fell away as he peered down at her.

The sundress showed off her shoulders, and her bare skin was like a feast for his carnal hunger. He'd never felt this way about another woman—he wanted her with everything in him, but he also just wanted to be *with* her. He loved spending time with her, talking to her, or just being in the same room.

He tightened his arm around her waist, pulling her closer. Her hair brushed his cheek as he lowered his mouth to her ear. "Have I told you how beautiful you look tonight?"

Her shoulders raised as a slight shiver ran through her, and he could hear the smile in her voice. "Yes, but tell me again."

He pulled back, just far enough to look into her eyes. "Sometimes I look at you and I think you're so damn beautiful that it makes my chest hurt, and I can't quite catch my breath."

"Oh," she whispered on a gasp, and he had a hard time not leaning down to kiss that perfect circle of her lips. Peering up at him from under her lashes, her gaze was sincere as she whispered, "You sure are making it hard for me not to fall in love with you, Cade Callahan."

His throat tightened at her words, and he leaned in to kiss her. He didn't care who saw them. Let the gossips of Creedence go crazy. He *had* to kiss her.

The song ended just as his lips brushed hers. She pressed her lips to his, a quick press of contact before she stepped away and joined in the round of applause for the band. It was a soft kiss but full of promise of something more to come.

"That's it for us, folks," the band leader was saying. "But we thank you all for coming out tonight and for supporting the Heaven Can Wait Horse Rescue. It's not too late to donate. If you've got anything left in your pockets, we'll be happy to take it off your hands." He held up one of the donation jars that had been set on the edge of the stage. "Remember every dollar you donate goes to helping these poor animals in need."

With the music over, people got up from the tables and

wandered off the dance floor. It didn't take long for the crowd to disperse as they headed for their cars. Cade was glad to see several people step forward and drop bills into the jar before they left.

He and Nora stood at the edge of the barn door and watched people hugging and laughing as they left. Nora slipped her hand into his and gave it a squeeze. Her smile was radiant as she beamed up at him. "Gosh, what a fun night."

"It was. But now the real fun is going to start."

"Yeah?"

"Yeah," he said, turning around to look into the barn. "Now Bryn's gonna make us clean all this up."

"True." She laughed with him, then her eyes caught something behind him and the color drained from her face. Her shoulders went stiff as she took a shuddering breath. "What the hell is he doing here?"

CHAPTER 21

NORA'S MOUTH WENT DRY AND HER KNEES THREATENED TO buckle as she watched the man walk across the driveway and toward the barn.

It can't be. What the hell was Geoff doing here?

Even though he walked with an air of confidence, he looked completely out of place. If the hundred-and-fifty-dollar designer jeans and Hugo Boss golf shirt weren't enough of a tip-off, he also wore Kenneth Cole loafers with no socks. Yet he strolled across the barnyard like he owned the place.

His mouth was turned in a general frown of disdain as he peered around, then his face lit as he spotted her. He smiled as he strode toward her. "Nora, baby, there you are." He leaned back and spread out his arms. "Aren't you happy to see me?"

She shook her head and tried to keep her mouth from falling open. "No, I'm not. What are you doing here?"

"I came to see you. Haven't you been getting my messages?"

Cade had turned around and was standing next to her. She couldn't see his face, but she felt him stiffen next to her. "Yes, I got them. And I ignored them. Which I thought was sending you back a message in return."

He tilted his head to look into the barn. "So this is where you've been hiding out? With the Beverly Farmbillies?"

She ignored his insult, not just because it was too stupid to justify with a response, but also because she was more interested in what the hell he was doing there. "Why are you here?"

"I told you, baby. I came to kiss and make up. You've had your little break, but now it's time for you to come home."

I am home. She thought the words but couldn't say them. "I'm not going anywhere with you."

He waved away her protest. "Come on, I miss you, baby."

She gritted her teeth together. *If he calls me baby one more time.* She'd hated the way he'd used the word when they were together, but it was especially grating now.

He reached for her arm but she pulled it away. "No."

His brow furrowed, and his mouth twisted into a sneer. "Don't tell me you actually like this place? It smells like manure. Although your mom told me you've been hitting it with a local hayseed. Is that why you want to stay, 'cause you're slumming it with one of these hicks?"

"My *mom*? What are you doing talking to my mom?" He had to be lying. She talked to her mom every day, and she hadn't said anything about speaking to Geoff. And there was no way Sheila Fisher would use the words "hitting it with a hayseed."

To her right, she saw Cade's hand tighten into a fist, but she purposely kept her eyes on Geoff. If she dared to even glance at Cade's face, Geoff would know there was something going on between them.

"I've had quite a few interesting chats with your mom lately," he said. "She's always liked me."

"That's because I didn't tell her what a jerk you really are."

He let out an exaggerated sigh. "Come on, this is enough now. We had a little fight. Things got out of hand. You said things. I said things. But I've already apologized. And you've apparently sowed your little wild seeds with some redneck. So now it's time to put this behind us and for you to come home." He reached up to take her arm, wrapping his fingers around her bicep.

"I'm not going anywhere with you." She tried to keep her voice firm, even though she was shaking inside. "I think you need to leave."

He leaned toward her, his brows creasing in a menacing glare as his grip on her arm tightened into a painful squeeze.

"I think the lady just asked you to leave," Cade said, his voice taut with hostility as he took a step forward.

Geoff's grasp loosened, but he didn't let go of her arm. He turned his gaze to Cade as if noticing him for the first time. Nora thought she saw fear for just a second, but he quickly masked it with scorn. "So this is the hick you've been screwing behind my back."

"I'm not doing anything behind your back. We broke up." She tried to pull her arm away, but he wouldn't let go.

He glared at Cade, the two of them locked in some kind of macho stare down, and then he dropped his gaze back to Nora as he bent closer to her. "We're broken up when I say we're broken up."

Cade took another step closer and spoke slowly, as if explaining something to a toddler. "How about *you* take your hand off Nora, and then *I* won't break your nose with my fist?"

Geoff turned his face slowly back to Cade. And laughed. "Break my nose? Are you kidding? Do you have any idea who I am?"

"Yeah, I do. You're the douchebag who is touching my girl and who is about to have his teeth knocked out."

Geoff's head wrenched back. "You lay one finger on me and I'll have you arrested for assault. Then I'll drag your redneck ass through court and sue you for every penny you've got stuffed in your little hayseed mattress."

This time it was Cade's turn to laugh. "That all you got, doc? A little threat? I tell you I'm gonna knock your teeth out and you try to intimidate me with litigation? You're not even going to attempt to fight like a man?" Cade's lips pulled back in a sneer. "Or do you only bully women?"

Geoff jeered back at Nora. "This is the guy you're screwing? A backwoods brawler who uses his brawn instead of his brain? Did he even graduate high school?" He curled his lip in condescension. "I changed my mind. You're not worth it. He can have you." He shoved Nora hard toward Cade.

Which was all the invitation Cade needed to throw a

roundhouse at Geoff's smug chin. His head jerked sideways with the force of Cade's fist, and Geoff took a stumbling step back. He grabbed his jaw and glared at Cade. "You asshole. You're gonna pay for that." He pulled out his phone. "I'm calling the cops."

"No need," a deep voice said from behind Nora. Ethan stepped forward and held up the badge that had been clipped to his belt. "I'm Deputy Rayburn. Something I can help you with?"

"Yeah, I want you to arrest this man." Geoff pointed to Cade. "He just assaulted me."

Ethan turned to Cade, who now stood next to Nora and had his hands pushed into his front pockets. "Cade, did you assault this man?"

Cade shook his head and offered his most innocent shrug. "Nope. I have no idea what he's talking about."

Geoff spat out a huff as he rubbed his jaw. "He just punched me right in the face. All these people saw it." He gestured toward Nora.

All these people? She turned around and was surprised to see Bryn, Elle, and Jillian standing behind her and Brody and Zane flanking Cade's sides. How long had they been there? Her cheeks burned with shame. Had they heard the terrible things Geoff had said about her?

Ethan turned to the group. "Did any of you see Cade assault this man?"

Zane took a step closer to Cade as he shook his head. "I didn't see anything."

"Neither did I," Brody said as he also moved closer.

"Neither did we," Bryn said as the three women formed a protective ring around Nora's back. There were a few other people who stood a bit behind them but none of them stepped forward.

"They're lying!" Spittle flew from Geoff's lips as he pointed at the women. "Those bitches are just sticking up for their friend."

Ethan's shoulders drew back, and he stood even taller. "I think it's time for you to go."

"*Me-e?*" He drew the word out like it was two syllables. Narrowing his eyes, he turned his contempt onto Ethan. "I think it's time for *you* to do your job. And arrest this son of a bitch."

Cade seemed to get calmer as Geoff got more furious. "Now that's not cool to say about my mom."

"Sorry, sir," Ethan said with a shrug. "I can't arrest him if you can't get anyone to corroborate your story. I can't very well take your word over all these other people."

"I saw something." A voice spoke from behind Nora.

"Finally. One person in this godforsaken place who has some sense."

Aunt Sassy strode forward until she was barely a foot in front of Geoff. She had on a fringed denim skirt, white cowboy boots, and a hot-pink fur-trimmed leather jacket. She pushed back the pink cowboy hat she wore and stared straight into Geoff's eyes. "I saw this douchesicle manhandling my friend, Nora. He had his hand around her arm, and it appeared to me that he was threatening her."

Geoff's mouth dropped open. "Are you freaking kidding me? What is wrong with this place?"

Ethan pointed toward the driveway. "Like I said, I think it's time for you to go. Unless Nora wants to press charges against you." He glanced toward Nora.

She shook her head, still dazed by the amount of support she was getting from this community of people.

"Against *me*? This is unbelievable." Geoff pointed a finger threateningly at Nora. "Fine. I'll go. But this isn't over, bitch."

Cade, Zane, and Brody all stepped forward, but Cade was the one who spoke. "Oh, you can be assured that this *is* over, Dr. Aaron. I don't care how many fancy lawyers you have, if you ever speak to or try to contact Nora again, you'll have me to contend with. And redneck justice is a lot harsher than a little punch to the face."

Geoff's face paled as he sputtered, "Screw you. And screw this place. I don't need this shit." He glared at Nora, then twisted around and stomped toward his car, stopping once to yell back, "You might think you're tough, asshole, but I make more money in a year than you'll ever see in your lifetime."

Cade turned to Brody and Zane. "Wow. Did you hear that? That guy makes more money than me? I'm crushed."

"You should be," Brody said. "That was a total burn."

Zane shook his head. "I'm still trying to figure out what 'redneck justice' is?"

Cade chuckled. "I have no idea. It was just the most hick thing I could think of to threaten him with." His face turned serious as he peered down at Nora. "You okay?"

She swallowed as she wrapped her arms around her middle. "I will be." Tightening her arms, she tried to contain the tremble in them. "I just can't believe he showed up here like that."

Elle put an arm around her shoulder. "Seems like once he heard you were happy and involved with someone new, his pride was hurt and he had to come try to claim you again."

"I agree," Aunt Sassy said. "He was just trying to throw his weight around."

"He didn't throw it very far." Nora peered at the group of people clustered around her. "Thank you all. For sticking up for me. I never expected…" Her words trailed off as emotion overtook her.

Elle squeezed her arm. "That's what friends do. And that's what you have here."

She snuck a glance at Cade, who nodded in agreement. "Thank you. It means a lot." She cleared her throat. "Okay, that's enough about me. What do we need to do to help get this placed cleaned up?"

"Don't worry about this," Bryn told her. "We're almost finished. You all go on."

"Oh no. I'm fine," Nora said. "I'm happy to help."

"I know you are. And there will be plenty more to do in the morning. I think you've got other more important things to take care of right now." Bryn nodded toward where Allie was still standing by their table. Luke was with her, his arm protectively wrapped around her shoulder. Her face was pale, and her knuckles were white as she gripped the handle of the knee scooter.

"You're right. But count us in to help in the morning," Nora said over her shoulder as she hurried toward the teenager.

Allie rolled the knee scooter forward to meet her, then flung her arms around Nora's waist. Nora could feel her shoulders trembling. "Are you okay? I was so scared for you. Who was that jerk?"

"Nobody important. Just my stupid ex-boyfriend."

"Did he hurt you?" She gingerly touched the finger-shaped bruises already visible on Nora's arm.

"No. I'm fine, really."

"Is he coming back?" Allie whispered.

"No," Cade said firmly as he wrapped them both in his arms and dropped his chin to the top of his daughter's head. "He is definitely not coming back."

"You were really brave, standing up to that jerk like that," Allie told him.

"I will always stand up to jerks who threaten the people I care about." His hand tightened around Nora's waist. "And I won't let anything happen to either of you."

"I think you should stay with us tonight," Allie told her. "Just in case he comes back. You can have my bed. Or you can sleep in Cade's bed, and he can sleep on the couch. I don't want you to be alone."

It meant a lot that Allie was so concerned for her. She glanced up at Cade.

He nodded. "I think she's right. You should stay with us tonight. I'll take the couch." He let go of the women and shook hands with Luke. "Thanks for staying with Allie during all the ruckus. I saw you over here with her, and I appreciate it."

"Yeah, of course," Luke stammered. "I was glad to. I'll call you tomorrow, Allie." He waved as he backed away.

Cade picked up Nora's jacket from the table and frowned as he handed it to her. "Feels like your jacket is buzzing. I hope it's not that asshole already trying to call you."

Nora pulled her phone from her jacket pocket. "It's not. It's another missed call from my mom. It looks like she's tried to call me several times, and she sent a text that says to call her right away."

"Let's go then," Cade said, gesturing toward the bunkhouse. "You can call her as we head back to the house." He put his arm around Allie and helped guide her scooter around the remaining tables.

Nora tapped the screen as she fell into step behind them. Her mom answered before she'd even gotten the phone to her ear.

"Nora, is that you? Are you okay?" Sheila's voice was shaky and frantic. "I've been so worried."

"I'm fine. What's going on?"

"Oh, honey, I'm so sorry. I'm afraid I did something terrible. I told that jerk Geoff where you are. I swear I didn't mean to."

So her mom *had* told him. "Why were you even talking to him?"

"I'm embarrassed to tell you. I feel like such a fool. I see now that he completely played me. And I fell for it."

"What happened?"

"He showed up at the house with these two gorgeous bouquets of flowers. He said one was for you and one for me and fed me some line about bringing flowers to the two most beautiful women in Denver—well, I see it was a line now. I guess at the time I just thought he was being sweet. Anyway, I invited him in, or he invited himself in, I'm not sure which, and we got to talking, and he just seemed so nice. He noticed my new hairstyle and commented on how pretty I looked and talked about how great it was that I kept myself in such good shape."

Her mom *was* pretty. She was a great cook, but also loved to walk and hike, which was why she still had such a cute figure. But it was a little weird of Geoff to comment on it. He must have really been fishing for info.

"I'm such an idiot for getting suckered in by him. But he's always been so charming and really good to me."

"Oh, I know all about his charms, Mom. Don't beat yourself about it."

"But, honey, I can't believe I fell for it. He just seemed so sorry for the argument you all had. He said he wanted to make amends, then he somehow got it out of me where you are. But something changed once he knew where you were. I can't put my finger on it, just something in his eyes that made me think he might be dangerous. And that he's not really the man he's pretending to be. Nora, I think he's driving up there now. For you."

"He's already been here."

She heard her mom gasp. "Oh no. Are you okay?"

"I'm good. I think the situation could have gone differently if I hadn't been surrounded by friends. I stood up to him and told him to leave. And then when he wouldn't, Cade sort of punched him in the face."

Sheila let out a soft laugh. "Good for him."

CHAPTER 22

"Mom, don't worry. I'm not upset at you. At all. This is all that asshole's fault. Not yours. I love you."

"I love you too."

"I'll call you tomorrow." She clicked off and pushed the phone back into her jacket pocket as they walked up the porch steps.

Cade wrapped an arm around her waist. "She okay?"

Nora nodded, touched by his genuine concern for her mom. She let herself lean into him for just a moment. "Yeah, she is now. Geoff tricked her into telling him where I am, and she was just worried about me."

The puppy raced around their legs as they entered the bunkhouse. Clementine opened her eyes to offer them a passing glance from her perch on the back of the sofa, then closed them again and went back to sleep.

"You get on your pajamas, and I'll let the puppy out," Cade told Allie.

"I'll change into my pajamas too," Nora told them.

"Grab your toothbrush," Cade said as they walked onto the porch. The puppy tumbled down the stairs and ran into the grass. He pulled Nora into a hug. "We're not going to let you out of sleeping over, although this is not exactly how I imagined I'd get you into my bed."

She pressed a kiss to his jaw, then spoke softly next to his ear. "How *did* you imagine getting me into your bed?"

"Which time?" he asked, grinning down at her.

His grin had a way of making her stomach both excited and nervous. Heat surged through her veins. She'd better go inside before everyone still working at the ranch saw her jump

Cade's bones on the front porch. "I'll go change. And I'll get my toothbrush."

His voice was low, slow, and sexy as he drawled, "Let me know if you need any help gettin' out of that dress."

Another wave of heat swept through her, this time her body felt hot enough that she worried her dress might melt right off her. "I can manage." She offered him a coy grin. "This time."

He chuckled, a warm laugh that did nothing to cool her heated skin.

"Be right back," she told him as the puppy scrambled back up the stairs and attacked the toe of his boot.

He leaned against the wall of the bunkhouse. "I'll wait."

"You don't have to."

"I want to." His voice took on a more serious tone this time, and it suddenly felt as if he were talking about something entirely different. "I'm not going anywhere. I'll be right here if you need me."

―――――――――

Nora woke the next morning to the smell of coffee and bacon. She snuggled into the pillow—Cade's pillow—one last time, luxuriating in the feel of being in his bed and the scent of him on the soft flannel pillowcase. Granted, it would have been better if he were in the bed with her, and they were naked, but it still felt pretty dang good.

They'd stayed up late talking the night before, and both had been tempted to sneak him into bed with her. But neither of them wanted to take a chance on waking Allie. She'd done her best to stay up with them but had fallen asleep on Nora's shoulder a little after ten. It had been so sweet watching Cade carry her to bed and tuck her in, as if she were still a toddler instead of a teenager. Nora had tried to help and was sure Cade had gotten a little misty-eyed as Allie had sleepily reached for the stuffed unicorn on her pillow and cuddled it to her side.

Nora stretched and yawned and slipped out of bed. The house seemed quiet as she tiptoed across the hall to the bathroom, but Cade was leaning against the counter studying his phone when she padded into the kitchen a few minutes later.

He looked up when he saw her, and a broad smile creased his face. "Good morning, beautiful."

She had to smile back, couldn't stop the grin if she tried. "Mornin', cowboy."

He reached for her, pulling her close and dipping his head to kiss her lips. The kiss started sweet, then deepened into something more—hunger and need mixed with promise and demand. He tasted like coffee and desire, and she was glad she'd detoured to the bathroom to brush her teeth before coming into the kitchen.

His hand slid under her pajama top, his fingers brushing across her waist, then up her ribs. Her nipples tightened with want, and she moaned against his lips as his palm cupped her breast and teased the pebbled tips.

A thud from Allie's room had them pulling apart.

Nora smoothed the front of her pajama top, then crossed her arms to cover her hardened nipples. "It seems they're demanding a little more of your attention." She grinned sheepishly up at Cade, whose grin was much more in the Big Bad Wolf realm than anywhere close to sheep.

He lowered his voice to that slow drawl that sent shivers of desire rushing down her spine. "How about tonight I sneak into *your* bed and give them the attention they deserve?"

She swallowed. "I think they, and I, will have a hard time waiting until tonight."

His lips turned up in a roguish grin. "They won't be the only thing having a *hard* time."

She playfully swatted his arm as Allie's door opened, and the teenager rolled out. Most of her hair was still in the braid from the night before, but it was just mussed enough to give her that adorable bedhead look as she yawned sleepily. "Morning," she said as the puppy raced out of the room behind her and headed for the door.

"Good morning, Allie Cat," Cade said. "You want some—?"

They all froze as the sound of a gunshot rang through the air.

"What the hell?" Cade said, sprinting toward the door.

Nora and Allie hurried after him. He put his body in front of theirs, motioning for them to stay behind him as he peered cautiously out the door.

Another two shots rang out. Then Zane's voice could be heard yelling, "Get the hell outta here!"

Oh no! Nora's blood ran cold. Had Geoff come back this morning?

"Stay here," Cade told them as he ran outside.

"What's going on?" Allie said, reaching for Nora.

Nora put her arms around the teenager and pulled them away from the door. "I don't know. But your dad won't let anything happen to us." She hugged Allie tightly. "It's gonna be okay."

Several long tense minutes later, Cade was back. His boots pounded the porch steps as he ran back into the house. He pulled them both into his arms. "It's okay. Zane was shooting at the coyote. But I still want you to stay inside."

"At Jack? Why was he shooting at Jack?" Nora asked.

Cade let out his breath. "Because he got into the chicken coop and was killing the chickens."

She gasped. "But why?"

"Because he's a coyote. And coyotes are assholes."

"But we helped him."

"I told you he's not a dog. He's a wild animal. It's in his nature. A coyote isn't going to change just because you do something nice for it."

Nora sunk back onto the sofa. She shook her head, fighting the wave of nausea churning in her stomach. "Did Zane shoot him?"

"No, he was just shooting warning shots. But he took off with at least one of the chickens. The chicken coop's a mess. That's why I want you to stay inside, just until we can get things cleaned up." He lifted the puppy from the floor. "I'll take Scout outside first."

He left with the puppy but was back a few minutes later. The dog raced in after him and ran to Allie. "You guys get some breakfast. I'll be back when it's okay to come out."

Allie wrinkled her nose. "Gross. I'm not eating now."

"I don't feel much like eating either." Nora pushed up from the sofa. "But I do need coffee."

The basket on the front of Allie's scooter rattled as her phone buzzed from inside it. Allie frowned as she checked the message.

"Everything okay?" Cade asked.

"No, everything is *not* okay," she snapped. Whoever had messaged her had caused a massive mood shift. "I woke up to gunshots and dead chickens and being scared to death. And now Aunt Di is messaging me, wanting me to make decisions about mom's funeral and asking if I want to speak during the eulogy thing."

"Anything I can do to help?" he asked.

She glared at him. "Can you bring my mom back?"

His shoulders fell. "No."

"Then I guess not." She yanked the handle of the scooter around, the rubber wheel leaving a mark on the floor as it scraped over it. "I'm going back to bed," she said over her shoulder as she wheeled into her room and slammed the door.

Cade's face was bewildered as he turned to Nora. "What the hell did I do?"

She shook her head. "Nothing. She's a teenager. They're already prone to rampant mood swings, but she's going through a lot right now. Her mom's funeral is tomorrow, and I'm sure she has no idea how to deal with it. You're just the easiest target to take all that frustration out on."

Nora fell even harder for him as he shrugged off his daughter's words.

"I can take it," he said. "I've got thick skin. If snarking at me is what she needs to get her through this, she can snark all day long."

━━━━━━━━

Allie stayed in her room all morning, but Cade was glad to see her outside and standing by the corral fence that afternoon as they worked with the horses.

He'd talked Bryn into taking on a couple of wild mares earlier that summer, and he and Zane had been slowly working to break them. They'd had some interest in them the night before, so they'd brought them back from the pasture, and he and Zane were determined to get them at least green broke by that afternoon. So far, the one Zane had been working with had seemed to be settling down. But the one Cade had been trying to break was still giving him a hard time. She'd already bucked him off twice.

He'd given the mare, and his sore ass, a break while they cleaned out the stalls and spent some time with the other horses. His mind hadn't taken a break though. For the first time in a long time, he let himself dream and imagine what his future could look like. A future with Allie and one that hopefully included Nora too. The fact that he was letting himself hope was a big deal. And frankly, scared the hell out of him. He wasn't a guy who dreamed big or made plans. He was someone who waited for the cards he got dealt, then figured out how to make the most of his hand. Or sometimes just folded and watched other people win.

But this time he felt like he was finally in charge. Like he was dealing the cards and had just picked up a royal flush. He was feeling so optimistic, he'd made a phone call that morning to Miss Pearl's daughter to inquire about her plans for Crooked Creek Ranch.

"You ready to get after it again with those mares?" Zane hollered as he headed toward the corral.

"Yep." Cade spread another armful of straw into the stable, then shut the gate and followed Zane. He couldn't help the smile that spread across his face when he spotted Allie by the fence.

She didn't return his smile. Her face was still pinched when he walked over. "Where's Nora?" she asked.

"She ran into town to meet someone for a physical therapy session," he told her. "She'll be back in a little bit. Something I can do to help?"

She wrinkled her nose, then shook her head as she crossed her arms over her chest. "No," she said then let out a weary sigh as if she carried the weight of the world on her thin shoulders.

"We're working on breaking these wild horses," he told her, hoping to get her mind on something else. "You can stick around and watch if you want."

She took a step closer to the fence and peered through the slats. "What do you mean by breaking? That sounds mean. Are you hurting them?"

"No. Course not. Breaking them just means teaching them to accept a saddle and the weight of a rider. It's just how we train them so they can be ridden."

"Why do you have to train them if they're wild?"

"That's a good question. Colorado has an act that protects and manages our wild horse population. The Bureau of Land Management manages the wild horse and burro population and they actually have places where people can go to view them in specific herd management areas. But oftentimes, the population expands beyond what the land can support, so the BLM rounds them up and makes them available for adoption. These two were adopted but then rejected, so I convinced Bryn to rescue them, figuring we could take them on, get them trained, then re-adopted by someone who really wants them. There's an outfit down by Gunnison that's interested in them if we can get them green broke."

"Green broke? Like make them good for the environment?"

Cade chuckled. "No, green broke just means a horse who's recently learned to be under saddle or to accept a rider on his back. Or in this case, *her* back. I've been working with that brown mare for a few weeks now, getting her used to the halter and the blanket and having a saddle on her. She does okay until I actually get in the saddle, then that seems to kind of piss her off. But I think I'm winning her over." He nudged her with his elbow. "I like that you ask questions. Stick with me, kid. I'm going to teach you how to cowboy yet."

She shrugged, but he thought he caught a hint of a smile playing at the corners of her lips before her mouth settled back into a frown.

Zane yelled for him again, and he held a hand up to Allie. "I gotta go, but I'll come back and check on you in a bit, okay?"

Allie shrugged again, which today felt like the closest he was going to get to an okay. But she was still standing there as he approached the horse and took the side of her halter in his hand. He patted her neck and spoke soothing words into her ear. "All right now, girl. We're gonna try this again. And this time, my girl is watching, so I'd really appreciate it if you didn't toss me on my ass."

He slowly reached for the saddle horn and carefully tucked his foot into the stirrup. "Whoa there," he said, as the mare stamped her front feet and tried to pull away. "It's okay. We're going to do this nice and slow." He pushed himself up so he was standing in the stirrup, holding that position for a few seconds before slowly swinging his leg over her rump and easing into the saddle.

The horse whinnied and took a few steps backward, then huffed and seemed to settle down a little. He looked over at Allie and gave her a thumbs-up. Clicking his tongue, he gave the horse a slight nudge with his heel to her flank, and she leapt forward, spinning and bucking as she tried to eject him from the saddle.

He tightened the reins in his hand, tensing his muscles as his neck whipped back from the jolt. Tightening his legs around the belly of the beast beneath him, he held on, knowing if he let up the slack for even a second, he'd lose the thin grip of control he had over the horse. Kicking her legs out behind her, she used the force of her body to try to throw him off her back.

Thanks to his overconfidence and showing off a little for Allie, he didn't have as good a hold as he should have. He lost his grip as she kicked and gave another whopping buck that sent his Stetson flying through the air about ten seconds before he followed suit.

He landed on his ass in the dirt, but the horse was still pissed and stamped next to him. He tried to scramble out of her way as she reared back, but her hoof caught him in the side of the forehead and knocked him backward.

His head hit the ground with a hard thud. And everything went black.

CHAPTER 23

CADE BLINKED AND GROANED AS HIS VISION CLEARED. A HAND clapped onto his back and supported his shoulder as he tried to sit up.

"You all right there, brother?" Zane asked, tilting his head to get a better look at Cade's face.

"Yeah, I'm good." He blew out his breath and gingerly touched the side of his head. He could feel a lump had already formed and his fingers had blood on them, but it wasn't bad as it could have been. "She just grazed me with her hoof. I've been kicked a lot harder than that."

"It's bleeding, and you're gonna have one hell of a bruise, but I don't think you need stitches. Brody's on his way over to drop off some dewormer. He can take a look at it and probably patch you up with a couple of butterfly strips. Unless you want to go into town and try to see a doctor who works on people instead of animals."

Cade shook his head, then grunted at the pain. "Nah. Brody can patch me up just as well as any fancy doctor. What's good enough for my horse is good enough for me. I'll be fine, soon as I catch my breath." Zane stood and held out his hand. Cade took it and pulled himself to his feet. He looked across the corral and saw Allie, her face pale and her knuckles white as she gripped the fence. "Let me tell Allie I'm okay, then I'll take another run at her."

"You sure?" He tilted his head toward the mare who was tied to the side of the corral. Her eyes held a wild look to them, and she let out a huff as she stamped her feet. "She still seems pretty mad at you."

"Course I'm sure. You know if I don't get right back on her, we'll lose all our progress." He lifted his shoulder in an offhand shrug. "Besides, I'm used to dealing with pissed off females, so there's a pretty long line that horse will need to get into if she thinks she's gonna get to me."

"Still, you took a pretty good hit to your noggin."

"Haven't you figured out by now that I've got a hard head?" He winced as he knocked the side of his temple with his knuckles. "And I've never been accused of making smart decisions. Especially when it comes to females."

Zane chuckled. "Offer still stands. I can do it."

"Nah, I started it. I need to finish. And I almost had her. I just lost my focus for a sec. Give me one more ride, and I think she'll get it."

His hat was lying in the dirt several feet away, and he picked it up as he walked toward Allie. Her face still lacked color, and her lips trembled slightly as she spoke. "You're bleeding."

He brushed at his head with the back of his hand, then wiped the blood on his jeans. "It's not bad. I'm okay."

"I saw her kick you and then you were lying so still, I thought…I thought you were…"

"Oh, honey," he said, reaching through the rungs of the fence to take her hand.

She pulled it away and wrapped her arms around her stomach.

"I'm okay, Allie. Really. I'm fine."

"You don't look fine."

He pointed to his head. He hadn't seen it, but it couldn't be that bad. "This is nothin'. Brody's coming out, and he'll patch me up."

"Don't you think you should put some ice on it?"

"Probably. And I will. In a few minutes. I just need to give that mare one more ride."

"What? You're going to get back on that horse *again*? After she almost just killed you?" Allie's voice rose to a shrill level.

"She didn't almost kill me. She barely nicked me." He gingerly pushed his hat back on his head, careful to avoid the lump. "This is how it works. I need to get back on her to show her I'm the boss."

"Well, I'm not gonna watch." She pushed away from the fence and turned the knee scooter around.

"Allie. I'm fine. And I'll get some ice. I promise."

She turned her back on him and rolled toward the bunkhouse. "I'm going inside. Just leave me alone."

He grabbed the fence rail, something telling him he should go after her. She seemed different than this morning, more upset.

Zane hollered from across the corral. "Cade, you getting back on this horse or not?"

He called her name again. "Allie."

She turned back, her eyes narrowed as she told him, "You'd better go take care of that mare. We all know how important horses are to you."

He clung to the fence, torn between going back to the horse and going after his daughter. But getting back on the horse had to be done *now*. And it would barely take any time. He could make up with Allie after that. Maybe it would be best to give her a few minutes to cool off anyway. "I'll just be a few minutes, then I'll come inside. We can get a snack or something."

"Don't bother." She pushed harder on the scooter as if she couldn't get away from him fast enough.

He watched her for another second, then let go of the fence with a sigh and headed back to the horse.

A few minutes turned into over an hour as Cade finally got the horse to settle with him in the saddle and then let Brody patch up his head. The vet had agreed he hadn't needed stitches. Instead, he'd cleaned the wound, gooped it up with some antibacterial, and closed it with a couple of butterfly bandages.

"Thanks, Doc," Cade told him. "What do I owe you for the house call?"

Brody offered him a Cheshire cat–type grin. "Let's see, I used two Steri-Strips, some disinfectant, and a good bit of antibacterial. That'll cost you three hours of babysitting. Which works perfectly, since Elle has been bugging me about taking her out on a date night. How about I drop Mandy off at your place next Friday night?"

Cade chuckled. "Works for me. I'm sure Allie would love it. But if you don't want your daughter to tear off your head or my freshly bandaged one, let's not call it babysitting."

"Good point." He snapped his medical bag shut. "You're going to have a heck of a bruise by tomorrow, but you can help lessen the swelling by taking some ibuprofen and giving it a little more ice."

"I'll do it now." He pushed to his feet. "I was gonna head back to the house to check on Allie anyway." He grabbed his hat and was walking out of the barn when he saw Diana's Subaru turn into the driveway. What the heck was she doing here?

Dust flew behind her as sped up to the house and gravel flew as she braked to a stop. She got out of the car and slammed the door before rounding on him. "What did you do?"

He reared back. "Me? I didn't do anything." He pointed to his head. How had she already heard about his injury? "You mean this? It's nothing."

She squinted at his bandage, then dismissed it with a shake of her head. "I'm not talking about your stupid thick head. I'm asking you what you did to Allie."

"Allie? I didn't do anything to her." He rubbed a hand across the back of his neck, the pain in his headache getting worse. "I'm confused. Why are you here?"

"Allie called me. She was crying and asked me to come get her and take her back to Denver."

Crying? "I don't know what you're talking about. She's been having a bit of a rough day today, but I thought it was because of the funeral. Honestly, I'm at a loss here."

"Whatever it was, she was angry enough to call me to come get her." She planted a hand on her hip, her head angled in a smug tilt. "She said she wants to come back to live with me."

"To *live* with you?" He reached out to steady his hand against the side of the barn as his knees threatened to buckle. What was going on? He knew Allie was upset, but he didn't think she wanted to leave. "I think you must have misunderstood her."

"I don't think so. She was pretty clear on the phone. And I'm here now so I'm taking her home with me."

He swallowed as he tried to think. His head pounded with the effort. He was prepared to fight for Allie, but he wasn't sure this was the best time to start the battle. The funeral was tomorrow anyway, so it wouldn't hurt to have Allie go with her aunt. And maybe she would cool down. He held up his hand. "Give me a minute to talk to her, would you?"

"Why should I? You're obviously why she's upset in the first place. I don't want you to make it worse."

"Diana. We've been doing fine together. Great, in fact. I don't want to upset her. I just want to talk to her, to find out what's going on."

Diana checked her watch. "Fine. You have five minutes. Then I'm coming in and getting her."

He dusted off his jeans as he strode into the bunkhouse. Pausing outside her room, he was surprised to feel his hands shaking. He could face down a wild bucking horse, but this ninety-pound teenage girl was bringing him to his knees. Taking a deep breath, he forced his feet to keep moving.

Her room looked like a tornado had hit it, the blankets on the bed in disarray and her suitcase spread open across it. The boxes and tubs they'd used to bring her things from Denver were stacked on the floor. The closet door was open, and the hangers were empty.

Cade swallowed. She really *was* leaving.

Scout lay curled on the pillow, her chin resting across the back of the stuffed unicorn as her eyes tracked Allie's movements. She looked up when she saw Cade, and her tail beat a happy rhythm as it wagged against the pillow.

He leaned against the doorjamb. "Hey, kid."

Allie's concentration was on filling her suitcase with her clothes, and she jumped when he spoke. She looked up at him, her mouth set in a tight line and tearstains on her cheeks.

Diana was right—she had been crying. His heart felt as if it had been kicked by that horse instead of his head. But he was also pissed at himself for not coming inside sooner, for not recognizing the signs that she was really upset. He took a step forward, but Allie backed away. "Allie. What is going on? Did you call Diana and ask her to come get you?"

"Yes." Her answer was one curt word.

"Why?"

For just a second, he thought he saw a flash of hurt in her eyes, but then she pushed her shoulders back and glared at him. "Because I don't want to stay here anymore. I can't."

"I don't get it. I thought we were doing okay, you and me."

"You thought wrong." She yanked a dresser drawer open and threw a pair of jeans toward her suitcase. They missed the bed and fell to the floor.

Cade reached down and picked them up. He folded them carefully, then laid them on the stack of clothes in her suitcase. His throat ached at the thought of her leaving. "But why? Was it something I said? Something I did?"

She shrugged, a gesture he was beginning to loathe. "It's everything," she muttered.

"Could you be a little a more specific? Because I don't get what the hell is happening. I thought things were pretty good. I thought *you* were doing pretty good."

She planted a hand on her hip and stared at him, her eyes hard and full of anger. "How would you even know? You've been my dad for like one week."

Her words hit him like a kick to the gut. What she said was true. "Okay. I deserve that. But I'm trying to figure it out. I've been doing the best I can."

"It's not enough." She turned back to the desk, where one of the photo albums he'd brought from Denver was spread open, the page filled with pictures of a laughing Allie and Amber at one of her birthday parties. A birthday party he'd either missed or hadn't been invited to. Her voice was soft, but Cade heard every word, each one slicing off another piece of his heart. "You're not Mom."

He took a shuddering breath, trying to figure out what to say, how to tell her how he felt. "I know. But things are different now."

She slammed the photo album closed and shoved it into one of the boxes. "*Are* they different? Why? Because you bought me some boots and learned how to braid my hair? Being a dad is about sticking around and being there when I need you. You haven't been there for me for the past nine years. Why should I start counting on you now?"

"Because *I'm* different now too. And I'm here."

"Only because you got stuck with me. If Mom hadn't died, would you even be paying attention to me?"

"Yes. I think so. That's part of why I moved here. And why I renovated the bunkhouse, so I could try to spend more time with you."

She laughed. A hard, dry sound. "I don't believe you. You've always put everything else in your life before me. There's no reason to think you'll change now."

"Is that why you're leaving? Because you think I can't change? You have to give me a chance here."

"No. I don't. I've already given you nine years of chances, and you haven't come through yet."

The screen door slammed, and Diana barreled her way into the bunkhouse. She brushed past Cade and gave Allie a hug. "Are you all right?"

Allie nodded, but Diana pushed back the girl's bangs and searched her face, as if looking for some kind of physical damage. Thankfully, the bruising around her eyes and forehead had mostly faded to a dull gray and yellow.

Cade felt another sickening blow to his chest. "I didn't hurt her, Di. I never. I couldn't."

Diana jerked her head back to glare at him. "Don't kid yourself. You've hurt her plenty." She pointed to the suitcase. "Is this ready to go?"

Allie nodded again. Her shoulders sagged as her eyes filled with tears again.

"I'll take this out then." Diana's movements were quick and efficient as she tossed in Allie's jacket and slammed the suitcase shut. She'd always been the organized one, decisive and competent. The opposite of her sister's flighty, impulsive personality. Amber could be fun and crazy but also spontaneous, and at times reckless, in her decisions to move her and Allie around, always chasing another dream, another job, or another man.

Diana wrenched the zipper around the case, the sound almost deafening in the otherwise silent room. She shifted one of the boxes onto her hip and pulled the suitcase behind her as she pushed Cade out of the doorway. "Can you at least carry those boxes for her?"

No. If he didn't take the boxes, he might have time to persuade Allie to stay. But Allie was already swinging her backpack onto her shoulder.

"Wait, I'm coming with you," Allie said, rolling the scooter after her aunt.

Cade picked up the remaining boxes, his heart breaking again as he saw she'd left the stuffed unicorn behind.

The puppy jumped off the bed and scrambled after them.

Allie's voice broke as she turned and held her hand out toward the dog. "You can't come with us. You have to stay here."

Cade jerked his head back. Now he knew something was seriously wrong. "You're not taking Scout?"

"She can't," Diana said over her shoulder as she barreled through the front door. "The apartment building doesn't allow pets."

The teenager bent and tears streamed down her cheeks as she stroked the puppy's head. "You're a good girl, Scout. You can go back to your mom now."

The puppy whined and tried to climb up her leg, but Allie stood and gently pushed the little dog away.

"Allie…" he tried again.

But this time she held her hand up to him. "I can't. I'm not a country girl. Or a cowboy. Or whatever you've been trying to turn me into. I'm not like you." She pushed out the screen door and let it slam behind her.

Cade winced at the sound as if she were also slamming the door on her relationship with him. Scout whined and scratched at the door. "I know the feeling, girl," he told the desolate little dog as he scooped her up in his hand and cuddled her to his chest.

Diana already had Allie's things loaded into the hatchback of her Subaru by the time Cade put the puppy back in Allie's room and made it outside. Diana marched toward him, taking the boxes he held and shoving them into the back with the other things.

Nora's car turned into the driveway and she parked next to the Subaru. Cade wondered if his face held the same bewildered expression hers did as she got out of the car. "What's going on? I thought we were bringing Allie down tomorrow."

He pointed to where his daughter was trying to load the knee scooter into the car. He took a step forward to help, but Diana glared at him and did the task herself. "Ask Allie. Apparently she called Diana to come get her. She's leaving. For good."

"For good?" Nora's voice sounded stricken. She hurried toward Allie and folded the teenager into a hug. "Are you all right, honey? Did something happen?"

Allie tightened her arms around Nora's waist, then pushed herself away and slid into the passenger seat.

Cade clamped his teeth together, biting them as hard as he could in an effort to hold it together. Apparently he didn't even rate a hug goodbye.

Diana slammed the back door, then rounded on him. "I don't know what you did to make her so upset, but I'm going to find out. I never should have trusted her with you. You couldn't protect her when she was little, and you've always been worthless as a dad. You've never been there for her. You missed birthday parties and school programs. We don't even refer to you as her dad. We just call you SD because that's all you've ever been—her sperm donor."

His head whipped back as if he'd taken a brick to the face. He couldn't breathe. It was taking all his concentration to keep his legs steady. *Sperm donor?* That's all he was to his daughter?

Allie had her chin buried in her chest but her shoulders shook as she sobbed. Having gotten in the last vicious word, Diana got into the car, slamming the door before starting the engine and taking off.

Nora stood frozen in place, her mouth slack as she slowly shifted her gaze from the car to Cade. "What happened?"

"I have no freaking idea." He shook his head slowly, the pain in his temple now radiating out through his whole skull. "She was watching Zane and me break those wild horses, and she got mad that I was going to get back on one after she'd bucked me off and scraped me with her hoof." He pointed to the butterfly sutures. "But she just went back to the house. She didn't say she wanted to leave. I should have followed her, but I was in the middle of the thing with the horse, then Brody showed up and patched up my head. I thought I was giving her a chance to cool down. I didn't even know she'd called her aunt until Diana pulled into the drive-way ten minutes ago."

"Are you sure she said she was leaving for good?"

"Oh yeah. She packed up all her shit and told me off. She's really gone."

"Oh, Cade," Nora whispered as she took a step toward him.

He held his hand up. "Don't." He was barely holding it together. If Nora so much as touched him, he was afraid he'd shatter into a million pieces. Or break down sobbing worse than Allie. And he didn't want to do either of those things.

He forced his feet to move and took a stumbling step back. "I've got some work to do in the garage. Bryn said that old tractor has been acting up again."

The look of hurt on her face almost had him changing direction and going to her. But he couldn't do it. His emotions were too raw. He needed a minute to be alone, to collect himself, to try to think straight and figure out what to do.

"I'll make some iced tea," Nora called to him.

He didn't turn around, just kept walking toward the rundown garage that sat behind Bryn's farmhouse. A rush of hot, musty air hit him as he slid back the large bay door. A long workbench ran the length of the far wall and farm tools and implements crowded the opposite side. The ancient tractor sat in the middle. Zane was the one who usually worked on it, he was almost as good with engines as he was with horses, but Cade needed something to do with his hands—a task that would take his mind off the sting of Diana's hurtful accusations.

He stomped to the workbench, sweat already forming on his brow from the heat of the garage. He blew out his breath and tried to focus. He assembled various-sized wrenches and sockets, some pliers, and a hammer on the counter.

His cell phone buzzed, and he yanked it from his pocket, hoping it was Allie. Maybe she'd changed her mind. He didn't recognize the number, but maybe she was calling from Diana's phone. He tapped the screen and pressed the phone to his ear. "Hello?"

"It's about time," a voice said. Cade hadn't spoken to Amber's dad in over five years, but he easily recognized the gravelly voice earned from a pack a day habit.

"I'm not really in the mood, Ed."

"Oh, sorry. Did I catch you at a bad time?" the other man asked in a mockingly sweet tone. "Tough shit. My daughter's dead and yours is still alive so I can damn well guarantee I'm in a worse mood than you are."

Cade inhaled a deep breath and tried to unclench his teeth. The man had a point. He eased back on his tone. "I'm real sorry about Amber."

Ed huffed, the sound dry as a husk. "I bet you are."

"What do you want, Ed?"

"I wanted to tell you to stay away from the funeral tomorrow. Nobody wants you there."

Cade sighed. So that's what this was about. "I don't think that's your call to make. If I show up, it will be for Allie. She's still my daughter, you know."

"Since when have you even cared about that? Oh, wait..." he said before Cade had a chance to answer. "Since she turned into your cash ticket."

"That's bullshit."

"Is it? We all know you've ignored her for most of her life, haven't even tried to get in touch with her. Until now, when there's a big life insurance policy at stake. Seems pretty convenient."

"I didn't even know about the life insurance until a few days ago."

"Yeah, sure you didn't. Doesn't matter anyway—we're not going to let you keep it or Allie."

"I don't think you have a say in the matter. Are you forgetting that I'm her father?"

Ed laughed again but his laugh turned into a hacking cough. "You haven't been her father in years. And even when you lived with them, you were a sorry excuse for a husband and a father. Amber told us about the abuse. That's not going to look good for you if you make us take this to court."

Cade reeled back as if he'd been slapped. "Abuse? What the hell are you talking about? I never abused Amber or Allie."

"Course you'd say that. Now. But you expect me to believe you over my own daughter? And who do you think a judge would believe? Sure as hell not the guy who hasn't given a shit about his daughter for years. Not until there's a big wad of cash involved."

The blood rushed to his ears. Cade couldn't believe what he was hearing. "You listen to me, Ed, and you listen good. I don't give one damn shit about the money. You and Diana can keep it for all I care. You can both shove it up your collective asses. But I do care about Allie. I might not have been there as much as I should have in the past, but I'm here now. I never laid a hand on her or Amber. But Allie is *my* daughter and if you think you're going to take her away or try to keep her from me, you better be prepared for the fight of your old, miserable life."

"Good luck with that." Ed chuckled again, a derisive laugh. "We'll see you in court, pal. But I don't want to see your ugly mug before then. You'd better not show your face at the funeral tomorrow." He clicked off before Cade had a chance to reply.

CHAPTER 24

Nora heard the last of Cade's call as she walked into the barn. He must not have seen her yet because he slumped down onto the weathered bench against the wall and closed his eyes as he leaned his head back.

"You okay?" she asked, taking a tentative step toward him. She'd never seen him look so defeated.

He opened his eyes but seemed to stare right through her. "I just got hung up on by Amber's dad," he said, pushing his phone back into his pocket. "He told me not to come to the funeral tomorrow and that they're going to fight me for custody of Allie."

Nora was stunned. "They can't do that. You're her father."

"Not a very good one. And apparently that's up for debate. Didn't you hear Diana? All I am to Allie is her sperm donor."

"She doesn't really think that."

"Yeah, she does. How many times has she called me SD? And I told her I thought maybe it stood for Super Dad. I'm such an idiot."

"You're not an idiot. This is just a temporary setback. You just need to get back on that horse and try again." She offered him a small encouraging smile, but his expression remained somber.

"Not this time."

"What do you mean? Aren't you going to go after her?"

"What's the use? She's better off without me." He bent forward and cradled his head in his hands. He looked broken, and it was tearing Nora's heart out.

"That's crazy. You've spent all this time trying to teach us how to cowboy. Now it's your turn to cowboy up and go get your daughter."

He shook his head. "Don't you get it? She doesn't *want* to be a cowboy. And she doesn't want me. I knew this would happen. I've been pretending I knew what I was doing. Like I finally understood how to be a parent. But I knew she'd eventually see me for the shit dad I am."

"I don't get it. You don't sound like the man I thought you were."

He lifted his head to look at her, the pain in his eyes almost shattering her. "That's because I'm not. You keep trying to see something in me that it isn't there, like with that stupid coyote. But I'm not someone you can count on, Nora. So you might as well leave too."

She took a step back, his words slicing through her. "Leave?"

The hurt in his eyes shifted to something harder, as if his defensive walls had just raised back up and slammed into place. "Yeah, leave. Go home. Allie's gone. There's nothing left for you here."

She reached behind her, gripping the side of the workbench for support, as she fought to take a breath. She'd done it again, jumped in with both feet and gotten involved with a man she barely knew. Although she did feel like she knew him. Like her heart knew him. So she'd given it freely to Cade, believing he'd take care of it.

But now she didn't know what to believe. He'd acted like they had something real and now he wanted her to leave? Just. Like. Geoff.

How could she have fallen for this again? She'd thought Cade was different. That they really had something. But once again she was wrong.

Apparently, Cade really was like that coyote. She'd seen them both as wounded and hurt and had extended an offer of friendship, but the animal had shown just that morning that in the end, he was still a coyote.

Her chest ached as she tried to make sense of what was happening. Cade had been trying to change. She knew that. She'd seen it. But what if he couldn't change? What if he was right, and she was just trying to see something in him that wasn't really there?

Cade pushed up from the bench, straightening his back as he huffed out a breath. "I'm done. I've been bending over backward trying to prove I've changed, that I can be a better man. But apparently I'm never going to change. So you'd better go too. Get out now. I can't be trusted to stick around so you should leave before I leave you."

She reached out a hand to touch his shoulder as he strode by her, but then pulled it back.

"I'm going for a ride," he said without turning around.

"Cade," she whispered, but he was already halfway to the barn.

She sagged against the garage door as she watched him walk away. *Please come back.* She pressed her fingers to her mouth, holding back the tears as she prayed for him to turn around and ask her to stay. To be the man she knew he could be. To prove that he had changed and that he wanted a life with her *and* his daughter in it.

But he didn't turn around. He kept walking. Which told her all she needed to know.

Once again, she'd blindly stumbled forward, throwing herself into a situation she thought was one thing but turned out to be another. She'd thought she and Cade really had something, that his feelings for her were real, and that they had been falling in love. But apparently, she was the only one who had been falling, and now she was holding out her hands, scraping them against the sidewalk, tearing up her heart as she fell on her face.

The barn door slammed as Cade disappeared inside. She turned toward the bunkhouse, the place she'd been calling home, and wanted to cry at the sight of the stupid tray of iced tea and cookies she'd set out on the porch. How had everything fallen apart so quickly?

A few hours ago, she'd thought she'd had everything—a place to call home and a chance at love and having a real family.

Now she was back where she started, brokenhearted and retreating to her mom's basement again.

Cade dug his heels into the horse's side, spurring the animal to go faster as they galloped across the pastures. Leaning forward, he drove himself and Gypsy to push harder, as if he could outrun all the pain and heartbreak of the last hour.

It was hard enough to accept that Allie had left him. Now he'd lost Nora too. And it was his own damn fault. He'd pushed her away.

He'd been falling for her—correction. Had already fallen for her. And he had it bad. But it would never work. He wasn't the kind of guy who could be counted on. Hadn't Amber told him that enough times?

But Nora isn't anything like Amber.

Maybe she really did see something in him. He hadn't even given her a chance to say anything. He'd just told her to leave and walked away.

He pulled on the reins, turning the horse around. Maybe there was still a chance they could talk things out. He'd told her to go, but what if she'd stayed and wanted to help him get Allie back? What if she hadn't given up on him too and was still waiting for him back at home?

Home? That was something he never believed he'd get the chance to have.

But maybe, with Allie and Nora…

Except he was too late. His battered heart shattered again as he galloped back into the ranch and saw Nora's car was already gone.

The traffic was light on the drive down the pass the next morning, but Cade still felt irritable and grumpy. His head hurt and his eyes were gritty from lack of sleep. He and the puppy had been up most of the night—both of them restless and missing Allie. Scout had whined on and off for several hours before finally crashing on the pillow next to him. He understood the feeling. He'd felt like crying too.

Once the puppy wore herself out, then the bunkhouse had been *too* quiet—the silence emphasizing the fact that Allie and Nora were both gone. Sleep had eluded him as his mind raced with all the things he should have said and done the day before and all the things he was going to try to do today.

All the tangled thoughts in his head came down to one focus. He loved two women, and if he wanted them in his life, he was going to have to do what Nora said—get back on that horse and try again. He woke up with a determination and resolve that had him rushing through his morning chores, anxious to get showered and on the road.

He was going after Allie. And Nora. But he needed to focus on Allie first. He knew the funeral today would be tearing her up, and he hated the thought of her hurting.

He glanced down at the puppy who lay curled in the seat next to him, her head on his lap, and hoped seeing Scout would bring her a little joy. He hadn't given much thought as to what he'd do with her when he got there—he hadn't really been thinking at all. He'd just been acting.

He had thrown in a little puppy crate of Bryn's, but he didn't really want to leave her in the truck the whole time. He'd called his cousin on the way down the mountain and after a few minutes of discussion, it was agreed that Milo and Mandy could skip the service and puppy-sit.

He told her he might be late, but Bryn assured him the kids could wait in the vestibule until he got there.

There was a scattering of cars in the church parking lot as he pulled in, but he didn't see any people. He'd purposely arrived just as the service would be starting so he could avoid running into

Amber's family. Not that he was afraid of them. He didn't give a rat's ass about Ed's threats or his warnings to stay away from the funeral. He just didn't want to cause a scene before the service.

He didn't want to cause any more pain or discomfort for Allie—today was going to be hard enough on her. Which was why he knew he had to come. The first step to showing Allie he had changed and that he'd be there for her was to show up. And despite the events of the day before, wild horses couldn't keep him away. *No pun intended*, he thought ruefully.

He eased the puppy off his lap and brushed the dog hair from his pants. The church door opened, and Mandy and Milo came out and ran toward him.

"You're just in time," Milo said. "It's about to start."

"Thanks for doing this," he told the kids. "I didn't want to leave Scout in the truck by herself."

Mandy had already climbed into the cab of the truck and had the still-sleeping puppy curled in her lap. "Don't worry about us," she assured him. "This is easy. And I doubt the service will even last an hour."

"Her dish is on the floor, and there's a bottle of water in the seat. You might want to give her some when she wakes up. And you can always come get me if you need me."

"We got this," Milo said, pushing him toward the building. "Now get in there before you miss it."

Cade waited until he heard the organ music, then slipped into the back of the church. His boot steps were silent on the thick carpet as he entered the sanctuary and eased into the last pew.

It had been a while since he'd been in a church, and he took it as a good sign that he didn't burst into flames as he crossed the threshold. He felt guilty that it had been so long, and he hated that Amber's funeral was what had brought him back.

It felt the same though. The plush red velvet cushions on the pews, the stained-glass window above the choir loft, the little pencils and offering envelopes tucked neatly next to the Bibles in the pew pocket, and the swell in his chest as the organist reached a crescendo in the hymn she was playing. The smell of roses filled the air, along with the faint lemon scent of wood polish.

A few bouquets of flowers decorated the front altar. Cade spotted the plant he and Nora had ordered and had delivered to the church. It had been Nora's idea. He would never have thought of it. But he was pleased to see their contribution, even if the thought of the little card reading both their names together had emotion choking his throat.

That wasn't the only thing choking him up. There was also the sight of the silver urn surrounded by a modest but elegant spray of white roses on the table in the center of the altar. Even from his spot in the back, he could clearly see the photo sitting next to the urn of a smiling Amber. They'd had their differences, but he would have never wished this on her.

He was surprised to see such a small gathering of people at the front of the church. Although Amber didn't have much family. Ed, Diana, and Allie were in the front row, and he recognized a couple of her cousins and their families sitting behind them. A handful of people he didn't recognize filled the rest of the rows on that side.

Allie looked so small in the long pew, her shoulders bent forward and her chin almost touching her chest. She wore a simple black dress and had switched out the pink splint she had on the day before for a dark-colored one. Her eyes were red and swollen, and her hair was pulled back into a tight braid down the back of her head. Diana must've done it because it was the opposite of how Allie liked her hair. She was always harping on Cade about how she liked her braids and ponytails looser, so they didn't give her a headache.

His chest burned at the thought that he finally felt like he knew his daughter. Or at least knew her well enough to know how she liked to wear her hair. And that she preferred honey with a peanut butter sandwich instead of jelly, but if there was only jelly, grape was her favorite. He now knew that she liked cozy socks and blue nail polish and dangly earrings and purple pens and anything related to the world of Harry Potter. He knew she preferred the outer edge of the cinnamon roll over the gooey center, poured about a gallon of syrup on every pancake, and hated mayonnaise.

They hadn't been together long but they'd learned so much about each other in the last few weeks. They'd even laughed and had fun together. They were finally building a real relationship. And he didn't want to give that up.

Just like he didn't want to give up the place he'd finally found—for both of them and, hopefully, Nora too in Creedence. He was touched to see the pews on the other side of the church filled with their new Creedence family. Bryn and Zane sat in one row with Aunt Sassy and Doc Hunter next to them. Nora sat solemnly in the pew behind them, squeezed between Jillian on one side and Elle and Brody on the other.

He stared at the back of Nora's head, willing her to turn around. He caught her profile as she turned to whisper something to Elle, and a queasiness fluttered in his empty stomach.

Bending his head, he prayed that he hadn't lost the daughter he was just getting back or the woman he was just beginning to love. He prayed for God to give him the right words to say to show them both he had changed. And he prayed he would have the strength to stay and fight for them, even if they both pushed him away.

He looked up to see Allie had turned in her seat and spotted him. He raised his hand in a small wave. She didn't wave back, but the hint of a sad smile turned the edges of her lips.

———

Just as Mandy had predicted, the service lasted just under an hour. Cade slipped out as the minister was giving the benediction. He checked on the kids and the puppy first—they were doing fine. Scout had woken up, and they'd given her water and been running around with her in the grass.

They were going to do a small reception in the church basement after the service, so he knew it could be a while before Allie was finished. After letting them play a bit more, he sent the kids back in and put the tuckered-out puppy in the crate. He'd parked in the shade under a tree and rolled the windows down, figuring she'd be okay on her own for a little bit.

Keeping the truck in sight, he walked back to the church and settled his back against the wall, determined to wait for his daughter.

The reception didn't last long. Several of the parishioners left right after the service and others must have given their condolences, then left soon after. If he knew Bryn and her bunch, they were probably clearing plates or in the kitchen cleaning up.

The front doors of the church hadn't moved in the last fifteen minutes. Cade was surprised when one of them swung open and Allie wheeled out.

She looked around, then turned the knee scooter when she spotted him and took a few rolling steps forward. "Grandpa said he told you not to come."

Cade shrugged. Not the greeting he was hoping for, but at least she was talking to him. "Regardless of what he may think, your grandfather's not in charge of me. So I don't care what he says. But I do care about you. How you holding up?"

This time it was her turn to shrug. "Not great. This sucks."

"Yeah, it does. I'm sorry, kid."

"I know. That's what everyone says."

A woman in a gray coat hurried back from the parking lot and up the steps as if she'd forgotten something. She yanked open the door and rushed through, heedless to them standing there.

Allie took a step back to let her pass. As the door closed, the back wheel of the knee scooter teetered on the edge of the top step, then fell over. Allie tried to overcorrect but lost her balance as the momentum of the knee scooter propelled her backwards. Her arm pinwheeled as she fell backward.

Cade saw the whole thing happen as if in slow motion. And it was like she was four years old again and falling down the stairs.

But this time, he *was* paying attention. He leapt forward, knocking the scooter out of the way as he slid onto the stairs as if he were a runner sliding into home base. But instead of earning the run, he reached out and caught Allie as she fell into his outstretched arms.

Hugging her to him, he pressed his lips to her forehead, kissing the scar that had been created the last time she fell. "I got you. I caught you this time." He pulled back and brushed her bangs away from her forehead. "I didn't catch you before."

"I know," she said. "Mom said that's why you left. Because I didn't mind you and stay in the living room where you told me to. And then I fell down the stairs and got hurt." She stared down at her lap. "I know it was my fault you left."

"What? No. It was *my* fault. I wasn't paying attention, and you got hurt." *What kind of bullshit had Amber been feeding her?*

"But then Mom said you stayed away because I was too much trouble, and you didn't want the responsibility."

Cade drew his fingers into a fist as anger swirled through him. How could Amber put that on Allie? He shook his head. "No, that wasn't it at all. You were *never* too much trouble. I guess it's sort of true that I didn't want the responsibility, but not how you think. You got hurt because I wasn't a good enough dad. I didn't feel like I was responsible enough to keep you safe." *Amber didn't think so either.* She'd done everything in her power to keep them apart. He wished he could tell Allie that. But he wouldn't talk bad about her mom now that she was gone.

"Mom didn't think so either," Allie said, twisting the frayed ends of the friendship bracelet from Mandy she still wore. "I know she kept me away from you."

He blew out a breath, not sure what to say.

"But you still could've tried harder. You could have done more to try to see me or call me."

He nodded, guilt settling into his stomach like a thick rock. "You're right."

"You always made me feel like everything else was more important than me. Especially the rodeo and all your stupid horses. That's all you talked about when you did see me."

"That's because I didn't know *how* to talk to you. I'd never had a kid before. And I knew I was letting you down, so I got so damn nervous every time I was around you. I didn't know what to say, so I just rambled about my horse and the stupid rodeo."

A flicker of movement had him lifting his head to see Nora standing in the doorway of the church. She stood motionless, one hand pressed to her mouth, the other to her heart. His eye caught hers and a ripple of hope fluttered inside him as their gazes locked. She didn't smile, but he still felt that bone-deep connection they had. Like she knew him better than anyone else ever had.

He wasn't sure how long she'd been there or how much she'd heard. But Allie had just said she felt he put everything else above her, so as much as he wanted to call Nora to them, he needed to keep his focus on his daughter.

"You scared me yesterday," Allie said quietly, fumbling with the clasp on her splint. "When you got bucked off that horse. And then you blacked out. You really scared me."

"I didn't mean to. I was just doing my job."

"I know. But you can't do stuff like that—dangerous stuff. Stuff that could get you killed. That's why I called Aunt Di. Because it freaked me out. I've already lost one parent." Her breath hitched and tears swelled in her eyes. "I can't lose another."

"Oh, honey," he said, pulling her close and hugging her to his chest. "Nothing's going to happen to me. Listen, I'm so damn sorry about your mom. I would do anything to bring her back for you.

But I can't. What I can do is be there for you. I can be your dad. Finally. If you'll let me. I know I haven't been much of one the past several years, but I want to change. I want to be there for you. To help you with your homework and to teach you how to ride that book-loving horse. I want us to be a real family." He smiled down at her, trying to convey his feelings.

He swallowed, emotion burning his throat as he waited for her reply.

Allie tilted her face up to look at him. "Me too. But not just us. Nora too. For the last week and a half, you and me and Nora have practically been inseparable. The three of us have always been together, laughing and helping each other—like we're already kind of a family. But today all three of us were apart. It felt bad. You guys weren't even sitting together. I *know* I was miserable. And you and Nora both looked awful too. It just seems to me that the three of us do a heck of a lot better when we're together than when we're apart."

"I agree." He looked up, the smile already on his face, ready to call Nora over to them. But his smile fell.

She was gone.

CHAPTER 25

CADE'S HEART SANK. *WHY WOULD SHE LEAVE?*

He let out a sigh as he peered down at his daughter. "I think I messed all that up. After you left yesterday, I was pretty down in the dumps, and I said some stuff to Nora that I wish I could take back."

"Like what?"

"Like that she was better off without me, and she should just leave too."

Allie's eyes widened, then she slugged Cade in the arm. "You dummy. Why did you say that?"

"Because I'm an idiot."

"Agreed. So did Nora leave?"

He nodded, the heaviness of her actions weighing down his chest.

"You *are* an idiot." Allie accompanied her statement with one of her eye rolls. "But she still showed up here today, so she must still care about us. Which means it's not too late." She poked a finger into his chest. "You need to fix this."

"It's not that simple."

"Yes it is. Unless you don't *want* to fix it."

"I do. But I don't know if Nora does." He rubbed his hand over her good shoulder. "Besides, you're my biggest priority right now. You and me and figuring out how we can be a family."

"But I already told you, Nora *is* part of our family. We're a team. And I already love her. Don't you?"

He nodded as he tried to find his voice. "Yeah. I do."

"Then you need to tell her."

"Okay, okay. But first, there's something else I have to tell you."

"What?"

"There's some money, I guess. For some reason, your mom named me the beneficiary on her life insurance policy, and that's causing some problems."

She waved his concern away. "Oh, I know. It's all Grandpa and Aunt Di have been talking about."

"Well, I don't want it. Especially if it's going to cause so much grief. They can have it. All I want is to have you with me. But you should know, they're threatening to take me to court. So I was thinking maybe if I gave them the money, they'll let that idea drop."

"Forget that. Don't listen to them. I'm old enough to have a say in who I live with. You're my dad. And I choose you."

One corner of his mouth lifted in a grin.

"I love them," she said. "But I've been with them the last thirteen years. I want to live with you now. And we're not giving that money back. I'm sure Mom chose you because she knew you'd spend the money on taking care of me. And we're gonna need it to buy our dream house."

"Dream house?"

She rolled her eyes again. "Yeah. Duh. The Larson ranch."

Cade grinned and that feeling of hope burst through him again. "I'm way ahead of you, kid. I already talked to Pearl's daughter yesterday morning. I put in a fair offer, and she said she's willing to sell us the place."

"You did? *Yesterday?*" Her eyes widened. "You mean before I left?"

"Yeah. I was going to talk to you and Nora about it at dinner. I wanted to show you that I was serious about you staying with me. I'm still learning all this dad stuff, but I swear, I'm not going anywhere this time. You're *my* daughter and I love you, Allie-Cat."

She threw her arms around him and buried her face in his neck. "I love you too, Dad. And I believe you that you've changed. And that you'll stay."

He hugged her tightly, her words meaning everything to him.

She hugged him back, then clapped her hand on his shoulder. "Now let's go get Nora."

"Good idea. But first, I have someone else in the truck who's been missing you almost as much as I have."

She inhaled a quick gasp, and her eyes lit with excitement. "You brought Scout?"

"I did."

She let out a squeal as she threw her arms around him. "You're the best dad ever."

He grinned as he hugged her back, the words healing some of the hurt of the past several years. "I'm trying my best, kid."

Cade knocked on the door, then took a quick glance back at the truck. After breaking the news to Diana and Ed, they'd swung by the apartment to pick up the rest of Allie's things. The puppy sat on her lap and gave a small yip as Allie gave him an encouraging nod from the front seat.

The front door opened and Cade tipped his hat to the woman who answered. "Hello, ma'am. I'm sorry to bother you, but I'm looking for Nora Fisher."

The woman smiled as she peered up at him, and he could see the resemblance to Nora. "You must be Cade."

"Yes, ma'am."

"Dang. No wonder it only took her an instant," she muttered.

"Pardon me?"

"I'm Nora's mom, Sheila." She peered around him. "Is that Allie in the truck?"

"Yes, ma'am."

"Nora's told me so much about you all. I feel like I practically know you. Your daughter is beautiful."

Cade face broke into a proud smile. "Yeah, she is."

"Oh, and that must be Scout." Sheila waved excitedly to the girl and the dog. "Mind if I go say hello?"

He chuckled, another spark of hope lighting in him that Nora had talked about them so much. "Suit yourself."

"Nora's in the basement." She waved him in. "Go through the kitchen. The stairs are on the right."

He walked through the house, grinning at the photos of Nora that lined the walls—Nora in a cheerleading uniform, holding up a fish, beaming at the camera from above a huge birthday cake. She looked young and fresh-faced in her senior portraits, but his favorites were the ones of her as a little girl, especially the goofy one where her front tooth was missing.

His feet carried him down the stairs and toward the sound of a familiar voice singing along to the radio. The song playing was bluesy and sad, and just hearing Nora's voice had butterflies dive-bombing his stomach. What if she didn't want to hear what he came to say? What if the reason she left the church was because she didn't want to see him anymore?

He was excited but nervous to see her. He still wasn't sure why she'd left the church. Maybe this whole thing between them was in his imagination.

Only one way to find out.

He leaned against the side of the door, his heart pounding as he watched Nora slide her dress onto a hanger. Her back was to him as she shifted clothes in the closet to make room. She'd changed into jeans, sneakers, and a teal top, and his gaze was drawn to the curve of her lush hips as she slowly swayed to the music. "Hey, beautiful."

She let out a shriek and sent the dress flying as she jumped. "Holy moly," she said, pressing her hand to her heart. "You scared the crud out of me."

Hmm. Not exactly the warm welcome he was hoping for. "Sorry."

"What are you doing here?"

"I came to see you." He shook his head. "No, I didn't just come to see you. I came to tell you that I worked things out with Allie and she's coming back to the ranch. And we want you to come back with us."

She narrowed her eyes. "You mean to finish Allie's therapy?"

"Well, yeah, I guess, but that's not what I'm talking about." He raked his hand through his hair. "Damn it. I'm totally blowing this. I'm here for *you*. To tell you how I feel and convince you to come back. I don't know, I guess I was trying to come in here and sweep you off your feet."

She sank down onto the side of the bed. "What? Like in one of Allie's books? Like some fairy tale where the handsome prince comes to find the princess?"

He offered her a roguish grin. "Are you saying you think I'm handsome?" He frowned. "I am the handsome prince in this story, right?"

She laughed. It was a small one, but it was still a laugh. His hopes lifted. "Yes, you dope. But I can't just jump on your horse with you and ride off into the sunset to your castle on the moors."

"Sure you can. Except I'm not exactly sure what a moor is, and I didn't bring my horse. But I can still ride you off in my pickup to my castle, if you consider a castle to be a slightly rundown farm-house with a cozy reading nook in the mountains."

She let out a small gasp. "You mean the Larson farm?"

He couldn't help but smile. "Yep. Pearl's daughter agreed to sell it to me, and Allie is all in. She wants to use the insurance money to help us buy it."

"*Us?*"

Cade reached for her hand and pulled her up to stand in front of him. She peered up at him, and he felt that click of connection again. "See, darlin', the thing about a fairy tale is that with one kiss from the handsome prince's lips, the beautiful princess falls in love with him and they live happily ever after. I don't know if it happened with our very first kiss, but I *am* in love with you." He pressed her hand to his heart. "I can't promise we'll always be happy—I can be a real idiot sometimes. But I can promise the ever after because I'm staying this time. For good."

"Oh, Cade." She let out a shuddering breath, but her eyes looked sad, her expression pained.

He rested his hand on her cheek, trying to pour all of his feelings into his touch. "Nora, I'm in love with you. Allie loves you too. So how about it? You ready to come back to the ranch with us?"

Instead of throwing herself into his arms, she took a step back. "I just…" She chewed on her lip as she stared at the floor. Not a good sign. She wrapped her arms around her stomach. "I can't. After everything that's happened, I just need some time to think about it."

Oh.

He hadn't seen a Mack Truck coming, but it sure felt like one had just hit him in the chest. He swallowed. "Then I guess that's my answer. Let me know what you think. But know that I'll still be here, no matter what you decide." He turned and strode from the room.

His heart ached as he pushed through the front door, not just from Nora's rejection, but from the thought of what he was going to tell Allie.

He'd failed her. And himself.

Nora's mom must have gone back inside because it was just Allie sitting in the truck. She leaned her head out the window. "Where is she? Where's Nora?"

He shook his head. "She's not coming. It's just you and me, kid."

———

Nora flung herself onto her bed and buried her face in her pillow. She'd done it. She'd stopped to think before jumping headlong into a crazy situation. She'd placed herself back on the sidelines, taken herself out of the fight until she had time to plan, to strategize her next move.

And it felt…terrible.

What the hell had she done?

Cade had come to her, offering her his love and a chance at building a life and a family together. And she'd told him she needed to think about it?

She'd made plenty of impulsive decisions in her life, and some had gloriously and spectacularly failed, but others had worked out great and taken her to places she'd never have gone if she hadn't been willing to jump in and take some chances.

Aunt Sassy's words came back to her. *You can't live your life in fear of making another mistake…for goodness sakes, if you get another chance to fall in love, take it.*

She was being offered another chance—a handsome cowboy prince chance—and she'd just let him walk out the door.

Maybe it wasn't too late. She pushed off the bed and raced up the stairs. Sprinting through the house, she burst through the front door. "Cade! Wait!"

He was standing next to the truck, looking so tall and gorgeous it almost hurt to look at him. He turned around, and she ran to him and jumped one more time as she launched herself into his arms.

Clinging to him, her words came out in a rush. "I'm sorry. That was so stupid. I don't need time to think about it. I love you too." She peered up at him. "I was just afraid of getting hurt again. But I don't care if I get hurt. It's worth the risk of being with you."

The smile that spread across his face sent her heart soaring. "You sure?" he asked.

"Yes, one hundred percent. It did happen quickly, but it still happened." This time she reached up to touch his cheek. "I am completely in love with you. And I want to build a life, and a home, with you *and* Allie. So what if it's impulsive? I love you and something tells me you are the best impulse I've ever had." She pushed up on her toes and kissed him.

He lifted her off her feet, pulling her close as he kissed her back—a kiss filled with promise and possibility.

He set her down as the truck door opened, and Scout jumped out and raced around their feet. Allie slid out of the truck, tears on her cheeks as she hopped the few steps into Cade's and Nora's arms.

Nora kissed the top of her head as she hugged them close. In her arms, she held everything she'd ever wanted, ever dreamed of—her family.

Scout yipped at their feet and Nora swooped him up as she beamed at Cade and Allie. "Let's go home."

THE END...
...AND JUST THE BEGINNING...

Looking for more cowboys? Keep reading for an
excerpt of the first book in the Cowboys of Creedence
series from bestselling author Jennie Marts!

CAUGHT UP
in a
COWBOY

Available now from
Sourcebooks Casablanca

CHAPTER 1

BITS OF GRAVEL FLEW BEHIND THE TIRES OF THE CONVERTIBLE, and Rockford James swore as he turned onto the dirt road leading to the Triple J Ranch. Normally, he enjoyed coming home for a visit, especially in the late spring when everything was turning green and the wildflowers were in bloom, but not this spring—not when he was coming home with both his pride and his body badly injured.

His spirits lifted and the corners of his mouth tugged up in a grin as he drew even with what appeared to be a pirate riding a child's bicycle along the shoulder of the road. A gorgeous female pirate—one with long blond hair and great legs.

Legs he recognized.

Legs that belonged to the only woman who had ever stolen his heart.

Nine years ago, Quinn Rivers had given him her heart as well. Too bad he'd broken it. Not exactly broken—more like smashed, crushed, and shattered it into a million tiny pieces. According to her anyway.

He slowed the car, calling out as he drew alongside her. Her outfit consisted of a flimsy little top that bared her shoulders under a snug corset vest and a short, frilly striped skirt. She wore some kind of sheer white knee socks, and one of them had fallen and pooled loosely around her ankle. "Ahoy there, matey. You lose your ship?"

Keeping her eyes focused on the road, she stuck out her hand and offered him a gesture unbecoming of a lady—pirate or otherwise. Then her feet stilled on the pedals as she must have registered his voice. "Ho-ly crap. You have got to be freaking kidding me."

Bracing her feet on the ground, she turned her head, brown eyes flashing with anger. "And here I thought my day couldn't get any worse. What the hell are you doing here, Rock?"

He stopped the car next to her, then draped his arm over the steering wheel, trying to appear cool. Even though his heart pounded against his chest from the fact that he was seeing her again. She had this way of getting under his skin; she was just so damn beautiful. Even wearing a pirate outfit. "Hey, now. Is that any way to speak to an old friend?"

"I don't know. I'll let you know when I run into one."

Ouch. He'd hoped she wasn't still that bitter about their breakup. They'd been kids, barely out of high school. But they'd been together since they were fourteen, his conscience reminded him, and they'd made plans to spend their future together.

But that was before he got the full-ride scholarship and the NHL started scouting him.

And he had tried.

Yeah, keep telling yourself that, buddy.

Okay, he probably hadn't tried hard enough. But he'd been young and dumb and swept up in the fever and glory of finally having his dreams of pursuing a professional hockey career coming true.

With that glory came attention and fame and lots of travel with the team where cute puck bunnies were ready and willing to show their favorite players a good time.

He hadn't cheated on Quinn, but he came home less often and didn't make the time for texts and calls. He'd gone to college first while she finished her senior year, and by the time he did come home the next summer, he'd felt like he'd outgrown their relationship, and her, and had suggested they take a mini break.

Which turned into an *actual* break, of both their relationship and Quinn's heart.

But it had been almost nine years since he'd left; they'd been kids, and that kind of stuff happened all the time. Since then, he hadn't made it home a lot and had run into her only a handful of times. In fact, he probably hadn't seen her in over a year.

But he'd thought of her. Often. And repeatedly wondered if he'd made the right choice by picking the fame and celebrity of his career and letting go of her.

Sometimes, those summer days spent with Quinn seemed like yesterday, but really, so much had happened—in both of their lives—that it felt like a lifetime ago.

Surely she'd softened a little toward him in all that time. "Let me offer you a lift." The dirt road they were on led to both of their families' neighboring ranches.

"No thanks. I'd rather pedal this bike until the moon comes up than take a ride from you."

Yep. Still mad, all right.

Nothing he could do if she wanted to keep the grudge fest going. Except he was tired of the grudge. Tired of them being enemies. She'd been the best friend he'd ever had. And right now, he felt like he could use a friend.

His pride had already been wounded; what was one more hit? At least he could say he tried.

Although he didn't want it to seem like he was trying too hard. He did still have a *little* pride left, damn it.

"Okay. Suit yourself. It's not *that* hot out here." He squinted up at the bright Colorado sun, then eased off the brake, letting the car coast forward.

"Wait." She shifted from one booted foot to the other, the plastic pirate sword bouncing against her curvy hip. "Fine. I'll take a ride. But only because I'm desperate."

"You? Desperate? I doubt it," he said with a chuckle. Putting the car in Park, he left the engine running and made his way around the back of the car. He reached for the bike, but she was already fitting it into the back seat of the convertible.

"I've got it." Her gaze traveled along the length of his body, coming to rest on his face, and her expression softened for the first time. "I heard about the fight and your injury."

He froze, heat rushing to his cheeks and anger building in his gut. Of course she'd heard about the fight. It had made the nightly news, for Pete's sake. He was sure the whole town of Creedence had heard about it.

Nothing flowed faster than a good piece of gossip in a small town. Especially when it's bad news—or news about the fall of the hometown hero. Or the guy who thought he was better than everyone else and bigger than his small-town roots, depending on who you talked to and which camp they fell into. Or what day of the week it was.

You could always count on a small town to be loyal.

Until you let them down.

"I'm fine," he said, probably a little too sternly, as he opened the car door, giving her room to pass him and slide into the passenger seat. He sucked in a breath as the scent of her perfume swept over him.

She smelled the same—a mix of vanilla, honeysuckle, and home.

He didn't let himself wonder if she felt the same. No, he'd blown his chances of that ever happening again a long time ago. Still, he couldn't help but drop his gaze to her long, tanned legs or notice the way her breasts spilled over the snug, corseted vest of the pirate costume.

"So, what's with the outfit?" he asked as he slid into the driver's seat and put the car in gear.

She blew out her breath in an exaggerated sigh. A loose tendril of hair clung to her damp forehead, and he was tempted to reach across the seat to brush it back.

"It's Max's birthday today," she said, as if that explained everything.

He didn't say anything—didn't know what to say.

The subject of Max always was a bit of an awkward one between them. After he'd left, he'd heard the rumors of how Quinn had hooked up with a hick loser named Monty Hill who'd lived one town over. She'd met him at a party and it had been a rebound one-night stand, designed to make him pay for breaking things off with her, if the gossip was true.

But she'd been the one to pay. Her impulse retaliation had ended in an unplanned pregnancy with another jerk who couldn't be counted on to stick around for her. Hill had taken off, and Quinn had ended up staying at her family's ranch.

"He's eight now." Her voice held the steely tone of anger, but he heard the hint of pride that also crept in.

"I know," he mumbled, more to himself than to her. "So, you decided to dress up like a pirate for his birthday?"

She snorted. "No. Of course not. One of Max's favorite books is *Treasure Island*, and he wanted a pirate-themed party, so I *hired* a party company to send out a couple of actors to dress up like pirates. The outfits showed up this morning, but the actors didn't. Evidently, there was a mix-up in the office, and the couple had been double-booked and were already en route to Denver when I called."

"So you decided to fill in." He tried to hold back his grin.

She shrugged. "What else was I going to do?"

"That doesn't explain the bike."

"The bike is his main gift. I ordered it from the hardware store in town, but it was late and we weren't expecting it to come in today. They called about an hour ago and said it had shown up, but they didn't have anyone to deliver it. I was already in the pirate getup, so I ran into town to get it."

"And decided to ride it home?"

"Yes, smart-ass. I thought it would be fun to squeeze onto a tiny bike dressed in a cheap Halloween costume and enjoy the bright, sunny day by riding home." She blew out another exasperated breath. "My stupid car broke down on the main road."

"Why didn't you call Ham or Logan to come pick you up?" he asked, referring to her dad and her older brother.

"Because in my flustered state of panic about having to fill in as the pirate princess and the fear that the party would be ruined, I left my phone on the dresser when I ran out of the house. I was carrying the dang bike, but it got so heavy, then I tried pushing it, and that was killing my back, so I thought it would be easier and faster if I just tried to ride it the last mile back to the ranch."

"Makes sense to me." He slowed the car, turning into the long driveway of Rivers Gulch. White fences lined the drive, and several head of cattle grazed on the fresh green grass of the pastures along either side of the road.

The scent of recently mown hay skimmed the air, mixed with the familiar smells of plowed earth and cattle.

Seeing the sprawling ranch house and the long, white barn settled something inside of him, and he let out a slow breath, helping to ease the tension in his neck. He'd practically grown up here, running around this place with Quinn and her brother, Logan.

Their families' ranches were within spitting distance of each other; in fact, he could see the farmhouse of the Triple J across the pasture to his left. They were separated only by prime grazing land and the pond that he'd learned to swim in during the summer and skate on in the winter.

The two families had an ongoing feud—although he wasn't sure any of them really knew what they were fighting about anymore, and the kids had never cared much about it anyway.

The adults liked to bring it up, but they were the only kids around for miles, and they'd become fast friends—he and his brothers sneaking over to Rivers Gulch as often as they could.

This place felt just as much like home as his own did. He'd missed it. In the years since he'd left, he'd been back only a handful of times.

His life had become so busy, his hockey career taking up most of his time. And after what happened with Quinn, neither Ham nor Logan was ever too excited to see him. Her mom had died when she was in grade school, and both men had always been overprotective of her.

He snuck a glance at her as he drove past the barn. Her wavy hair was pulled back in a ponytail, but wisps of it had come loose and fell across her neck in little curls. She looked good—really good. A thick chunk of regret settled in his gut, and he knew letting her go had been the biggest mistake of his life.

It wasn't the first time he'd thought it. Images of Quinn haunted his dreams, and he often wondered what it would be like now if only he'd brought her with him instead of leaving her behind. If he had her to wave to in the stands at his games or to come home to at night instead of an empty house. But he'd screwed that up, and he felt the remorse every time he returned to Rivers Gulch.

He'd been young and arrogant—thought he had the world by the tail. Scouts had come sniffing around when he was in high school, inflating his head and his own self-importance. And once he started playing in the big leagues, everything about this small town—including Quinn—had just seemed…well…small. Too small for a big shot like him.

He was just a kid—and an idiot. But by the time he'd realized his mistake and come back for her, it was too late.

Hindsight was a mother.

And so was Quinn.

Easing the car in front of the house, he took in the festive balloons and streamers tied to the railings along the porch. So much of the house looked the same—the long porch that ran the length of the house, the wooden rocking chairs, and the swing hanging from the end.

They'd spent a lot of time on that swing, talking and laughing, his arm around her as his foot slowly pushed them back and forth.

She opened the car door, but he put a hand on her arm and offered her one of his most charming smiles. "It's good to see you, Quinn. You look great. Even in a pirate outfit."

Her eyes widened, and she blinked at him, for once not having a sarcastic reply. He watched her throat shift as she swallowed, and he yearned to reach out to run his fingers along her slender neck.

"Well, thanks for the lift." She turned away and stepped out of the car.

Pushing open his door, he got out and reached for the bicycle, lifting it out of the back seat before she had a chance. He carried it around and set it on the ground in front of her. "I'd like to meet him. You know, Max. If that's okay."

"You would?" Her voice was soft, almost hopeful, but still held a note of suspicion. "Why?"

He ran a hand through his hair and let out a sigh. He'd been rehearsing what he was going to say as they drove up to the ranch, but now his mouth had gone dry. The collar of his cotton T-shirt clung to his neck, and he didn't know what to do with his hands.

Dang. He hadn't had sweaty palms since he was in high school. He wiped them on his jeans. He was known for his charm and usually had a way with women, but not this woman. This one had him tongue-tied and nervous as a teenager.

He shoved his hands in his pockets. "Listen, Quinn. I know I screwed up. I was young and stupid and a damn fool. And I'm sorrier than I could ever say. But I can't go back and fix it. All I can do is move forward. I miss this place. I miss having you in my life. I'd like to at least be your friend."

She opened her mouth, and he steeled himself for her to tell him to go jump in the lake. Or worse. But she didn't. She looked up at him, her eyes searching his face, as if trying to decide if he was serious. "Why now? After all these years?"

He shrugged, his gaze drifting as he stared off at the distant green pastures. He'd let this go on too long, let the hurt fester. It was time to make amends—to at least try. He looked back at her, trying to express his sincerity. "Why not? Isn't it about time?"

She swallowed again and gave a small nod of her head.

A tiny flicker of hope lit in his gut as he waited for her response. He could practically *see* her thinking—watch the emotions cross her face in the furrow of her brow and the way she chewed on her bottom lip. Oh man, he loved it when she did that; the way she sucked her bottom lip under her front teeth always did crazy things to his insides.

"Okay. We can *try* being friends." She gave him a sidelong glance, the hint of a smile tugging at the corner of her mouth. "On one condition."

Uh-oh. Conditions are never good. Although he would do just about anything to prove to her that he was serious about being in her life again.

"What's that?"

"I need someone to be the other pirate for the party. I already asked Logan if he would wear the other costume, and he refused. I was planning to ask Dad, but I have a feeling I'll get the same response."

He tried to imagine Hamilton Rivers in a pirate outfit and couldn't. Ham was old-school cowboy, tough as nails and loyal to the land. He wore his boots from sunup to sundown and had more grit than a sheet of sandpaper. The only soft spot he had was for his daughter. And Rock had broken her heart.

If there hadn't been enough animosity between the two families over their land before, Rock had sealed the feud by walking away from Quinn.

And now he had a chance to try to make it up to her. And to keep an eight-year-old kid from being disappointed. Even if it meant making a fool of himself.

He squinted one eye closed and tilted his head. If he was going to do it, might as well do it right.

Go big or go home.

"Aye, lass," he said in his best gruff pirate impression. "I'll be a pirate for ye, but don't cross me, or I'll make ye walk the plank."

Her eyes widened, and she laughed before she could stop herself. An actual laugh. Well, more like a small chuckle, but it was worth it. He'd talk in a pirate accent all afternoon if it meant he could hear her laugh again.

She took a step forward, reached out her hand as if to touch his arm, then let it drop to her side. "All right, Captain Jack, you don't have to go that far." She might not have touched him, but she offered him a grin—a true grin.

Yeah, he could be a pirate. He could be whatever she needed. Or he could dang well try.

The front door slammed open with a bang, and Quinn jumped. As if on cue, her brother stepped out on the front porch.

Anger sparked in Logan's eyes as he glared at Rock. "What the hell are you doing here?"

CHAPTER 2

QUINN WAS THINKING THE SAME THING.

What the hell was Rockford James doing standing in front of her? And offering to fill in as the pirate at her son's birthday party, no less.

But the righteous indignation was hers to carry, and she held up a hand to her brother. "Rock gave me a ride home. That stupid car broke down again, and I would have had to walk the whole way if he hadn't stopped to give me a lift."

"Why didn't you call me?"

"I forgot my phone."

He gave a grudging nod to Rock. "Well, we've got it from here. Thanks." He pulled the screen door open, then turned back and mumbled, "Sorry to hear about your head. That guy was an asshole."

She felt Rock stiffen beside her. He obviously didn't like to talk about it. But she was glad to see her brother being civil—maybe this could be the start of a truce between the Rivers and James families. She tried to keep a light tone in her voice. "Rock is coming to the party. He's going to help out by filling in as the other pirate."

Her brother raised an eyebrow, then shook his head, any remnants of a truce disappearing behind his scowl. "Like hell he is. We don't need another pirate. And we dang sure don't need *his* help."

Leaving the bike on the porch, she automatically reached for Rock's hand and pulled him up the stairs. "Too bad. He's staying. Max wants a pirate, and I'm giving him a pirate." The nerve of her brother, telling her what to do. She fought to hold back the eye roll. He was only two years older than she was, but she'd always be his baby sister. Annoying.

It wasn't until they had stepped onto the porch that she realized she was holding Rock's hand. The shock of touching his skin and having her hand in his after all these years took her breath away. His fingers curled around hers, making her hyperaware of the wall of male standing next to her.

"You heard the lady," Rock said with a smirk.

She led him through the house and into her bedroom, where the other costume was. It was strange having him in her room again.

He looked around with interest. "Wow, you're still in your old bedroom. You've changed it up though. Got rid of the pom-poms and the boy band posters."

Pushing the door shut with her foot, she dropped his hand as if it were on fire. "That's because I'm an adult now. And a mom. I have my own boy, and he's the one I cheer for."

Memories of Rock being in this room with her flooded her mind, and her heart ached at flashes of recollection. Lying on the floor as they listened to music or worked on homework, curled on her bed kissing and touching in the frantic way that teenagers discover each other. The pictures in her head were as clear as if they had happened yesterday.

But they hadn't. She pushed the memories away—back into the spaces where she kept them, sealed off so they couldn't hurt her. That was the past. She needed to focus on the present, on Max and the birthday party that was going to start any minute now.

She pointed to the pirate costume laid out across her bed. The outfit consisted of a thin muslin shirt, a faux leather vest, and a pair of brown, striped pants. A long scarf served as a belt, with a black hat and a sword completing the costume.

"You can put that on. The guests will be here anytime, so we've got to be ready. If the pants don't fit, just wear your jeans." She glanced at his thighs, thick and muscular from years of ice skating. "Yeah, you should probably just wear your jeans."

He chuckled as he reached for the hem of his T-shirt and tugged it over his head.

She sucked in her breath.

Holy hot cowboy. The guy's chest was a solid mass of muscle.

The last time she'd seen him without a shirt, they'd been teenagers. He wasn't a teenager now. He was a man with a man's body.

The muscles in his arms flexed as he tossed the shirt onto the bed, and she almost choked at the size of them. He had the body of an athlete, toned and firm. A tattoo of his team's logo covered the top part of his right arm. She hadn't known he'd gotten a tattoo.

She didn't really know anything about him anymore. Just the bits of gossip around town and the occasional stories she heard about him from his family or on one of the sports channels on TV. She wouldn't admit it to anyone else, but she'd seen several of his games, watching him when he was on the ice and searching the player's box for glimpses of him when he wasn't.

She tried to look away but was mesmerized by his body, so foreign yet so familiar. Her gaze traveled over him, discovering new scars and marks that hadn't been there before, that he must have earned in his years on the ice.

His hair was still a little too long, curling along his neck, but it had darkened to a dirty-blond color, and his eyes were still the same greenish blue. She'd always thought they were the same color as the pond they learned to swim in, a mixture of the shades, depending on his mood or what color clothes he was wearing.

There were so many new things about him, yet he still felt like the same guy that she'd grown up with—the one who'd shown her how to ride a horse, who'd tutored her in chemistry, and who had taught her how to French kiss. And he'd been quite a teacher.

He reached for the shirt on the bed, turning slightly, and she gasped at the mass of ugly purple bruising down the side of his rib cage. She reached out as if to touch him, heard his sharp intake of breath as her fingers barely skimmed his side, and quickly dropped her hand.

"Is that from the—" She didn't want to bring up the fight again. Apparently, she didn't have to.

A scowl settled on his face, and he swiped at the discoloration as if to wipe it away. "Yeah, I guess. It's no big deal though—just a few bruises. We're always getting banged up. These are already starting to fade."

They didn't look like they were starting to fade. But the subject obviously made him uncomfortable, so she let it go and concentrated on a problem that had just surfaced in her mind. "They didn't send along any boots or shoes."

He pulled the shirt over his head. It was snug, hugging his muscled chest and stretching over his thick upper arms. "My boots will do fine."

She glanced down at his leather, square-toed cowboy boots. "A pirate wearing cowboy boots?" Oh geez—that sounded kind of hot, especially when the cowboy/pirate was Rock.

Stop it. This was the man who'd broken her heart—who'd left her behind. She wasn't about to fall victim to his charming grin and a few well-toned muscles.

He tugged on the vest and picked up the long, red scarf, a baffled look on his face. "What do I do with this?"

"You tie it around your waist. Like a belt." She sighed at his blank look and took the scarf. Sliding her arms around him, she wrapped the scarf around his waist and tied it in a knot at his hip. Her hands shook a little as they brushed over his hard abs, their solidness visible through the thin shirt.

Taking a step back, she picked up the sword from the bed and passed it to him. They needed to get out of her bedroom. She could try to push the memories away, but the ghosts of them as a couple—as young lovers—were thick. As if their souls were floating in the air, taking up all the space and making it hard for her to breathe.

The sound of a truck coming up the driveway pulled Quinn

from her thoughts. Thank goodness. The guests were starting to arrive.

The door of her room burst open, and Max rushed in. "Mom! Mom! They're here! Come on! The party is starting!" He grabbed her arm and pulled, then stopped when he caught sight of Rock.

He pushed his small glasses up his nose and grinned at her. Her heart did that gushy mom thing it did every time her son smiled because she'd gotten something exactly right. "You found a pirate."

That smile on her son's face made every awkward moment with Rock worth it. "Yep, this is Captain…um…James." That was original. She gave Rock a small shrug of her shoulders, hoping he would play along. "He sailed the seven seas to be here for your birthday party today."

Max's eyes widened as he looked at Rock. "You're a pretty big pirate," he whispered.

Rock puffed out his chest and lowered his voice, affecting a deep, pirate accent. "Aye. That's from spending so much time working aboard me ship, matey. I heard some scallywag named Max was having a party, and I thought I'd stop by for some rum." He glanced up at Quinn. "Er, I mean some grog. You got any grog, boy, or am I going to have to make you swab the poop deck?"

"You said 'poop.'" Max dissolved into giggles as Rock wielded his plastic sword in the air. "You're funny."

He *was* funny. Was he seriously *still* doing a pirate voice?

She tried to keep from laughing, but the sound of Max's giggles was too much. Shaking her head, she looked down at her son. "Why don't you go say hello to your guests, and I'll try to find the Captain here some *grog*."

"Okay, Mom." Max offered Rock a wave, then raced from the room. "See ya later, Captain James."

"Nice work, matey," she said, trying to mimic his accent as she held the door for him. "You think you can keep it up long enough to entertain a dozen hyper eight-year-olds?"

"Aye. I love a challenge." He crossed the room, stopping behind her and lowering his voice as he leaned closer to her ear. "And might I add, ye've got the finest pirate booty I've ever laid me eyes on."

She raised an eyebrow, trying to hold in a laugh. "Are you seriously flirting with me using pirate lingo?"

He winked and gave her a sharp nod of his head. "Aye, me beauty. Would you like to shiver me timbers?"

Her eyes widened, but even he couldn't hold a straight face for that one, and they busted out laughing.

It had been a long time since they'd laughed like that together. It felt good. Right.

He held up his hands in surrender. "Sorry. That one went too far. It sounded better in my head."

"Keep that up, and you're gonna be the one walking the plank." She tried to sound gruff but couldn't quite pull it off. With a slow smile, she turned and headed for the kitchen, ignoring the butterflies careening around in her stomach at the fact that not only was Rock in her bedroom again, but he was flirting with her—and she kind of liked it.

Three hours, seventeen cupcakes, and three water-balloon fights that Rock instigated later, she sank onto the bench seat of the picnic table.

He dropped down next to her and pulled off his pirate hat. The scent of his aftershave wafted around her, and his thigh came dangerously close to touching hers. His hair was tousled from the hat and the warm day, and she had the strongest urge to reach out and smooth it down.

Her dad and Max had left to take the last of the kids home, and the scent of grilled hot dogs and sunscreen lingered in the air.

She'd thought her dad would have a coronary when he saw Rock at the party, but she told him he was doing it for Max and to chill out. Ham had grunted, and the two men had mainly stayed out of each other's way.

"Wow. You were right. Eight-year-olds are tough." He puffed out a breath, sounding more like he'd gone into triple overtime instead of wrangling up a group of rowdy children.

"You were pretty great with them." Surprisingly great. She'd had no idea he could work a crowd like that. He was funny and charming, and he'd had the kids and half of the parents eating out of his hand. Especially the moms.

One of the kid's moms fell all over herself trying to help Rock pass out the cupcakes.

And speaking of falling, if Carolyn Parker had displayed any more of her cleavage, her boobs would have popped right out of her top. Not very becoming of the PTA president and self-professed "room mom."

The moms were bad enough, preening around Rock, but the dads were just as ridiculous, trying to act cool and buddy up with him. So what if he was a famous hockey player and on television? He was still the same guy that half of them had gone to school with. Why were they treating him like such a celebrity?

Because he was. He wasn't just *some* hockey player. He was Rockford James, the star, the hockey-playing cowboy and a major player on the Colorado team. A team he was going back to, she reminded herself.

"They were fun." Rock's deep voice rumbled through her and dragged her out of her musings. "And I do have *some* skills." He nudged her leg and cocked an eyebrow. "But I do my best work when I'm not in front of a crowd."

She shook her head, the start of a smile tugging at her lip. "You're awful."

"Awful handsome for a pirate, you mean?" He flashed her one of his charming grins, teasing her as he bumped her leg with his again, then leaving his knee lightly against hers.

She could feel the heat of his skin, even through his jeans. The cotton texture of the denim rubbed against her bare leg, causing her earlier butterflies to return, swooping and swirling wildly in her belly.

Was he flirting with her? Or just laying on the charm like he'd been doing all afternoon with the other guests? Ugh. The very thought of him flirting with Carolyn Parker made her stomach go sour.

What was that about?

Actually, she knew what it was about.

The green-eyed monster was rearing its ugly head, and she didn't like it. Not one bit. She wasn't usually jealous. But who would she have to be jealous of? So much of her life was spent focused on her role as a mom: laundry, bath time, making lunches, tucking Max in at night, and reading books with him. So many books. That kid loved to read and loved being read to.

She didn't have time to think about men or flirting. Not until now, when she had Rock James sitting in front of her, the ridiculously cute guy she'd loved for half of her life, the one whose leg now pressed snugly against hers as he'd somehow moved even closer.

And the one who had torn her heart to shreds when he'd broken up with her.

No matter how cute and charming he was, there was still that.

She sighed. "What are you doing here, Rock?"

His playful grin fell, but before he had a chance to answer, her brother walked up holding a chocolate cupcake and leaned his hip against the edge of the picnic table next to her.

"Looks like you two were the hit of the party," Logan said. "Your picture will probably make tomorrow's news as the pirate couple of the year."

"What are you talking about?" she asked.

"Didn't you see Carolyn Parker taking pictures of you guys? I'm sure you'll be in tomorrow's edition of the *Creedence Chronicle*. She just got hired on there and is trying to start some new section like the society pages. I'll wager that you'll be her feature story." He peeled back the wrapper of the cupcake and took a bite. "Unless she sells the pictures to that reporter who was lurking out front earlier," he said around a mouthful of cake.

Rock's head snapped up. "What reporter?"

CHAPTER 3

SO THAT'S WHAT THIS IS ALL ABOUT.

It didn't have anything to do with her. Or with him wanting them to be friends again. She should have known.

Pushing his leg away, Quinn stood up and turned on him. She could feel the fury building in her chest, like bile filling her throat.

No. She would *not* cry, damn it. It was easier to be mad than to let him know he had gotten to her.

Her hands landed on her hips, and her heart slammed against her chest. "You brought a reporter to my son's birthday party? To our house? So this was all just a publicity stunt?"

His face registered shock as he sputtered, "No, of course not. Quinn, I—"

She held up her hand. "Save it. Save your excuses. This didn't have anything to do with you wanting to be my friend or trying to help make an eight-year-old's dream come true. It all has to do with your almighty career. Just like everything else in your life, hockey comes first."

"Quinn, come on. I had nothing to do with this. I hate the press. Please—" he tried again, but she cut him off.

How could he say he hated the press when he showed up in the news all the time? She didn't know what to believe.

"Just leave, Rock. Go home."

Turning on her heel, she hurried into the house, determined not to let him see the emotions she knew were evident on her face. She'd never been able to hide her feelings from him.

And she damn sure didn't want him to know he'd gotten to her. Again.

Just like he always did.

Rock slammed the front door and stomped into the living room of the two-story farmhouse he'd grown up in.

"What in the Sam Hill are you wearing?" his mother, Vivienne, asked. She stood at the kitchen island, elbows deep in a sink full of sudsy water.

"Ahoy there," one of his younger brothers, Mason, called from the recliner in front of the television. "Nice pirate duds. I hope you brought some rum and a couple of wenches home with you." He glanced over at Vivienne. "Sorry, Mom."

Rock had wanted to follow Quinn into the house, to explain and to get his shirt back, but her brother had stopped him. Not that Logan could really have stopped him if he'd wanted to get past him. He'd checked bigger guys than Logan Rivers into the boards without even a blink.

But he'd kept his cool long enough to realize that getting into a fight with her brother wouldn't help anything. The last thing Rock needed was to fuel the feud between their two families; that would only piss Quinn off more. Instead, he'd chosen to take his pirate sword and leave.

"Shut up," he growled at his brother as he sank onto the sofa.

"Geez, nice to see you too, Bro."

"Rockford James, you get your butt up off that couch and come give your mother a proper hug." Vivi was already drying her hands on a towel, and he was struck as he often was by how young and beautiful she still looked.

The combination of her being tall and constantly working in the house and on the ranch allowed her to eat cookies and macaroni and cheese and still stay slim, but it was more than that. More than the fact that her hair was still blond and worn long around her shoulders.

Vivienne James had a big heart and an easy laugh and a zest for life that drew people to her. Today, she wore jeans and a yellow cotton top, but her feet were bare, and as she padded across the kitchen toward him, he noticed her toenails were painted bright pink.

He stood and offered her a sheepish grin. Stepping forward, he wrapped his arms around her and tipped his head to her shoulder. "Sorry, Mom. I don't know what I was thinking. Bad day."

Everything felt off-kilter. Normally, he would go straight to his mom and wrap her in a hug. But nothing had been normal about the day he'd had.

She must have realized in her spidey mom-sense that something was off, because she squeezed him tightly, then pulled back, searching his eyes, her brow furrowed in concern. "How are you? How's your head?"

"I'm fine, Ma."

"You're *not* fine. You suffered a concussion serious enough that your coach sent you home to recuperate. I'm still not happy that you drove yourself up here." She slapped his arm with the damp dish towel. "But Lord knows the last time you listened to me."

He chuckled. As if.

Both he and his brothers knew that when Vivi James had something to say, they dang well better listen. Their dad had died when Rock was about Max's age, and Vivi had raised him and his two younger brothers on her own, with steady discipline and a fierce love.

She moved to the sofa and patted the seat next to her. "The rest of the dishes can wait. Tell me what's got you so worked up."

He glanced in the kitchen, then back at her. "I don't know why you're washing the dishes anyway. Why don't you use the dishwasher I bought you?"

He'd paid to remodel the old house the year before, updating it with modern appliances and tearing down the center wall to turn the kitchen and the living room into a great room. His mom had complained that she didn't want to be in the kitchen and miss one of his games, so he'd bought a flat-screen television that she could see from the big center island.

She'd accepted the new floor plan, the hardwood flooring, and most of the new furniture, but she still had some of her antiques scattered throughout, giving the house a more country look and keeping the homey feeling.

"I do use it. But sometimes I still like to wash up the supper dishes by hand. Helps me to think."

A worried expression crossed her face—just for a second, then it was gone, replaced by her normal, open smile.

What did she have to worry about? Was something going on with the farm? Mason hadn't told him of any problems. Not that he would.

Mason was the stable one, the one who always made sure things were taken care of. He had a head for business and the steady work habits of an ox. He and their youngest brother, Colt, had both stayed to help their mom run the ranch. But it seemed to suit both of them.

Mason had made some changes, put in some upgrades, and things seemed to be going smoothly. Although you wouldn't know it, listening to Mason talk, his little brother never gave himself enough credit for a job well done.

He glanced at his brother as he passed him a bottle of beer. Tiny bubbles fizzed against his lips as he tipped the bottle up and took a long swig. The cold beer felt good on his throat, and he slumped back against the sofa.

"Thanks, Brother. Sorry for being a jerk. It's been a weird day."

"Says the guy in the pirate shirt." Mason crowed with laughter as he sank back into the recliner.

Rock grabbed a throw pillow from the couch and flung it at him.

It felt good to be home.

The morning sun shone through the curtains of his old bedroom the next day as Rock cracked open one eye and squinted at the digital clock on his bedside table.

Eight thirty. He had a moment of panic, thinking he had overslept and should have been on the ice by now.

Then he remembered. The game. The fight. The feel of his opponent's stick across his back and the sickening thud of his head cracking against the boards.

He tried to close his eyes again but felt the insistent poking of his shoulder that had woken him up in the first place.

Rolling over, he came face-to-face with Quinn's son, Max.

He reared back against his pillow. "What are you doing here?"

"Trying to wake you up. You snore really loud." He scrunched his small nose and pushed his glasses back. He was a cute kid, his white-blond hair sticking up in messy spikes, and his glasses giving him a bookish look.

"No. I mean what are you doing *here*? In my bedroom?" A glimmer of hope sparked in his chest, and he craned his neck around Max to see out the door, but the hallway was empty. "Is your mom with you?"

"No. She dropped me off 'cause she had to work at the coffee shop this morning," he said, as if this explained everything.

"So she dropped you off here? Why?"

Max gave him a funny look like he didn't think that was a very smart question. "Because I'm only eight. And she thinks that's too young to stay home by myself. I told her I'd be fine. It's only for a few hours, but she doesn't listen to me."

"Welcome to the world of women, pal." Rock sat up in bed and ran a hand through his hair. "And I do *not* snore."

Max raised an eyebrow at him, the same look of skepticism he'd seen Quinn give him many times. "Yeah, dude. You do."

With the number of times he'd had his nose broken, there was a slight possibility that the kid might be right, but he wasn't giving in. Better to change the subject. "Does your mom drop you off here often?"

Max shrugged. "Couple days a week, if my grandpa or my uncle are busy. It's not so bad. I like Miss Vivi."

Hmm. Maybe the family feud didn't affect the women of the family. He smiled. "I like her too."

"We're makin' blueberry pancakes. She said they're your favorite and to come wake you up and tell you to get your behind downstairs if you want any." His blue eyes sparkled, and he laughed at the word *behind*.

"Blueberry pancakes, huh? Those *are* my favorite. Tell Miss Vivi that I'm jumping in the shower and will be down in five minutes."

Ten minutes later, he was sitting at the table, mopping syrup off his plate with the last of his pancakes. He stuffed the bite in his mouth just as the front door opened, and Quinn walked in, a happy smile on her face.

He tried to swallow, but the pancakes stuck in his throat.

She stole his breath, she was so beautiful. He'd seen her only yesterday, but she looked different today. Maybe it was the smile, maybe it was the fact that she wasn't in pirate garb and instead wore a pink cotton T-shirt, brown leather cowboy boots, and snug-fitting jeans that hugged her generous curves. Maybe it was the temporary truce they'd eased into the day before.

Well, they'd called it a truce. Right up until she'd pegged him for a liar and stormed into the house. So maybe not a truce anymore.

It didn't matter.

Whatever it was, she looked good.

Her smile fell as she caught sight of Rock. It obviously hadn't been meant for him. "Oh, sorry. I thought you'd still be asleep."

"Nope. Mom made pancakes. Well, Mom and Max, I guess. Want some?"

She shook her head, and he hated the look of hurt he saw in her eyes. "No. Thanks. I'm good."

"Listen, Quinn, I didn't have anything to do with that reporter showing up there yesterday. I *hate* the press. I would never willingly bring them anywhere, least of all back to Creedence. I swear."

She slumped into the seat across from him and picked at the remaining pancake on the platter. "Okay. I believe you, I guess."

His mother came out of the laundry room off the kitchen and smiled at Quinn. "Oh good, you're here. I need you and Rock to help me with something."

He cocked his head. He knew that tone. His mother was up to something.

———

Quinn followed Rock out to the barn, trying not to look at his butt in his well-fitting Levi's. There was something about the way a guy's butt looked when he wore boots.

But this guy also wore skates. And his time spent in his skates obviously meant more to him than his time in his boots.

His mom had said she needed them to fix the gate on one of the stalls in the barn, that Mason hadn't had a chance to get to it, but she had a sneaking suspicion that Vivi was using the task to put her and Rock in closer proximity.

She wasn't sure yet if she minded or not.

She was still mad from yesterday—hell, she was still mad from nine years ago when he'd left the first time. But something about him still drew her, made her want to spend time with him, just be in his presence.

Why she was subjecting herself to this twisted kind of torture, she had no idea. He'd already told her that he was home only for a short time, just while he recuperated from the concussion, and then he'd go back—would leave again. So why bother spending time with him now? Why risk getting her heart hurt again?

One of the farm dogs raced up to Rock, who knelt down, laughing as he rubbed the collie's black-and-white neck, and the dog covered his face with licks.

That was why.

Listening to Rock laugh, seeing that smile on his stupid, handsome face, that was why she would subject herself to hanging out with him. Just for a little bit.

"I miss having a dog around." He held open the door leading into the barn.

She stepped through the door, her eyes adjusting to the dim interior. The scent of hay, grain, and horses filled the air, and she heard the stomp of feet followed by a soft whinny from the horse in the far stall. She hadn't been in here in years and took a step back as the memories flooded over her, almost like a physical punch to her stomach.

They'd spent so much time here, riding horses, putting up hay, laughing and talking as she watched him do his chores. Her gaze drifted to the back corner of the barn, the spot where they'd piled hay and covered it with an old quilt and lost their virginity to each other.

She tore her gaze away, hoping Rock hadn't noticed. Too late. He'd caught her looking, and his eyes shone with amusement as a smile tugged at the corner of his lip. Maybe he wasn't thinking about the same thing she was. "Lots of memories in here." His gaze drifted to the back corner.

Crud. Warmth crept up her neck.

Yeah, he knew exactly what she was thinking about. It was just the single most pivotal part of a girl's life. It was only natural that she was thinking about it. But they sure as heck didn't have to *talk* about it. Time to change the subject. Quick.

"So why don't you get one? A dog, I mean."

He gave her a knowing smirk, then turned to the workbench and rummaged for tools. "I've thought about it, but I'm on the road too much. Wouldn't be fair to the dog."

"Don't you have someone you could leave it with during the day? Like a girlfriend?"

Seriously? Where did that come from? Thank goodness his back was to her and he couldn't see the heat flaming in her cheeks.

His hands stilled on the hammer he'd just grasped. His tone was light, but she felt the weight of it, like their conversation was hanging in the air. "Nope, no girlfriend. How about you? Got a man in your life?"

"Yeah, I've got three."

He dropped the hammer and turned around, his eyes wide. "Three?"

She laughed. That was too easy. "Yeah, but they're all related to me. My son, my brother, and my dad. I don't have the time or the inclination for anything else."

Arching an eyebrow, he parted his lips as if to comment—why was she looking at his lips?—but he let the subject drop. Instead, he pointed at the broken stall door. "Let's take a look at the damage."

She followed him across the barn and stood back as he leaned down and assessed the gate.

"It looks like the screws are stripped on this hinge. It shouldn't take but a few minutes to fix it. You can…"

She had been busy checking out his butt again as he'd leaned down and didn't notice when his words drifted off midsentence. Not until he made a grab for the fence post and swayed on his feet did she catch on that something was wrong.

Reaching out, she grabbed his shoulder for support. "Whoa there, you okay?"

He brushed her arm away, his voice gruff. "I'm fine." But his pale coloring told her otherwise.

"Why don't you sit down?"

"I don't need to sit down."

She narrowed her eyes, glaring at him with her best Mom stare.

"Fine. I'll sit down." He sank to the ground, resting his back against the fence post.

She sat next to him, her shoulder barely grazing his. "How bad is it?"

"I don't know. Pretty bad, I guess. Bad enough to have the coach send me back to the ranch to recuperate."

"Why to the ranch?"

"Just so I'll have somebody around if the symptoms get worse."

Panic filled her chest, and she pushed to her feet. "Was this worse? Should I call someone? Should I call 911?"

He chuckled and grabbed her hand, stopping her and pulling her back down next to him. "Hell no, you don't need to call 911. I just stood up too fast. Got a little dizzy. Could have happened to anyone."

She settled in next to him again, satisfied with his answer. For now.

Glancing up at his head, she noted the cut above his left eyebrow and wondered if it had resulted from the same fight. "It was a pretty good hit. And a total cheap shot. That guy's such an asshat. I'm glad he got suspended. They're not gonna let him play for the rest of the finals, even if they get a run at the Cup."

His body was turned slightly to hers, and he cocked his head to the side, his eyes wide with disbelief.

"What? Didn't you know he got suspended? He's out for the rest of the season."

A cocky grin pulled at one corner of his mouth, then slowly turned into a full-fledged smile. "If you saw the hit, that means you were watching the game. You were watching me play."

He said the words like an accusation, and she felt like a naughty kid who'd just been caught with her hand in the cookie jar.

"I didn't say that," she sputtered. "I never said that I watch you play. I don't even like hockey."

"Then how do you know about the Cup?"

"Everybody knows about the Stanley Cup. It's a thing. Like the Super Bowl. That doesn't mean I watch *you*, specifically."

"Then how'd you see the hit? Or know the guy is an asshat? Which he is, by the way."

Her mind raced, searching for a plausible explanation. She could say that she saw it on the news. They showed the replay often enough. But then she'd just have to spin another lie to keep that one going.

She let out a sigh. "Okay, yeah. I was watching you play. I catch a game sometimes. And it *was* the playoffs."

"Which we are now out of," he said with a grimace. "Thanks to my not paying attention."

"What? Are you kidding me? That wasn't your fault. You couldn't have anticipated that. It was a cheap shot, and boarding is bullshit," she said, referring to the term used when one player rams into the back of another and shoves them into the sideboards. The move was illegal and often resulted in the player getting kicked from the game.

But this time, it resulted in Rock's head hitting the boards and knocking him out. She'd never forget the sight of his head cracking into the sideboard and the feeling of panic in her chest as she'd watched him sink to the ice.

Even now, just thinking about it, it still made her mad as hell. "I don't care if the guy was a rookie. He should have known better."

She glanced up at Rock. His grin was back.

"Yeah, it sounds like you just catch an occasional game."

Heat crept up her neck, and she shoved against his shoulder. "Oh, shut up. Quit giving me a hard time."

"What kind of a time would you like me to give you?" He lifted his arm and dropped it easily around her shoulders, his expression going from playful to sinfully sexy in a matter of seconds.

All the air felt like it had been sucked from her chest. She hadn't been this close to him in years, yet the pressure of his arm across her shoulders felt exactly right. The scent of him surrounded her—soap and aftershave and a hint of maple syrup.

She couldn't move, couldn't breathe. Her body felt frozen as she watched his gaze travel down from her eyes and land on her lips.

He leaned down, just an inch, then stopped, searching her face for—what?—permission? She couldn't give it but couldn't deny it either. She couldn't do anything. Except wait.

And try to breathe.

All she could do was hold perfectly still as he leaned even closer, his lips just a fraction of an inch from hers.

She closed her hands, tightened them into fists at her sides as the sensation of butterflies plunged and careened into the walls of her stomach.

He was still looking at her lips, regarding them as if he were a starving man and they represented his last meal.

Reaching his hand up, he skimmed his fingers across her neck before they came to rest on the side of her face. His thumb brushed across her bottom lip.

She sucked in her breath, a quick gasp, as a shiver tingled down her spine.

Every nerve in her body was on hyperalert, anticipating, craving, waiting, dying—for the touch of his lips.

With the softest touch, he leaned closer, his palm still holding her cheek, and with just a passing graze, the lightest glance, his lips brushed hers.

CHAPTER 4

IT WAS BARELY A KISS, JUST THE SLIGHTEST TOUCH OF THEIR lips, but it was Rock's lips—lips that even after all of these years, felt as familiar as her own.

Her breath caught in her throat, but she didn't pull away, couldn't pull away.

His mouth slanted across hers, deepening the kiss as she melted into him. Literally melted against his body as if all of her bones had vanished, replaced with molten heat that surged through her veins, warming her from the inside out.

He tasted like maple syrup and blueberries and Rock—and the smallest of sighs escaped her lips. His hands cupped her cheeks, holding her face in a tender embrace.

She gripped his shoulders, holding on, forgetting everything as she kissed him back. Sinking in to the feeling—to the sensation of being thoroughly kissed—it felt so damn good. Oh God, he felt so good.

The scent of him, his soap, his aftershave—something musky and expensive—swirled around her, both familiar and mysterious. She wanted to climb into his lap, to wrap her legs around him, to slide her hands under his shirt and explore the new contours of his muscles, to kiss and touch every scar, every inch of his body. A body that she knew, yet didn't.

Memories swirled through her, memories of kissing him, touching him. He was her first love, her first kiss, her first every-thing, and she had loved him with everything she had to give.

They had loved each other. And he had walked away, left her behind.

Holy shit.

What the heck was she doing?

She pulled back, her palms flattening against his shoulders as she straightened her arms. "I can't." Gasping, she ignored the sting of gravel that bit into her hands as she scrambled backward. "I can't do this."

"*Quinn.*"

"No. No. No." She shook her head, trying to clear her muddled thoughts. It was as if she'd been swimming in a beautiful perfect lake, the water warm and fluid around her, then something had brushed past her leg, and she remembered that the lake held a monster that swam just below the surface, and suddenly she couldn't get out of the water fast enough.

She backpedaled, then pushed to her feet, determined not to get pulled down into the water again, not to get sucked in to the whirlpool that was Rockford James.

"I gotta go." She took two steps forward, then stopped and stomped her foot, a small cloud of dust kicking up around her boot heel. "Damn it. I can't just leave you here."

A grin tugged at the corner of his beautiful mouth.

"Not because of that," she sneered. Her shoulders fell as she let out a sigh. "Because you're hurt."

His cocky grin fell, replaced by a scowl. "Let me get this straight—you're pissed but you're not gonna walk away because you feel *sorry* for me? Well, screw that. You can keep on walking, lady."

"I can't. That's not who I am. I don't walk away when someone needs me."

He winced. "Who says I need you?"

A flash of pain pierced her heart. No one. No one had said that. And Rock didn't need her. Apparently, he didn't need anyone except himself. "It doesn't matter. I'm a mom; it's what I do. You're hurt, and I'm not walking away."

"You guys need a hand? Somebody hurt?" A younger version of

Rock walked around the barn, a copper-colored golden retriever on his heels.

"Nobody's hurt," Rock growled. "I'm fine."

"Hey, Colt. I'm glad you're here," Quinn said to Rock's baby brother. He looked so much like Rock, the same sandy-blond hair, the same broad shoulders, sometimes it was hard for Quinn to be around him, just the sight of him bringing up too many painful memories. "I've got to go. Can you watch him?"

"Nobody needs to watch me. I'm not a child."

The golden ran over to Rock and set to licking his face in greeting.

No, he wasn't a child. And he wasn't the teenage boy who'd left her behind, the boy who still lingered in her mind and haunted her dreams. No, he was a man. A man who with one kiss, had just turned her inside out and shaken her to her core.

Shoving her hands in her pockets, she tried to control their trembling, then turned on her heels, and walked back to the house.

———

Rock held out his hand and let Colt pull him up. "How you doing, little brother?"

The younger man pulled him into a bear hug. "A lot better than you, by the looks of things. What's going on with Quinn? I don't think I've ever seen her so rattled."

"Yeah, me neither." He wasn't sure if he wanted to share that it was his fault, or that it might have something to do with the fact that he'd just kissed her. Okay—it had everything to do with the fact that he'd just kissed her.

But he needed to mull that over a little on his own first—because he also wasn't sure if he was ready to face how rattled he felt either.

"Sorry I missed you last night," Colt said.

"It's cool. Mom said you were working a late shift at The Creed," Rock told him, referring to The Creedence Tavern, the local pub and restaurant in town. "Since when did you start working there?"

"I don't work there. I was just filling in for Dale last night because his wife went into labor."

"No way. I didn't even know she was pregnant."

He shrugged. "It's only been for about the last nine months now."

Rock elbowed him in the side. "I was gonna come down and see you, but Ma wouldn't let me out of her sight last night."

His brother chuckled. "Yeah, I bet. So, how's your head? For real."

"For real?"

Colt nodded, his gaze solemn.

"For real, it hurts like a bitch sometimes and other times not at all. I'm sore and pissed and embarrassed that I let that punk get the drop on me, and I feel like I let the whole damn team down and we're out of the finals because of me."

"Whoa. That's a lot. I know you've got some pretty broad shoulders, but I didn't realize you carried the whole team."

He sighed. "Shut up. You know what I mean. I just feel like I let 'em down. And I hate that the coach sent me home to 'recuperate.'" He lifted his fingers to make air quotes.

"It must have been pretty bad then."

"It's a few dizzy spells and some bruises. But I'm not a freaking invalid, and regardless of what Quinn Rivers has to say about it, I do *not* need a babysitter."

Colt held up his hands. "All right, dude. Although you'd be hard-pressed to find a prettier babysitter than Quinn. She used to babysit me, and I never seemed to mind."

Rock let out a chuckle. "Point taken. I just don't want her, or anybody, making a fuss over me. That includes Mom."

"Good luck with that one." He gestured toward the pasture.

"I'm headed out to check on the calves. Want to keep me company? Stretch your legs a little?"

"Sure." He picked up a stick and threw it for the dog as he fell into step behind his brother. It *would* be good to stretch his legs and to focus on something besides the blond cowgirl who smelled like vanilla and whose kiss still sent him reeling, making him dizzy in ways that had nothing to do with the concussion.

ACKNOWLEDGMENTS

As always, my love and thanks goes out to my family! Todd, thanks for always believing in me and for being the real-life role model of a romantic hero. Thanks for making so many suppers so I could write and listening to a million plot-storms and book ideas as we traversed the trails on our walks. You make me laugh every day and the words it would take to truly thank you would fill a book on their own. I love you. *Always*.

I can't thank my editor, Deb Werksman, enough for believing in me and this book, for loving Cade, Nora, and Allie, and for making this story so much better with your amazing editing skills. I appreciate everything you do to help make the town of Creedence and the motley crew of farmyard animals come to life. Thanks to my project editor, Susie Benton, for all your encouragement and support, and a huge thanks to Dawn Adams and Stephanie Gafron for this gorgeous cover and every other awesome cover you've given me! I love being part of the Sourcebooks Sisterhood, and I offer buckets of thanks to the whole Sourcebooks Casablanca team for all of your efforts and hard work in making this book happen.

A big thank-you to my parents—all of them. I appreciate everything you do and am so thankful for your support of this crazy writing career. Thanks to my mom, Lee Cumba, for so many lunches where we talk writing and plots. And thanks to my stepmom, Gracie Bryant, for your encouragement and support, and to my dad, Dr. Bill Bryant, for spending hours giving me ranching and farming advice, plot ideas, and guiding me through some of the tough aspects of rescuing horses.

Special thanks goes out to Melissa Marts, my sister-in-law and BFF, who this book is dedicated to. We have seen each other through so much since our friendship began in Advanced English in eighth grade. I cherish our friendship and can't thank you enough for the hours spent talking writing, books, family, and life. Thanks for the fun afternoon at the cabin spent chatting about all things horses and how to incorporate them into the plot of this book. Your encouragement and belief in me mean so much.

A huge thank-you goes out to Julie Feuerbach for your expertise on physical therapy and your guidance on all the injury and PT areas of the book. Any mistakes are mine.

Special thanks goes out to Drs. Rebecca and Corbin Hodges, my sister and brother-in-law, and my dad, Dr. Bill Bryant, who are always willing to listen and offer sound veterinarian counsel on my crew of farmyard animals.

Shout-out and thanks to Andrea Reynolds for always listening and offering fun and crazy ideas to spark new book ideas. I treasure your friendship and value all the time we've spent cracking each other up.

Thanks always goes out to my plotting partners and dear friends, Kristin Miller, Ginger Scott, and Anne Eliot. The time and energy you all take to talk through scenes and run through plot ideas with me is invaluable! Your friendship and writing support means the world to me—I couldn't do this writing thing without you!

Huge thank-you to my agent, Nicole Resciniti at The Seymour Agency, for your advice and your guidance. You are the best, and I'm so thankful you are part of my life.

Special acknowledgment goes out to the women who walk this writing journey with me every single day. The ones who make me laugh, who encourage and support, who offer great advice and sometimes just listen. Thank you Michelle Major, Lana Williams, Anne Eliot, and Ginger Scott. XO

Big thanks goes out to my street team, Jennie's Page Turners, and for all of my readers: the people who have been with me from the start, my loyal readers, my dedicated fans, the ones who have read my stories, who have laughed and cried with me, who have fallen in love with my heroes and have clamored for more! Whether you have been with me since the first book or just discovered me with this book, know that I write these stories for you, and I can't thank you enough for reading them. Sending love, laughter, and big Colorado hugs to you all!